FORCE OF HATE

By Graham Bartlett

Bad for Good

Force of Hate

FORCE OF HATE

GRAHAM BARTLETT

Allison & Busby Limited
11 Wardour Mews
London W1F 8AN
allisonandbusby.com

First published in Great Britain by Allison & Busby in 2023.

Copyright © 2023 by Graham Bartlett, South Downs Leadership
and Management Services Ltd.

A CIP catalogue record for this book is available from
the British Library.

First Edition

HB ISBN 978-0-7490-2867-1

TPB ISBN 978-0-7490-2872-5

Typeset in 11.5/16.5 pt Adobe Garamond Pro by
Allison & Busby Ltd

Printed and bound by
CPI Group (UK) Ltd., Croydon, CR0 4YY

For all those who come in hope. May we not let you down.

I always tell authors that the story and characters must come first. With that in mind, this is a work of fiction, hence some structures, titles, locations, even some police procedures, have been modified to serve the story and the characters for your enjoyment.

1

It took all Ajee had to suck in the faintest breath.

The lung-crushing stench pervading the impossibly tight fissure she'd wedged herself into tempted her to succumb to suffocation.

This was the third, or was it fourth, leg of her month-long escape, hidden in pitch-dark trailers. This was meant to be the shortest yet but had cost her tenfold the other trips, but she'd been told it was worth it.

The other journeys, nestled among boxes of offal and seafood, had been unbearable but nothing as revolting as this. There was barely room to blink; the sweat and halitosis of the fifteen or so other migrants seeped into every pore and tainted every gasp of air. It made her wonder whether the job, apartment and papers she'd been promised would be worth it.

Ajee had sensed that they had cleared the port. She'd learnt to read the list and rattle of the lorry's stops and starts and knew they were now on the open road. The crossing had been rough but nothing like the open boat across the Aegean Sea from Turkey.

The smugglers in Dieppe had told them the journey through England would take three to four hours before they would be dropped off to meet the uncle who would look after them. So why were the brakes hissing so urgently now? And why had the lorry swung so sharply that she had to brace against the walls of her hollow?

Even though she couldn't see them, the other stowaways' unease rippled through the trailer. A few panicked voices were hushed by others demanding silence.

It was probably nothing. A broken-down car? A closed road? It would be fine. After all she had been through on her 3,000-mile flee from the city – and people – she loved, why would it all end now?

Then, voices. Official. Muffled but definitely police. Or customs. Soldiers? She'd learnt English whilst studying for her nursing degree at the University of Aleppo so managed to pick up a few words, and they terrified her.

Ajee shuffled away from the crates, praying she was moving to the edge of the trailer not deeper into its core. She had no idea whether this was the smartest or dumbest thing to do but instinct drove her on. All around others were doing the same.

She listened carefully. As she touched the lorry's canvas walls, the voices became clearer.

'Can we have a look in the back then?'

'*Mais oui*, officer,' came the reply, a little too loudly for Ajee's liking.

Her heart trembled and beads of sweat bubbled on her brow.

Footsteps.

She must be low down as they'd sounded right next to her, yet faded off to her left. They'd be heading to the back doors, she guessed, so she must be close to the cab. Low, on the front left side, she decided.

Perfect.

She fumbled in her right-hand jeans pocket. Empty. Oh no. Her left. Oh, please don't say she'd dropped it. She'd guarded that knife since Istanbul. Having fled the would-be rapist, she'd paid fifty dollars she could ill afford, and now for the first time she needed it. She frantically frisked herself, then, as if Allah was watching over her, remembered the hidden pocket in the lining of the gilet she'd found in France. She heaved a silent sigh of relief and squeezed the cold metal to her calloused palms.

The clank of rods and locks being unbolted snapped her back. Panic was now all around her as her faceless counterparts scurried around. She dared not add to the mêlée by shouting to them to stay still. She knew the game was up.

As the doors were wrenched open, the bright morning sun floodlit the trailer. The reek of bodies and fear must have hit the police officers as they beamed their torches around the cargo.

'Stay where you are,' came the shout, then, 'Charlie Bravo 34, urgent. Charlie Bravo 34, can we have back-up on the A27 westbound by the Amex Stadium. We've stopped a lorry full of migrants.'

It was now or never. Once more police arrived, she'd be done for. All those months, and wasted dollars, running from everything she knew. For what? She had to run now, and take her chances, or she'd be sent back to certain death.

She flipped the blade open and stabbed at the canvas. The knife snagged and nearly flew out of her hand, but she gripped it tighter and with all she had, slashed downwards, just enough for her slim frame to squeeze through.

Someone was heaving themselves into the back, shouting, 'Stay where you are.'

She banked on only two police and surely one would be guarding the driver, so the other would no doubt be focused on those closer to the doors.

She pulled herself up and glimpsed the outside through the tear. A narrow pavement gave way to green fields trimmed with hedges. No police. Euphoria and panic drove her as she shouldered her way through then leapt onto the tarmac.

In three strides she was at the chain-link fence, and in one bound over it. She risked a backward glance to see the police slamming the trailer doors shut and frantically bellowing into their radios, the driver handcuffed by their side.

It wouldn't be long before they found the cut wall. Hugging the perimeter hedge and crouched on her haunches, she powered away, determined to put as much distance between her and the lorry before they did.

2

Four weeks later

Chief Superintendent Joanne Howe detested these charades.

Under Brighton and Hove City Council's previous chief executive, Penny Raw, like divisional commanders before her, she'd happily breeze into Hove Town Hall when the mood took her, amble up the open staircase to Penny's office and, whilst she waited, make small talk with the directors and their PAs.

Since the local election last year when the British Patriot Party had somehow swept to power, everything had changed. First, Penny and her top team were sacked overnight; then, just as quickly, a ready-formed band of fascists took the helm. Now, in a playground muscle-flex, new Chief Executive Russ Parfitt delighted in making her wait in the foyer. It wouldn't be so bad if he kept to time, but it seemed no coincidence that each week, he sent for her exactly nine minutes after their appointment time.

She tried not to let her anger show and had taken to wearing plain clothes to be less obvious, but within she seethed.

True to form, at 9.09 a.m. Russ's personal assistant Debbie ran down the open marble staircase mouthing 'sorry' as she did so.

Jo walked over to the security barriers and waited for Debbie to zap her through.

'Morning, Debbie,' said Jo. 'Tied up on a call, was he?'

Debbie shrugged. 'I'll get you a drink.'

Jo followed her up the stairs in silence, through two more security doors. As Debbie peeled off into the kitchen, Jo entered Russ's office which, given his bulk, seemed even more cramped than it actually was.

'Morning, Russ.'

'Ah, morning, Jo.' *No apology then.* 'Take a seat.' He'd barely looked up from his phone. Jo waited, wondering how the moons of sweat already darkening his armpits could appear so early on a chilly morning.

These weekly meetings were supposed to be their opportunity to thrash out any political or operational hot bricks so, to the public at least, the two most powerful city leaders could show a united front. In fact, they had turned into Parfitt making outrageous – often unlawful – demands and Jo being the voice of his disappointment. Today would be no different.

'Jo, I've had the Leader of the Council onto me about the travellers who've pitched up in both Preston and Stanmer Parks. We'd like them evicted.'

'When you've done what you need to do – as landowners – I'll ask Gary Hedges to have a look and see what powers we have.'

'I don't think you understand,' said Russ, edging forward. 'We want them gone.'

Jo held her ground, accustomed to his misogynistic bullying. 'And when you've done your bit, we'll have a look at ours.' She glared at him. 'Understand?'

Russ blinked first and Jo took that tiny victory.

'Talking of Superintendent Hedges,' Parfitt continued, 'Why didn't he clear the protestors out of the chamber during the council meeting last week? Both the Leader and the Mayor asked him to, but he flatly refused.'

Jo knew this was coming and regurgitated the rationale her deputy, Gary, had given her half an hour earlier. She paused for effect on the words 'democracy', 'rights' and 'freedom of speech', three concepts Parfitt despised. When she finished, he ranted on about the 'great unwashed', 'foreigners' and the need to look after the 'decent people', three groups Jo refused to recognise.

When he'd finished, it was Jo's turn. 'As I have told you time and again, we are not your personal army. We will do what is right, within our powers, when it's necessary. We are no one's puppets and will certainly not be part of any eye-catching, vote-winning agenda you and this new council might have.'

The chief executive stood, his ruddy jowls quivering.

'Don't fucking take me on, little lady. This city is going places with or without you and unless you start toeing the line, I'll have you removed. Just one call to Stuart Acers and you'll be gone.'

'The chief constable doesn't answer to you.'

'Are you sure about that?'

Jo stood, grabbed her case, turned for the door then threw a look back.

'Never threaten me. And I'm no one's little lady.' She grabbed for the handle, only to find the door open and the Leader of the Council, Tom Doughty, blocking her exit. He looked over her shoulder, as if she weren't there. 'All sorted, Russ?' he asked.

'I think so, Tom.'

'Don't fucking bank on it,' hissed Jo, as she barged past the councillor and fled for the outer door before a career-threatening tirade escaped from her mouth.

Jo Howe vowed, not for the first time, to resolve the police station parking once and for all. It would mean forgoing her designated bay that she had just pulled into, but she was sick and tired of seeing the response cars stacked up in front of one another. The inevitable synchronised shunting whenever there was a 'blues and twos' shout was a nonsense she should have eradicated months ago.

As she zapped herself in through the back door, her phone buzzed.

'Hi, Gary. I've just parked up. You in the office?'

'I am and I'm bloody seething.'

'Whoa. What's the matter?' replied Jo as she held a door for a PC who seemed to be heading for the car park in a hurry.

'Have you seen the chief's latest?'

'No. I'll be with you in two minutes. Hold that rage.'

As she weaved her way through the corridors and up the stairs to the second-floor office they now shared, Jo opened her emails on her phone and scanned the one from Stuart Acers. Whilst it was the usual ill-spelt, hastily thumped out rant, she got the gist of it.

Jo pushed the office door open to see Gary pacing the floor.

'It's fucking outrageous. Is it too much to expect some back-up from that wanker?'

'Maybe this is one of those chats best held with the door closed.' Jo then poked her head back out and called to Fiona, her PA, to bring in a mug of iron-strength coffee and one of hot water. She eased the door shut.

'Please, tell me you've not replied to him yet.'

'I tried to call him but apparently he's in a meeting.'

'Thank God,' sighed Jo. 'Look, we both know what's going on here. Parfitt is in his ear about the council meeting and he's snatched at the opportunity to give us another kicking.'

'Me, not us. He's having a go at me. My judgement and my bottle, for Christ's sake. Just because I wouldn't eject a few gobby objectors – who had a point, I might add. I mean, for fuck's sake, who's pulling the strings here?'

'We both know the answer to that. Rise above it.'

They were each sitting with their back to their respective desks, Jo's looking like a burglary, Gary's like a furniture catalogue.

'He's the one with no bottle. Never has had. It was probably the only thing Phil Cooke can be proud of as PCC, getting rid of that bastard. Then he rubs salt in by slinking back.'

'He's always been more worried about the pennies and politics than real policing, but we have to work with it. There's no point in grappling with him as, like it or not, he has the upper hand. I haven't got the energy to take on another chief.'

'I can't bloody stand this though. It's not like he's even got any experience to draw on.'

'Lucky he's as thick as pig shit then.'

Gary looked quizzical.

Jo explained. 'If he had anything nudging a double-figure IQ he would have at least waited a week or so after Parfitt had a go at me. But he couldn't wait to sound off, so now we know.'

'Know what?'

'That those two time-share a brain and a tiny one at that. We should be cautious about what we say to each of them, for sure, but we can also play their bromance to our advantage.'

'How?'

'We do nothing just now, but when the need arises we can have great fun feeding them what we want them to share and watching the fireworks that follow.'

'Christ, I'd hate to cross you,' smirked Gary.

'Very wise.'

3

One week previously

The day she ran from the lorry, the helicopter and sirens had terrified Ajee more than the Macedonian soldiers who guarded the sealed border.

She had skirted the open fields and hid in ditches whenever she felt they were onto her but the longer she remained undetected, the more her confidence grew that they thought they'd trapped everyone in the lorry until help arrived. Surely they'd have spotted the cut in the canvas though.

Over the following three weeks she had surprised herself at how resourceful she'd become since fleeing Syria. In fact, before then. She'd lost everything – her family, her beautiful home overlooking the river, and her nursing career – but somehow she'd not given up. The memory of what had happened to her parents and brother and wondering what became of her boyfriend when Assad's thugs snatched him off the streets kept her going. If only for their sake.

Life had been good in Aleppo until Assad's troops and opposition forces entrenched themselves on either side of the city. Since then, to the outside world, the situation had eased but to Ajee, the threat of exploitation and death was ever-present and she lived on her wits.

Hiding among Brighton's homeless was easier than Ajee could have imagined. She was not the only illegal in their midst and, as she kept herself pretty much to herself, she never attracted the interest of the few police she saw. There were plenty of others whose drunken rants or drugged stupors diverted their attention.

One evening, whilst she was begging outside a Tesco Express on Western Road, her luck changed. She'd been sitting by the cash machine for a couple of hours, never speaking but relying on her pitiful look and the McDonald's cup to do the talking. Every once in a while, she'd pocket the banknotes the more generous Brightonians had dropped in and nibble on the meal deals those who didn't trust her with cash gave her.

'You must be freezing,' a silky, deep voice said.

Ajee lifted her head just enough to see a pair of black mirror-shined shoes and razor-sharp herringbone trousers. She dared not risk a reply.

'Can I get you anything?'

Again, she remained silent.

'It's OK my dear, I'm just worried about you.'

Ajee struggled with English accents but this voice had a kindness. Friendly. Educated. She braved it.

'I OK. I well. Allah watch over me.'

'That's good. Very good. But you look so cold. Would you like me to help you? Find you shelter. Somewhere to get cleaned up, maybe?'

'You very kind but I'm OK. Thank you, sir.'

The man bid her goodbye and walked off.

The next evening, he was back. Then the next and the one after that.

A week after that first encounter, George – he'd told her his name a couple of days before – bought her a hot shawarma and chips. Three days later they were chatting like old friends, although Ajee was careful not to reveal where she'd come from or how. George, on the other hand, told her he'd been married for thirty years, and had two grown-up daughters who each had a baby son. He showed her photos of him and a grey-haired lady Ajee took to be his wife, cradling a newborn between them, their rapt joy beaming from the screen.

Now, two days later, he'd persuaded her to go with him to a flat he owned, just for a shower. They had walked for about fifteen minutes, chatting easily, when George stopped outside a tall, converted house in a big square overlooking the sea.

'Here we are,' he said.

Ajee backed off, suddenly anxious at her own gullibility. 'What is this?'

'My flat, of course.' He handed her a key. 'I'll wait out here. You go and pamper yourself.'

'I sorry, Mr George. It's just I . . .'

'I understand. Honestly, you can trust me.'

'Thank you,' she muttered. 'You very kind.'

The first-floor flat was sparsely furnished and there was no bed. That suited Ajee, as she had no intentions of abusing George's kindness by making him feel obliged to let her live here.

The shower was sheer luxury. Shards of scalding water pummelled her grimy skin and the fragrant shower gel and shampoo, which she lathered herself top to toe with, made her tingle with delight.

It was only as she wandered around, towelling herself with the fleecy bath sheet, that she spotted the new clothes draped over an armchair in the lounge. George had not mentioned them, but surely they were for her. There were no signs of anyone else living here, after all.

Ajee slipped on the sports bra, big knickers, slightly roomy black jeans and green Nike hoodie. She felt like a new woman. As she looked in the mirror, she grinned. George must have bought these himself. He had no idea what nineteen-year-old Muslim girls wore these days.

Once she was dressed and had brushed her hair, Ajee wiped over the bathroom surfaces, folded the towel over the rail and bundled up her old clothes – careful to recover what money she'd collected and her knife – then dumped them in the kitchen bin.

She glanced round one last time, scolding herself for wishing she could stay, closed the door and walked down the communal stairs and onto the busy street.

'Wow, look at you. You look like a new girl,' said George.

'You very kind, Mr George. How I repay you? These clothes are, how you say, beautiful.'

'Stop teasing me,' he replied. 'They were the best I could do. A young girl like you shouldn't be wearing the same clothes day in day out. It's you who are beautiful.' Ajee recoiled. 'Oh my dear, please don't take that the wrong way. I'm practically old enough to be your grandfather. I just mean you look so much – er – fresher now you're all cleaned up. Can I buy you something to eat? What do you like? Mando's?'

Ajee smiled. 'Yes, thank you, Mr George. I like *Nando's*.'

George flagged down a cab and they travelled in silence the short distance to Goldstone Retail Park. When they arrived, he held the door for her as they entered the restaurant. Once Ajee had briefed him on the ordering system, they chose then waited for their food.

Ajee felt more at ease now. She'd been slow to trust since the civil war but, even with her antennae on full alert for anyone who might harm her, she had found nothing but warmth in this quirky Englishman.

'I know you don't like talking about where you come from, but what are your plans? Surely you don't want to live on the street for ever?'

'No, of course not,' she said, then paused as their Butterfly Burgers and fries arrived. 'I train to be a nurse in my country. It was all I wanted since I was a child but I had to leave. Now that will never happen.' She felt a sting in her eyes and took a deep breath.

'Never give up on your dreams,' said George, as he reached over to squeeze her hand. She did not pull away.

A silence hung between them. George seemed deep in thought.

'My dear. Would you give me a moment? I just want to make a quick call.'

'But your chicken, Mr George?'

'I'll only be a minute.'

Ajee watched him as he slid along the bench seat and out of the booth. He was dialling as he made for the door and she watched him chatting on the phone through the window. A steeliness she'd not seen before flashed across his face. She let it pass and tucked into the food.

When George came back, he was his usual affable self. He sat back down but ignored his dinner.

'Ajee, look, I might have overstepped the mark but I think I have an opportunity for you.'

She furrowed her brow.

'A friend of mine has a string of nursing homes across the city. It's not what you had in mind when you started your studies. This is all old people, dementia sufferers mainly, seeing out their days with care and dignity. Anyway, I just spoke to him and, as I thought, he's looking for staff.'

'That's very kind of you, Mr George, but I have no papers. I can't work. They deport me.' She was practically whispering now.

'He understands that. He has several girls in your position. The pay's not great but it's cash in hand and each of his homes have a few rooms where you can live, free of charge. They even provide your meals.'

'That is kind but I'm not qualified. I didn't finish my degree.'

'My dear, you are more qualified than most. Anyway, why don't you have a chat with him at least? He can see you later today if you like.'

'This is all very fast, Mr George.'

'Sometimes you have to act fast. What have you got to lose?' For once his smile stopped short of his eyes.

Ajee weighed it up as she mopped up the last of the ketchup with her bap. It's not like she was fighting off offers of work or somewhere to live. She could trust him. He was right, what was the harm in a meeting? She could always say no if it didn't feel right.

'Thank you,' she smiled. 'I'm sorry I didn't seem very – how you say – grateful. It's just a shock.'

'Don't worry. Some things are meant to happen. He'll collect you from here in thirty minutes.'

'With you?'

'I'm afraid not, I have to get back, but the best of luck. I'm sure you'll get on famously.' He put a £20 and £10 note on the table and stood up. 'Take care, my dear. I'll see you soon.'

Ajee remained seated, the hope of changing luck glowing through her. 'Yes, thank you. See you soon, Mr George.'

As George had promised, a car pulled up outside Nando's exactly thirty minutes after he had vanished. The driver was surly, speaking only to confirm her name. That suited Ajee. The last thing she needed was conversation with a stranger. She was already fretting about how much she'd divulged to George, but at least that gave her the chance of a job – a fresh start.

When the car crunched to a stop on the sweeping gravel driveway, she stared in awe at the double-fronted two-storey mansion that threw its shadow across immaculately manicured lawns. The white stippled render and black-stained wooden window frames reminded her of the picture books she'd pored over as a child. English history had been one of her favourite subjects and she'd yearned to live in one of those grand Tudor houses. Could this be the paradise she'd imagined?

Ajee stepped out of the car and closed the door just in time as its wheels spun on the shingle, peppering her shins as it sped away.

She was about to rap on the huge black door when it was yanked open. A skinny woman in a stained white tunic, bearing a badge which labelled her as 'Peggy Squire – Manager', glared at her. 'Can I help you?'

Ajee bowed her head. 'My name is Ajee. Mr George said I was to meet his friend. He have a job for me.'

Peggy craned her sinewy neck and looked left and right. 'You'd better come in. Where are your things?'

'This is all I have,' she said, her arms out to indicate she was wearing the sum of her worldly goods.

Peggy turned and marched down a long corridor which smelt almost as vile as the lorry. Ajee presumed she was to follow, so closed the door and jogged to keep up. Peggy turned into a doorway on the right opposite a lounge, from which weary cries echoed. Ajee wondered whether she should go and see if someone needed help but thought that might be a little presumptuous.

By the time she caught up, she found Peggy was sitting behind a cluttered desk which barely fitted in the narrow space. Ajee perched opposite on a grey plastic moulded chair which reminded her of school. She tried to ignore the mysterious stain but positioned herself so it would not ruin her new jeans.

'You want to work here then,' said Peggy, more a statement than a question.

'Mr George, he say you might have job for me and we should speak about it. He tell you that, no?'

'I don't deal with George. I have enough to do here but I was told you'd be coming. Do you have papers? A passport, ID card?'

'No, nothing. I lost everything on way to England.'

'Empty your pockets,' said Peggy.

'Excuse me?'

'You heard me. Everything on the table.'

Ajee hesitated, then slowly put all her possessions on top of a file on the desk. It didn't amount to much. A total of £34.76, a few tissues, lip balm, three tampons and her knife. Peggy stared at the switchblade, then at Ajee.

'What is that?'

Ajee shrugged, stuck for an explanation this scary woman would understand.

'I won't tolerate any trouble here.'

'What is "tolerate"?'

'Put up. I won't put up with trouble.'

'I just work hard.' Ajee wondered if she was sounding a bit too desperate.

Peggy swept up the cash and knife and indicated to Ajee to pick up the remaining debris.

'Why you take my money?' Ajee protested.

'Call it rent,' replied Peggy. 'You start at six tomorrow morning. You will live here. I'll show you the room. The shifts are thirteen hours, days and nights. The pay is five pounds per hour but we will hold that for you. All your meals will be provided. You will not leave here without permission and an escort and you may not contact anyone from the outside.'

'But, but—' Ajee's head was spinning. A couple of hours ago she'd been feeling like royalty, all showered and pampered, and now this. It sounded like a prison. 'I think there is some mistake. I will find something else. Thank you, Mrs Peggy, for your time.'

'There's no mistake, Ajee.'

A click behind her made Ajee spin round. She'd not heard the man slip in until he locked the door.

'This is your life now. If you cause trouble or try to leave, we will hand you over to the authorities and you'll be on the first flight back to whatever hellhole you've come from.'

4

One week later

If there was one thing PC Wendy Relf hated more than her crew-mate's post-curry wind, it was his dad jokes.

Parked in the lay-by between the Palace Pier and the Sea Life Centre on a rare break between calls, all Wendy wanted was to write up the last two burglaries they'd been to – but PC Dan Bilkham, having swerved the paperwork as usual, was practising his stand-up act.

'Here, you'll love this one Wend. What do you call a vicar on a motorbike? Rev.' Dan creased up whilst Wendy just kept typing away on her smartphone.

'How about this? What did the football manager do when the pitch flooded? Brought on the subs.'

'Dan, I'm trying to work here,' said Wendy, but she couldn't resist a smirk at that one.

'Charlie Romeo Zero One,' came the voice over the radio.

'Zero One, go ahead,' replied Dan, flipping to professional mode.

'Charlie Romeo Zero One, can you start making for Al-Medinah Mosque, Brighton? We're getting reports of a group of youths shouting racist abuse at the congregation as they leave. Reports too of bottles being thrown. If you start making, I'll find you some back-up.'

'Roger, on our way. ETA five minutes,' said Dan.

Wendy flicked on the strobe lights and siren and elbowed her way into the logjam of tourist traffic snaking along the coast road.

'Move, shit for brains,' she yelled at the driver of the car in front, who seemed to have been frozen to a standstill by the sight of a speeding police car bearing down on him.

'You know he can't actually hear you shout, don't you?' checked Dan.

'Maybe not, but it makes me feel better,' replied Wendy.

Squeezing through impossible gaps and narrowly avoiding countless oblivious or confused pedestrians and cyclists, in no time Wendy reached the junction with West Street, Brighton's nightlife hub. Pausing only briefly for the red light, she powered through and dodged the Deliveroo moped scooting down the outside of the line of oncoming traffic.

'Can we try to keep the number of corpses we leave in our wake to single figures, please? You know my aversion to paperwork.'

'You should try it one day; you might like it.'

'What, mowing down innocent road users?'

'Getting your pen out.'

'What pen?'

The radio interrupted their banter. 'Charlie Romeo Zero One, an update for you. We are getting reports of upwards of twenty men now fighting and witnesses are reporting seeing baseball bats and one says an axe. Approach with caution and hold back until back-up arrives.'

Wendy swung the car right into Bedford Place, against the one-way traffic. 'Did you hear that?' she said.

'Which bit?'

'Something about holding back.'

'No.'

'Me neither.'

Her assertive driving and the incessant sirens forced cars onto pavements and into the side roads as Wendy pushed her way up the hill to the mosque. As they approached, the ferocity of the situation hit them. A sea of bodies blocked the road, clashing and charging at each other. Thrown punches, fleeing men, bins and rocks careering through the air snuffed out any thoughts of talking their way out of this one.

Wendy stopped the car as close as she could, resigned to the fact it would probably end up trashed. Not for the first time.

'Ready?' she said as she drew her baton.

'You bet. Stay in sight,' said Dan as he did likewise and, as one, they threw open their car doors and racked open their truncheons.

'Let's go,' shouted Wendy as both sprinted towards the warring masses, yelling 'police' for what that was worth.

In the mêlée, Wendy broadly made out two groups. One consisted of white, fat, red-faced men, most with armfuls of tattoos and hate in their eyes. The other were darker-skinned, fitter men wearing traditional thobes and kofis.

At first glance it seemed the white men were the aggressors, pushing forward and throwing missiles at the mosque; but the other group were more heavily armed, every two or three swinging baseball bats indiscriminately at their opponents.

Wendy knew not to over-analyse the situation, and instead to just do whatever the hell she could to stay alive and stop anyone getting seriously hurt.

She waded in, flailing her baton at any arm holding a weapon, fending off punches and kicks as she pushed through. She'd spun her head to see where Dan was, as much for his safety as hers, when she was jolted forward against a stationary car. Through the passenger window she could see a young woman, terror in her eyes, trying to placate two hysterical toddlers in the back.

Wendy shouted, above the din, 'It'll be OK,' but knew the mum couldn't hear – and even if she could, she'd know the promise was empty.

Suddenly she caught a glimpse of Dan, his hand gripped round a white man's throat, propelling him back towards a shopfront opposite the mosque. He was about three metres away but might as well have been thirty, such was the impenetrable crowd between them.

Like a tidal swell, the crowd bulged in Dan's direction lending Wendy a metre or two of space. At first she thought it was the start of a dispersal. Then, to her horror she saw it for what it was. Half a dozen white men had spotted Dan's arrest attempt and were charging to their friend's aid.

'Dan! Behind you!' she said, but her cries were swamped by the taunts and roar of the crowd. She strained to keep sight of her crew-mate and grabbed two men twice her size, flinging them out of her path, tears blurring her vision.

'Fuck off, pig,' was one discernible insult she picked out. Instinctively she floored the thug with one punch. That created more space and she pushed forward without breaking stride. As she was within a metre of where she'd last seen Dan, the crowd around where he should be suddenly pushed back, running in every direction. Wendy did the opposite, desperate to find her irritating friend, praying he'd moved elsewhere but unseen by her.

In seconds her worst fears were realised and she jabbed the red emergency button on her radio.

'Charlie Romeo Zero One, officer down, multiple stab wounds. I need ambulance and back-up urgently. Shit, he's bleeding out.'

There wasn't much that could persuade Jo to set foot in a hospital, especially the Royal Sussex County where her father had shrivelled to his death, but a stabbed PC in the Intensive Care Unit was an exception. She'd been desperate to visit him from the moment she heard about his vicious attack outside the mosque, but he'd been in surgery most of the night, so this was the first chance she'd had.

When she was buzzed through to the ward, she wondered why she was shocked to see the tangle of wires and tubes and the suck and puff of the machinery by his side. What did she expect?

She nodded at Dan Bilkham's dedicated nurse, then pulled up a chair next to PC Wendy Relf, who was gently holding her partner's hand.

'How is he?' Jo asked.

'Oh, hello ma'am. Sorry, I didn't see you come in,' said Wendy as she went to stand up.

Jo touched her shoulder. 'It's a Jo day for you.'

'They say he's stable but the next forty-eight hours are crucial.'

'Sounds like a stock prognosis.'

They were sitting in silence for a moment.

'Shall I tell you one of his worst jokes?' said Wendy.

'If you must.'

'Where is the worst place to play hide and seek in a hospital? ICU.'

Jo smiled. 'That's truly terrible.'

'See what I had to work with now?'

'*Have* to work with. We can always change your partner when he gets out of here.'

'Please don't though.' Wendy started to cry.

Jo hugged her. 'I thought you'd say that.'

Jo looked around, humbled by the love and care the staff gave every patient, but she couldn't shift the thought that this was God's waiting room.

'You know, there was real hate in their eyes,' said Wendy when she'd composed herself.

'You don't have to talk about it.'

'I want to. Dan was so brave. If they'd not stabbed him, they would have attacked all those poor Muslim boys and God knows what they'd have done to them.'

'But I thought it was them who had the bats?'

'Only to protect their mosque. And the women and children. Those fucking fascists started it. And did this.' She waved a hand towards Dan. 'Pardon my language.'

'You forget I share an office with Gary Hedges. That's pre-watershed by comparison. We'll find who's behind this, you know. They will pay for it.'

'Promise?'

'Pinky.'

Wendy threw her a curious look.

'Sorry, it's what I say to my kids. It's the most solemn vow I can make.'

For the first time Wendy smiled. 'In that case I believe you.'

As soon as she left the hospital, Jo was straight on the phone to Gary Hedges.

'This has got to stop, and not just because it's one of our own.'

'How is he?'

'Not good. I take it you have a team investigating it? I want these thugs found.'

'Obviously, but everyone's saying it's the people from the mosque who had the weapons and the white blokes were just protecting themselves.'

'That is utter bollocks,' said Jo, oblivious to the stares she was drawing from the crowd at the bus stop. 'What were they doing there in the first place? And what's their excuse for stabbing one of our PCs half to death? I'm not having that shit.'

'I know all that, but have you seen the *Chronicle*?'

'No. Why?'

'I'll send you a link.'

As she reached her car, her phone pinged with a WhatsApp message. She opened the link and froze when she saw the picture alongside the headline.

'What the hell are they doing? "PC Stabbed Outside Mosque" might be factually accurate but the picture of the Muslim lad with a baseball bat is bang out of order.'

She started her car and eased out into the traffic.

'I've spoken to the editor. He just said it was the best picture they had from the scene.'

'Best as in clearest, or best as in it suits their warped racist narrative?'

'Funny, he wouldn't elaborate. Have you seen the council comment?'

'No, I'm driving. Read it to me.'

'A council spokesman said, "We utterly condemn the violence outside the Al-Medinah Mosque yesterday. This city will not tolerate thugs arming themselves with baseball bats and the like to attack our citizens as they go about their lawful business. We call on the Imam to restore order in his community and turn those responsible over to the police." And before you ask, no one asked for a comment from us.'

'No condemnation of racists trying to murder a police officer then? That's bloody it. I need to talk to Parfitt, he's got no right to comment on active criminal investigations.'

'Jo, do you think you should calm down first?'

'That's a terrible idea.'

Jo diverted from Eastern Road and took the back streets around the rush-hour traffic, rehearsing in her mind what she would say to the chief executive, determined to look him in the eye and demand an explanation.

She pulled up outside Hove Town Hall and abandoned her car in a police-only bay opposite the front door. Marching through the doors, she took her chance when she saw the security barrier wedged open by a couple of deliverymen trying to manoeuvre a huge cabinet.

'Excuse me,' she muttered as she squeezed through and up the stairs, seemingly unseen by the flustered reception staff.

As she entered the executive suite she deliberately did not look into Debbie's office and hoped she hadn't spotted her. The last thing Jo wanted was to make what she was about to do seem to be the PA's fault.

She couldn't believe her luck when she saw both Parfitt and Doughty were in the chief executive's office. *Two vultures with one stone*, she thought.

'Can you explain this?' she said as she burst through the door, phone outstretched. Both men looked first startled, then livid.

'What do you . . .' Parfitt started. He looked even shabbier than usual.

'Do you know where I've just come from? The hospital, where one of my PCs is lying wired up to God knows what, having whatever it's taking to keep him alive pumped into him. Why? Because he was attacked by a mob of racist thugs and almost hacked to death.'

'And that's our fault, how?' asked Doughty with a sickening smirk breaking out.

'It's the tone you've set so your supporters think they have carte blanche to do whatever they want in this city. And then you underscore it with a press statement which blames the victims. The least you could do is show some support for those trying to keep a modicum of peace.'

'If your officers are going to disobey orders and put themselves in the middle of a race riot when they are told to hold back, I don't see how that's the council's fault. You need to get a grip and stop your lot acting the hero just to protect the foreigners who think they can bully those who are legitimately protesting,' said Doughty.

Jo was caught off guard. 'What do you mean "disobey orders?"'

'What I said. I'm surprised you don't know. They were told not to go in.'

'Who told you that?'

Another smirk that Jo wished she could punch off the council leader's face, coupled with him tapping the side of his nose.

'Let me just say, things are going to change round here. Russ here has just come from a very useful chat with your chief constable. They both agree that a new policing style is needed in this city, if we are going to give the voting public what they want.'

Jo glared at Parfitt who just nodded.

'And,' Doughty continued, 'it seems Stuart agrees with us, whether that's you delivering it or someone else. The choice is yours. You won't be missed.'

5

One week previously

Ajee's hunger screamed as she staggered up the stairs at the end of her first shift. She'd survived all day on two pieces of toast, a digestive biscuit and the remains of a chicken leg left by a resident. There had been no breaks to speak of and the couple of times she'd sneaked a sit-down in one of the rooms, Peggy had yelled at her for taking so long.

Perhaps if she'd slept better the night before, she'd feel stronger.

As she finally got to the top floor, she pulled the unmarked door open. The two metres by three windowless room boasted three iron bunk beds, one against each wall, with a narrow walkway down the middle, made smaller still by an army camp bed on which an African girl, about Ajee's age, now snored.

She'd been told the night before by an Afghan woman that ten of them shared the room but, as there were always at least four on shift, it wasn't so bad. Ajee begged to differ.

Each bed had a thin sleeping bag and grimy single pillow. The girls seemed to have made some effort to keep their clothes tidy. As it was all work and sleep, none had an extensive wardrobe, but the makeshift washing line, strung across both diagonals, made standing hazardous.

Chipped avocado-green plates were stacked up by the door. To Ajee's disappointment, any leftovers had already been swiped.

She counted three beds occupied, fewer than last night, so maybe she could get one furthest from the door tonight.

'Excuse me,' she said to the girl on the camp bed. 'When do we eat?'

The girl opened her eyes but no other part of her moved. She looked so tired Ajee guessed she couldn't if she tried.

'Our meal,' she repeated. 'When do we get food?'

'You eat on your shift. When you finish, you sleep. No eat.'

'But I'm hungry. I need food.'

'You must take what food you can when you work. Too late now.'

Ajee's heart sank. How would she get through the night, let alone the next day, without something inside her?

'Where can I bath? Shower?' She could tell the African girl was getting annoyed with her constant questions, but she needed to scrub off the grime of the day.

'Basin in toilet next door. No bath. No shower.'

Ajee's mind yearned back to the previous afternoon at George's flat. She wondered whether she could get hold of George. Surely he would get her out of this; realise what his friend was up to. Then she recalled the flash of ice when he'd implored her to come here. The way his face had hardened when he was on the phone.

It hit her that this was all part of his plan – or someone's plan at least. Having dodged robbers, rapists and killers across Europe, she'd fallen for the charms of a kindly old bumbling grandad who had lured her into this bar-less prison.

She plonked herself on the bottom bunk by the back wall, laid her head on the rancid pillow and silently sobbed herself to sleep.

6

One week later

Jo darted into a rare parking space on Upper Drive. These visits were her little secret; a promise she made to someone once very dear to her but who could no longer make them himself.

She grabbed the purple irises from the front seat, stepped out of the car, darted between the queuing traffic and walked up to the imposing black front door of Sycamore Care Home.

In the hallway, so you couldn't miss it, was a large mahogany table with a printed red laminate pinned to the wall above it, instructing *All Visitors – Sign In Here*. The entrance always looked neat and pristine, but no amount of air freshener could mask the reek of urine that hit you the moment you breathed in. That and the faceless cries and shouts that were the home's muzak broke Jo's heart.

She hated providing her real name, but on balance that was better than having to answer awkward questions if she used a pseudonym. A scribbled, barely legible, signature seemed a reasonable compromise.

She unclipped the safety gate at the bottom, then the top of the single staircase – were they even allowed? – then gently tapped the second door on the left. Waiting a beat, she opened it and walked in.

Mary Cooke was slouched in a pink plastic chair, her winceyette sky-blue dressing gown stained with what Jo hoped was today's breakfast but could have been weeks-old debris. Her head lolled to one side and Jo grabbed a tissue to wipe the drool tracking down her chin.

'Hello, Mary, it's me, Jo,' she said as she squeezed the old lady's icy hand. 'How are you today?'

Mary didn't reply. She never did. Jo wondered whether she'd even registered her being there, but a promise was a promise.

She looked around the room as she sat at Mary's side. The photos, some sharper and newer than others, catalogued a life well lived. Happy snaps of children and grandchildren frolicking in the sea by Brighton's Palace Pier. Mary at her only son's wedding and later shots of one of her grandsons holding a trophy aloft and the other, eyes closed as the strum of his bass guitar seemed to boom through him. Jo had to look away.

It was a small mercy that Mary's dementia had gripped her before these carefree scenes had shattered a few brutal months ago. To Mary, her happy family was still intact.

Jo watched the rise and fall of the food stains as Mary slept. She had nothing really to say to her but had promised her son Phil she would visit every couple of weeks; just sit and hold her hand and see that all was well.

Jo's bond with Phil had been stretched by the last year's events. Given everything that had happened, her instinct was to hide away from anything connected with the Cookes. The guilt and terror those few days had piled on her made restful sleeps a wild fantasy, even now. But the torch she held for him still flickered since their affair sixteen years ago, so, when he'd called her, a week after he was remanded in custody, and begged her to be there for his mother, how could she refuse?

She made a point of never arriving in uniform, and to the staff – who rotated more frequently than football managers – she was a close family friend. To be honest, none were that interested, but some would confide in her over Mary's health and ask if she needed anything. Probably the hampers Jo dropped in occasionally loosened their tongues more than was appropriate for a non-family member.

After what seemed like an hour but was probably around fifteen minutes, Jo unlocked her hand from Mary's and set about tidying her room. The staff did the basics – emptied the bin, cleaned round the basin, sluiced the commode – but Jo added the finer touches. Having thrown away the wilting tulips she'd brought last time, she arranged the irises then spruced up the bed, shelves and sink area. Lastly, she freshened up Mary's neck and dressing gown with a squirt of Chanel Coco Mademoiselle, brushed her willowy grey hair, pecked her on the cheek and left.

Stepping out onto the landing, she caught sight of a carer.

'Morning.'

The young, wiry Asian girl spun round, eyes like frisbees.

'I'm sorry,' said Jo. 'I didn't mean to scare you.'

'It's fine,' she replied, as she twiddled her pretty silver double-crescent necklace.

'I don't think I've seen you before. I'm Jo.' The girl hesitated then took the offered hand. An awkward moment stretched out between them.

'And you are?' Jo prompted.

'I—I, er. My name is Ajee,' she replied as she pulled her bony hand away.

'Well, it's lovely to meet you, Ajee. I wonder if I could trouble you?'

Ajee looked around as if checking that no one would overhear.

Jo continued. 'It's just that I've popped in to see Mary Cooke and I wonder if someone could change her robe? She's spilt something down the one she's wearing. I'd do it but I'm not allowed to lift her.'

'Yes, of course. I do it straight away.'

'Also, I was just wondering. Is Mary OK? You know, is she well?'

'Yes, yes. She very well.'

'Thank you,' replied Jo, finally allowing the flustered carer to go on her way.

Jo walked down the stairs, signed out and breathed in a lungful of air to expel the rancid stench that defined the home. She was relieved her obligation to prisoner AK7061 was discharged for another two weeks.

* * *

As was becoming more frequent these days, Russ Parfitt was in the foulest of moods when he stormed through his front door. Whilst, politically, you couldn't get a fag paper between him and Tom Doughty, the Leader of the Council's interpretation of the possible was rooted in fantasy.

Today it had all been about introducing by-laws to ban gypsies and travellers from any public space – and he meant *any* public space; effectively prohibiting them from the city. When Russ had argued that it would be unlawful, unethical and impossible to police, Doughty threatened, not for the first time, to replace him with someone more committed to 'the cause'.

Russ hoped, for her sake, his wife Heather had his dinner ready and their four- and six-year-old girls were in bed.

He stormed into the open-plan kitchen-diner and saw Heather through the bifold doors reclined on a patio chair, sipping a glass of white wine, phone wedged to her ear. Without breaking stride, Russ dropped his bag by the island unit and marched outside.

Heather's terrified look when she saw him was matched only by Russ's thunderous glare. Quickly ending the call, she stood up, spun round and took a step back, all in one movement.

'Hi, darling. I, er, I wasn't expecting you home so soon.'

'So I see. Why can't I smell cooking?'

'Oh, I thought . . . I wondered if you'd like a Chinese tonight.'

Russ turned and went back inside, knowing full well that the offer of a takeaway was cover for spending the day on her lazy arse, quaffing Chardonnay and gassing to the other yummy mummies.

She'd pay for that.

Heather followed Russ in, muttering apologies and pitiful attempts to change the subject.

'Shall I get on and order?' she asked.

'Best you had, I'm starving,' he replied as his phone rang. 'Fucking hell.'

'The usual?' she checked, but Russ ignored her as he answered the call.

'Tom. What can I do for you?' said Russ, hoping he'd masked his irritation.

'I need to see you,' said the councillor.

'What now? I only saw you half an hour ago. Can't it wait?'

'I'll be round in ten,' said Tom before killing the call.

Russ slammed the phone down on the granite worktop, startling Heather. The council leader's personal life was an enigma. The two had known each other as young activists but then Tom had gone off the radar, returning as the British Patriot Party's shining light.

Rumours of him training the youth wing of the English Defence Corps, and some unsavoury blurring of punishments and rewards, were never proved.

Now, it was all work work work, fuelled by an insatiable urge to create a supreme state, akin to Hitler's, right here in Brighton.

'Tom's on his way round. Make yourself scarce and keep those brats away from me.'

'Shall I still order the food?'

'Well, yes,' said Russ as he grabbed his bag and his phone, then stomped off to the study that overlooked the gated driveway.

He collapsed his flabby frame into his favourite leather armchair and fired up his laptop. A quick scan of his emails revealed no breaking disasters since he'd left the office. As ever, therefore, Tom had probably imagined some impending doom on his way home and diverted to shift his paranoia onto his chief executive.

As the Range Rover swung up to the entrance, Russ pressed the remote control allowing the iron gates to grant Tom access. He waited for him to step from the car before he went to open the front door.

'Russ, thanks for making time for me,' said Tom, not looking or sounding grateful at all.

'No worries, come in.'

Tom barged past his host and made his way straight for the study. This was not his first time encroaching here.

'Beer?' said Russ in his wake.

'Please.'

Russ took out his phone, opened his WhatsApp, and punched a demand to Heather for *Two Beers.*

In less than a minute she tapped on the door and delivered two ice-cold Chang lagers.

They waited until her footsteps disappeared down the hallway.

'Russ, I'm not having that bitch cop coming and throwing her weight around again. That's the second time in a week.'

'It's not like I invited her.'

'I don't care. What I care about is her poisoning this city with her namby-pamby leftie ways. She's a fucking liability.'

'In fairness, one of her officers did get stabbed and is on a life support machine. Even we should cut her some slack for the moment.'

'Bollocks we should. If those two numbskulls were dumb enough to wade in on their own, then they should expect what they got.'

'But the bloke's at death's door.'

'More fool him,' said Doughty.

Parfitt wandered to the bay window, trying to process how heartless the councillor could be. He watched helplessly as a ginger tomcat took a dump on his pristine lawn.

'OK. I'll speak to Stuart Acers again.'

'Make sure you do. Anyway, yesterday's events have brought things into focus for me. We're not making enough progress.'

'But . . .'

'This druggy, permissive, welcome-all-comers image has got to stop. We are a laughing stock and it's pissing off decent, normal people. What about their wishes and rights? The people who've voted for us. I've been going through the budget. Do you know how much we spend on gay rights, black rights, refugee rights, every other bleeding heart versus helping decent, hard-working English people like you and me?'

'But this new world you want to create has to be a long-term plan,' *and is therefore not urgent*, he wanted to add. 'We have to get people on board, nudge them in the right direction. You're going to need at least two four-year terms to get anywhere close to your dream.' *How often had they had this conversation?*

'Not good enough. From tomorrow I want direct action. Start by planning to cut all support for the mosques then anything we give to those LGBTQ, or whatever they call themselves, freaks. I've got plans for Pride, by the way, whatever the courts have said about us banning it. This year will be the last. No more spending on racial cohesion either. They come to our country, they earn their keep and play by our rules. I want the police to crack down on the filth bags coming and protesting about everything from the weather to the lack of vegan kebab shops. That's on top of the travellers' ban you're on to.'

Russ was speechless. Tom had had these scattergun rants before but this time he sounded desperate. He clearly had no idea change didn't happen like that. Arguing, however, was not an option. Chief executives, with their £200k salaries, were as disposable as bog roll these days.

He was grateful to see a moped stop at the gates. He zapped the Deliveroo boy in and met him at the front door. Taking the bag of Chinese into the study, he saw Tom lick his lips.

'Want some?'

'Go on then,' said Tom, suddenly much cheerier.

Russ picked up his phone, opened WhatsApp and typed, *Two more beers. Two forks.*

The ever-reliable Heather was at the door in thirty seconds this time. 'Open yourself a tin of beans,' whispered Russ as he snatched the cutlery and bottles, 'and wipe those fucking tears away.'

When his phone rang, Russ Parfitt's hangover felt he was in for the long haul.

The searing headache and crippling nausea following one of Tom Doughty's after-hours visits were as inevitable as the rising sun. Those evenings followed a pattern: outrageous demands, beer, food, more beer which then lubricated debates into the small hours covering topics such as what it meant to be British, gay marriage and when Brexit would deliver us our borders.

It was just shy of 1 a.m. before Tom finally snoozed off and Russ instructed Heather to call him a cab. Once he'd seen the council leader off the premises, he stumbled to bed and after some clumsy thrusting, for which Heather seemed bloody ungrateful, he collapsed into a stupor.

'Parfitt,' he slurred into the mouthpiece.

'Russ, are you going to be long?'

'What the fuck . . .' He glanced at his watch. 'Shit,' he muttered.

'Russ, are you there? It's Stuart, Stuart Acers. Shall I order for you?'

'Shit, sorry Stuart. No, I'll be right with you. Give me twenty minutes.'

'OK, but I have got other meetings.'

'Twenty minutes I said.' He jabbed the call to an end.

'Heather,' he shouted. 'Heather.'

He threw back the crumpled Wedgwood-blue duvet, scanned the floor for his boxers, pulled them on – back to front – and stumbled onto the landing.

'Heather. I need you to take me to Rick's caff. I'm meeting the chief constable there and I'm late.'

His wife peered up from the hallway below, her eyes red and moist.

'But I'm just about to drive the kids to school,' she pleaded.

'I'll be five minutes. Drop me on the way.'

Russ slammed the door and staggered over to the en suite shower. The jets of scalding water did nothing for his headache but at least they swilled away yesterday's grime and made him feel moderately ready for the day ahead.

He dabbed himself with a fluffy towel, noticing he had yet to shave, aimed a couple of blasts of deodorant in the vicinity of his armpits, and threw on a neatly pressed crisp white shirt and freshly dry-cleaned blue single-breasted suit.

A rudimentary scrub of his teeth over – or close to – the sink and he was done. He grabbed his electric razor and dashed out onto the landing.

'Heather, kids, I'm ready. In the car. Now.'

He thundered down the stairs, nearly trampling his daughters as he bolted across the hallway.

'Watch where you're going,' he said, not noticing Heather pull them both into her and whisper something into their hair about Daddy being tired.

Russ snatched his briefcase from the table, opened the front door and trotted across the gravel to the passenger side of their white BMW X5.

'Unlock the bloody thing,' he said, as he pulled on the unyielding handle.

A couple of bleeps and he was in, razor already hacking through his patchy stubble.

He cursed at Heather's fannying around, clipping the girls into their car seats behind him.

The back doors clicked shut. Heather climbed into the driver's seat, pressed the ignition button and eased the car forward, mounting the lawn to edge round Tom Doughty's Range Rover.

'Take that back to his house later. The keys are in the study,' said Russ.

'Why can't he—'

'You'll have to get a cab back. Make sure it's before lunchtime.'

'Can't he—'

'By one.'

Heather pulled out into the snake of traffic that lined Dyke Road Avenue and thumbed a thank you to the cabbie who'd shown her the first, and probably only, act of kindness she'd receive that day.

The girls, as always, were quiet throughout the drive, the only sound being the buzz of Russ's shaver.

He huffed at the gridlock. 'Take the back routes.'

'But they're always just as bad,' Heather replied.

'It's only a mile away, just take the fucking rat runs.'

Heather threw him a look that said, *The children.*

'Sorry girls,' muttered Russ, then hissed to Heather, 'Just do it.'

She meandered, in thick silence, back and forth along the residential streets that ran parallel to the main route into the city.

Finally, she pulled up outside Rick's Café in Upper Hamilton Road. Russ picked up his case, murmured 'Bye', to which he heard no reply, and stepped out of the car.

The bell on the door grated as he burst in. He glanced around and saw the chief constable sat at a corner table, deep in a phone conversation.

'Sorry I'm late. Trouble at mill,' he quipped, as he pulled out a ladder-back, blue wooden chair and sank his hefty frame down.

'Got to go,' Acers told the person on the other end of the call, then looked up. 'No problem. How are you?' He stretched out his hand, which Russ felt obliged to shake.

'Fine, fine. You ordered?'

'Not yet.' Russ beckoned over a waiter.

'I'll have the Big Breakfast,' said Stuart.

'Just coffee and toast for me,' said Russ, ignoring Stuart's raised eyebrow.

The waiter scurried off and Russ explained, 'Heavy night.'

'That's why I'm teetotal,' said Stuart. 'It all got a bit much for me, at my age.'

'I'm sure,' said Russ with a knowing look. 'Anyway, where are we with that bloody Howe woman?'

Stuart shuffled on his chair. 'Well, I've sent a shot across her bows, and Gary Hedges', but there's not much more I can do, to be frank. They are both right and after what happened yesterday . . .'

'Don't give me that. Those two idiots brought it on themselves.' He knew he was sounding like Doughty's mouthpiece.

'Hold on a minute . . .'

'No, you hold on. Everyone is bleating on about the poor PC – who should have known better by the way – or those bloody Muslims. It's all crap. They were the ones with baseball bats and your copper got in the way. Jo Howe has blood on her hands by not being robust enough. You keep telling me that policing is one huge shade of grey. Surely you can find a reason to either make them step in line or ship them out.' Russ then spelt out, with a little exaggeration, how Jo had burst into his office the day before.

'I'm sorry about that. I will speak to her, but I've got to give them a chance to respond before we turn the screw any more.'

'You seem to be under the impression that time is on our side. I've got Doughty breathing all sorts of shit down my neck, and you want to play the wait and see game?'

'All I'm saying is that it was only the other day that I bawled them out and now they are dealing with the attempted murder of a cop. Unless they cock up again, I can't be seen to up the ante.'

'But they've no backbone. How are those two snowflakes going to implement what we've agreed? It's going to be tough enough kicking the travellers out of the city, banning Pride, moving all the foreigners into one place – but without our police there to back us up when it goes tits up, well.'

'Banning Pride? You've already tried that and the courts were having none of it.'

'Watch this space on that. None of this is going away, you just need to get those two apologies for police officers to do what they're told.'

'It's hard to order them to—'

'Hard?' Parfitt said, a little too loudly. 'Hard?' he whispered. 'I thought you said you ran a disciplined service. At least you only have a Police and Crime Commissioner to appease. I've got a whole bloody council and, believe me, they don't all sing Tom's tune. I'm not asking, I'm telling you. If they don't come in line, shaft them. Like you did with Phil Cooke.'

Acers winced. Few people mentioned that man's name in his presence, especially those who knew what last year's events meant for the force.

'I'll see what I can do, but I can't promise that, even if I could find a reason to put them out to grass, their replacements will be any more malleable.'

Parfitt leant in. 'Then you'd better spark up that old ingenuity of yours, because you really don't want your little secret to leak out, now do you?'

Acers gulped.

'Get them in line or get rid, otherwise it's not just your reputation that will be in tatters. Understood?'

'Fully,' quaked the chief.

7

Unable to get through to Chief Constable Stuart Acers to brief him on PC Dan Bilkham, Jo took the opportunity to pop in to see Mary Cooke on the way into work. She'd yet to find the right time to tell her husband, Darren, that she was visiting Phil's mum, in much the same way as she'd yet to mention her affair with him, even though its break-up had indirectly led to her and Darren meeting.

Jo had not had time to pick up flowers but she doubted whether Mary noticed one way or the other. In fact, she wasn't sure who benefitted from the visits, but it went some way to salve her conscience after bringing down her former lover.

She parked just outside the home and, once again, tugged open the door. She was about to sign in when she spotted a familiar girl come out from the lounge.

Jo never forgot a face. Much to Darren's amazement she could always recite just about every actor's filmography the second they appeared on TV.

'Morning, Ajee,' she said. Once again, the girl turned round with a start. She was about to dart into a corridor when Jo called out. 'Ajee, it's me, Jo. We met the other day?'

With apparent reluctance, Ajee stopped and turned back round. 'Good morning, Mrs Jo.'

'It's just Jo. Twice in two visits? I hope they give you some days off.'

'I work hard. For my family. I must work now.'

Jo saw a sadness in Ajee's eyes as she moved to walk off.

'Where are your family?'

'Turkey, they are in Turkey,' she lied.

Jo wondered whether that was true but let it pass. 'You like working here?'

Again, a pause. 'Yes, very much. Thank you.'

'It's good to see young people looking after the elderly. I visit my friend's mother whilst he's away. It's nice that she sees people with their lives ahead of them. I'm sure it helps.'

'Thank you.' Ajee seemed a little more relaxed. 'You visit Mary. Mary Cooke, yes?

'You remembered. That's right.'

'I change her robe, like you ask. She very lucky lady to have you.'

Peggy, the manager, walked past and sized the two of them up. Ajee's stance tensed again.

'Thank you,' said Jo. 'It's lovely to chat. You have a good day now and I might see you next time.'

'Thank you, Mrs Jo,' replied Ajee, then disappeared from sight.

Following the uneventful visit, Jo was a little saddened that she didn't bump into Ajee on the way out. There was something fascinating yet deeply concerning about the girl. Her natural nosiness nudged her to find out more when she next visited.

As she walked to her car, she tried one more call to the chief. This time he picked up.

'Talk of the devil,' he said, before she had a chance to speak.

'That sounds ominous. Should I be worried?'

'Where are you? We need to talk.'

Jo let the fact that she'd been trying to do that since about seven that morning slide.

'Isn't that what we are doing?'

'I mean face to face.'

'I'm in Hove,' said Jo, determined not to give any more away.

'Snap,' said Acers. 'I'll meet you at the Hill Top Café at the top of Dyke Road Avenue. I'll buy you a coffee.'

'I don't drink coffee, but I can be there in ten.' It would actually take her five minutes, but she added some time so she could call Gary to find out whether there was anything she needed to know which Acers might ambush her with. He was as oblivious as her, so she drove the short distance to the rendezvous.

Acers was already there, pacing up and down the small gravel car park, phone wedged to his ear with one hand, the other gesticulating like a haywire windmill.

Jo stepped out of her car and leant against the bonnet, enjoying the sun on her face as she waited patiently for her bollocking.

After a good ten minutes, Acers paced over.

Seizing the initiative, she spoke first. 'I suppose you want to know about Dan Bilkham.'

Acers looked lost for a moment, so Jo helped him out. 'The PC in the ICU who those racist thugs stabbed?'

'Yes, yes, of course. How is he?'

'Still being kept alive by the combined talents of machinery and the medical profession. Are you planning on visiting him?'

'Indeed. I'll, er, ask my PA to arrange it.' He tapped out a brief message on his phone. Jo struggled with why he couldn't pop in on his way back to Lewes HQ, but so much about this man escaped her.

'You wanted to see me?'

'Oh yes. What's all this about you gatecrashing a meeting between Tom Doughty and Russ Parfitt yesterday?'

'So, you didn't want to talk about the poor PC fighting for his life, only my reaction to it?' Jo knew that was incendiary but couldn't help herself. Luckily for her, a couple who'd parked two spaces along walked within earshot, making their way to the café.

Once they were clear, Acers let rip.

'You can't bloody help yourself, can you? Can't you see I'm trying to protect you? You can't go throwing your weight around among the city's senior leaders. Do you understand?'

'Perfectly, *sir*. But what do you expect when they openly supported the fascists who nearly killed one of my PCs? They're blaming him and the Muslims who were defending their place of worship.'

'With baseball bats.'

'Granted, but they weren't the aggressors here. PCs Bilkham and Relf certainly weren't either. Yet if you listened to Doughty and Parfitt, it's the ones who put Dan on life support we should be feeling sorry for.'

'Just rein it in. We have to work with these *elected* members and their appointees, not against them. They have the mandate to do what they want. We have to support them.'

'Since when? Didn't we both take the same oath to serve impartially? I was always told that meant we don't side with politics.'

'Are you really that naive?'

'Every time they bark, you're on at me. What have they got on you? I know you're my boss, but you need to grow a pair and stand up to those yobs before it comes back to bite you.' She knew she'd long-jumped rather than overstepped the mark. To her amazement, the barrage she'd been expecting didn't come. Acers just stood there staring at her. Was that a tear in the corner of his eye? She left the silence for him to fill which, after what seemed like an age, he did.

'Jo, there are things you can't know but please, for my sake and yours, just toe their line. It won't be for ever but more hinges on it than you can ever know.'

The chief constable trudged over to his Mercedes, and with not so much as a goodbye, zapped it open, slid in and the car purred off.

Jo stared as his car disappeared. What on earth had got into the man? He'd be perfectly within his rights to rip into her, but something was up – and his desperation said that what she did next could destroy him.

* * *

The last time Detective Inspector Bob Heaton had been in a suspect interview room, he was on the other side of the table facing a murder charge.

The two months he'd spent on remand in Her Majesty's Prison Bullingdon for killing a murder suspect, before he was exonerated when the incompetence of the Independent Office of Police Conduct was revealed, had crushed his spirit and all confidence in the criminal injustice system, as he now called it. He'd been lucky to survive both prison and what followed. Against his better judgement he'd taken the offer of re-joining Sussex Police at his previous level.

Protocol demanded a rank differential between investigator and suspect when the latter was a serving police officer, but he was grateful to the helpful DS by his side whose familiarity with the recording equipment outstripped his own.

Bob felt for the officer opposite, despite what he'd done. He was the only one in the room who knew for certain the brutality Sergeant Harry Masters was facing. Being a copper in prison was bad enough, but being a rapist as well guaranteed horrors beyond even Bob's imagination.

Bob had arrested the firearms unit sergeant as he arrived for work at 7 a.m. that morning after his wife had revealed a decade of physical and sexual abuse at the officer's hands. The evidence she'd amassed was unusual in domestic abuse cases, but she was a serving DC so knew what was required.

Having reminded Masters of the caution, he then introduced himself as DI Bob Heaton of the Brighton and Hove Safeguarding Investigation Unit, before trotting out some confirmatory questions regarding the arrest and there having been no off-the-record interviews.

'Harry, are you sure you don't want a solicitor?' asked Bob, wondering whether Masters knew how deep a shit he was in.

'I don't need one. I can explain everything.'

'Your call. Now, listen to this voice recording your wife made during the last rape.'

Bob tapped play on his laptop.

Masters blanched as the shouts and screams echoed round the room. When it was over, Bob said, 'Can you explain what's happening?'

Masters coughed, then said, 'No comment.'

Bob sighed. Some of the cleverest – and most stupid – people Bob knew were in the job. Harry Masters was firmly in the latter camp.

'You need to explain, Harry. Your wife says that's you raping her and it sounds pretty much like that to me.'

Masters' eyes welled up, his lips quivered. 'No comment.' It was plain to Bob that he had not been expecting to get caught. They never did.

Of all the offenders he'd dealt with over the years, Bob hated rapists the most. Why he'd accepted a job in the SIU, therefore, was beyond him – but at least being a DI meant he rarely came face to face with these monsters.

'Don't you dare start feeling sorry for yourself. If you're going to feel sorry for anyone, make it your wife.'

'No comment.'

'That wasn't a question.' Bob then read out a list of injuries the Forensic Medical Examiner had documented. 'Your wife says you caused those during this same attack. Did you?'

'No comment.'

The interview continued for another thirty minutes, during which the soon-to-be-ex sergeant stuck to the silence a solicitor would have advised him to observe.

As all three rose to attend to the question of bail and Masters' immediate suspension from duty, Bob's phone buzzed in his pocket. 'Unknown Number' usually signalled the control room or one of his more cautious colleagues. Either could be urgent, so he nodded to his DS to take the prisoner to the custody officer, sat back down and tapped 'accept'.

'DI Heaton.'

'Morning, sir, it's DC Jake Briers. Have you got a minute?'

'Depends what for. I'm up at custody with a prisoner.' Bob could tell by the pause that the young detective could not compute one of his bosses being so hands-on.

'Oh, right. It's just I'm at a sudden death at a care home in Hove and I'm not happy with it.'

'Tell me more.'

'Well, it's an eighty-five-year-old chap. He had dementia but physically he was quite well. Early this morning he suffered a heart attack and died.'

'I'm guessing there's more.'

'Well, yes. No one tried CPR or anything. They just let him die.'

'Well, that's not wholly unusual. What have the staff said?'

'This is where it gets really odd. First of all, I couldn't find anyone who knew much about him. He'd only been here for about ten days. His next of kin live in Scotland. Then, after about half an hour of me asking, up pops the manager waving something called an advance care plan at me. In that is a DNACPR clause.'

'Do not attempt CPR?'

'Exactly. The odd thing is that, by all accounts, this bloke can't really communicate, yet the GP who put this in place did so the day he moved in. I've not dealt with anything like this before, but it all seems a bit convenient. Sorry if I'm panicking but I'd really like you to come and take a look.'

Bob could have hugged the lad. He'd spent the best part of his career telling junior detectives to listen to their instincts and act on them. And here was a DC, barely out of uniform, doing just that with no prompting.

'Give me the address,' Bob scribbled it down. 'I'll be with you in fifteen.'

DI Bob Heaton abandoned his silver CID Ford Mondeo by the recycling bins, grabbed his document wallet and marched up to the entrance of Sycamore Care Home. He pressed the buzzer, looked up at the CCTV and a click granted him access. Heaving the front door open, he scanned the corridor and offices for anyone who could point him to where he needed to be.

A young girl, late teens or early twenties, in a sky-blue tunic and navy trousers appeared from what looked like a lounge to his left.

'Excuse me, I'm from the police. I'm looking for my . . .' The girl turned and dashed off the way she'd come. 'Suit yourself,' muttered Bob.

'Can I help you?' came a voice from a poky office opposite. Bob glanced in and saw a woman in white sitting behind a desk, the state of which reminded him of Jo Howe's.

'Oh, hi.' He reached into his inside pocket and pulled out his black warrant card wallet. Flipping it open, he said, 'I'm DI Heaton from the police. I'm looking for my colleague, DC Briers?'

'Certainly, I'll show you to him. Poor Mr Moore. Very sad.' She eased her slender frame past the desk, picked up a bunch of keys and squeezed by Bob. 'I'm Peggy Squire, by the way. The manager. I must say, all this is a little unusual for a sudden death, isn't it?'

'Oh, there's probably nothing to worry about. The officers often ask for supervisors to come to this sort of thing,' he lied. 'Two heads are better than one, and all that.'

Peggy huffed then led Bob through a web of corridors and closed doors that seemed testament to numerous successful yet ill-thought-out planning applications over the years. Having passed the waft of boiled cabbage, which Bob took to be either coming from the sluice or the kitchen, Peggy tapped on a door marked 31.

DC Briers opened it and, just as Peggy was about to enter, Bob stepped in front of her. 'Thanks, Peggy. We'll call you when we need you.' She was about to reply when Bob cut her off. 'I'll find you when we are done.' He smiled as he eased the door closed.

'Thanks boss. She's been gagging to come in all morning.'

'I bet. What have we got?'

Bob glanced at Arthur Moore's body tucked up in bed. He looked like he'd surrendered quietly to whatever took him. The DI wondered what joys and horrors those now sightless eyes had witnessed.

Jake repeated what he'd been through on the phone, accepting how he might be wrong and could be panicking. His humility was refreshing and Bob coaxed him into voicing why he was worried. Gut feelings are always born out of something. Talking it through helped name it.

'To summarise,' Bob said. 'On the day he arrived the GP rocks up, spends five minutes with him and signs the DNACPR forms. He's got no history of heart disease, for his age he's physically quite healthy and no one's been in touch with the next of kin. That it?'

'Yes. He's got one son, who lives in Glasgow with his wife and two teenage children. I spoke to him on the phone. One of the kids has cystic fibrosis so they couldn't move Arthur up with them. He's phoned here a couple of times over the last few days to check how he was settling in, but that's it.'

Bob considered that. They would need to speak to the son again. He'd probably thought in finding a home for his dad, he'd have one less worry. Was he told that the doctor had put a DNACPR in place? If so, surely he'd have been down here like a shot.

'Have you spoken to the GP?'

'No, the paramedics declared life extinct. I'm hoping to catch the doc on his rounds. He's due about twelve.'

'OK, here's what we do. Get all Arthur's records. Speak to the GP when he arrives. Interview the staff who attended to him in the night and find out how many DNACPRs there are in place here. I'll phone the son and adult social care.'

'Any chance you could get someone up here to help me with the interviews, boss?'

'Sorry Jake.'

The DC's shoulders sagged. Bob hated himself for lumbering the lad, but what could he do? Even safeguarding had been slashed to the bone.

8

Both blacked-out panel vans slipped off the A27 at the Brighton exit. Turning right at the roundabout would have delivered them into the affluent Patcham estate or the main road into the city centre.

They turned left.

Both eased to a stop on the gravel lay-by. The driver and passenger of each – one a Renault, the other a VW – got out and huddled by the locked-up burger van which did a roaring trade by day.

'All set?' asked Leigh, the team leader. He'd been chosen as such for no other reason than because his dubious army career – which had spectacularly crashed following allegations of him torturing black recruits – suggested he had the best chance of keeping the other three thugs in order.

'Yep,' replied the monosyllabic driver of the VW. The other two just nodded.

Leigh checked his watch, then glanced skywards with a self-satisfied grin. He'd insisted they wait for cloud cover and a new moon which infuriated the controller, who wanted to carry out the attack sooner. However, he'd never seen combat and wasn't the one who'd be identified if it felt like they were under floodlights. Leigh sent his passenger down the pitch-black lane to check the gate to the travellers' site was open. His earlier recces suggested it would be, but he'd never leave such things to chance.

A couple of minutes later the red-headed lad returned and nodded.

'Listen in. Ginge and I will lead, lights off, and turn right when we get in. You turn left, then pull over about twenty yards in. Watch for a flash of my torch, then we go. So far?'

All three nodded. They had been through this several times but it didn't hurt to remind them.

'You go to the three nearest caravans, we'll do the ones on the right. One of you cut the gas pipes at the back of each, the other light the petrol bombs and launch them. Aim near the gas. Then get back in the van and fuck off. Whatever you do, don't hang around. In and out in fifteen seconds max. Can you count that high?'

Leigh expected at least one to react. Shit, this lot really were brain-dead.

'Right, let's go.'

All four slipped into their respective seats and clicked their doors closed.

Leigh moved off first. Ginge would be the pipe-cutter, as Leigh gauged the risks of throwing the Molotov cocktails were far lower than getting up close and personal with thirteen kilograms of volatile propane gas.

'Got the knife?' he checked.

Ginge grunted what Leigh hoped was a yes.

He coasted down the gentle slope, the car lurching into each pothole. Leigh checked in his mirror that the others were following. As he coasted through the open gate and past the shower block, Leigh turned right and, as arranged, sensed the others turn left. Happy they were ready, he blinked his phone light once and all four doors eased open.

'Go,' Leigh whispered, and Ginge sprinted to the furthest caravan whilst he went to the back of the Renault and opened the doors. Leigh could just make out Ginge dashing from the first caravan to the second. As he sprinted from the third, Leigh flicked his lighter and touched it on the rag drooping from the first milk bottle. It flared, then like a Test Match bowler, Leigh launched it, then the second, then the third blazing bomb towards their targets.

The first boom – then a scream – from the other side of the site came just as the third bottle left Leigh's hand. He and Ginge darted back to the van. As he floored the accelerator, tyres spinning on the damp concrete, the explosions lit up the surrounding downland, rupturing the silent night air.

He slowed for the gate, then glanced in the mirror. He could just make out the VW falling in behind him but, just as he was about to look away, spotted a whole pack of men sprinting towards them.

He kicked down again, momentarily losing control, the van glancing off the metal sign that welcomed all-comers to Horsdean. Ginge just stared ahead, mute with not a spark of emotion showing. Leigh powered up the hill, satisfied he was gaining ground. They'd soon be chasing them in cars, vans and motorbikes and he didn't fancy falling into the clutches of a gang of raging gypsies whose rancid homes he'd just torched.

As he wrenched the wheel towards the roundabout, he glanced back at the shimmering orange glow illuminating the rise of the hill.

He slammed into the motorbike before he saw it.

The thud, then the figure flying up his windscreen, was the first moment he realised what he'd done. The bike itself was ricocheted to the right, allowing Leigh to instinctively surge forward and away. The image in his mirror of the second van smacking into the biker as he, or she, was dumped off his own roof made him retch. Leigh just prayed they wouldn't be so stupid as to stop.

'Thank fuck,' he said as he spotted the VW closing on his tail. 'Just fucking follow me,' he hissed.

He was nearing sixty miles per hour over the A27 bridge as he approached the second roundabout. No way was he slowing but, thankfully, it was clear. He raced over the next and up Mill Road, desperate to reach the South Downs.

He checked again. The others were keeping up.

As he got to the top of the hill, he took the Devil's Dyke turn-off and urgently scanned for a lay-by or one of the ubiquitous sightseeing car parks. Soon, he spotted one marked 'Poor Man's Corner'. He swung in and his euphoria at the sight of the inferno across the valley was immediately doused by the ribbons of blue strobes racing towards it from every angle.

'Out,' he told Ginge, as the Renault crunched to a halt. 'Get the petrol and torch the vans. We'll have to tab the fuck out of here.'

The VW driver leapt out of his van and Leigh gave him the same order; then bile rose, singeing his throat. 'Where's the other idiot?' he said.

'He didn't make it to the van. I had to go.'

'You fucking left him?' Leigh screamed, his hands now round the other man's throat. 'You NEVER leave a man behind, you fucking twat. Never.' The man tried to fight back but Leigh's red mist had taken over. He swept the struggling man's feet from under him and landed on top of him as he hit the deck, his thumbs still crushing his trachea. Eventually the thrashing of his legs, arms and head slowed and finally stopped.

Leigh fell off him, panting.

'Help me get him in the back of the VW,' Leigh said to Ginge, who had been transfixed, the petrol can at his feet. 'Fucking now!'

Both men dragged the corpse through the double doors then Leigh slammed them shut. He grabbed the can and sloshed it inside the driver's compartment of each, then in the rear, making sure the body was drenched in the stuff.

'Get ready to run,' shouted Leigh, as he ignited a splash of petrol in each van. 'Fucking go,' he said, and they both sprinted across the boggy fields, with no plan other than to get the hell away.

9

Since becoming a chief superintendent, disturbed nights were fewer and further between for Jo Howe. Her previous job as Head of Major Crime meant rarely a week went by without at least two 'just to let you know' calls or full-on call-outs.

Now, other than the odd week when she was the duty Force Gold, designated to command the highest-level critical incidents, on a good night, she could snatch up to six hours interrupted sleep. Kids, and nightmares, permitting.

So, when her phone rang her first thought was a family emergency. Her heart returned to its normal beat when she slipped her glasses on to see Bob Heaton's name come into focus.

'Just a sec,' she whispered as she slid out of bed and the room, careful not to wake Darren or the boys.

She tiptoed downstairs, avoiding the creaky floorboard. As she flicked on the kitchen light and perched on a breakfast bar stool, she said, 'All right, go ahead, but you know I'm not Gold, don't you?'

'Thanks ma'am. Yes, Gold is already aware but you need to know this, as divisional commander.'

Jo had hammered home to all her inspectors that she, or Gary Hedges, were to be called if anything happened on the division which was likely to affect its reputation, resilience or resourcing. Some Gold commanders objected to this but, as Jo reminded them, she was the one left to pick up the pieces of whatever carnage had befallen the city. And, anyway, she'd return the compliment when the tables were turned.

'Go on.'

'You are sitting down, I take it.'

'Just spit it out.'

'Right, first things first, we've had an arson attack up at Horsdean. At least six caravans firebombed and ten people, including four children, taken to hospital.'

Jo's heart raced, 'How are they?'

'Thankfully most got out quick, so four adults and two children are expected to be discharged soon. The remaining casualties are in a critical condition.'

'Right?' Jo sensed there was more.

'The fires are out but, as you can imagine, the other residents are baying for blood. There's two police support units up there now.'

'Well done to whoever rustled up two PSUs at this time of night. What else?'

'It seems that as the attackers drove off – witnesses say they were in two vans – one of them, maybe both, have broadsided a motorcyclist on the roundabout.'

'Shit. How are they?'

'Declared dead at the scene.'

'I take it that's being investigated along with the arson.'

'Yes. Does the name Loretta Briggs mean anything to you?'

'The Council Finance Director? What's she got to do with it?'

'I'm afraid she's the motorcyclist.'

Jo took a moment. Loretta was the one director with whom she could have a sensible conversation. She was also the only woman among Parfitt's top team.

'Bloody hell. Has her next of kin been told?'

'Happening now.'

'Chief exec and leader?'

'Not yet. Would you like me to do that?'

'No, I'll do it, but only after her family know. Give me about thirty minutes and I'll be in.'

'One more thing.'

'What do they say about things in threes? Go on.'

'What we think are the two vans have been found burnt out at the Dyke.'

'And?' Jo knew a burnt-out vehicle up there was hardly worthy of mention.

'There's a body in the back of one.'

Jo gulped down the rising cobra of terror that these high-threat incidents always brought nowadays, coughed and said, 'Make that fifteen.'

By the time Jo reached her office, the station felt like it did at the height of a protest.

The corridors were crammed with dozens of Kevlar-clad PSU officers she did not recognise, but from the mumbles of 'morning, ma'am' that greeted her, even wearing her tracksuit top, most knew her.

Radios blared, phones rang unanswered, and sirens wailed as yet more units sped to Horsdean.

Amongst all the mayhem, she could have hugged Gary Hedges when she saw him, alongside a tactical advisor and a face in a suit she couldn't place, pacing towards their shared office.

'What the hell are you doing here?' she asked.

'Nice to see you too. I'm Gold tonight. Swapped with some Kent chief super. Some fucking ACC's leaving do or something. Anyway, I take it I can leave the politics to you and I can get on with the real policing.'

'Be my guest. Who's SIO?'

The smartly dressed Asian man she hadn't been able to place a moment ago stepped forward.

'DCI Faisal Hussain, ma'am. Hampshire originally but I took over from Scott Porter on the Major Crime Team.'

'Anyone who replaced that corrupt bastard is more than welcome on my division,' she said as she warmly shook his hand. This detective had a reassuring air about him.

'As we've not worked together before, can I just ask that you keep me updated on the investigation? I'm sure Gary will have briefed you on the politics of this city, but an attack on the travellers' site coupled with the death of a council director is pretty rare, even for here. It's going to send the so-called great and good into a flat spin.' She didn't mention what they'd think of a Pakistani man leading the murder hunt. 'Oh, also, if the chief asks anything, play dumb until you've checked in with Gary or me. Suffice to say, we're going through a rocky patch where he's concerned.' She flashed the DCI a smile.

'Well, forewarned and all that,' said Faisal, looking slightly less confident than he had a moment ago.

Gary's phone rang and his face froze. Jo watched him intently as he listened hard, interrupting with only the odd 'I see' and 'OK'.

He lowered the phone.

'One of the children and her mum have just died,' he said, more sombre than she'd ever seen him.

'The other two?'

He shrugged. 'Not looking good.'

Jo sat at her desk, pulled out her blue investigator's notebook and started scribbling. Then she looked up.

'Faisal, has Loretta Briggs' next of kin been informed?'

'Yes, about fifteen minutes ago.'

'Good. Any objections if I inform the Council Chief Executive and Leader? It'll be better coming from me.'

'After the briefing you've given me? None at all.'

Jo took herself off to her PA Fiona's office to give Gary some space.

Delivering bad news to Parfitt was one of her favourite pastimes, but this was a message she dreaded giving.

The phone rang for so long Jo almost gave up. Just as she was about to hit the red icon, a muffled 'Russ Parfitt' spluttered down the line.

'It's Jo. Jo Howe,' she said, spitefully loud and sprightly.

'Fuck do you want?'

'Take a moment Russ, as you definitely want to be fully awake for this.'

He huffed, then she heard shuffling before a more emphatic, 'I'm all ears. This better be worth waking me up for.'

'Two things. Firstly, there's been a multiple firebomb attack at Horsdean Travellers' Site. Two dead so far but likely to rise to four, six caravans gutted and there is serious unrest among the other residents.'

He was silent for just a moment too long in Jo's judgement.

'That sounds like a police matter. Why are you bothering me?' he replied a little sheepishly and without the shock of a decent person.

'Aside from the fact that the council own the site, you have duties to rehouse the occupants – unless you want them camped up across the city's parks. This is a critical racist incident, one that will have unprecedented repercussions for us all. You might want to be on top of it.'

'Racist? They're only pikeys.'

'Never use that term again. They are human beings.'

'You said two things, what's the other?'

'When the arsonists fled, they hit a motorcyclist. Killed her outright.'

'And?'

How can anyone be this cold, thought Jo.

'It was Loretta. Loretta Briggs.'

Jo could almost hear the pieces falling into place.

'What was?'

'The motorcyclist. Russ, Loretta's dead.' As death messages went, this was probably the brusquest she'd given. That was a shame as she liked Loretta, but she hated Russ so couldn't bring herself to soft-soap him.

'Jesus, Jo. What happened?'

Finally, some interest.

'It's early days but it looks like she was hit on the roundabout by the site. Killed instantly.'

'That's dreadful.' Was that a quiver in his voice? 'Does her family know?'

'Yes, DCI Hussain has arranged that.'

'Hussain?'

'The senior investigating officer. We are very lucky to have him on this.' She sensed Parfitt would be fuming.

'All right, well I'd better tell Tom Doughty. Anything else?'

'Oh, we have found a body in a burnt-out van, which we believe is connected, up at the Dyke. Would you like any more details on the travellers who were killed, their families?'

'Not really. I need to speak to Tom.'

Jo clenched the phone, and engaged every muscle to stop a fireball of invectives spitting out of her mouth. She counted to five, then said, 'I've got to go, someone needs me.' She terminated the call, seething. Parfitt's predecessor Penny Raw would have been out of the house before the call finished. She'd be up at the site, leading not only the condolences but also ensuring the council did their very best for the bereaved and displaced. She'd be fronting the press, then straight round to Loretta's family doing all the things a good boss should do.

Russ would do none of that but, underneath Jo's anger, she could tell something was bothering him. Almost as if he was expecting this to have happened.

Russ was a maelstrom of panic as he thrust the £10 at the taxi driver.

'Keep the change.'

'50p! Thank you, sir.'

Ignoring the jibe, he marched up to Councillor Tom Doughty's front door, a terraced two-up two-down he kept as a front in the hillside Hanover district of the city. His main home, a sprawling cluster of renovated farm buildings nestling in the Kent countryside, was hidden from the Brighton electorate.

It took three increasingly vigorous raps on the chrome knocker before the bleary-eyed leader appeared in the sliver between door and frame.

'Never heard of the telephone?' Doughty slurred.

'Let me in. We need to talk.'

Tom hesitated. 'I've got company.'

'I don't give a shit, we need to talk.' Russ couldn't remember being this brazen with his boss before.

He pushed his way through and led the way to the lounge, which resembled the aftermath of a freshers' party.

'Where?'

'Here's fine. I'll shut the door. This better be good.'

Russ gestured Tom to sit, ignoring the fact he was the guest.

Russ repeated, almost verbatim, what Jo had told him but with more profanity and xenophobic slurs. As he did so, Tom paled. Once he'd finished Russ paused, then asked, 'Is this down to you?'

Had Tom answered straight away, Russ's trepidation might have waned, but the pause was telling.

'In what way?' asked the councillor.

'In any fucking way, Tom. Holy shit, if you even so much as knew about this, they'll find out. It'll come back to you. To us.'

'How?'

'It just will. Four dead gyppos . . .'

'You said two.'

'It'll be four. Loretta wiped out and one of the attackers crisped in the back of a van. This is not going away.'

Tom rubbed his eyes, took a sip of something clear from a glass and shook his head.

'Tom, Loretta's dead.'

'I heard you. I'm sorry about that. I know how much you liked her, but we need to nip this. Speak to Stuart Acers.'

'It's beyond him. They've got some Paki from Major Crime running it. You think six bodies, one of whom happened to be a close personal friend, can be swept under the carpet?'

'I need to make some calls. Have they identified the bloke in the van yet?'

'I don't know.'

'Didn't you ask?'

'Jesus, Tom, don't you think that might have been a bit obvious?'

'You need to find out. And start acting like a chief exec. Get yourself in front of the TV cameras. Abhor the attacks, mourn the victims, shoulder to shoulder with the police, rebuild the community. All that old shite.'

'Isn't that your job?'

Tom stood up and marched to open the door. The meeting was over.

'I'm going to be busy for a bit. Calls to make. You do it.'

Russ slid out, wondering whether to advise his boss not to use his own phone for whatever those calls might be.

He chose not to.

10

Ajee wondered how others, those who had not endured what she had over the last six months, coped with this.

Hunger, debilitating fatigue and abused trust had become natural for her during her three attempts to flee Turkey, after that blistering dash from Aleppo where she'd been robbed of her parents and little brother. Then on the journey, countless new-found friends and the lovely man she met who was trying to find a safer life for his wife and children – all now slept at the bottom of the Aegean Sea. All discarded by the predatory smugglers, who brazenly took their life savings, promising salvation, but jumped from the boats, leaving seventy or so people to fend for themselves.

Loss and grief were daily occurrences and that made her mistrust just about everyone. Yet here she was. Sucked in again by a friendly old gent who'd promised her a new start; but in the end he was no better than the ruffians who'd condemned her newfound friends to drown.

Ninety minutes into her shift, the exhaustion of just two hours' sleep was starting to bite. It helped that she was assigned to the rear wing of Sycamore Care Home, which just so happened to house the kitchen. Her weeks on the run had taught her resourcefulness, so filching the odd crust of bread – if that's what you could call the squares of cotton wool that masqueraded as such – was child's play. She could do this for as long as she had to but was already planning her escape. The actual leaving would be the easy bit, just a case of dodging the security, but staying hidden in this city, which felt like a village, would take every ounce of her ingenuity. That detective turning up yesterday had terrified her, and she prayed to Allah he would not come back and ask questions. The thought of deportation was too horrifying to imagine.

Glancing at the name scribbled on the door sign – next to the one where the man had died yesterday – she tapped lightly.

'Good morning, sir,' she said, easing the door open, gagging as she stepped in.

Her eyes took a moment to adjust to the dark. She made out the empty bed at the same time as she heard the groan. Mr Johnson resembled a bundle of rags, face down yet huddled over on the floor.

Ajee flicked the light on, pulled the emergency cord and knelt beside him, thankful for once that her stomach was all but empty.

'Oh, Mr Johnson. I help you.'

An ambiguous groan did nothing but confirm he could hear her.

'Help is coming. Oh, sir. How long you been here?' She checked him over and soon found the graze on his forehead and the dried blood caking his nostrils. She touched his right arm, triggering a shriek.

'It's OK. You stay. We help, then clean you.'

Ajee put her hand down to lever herself up, but the slime of the blood got the better of her and she narrowly avoided slipping on top of the old man. Her second attempt to get up was more successful but she retched when she realised what she'd put her hand in.

'Help is coming,' she said as she scrubbed his blood off her hands in the basin.

Ajee pulled the door open and said, 'Help. Please.'

Thankfully, the manager, Peggy, emerged from the kitchen, chewing.

'Mrs Peggy, I need help. Mr Johnson, he fall. He hurt. I pull the cord.'

Peggy scoffed, then, with a sigh, 'Get one of the girls then. Can't you see I'm busy?'

'But he bleeding. He bang his head. Please help. He need an ambulance.'

Peggy stopped and glared at Ajee. 'Then get one of your friends. I can't drop everything every time he falls over. And no, he does not need an ambulance. Pick him up, clean the shit off him and I'll get Dr Harper to give him the once-over on his rounds.'

As she stormed off, Ajee wondered how she knew the old man had messed himself.

She darted to the conservatory that overlooked the herb garden at the back of the home, hoping to find some help.

Her luck was in. The African girl, who had been so unwilling to talk the other night, was just finishing off cleaning up an old woman's sick.

'Please, please. Can you help? Mr Johnson. He fallen.'

The girl's tired eyes seemed to take an age to connect with Ajee's. 'I'm sorry?'

'Please come. I need help.'

She paused then shuffled after Ajee.

When she reached the door, Ajee again knocked then turned to check she still had back-up, before opening it.

'I have help, Mr Johnson.'

Something seemed to spark in her colleague and she crouched by him – seemingly devoid of a sense of smell – and murmured comforting words, then took charge.

'Please, you check where the bleeding's from.'

'I have. His head.'

'Sorry, what is your name?'

'Ajee. And yours?'

'Neela. He does this all the time. We just have to check him, clean him, then make him comfortable. I'll get his walking frame.'

Ajee immediately warmed to Neela. Someone she could learn from, be friends with. Trust? She checked herself; not trust.

The two young women moved around like ice dancers. Each predicting and helping the other, getting Mr Johnson to his feet, checking for breaks or bruises, helping him to the bathroom, stripping him and lowering him onto the shower chair.

Ajee gasped.

'What is it?' asked Neela.

Ajee could only point.

Neela looked, and nodded, as if seeing the expanse of blue, green and scarlet across every visible patch of skin for the first time.

'You'll get used to that.'

'But he is so hurt,' said Ajee. 'Those are old.'

'Ajee, please remember. These people are very frail. They fall. They bump. They do not heal like you and I. Also, their white skin. It shows everything.'

'But he is hurt. We must help him.'

Neela turned on the shower, checked the temperature and gently doused the old man with its warm flow. Ajee cleaned his head wound with a flannel then took the sponge and dabbed the crusted faeces from Mr Johnson's bottom, legs and back.

'Please. You need to understand. All we can do is this. Many residents, they fall, they make a mess and we ask no questions. Some, they shout, swear, hit out. Special nurses come and then they stop. Sometimes they cry afterwards, sometimes they bruise. Sometimes Peggy, she tells us they not hungry for two days. We just accept this. We look after them as much as we can, but we look after ourselves more.'

'But, this. It's not right. He's someone's father, grandfather.'

Neela turned the shower off and wrapped him in a towel, then looked at Ajee like a schoolteacher about to explain something profound to a callow child.

'I don't know how you ended up here, but where you've come from must have been worse. Just do what they tell you, look after yourself and don't ask questions. Then one day, *inshallah*, we will be free to live the dream that brought us here. Until then, how they say, keep your head down.'

'But . . . ?'

Neela raised her finger to her lips. 'Farah, the girl who slept in your bed last week. I don't know where she's gone but Peggy, she was very angry with her. Something about phoning family. I never see Peggy so cross, then Farah, she leave. They came for her in the night.' Neela left a pause. 'I think I like you. Please, don't end up like Farah.'

DI Bob Heaton was in two minds whether to go home once he'd briefed DCI Hussain and handed the enquiry over to the Major Crime Team. It was that awkward period when to stay on duty would mean an impossibly long day ahead, yet to go home would have served no purpose other than to wake his partner, Steve. On top of that there was no way he could sleep after what he'd seen. The images of those charred toddlers would haunt him for ever.

Three coffees in, he reckoned that he'd keep going long enough to put a respectable shift in.

As he plodded past Jo Howe's office, she frantically waved him in.

'Ma'am?' he said.

'Bob, no one's listening. After all we went through together last year, you of all people can dispense with the formality.'

'If you're sure, ma'am. I mean Jo,' he quipped.

'Sit down.' Bob did as he was told. 'How are you? It can't have been pleasant.'

'I'll get over it,' he replied, his look suggesting that was the last thing he'd do.

'Well take care of yourself. You're no good to anyone otherwise, especially Steve. How are things going between you?'

'He's an absolute dream. I've not got a great track record of picking men but I reckon he's a keeper.'

'Good. Have you had any contact with Phil?'

If anyone else had asked, Bob would have thought it was a trap. Even though the disgraced former Police and Crime Commissioner and he had been friends for years, he kept his contact to himself.

'One or two letters. You?'

'Same.' Jo paused. 'Well, a bit more than that.'

Bob tensed, unsure whether he wanted Jo to go much further. He'd discovered in the aftermath of last year that she and Phil had a fling, years back, and that she felt an ill-placed guilt for his incarceration. If she was trying to make amends, he'd rather not know.

'I'm visiting his mum for him.'

Bob felt his rigid shoulders relax. 'Well, that's nice. I take it that's not common knowledge.'

Jo's tilt of the head confirmed she'd taken him into her confidence.

'How is she?' Bob asked, relieved to switch to small talk.

'Truth? Not so good. I'm not even sure she knows who I am, and the care home only seem to do the basics.'

'Like me to pop in from time to time? You know, relieve the burden.'

'Are you sure? It is a bit of a chore sometimes and I literally take some flowers, sit with her and wipe a cloth round.'

'Sure. She might even remember me from the old days.'

'Doubt it.'

'Where is she?'

'The Sycamore in Upper Drive.'

Bob paled. 'The Sycamore?'

'Yes. Do you know it?'

'Only since yesterday. Look, it's probably fine but any chance Phil could have her moved?'

'Why? She's not got long left and a move could kill her.'

'So might staying there.'

Jo was rapt as Bob described the events of the previous day and how he and Jake Briers shared a deep concern over Arthur Moore's death.

'Maybe it was a one-off,' said Jo. 'People die in nursing homes all the time.'

'Sure, but most of the time someone at least tries to save them. All I'm saying is that there's something going on there and I'm determined to get to the bottom of it. In the meantime, keep a very close eye on Mrs Cooke. I certainly will.'

* * *

A few minutes later, Bob was back in his room, a glass Tardis hastily erected in the corner of the general Specialist Investigations Unit office.

As soon as he sat down he called up the incident log for the arson attack, keen to be the first outside MCT to know if and when arrests were likely. 'Shit,' he muttered when he read the other mum and child had died too.

Just then he glimpsed a Lycra-clad DC Jake Briers sidle into the office. Jake was a fitness freak and ran the six miles to work from Portslade and home again. Bob felt exhausted just thinking about it.

'Jake, you got a minute?' Bob called out as the young detective passed.

'Er, can I get showered and changed first?'

'It won't take a moment,' said Bob. 'How are you getting on with the Sycamore?'

'Slowly I'm afraid, boss. By the way, what's going on? MCT are all over the place and I've never seen so many top brass here this time of the morning.'

'Later. The DNACPR?'

'As I say, I'm not exactly being overwhelmed with cooperation. I've left so many messages for this Dr Harper . . .'

Bob raised an eyebrow.

'The GP who signed the form and who attended on the night. I can't seem to get past the practice manager.'

'Get yourself changed and meet me in the back yard,' said Bob, remembering his pledge to Jo Howe.

A quarter of an hour later, Jake was at the wheel of a grey Toyota Avensis and heading out to Hove, the DI riding shotgun.

'I really could do this on my own, guv,' said Jake as he weaved his way through the North Laine area towards Hove.

'What, and deprive me of all the fun? I've had a shitty night and going head to head with a jobsworth GP seems the perfect antidote.'

'Bad?'

'As it gets,' said Bob.

Neither spoke for what seemed like an age.

As they approached Goldstone Medical Centre on Woodruff Avenue, Bob perked up.

'You do the talking first. I'll chip in once it's clear we aren't getting anywhere.'

'Righto.'

Jake pulled into the three-space car park in front of the surgery.

'In there,' said Bob, pointing to a bay denoting it was reserved for Dr Harper.

They got out of the car and walked to the front door. Despite the notice making it clear the surgery opened at 8.30, in fifteen minutes' time, Bob rapped on the door.

It took three knocks and him pounding the window to the left before he provoked a response. The first was a forty-something woman with a fierce grey buzz cut waving him away and pointing to her watch. Bob's retaliation of thrusting his open warrant card at the glass appeared fruitless, so he accompanied it with a further pounding that would have shattered a weaker pane. Eventually, the woman strutted over and Bob stepped back.

She'd barely opened the door three inches before she launched her invective. 'The surgery is closed. Whatever you want, come back at eight-thirty.'

'Good morning, madam,' said Jake. 'I'm DC Briers and this is DI Heaton from Brighton and Hove Police. We'd like a word with Dr Harper before surgery starts.'

'By the very fact you've parked in his bay, you will know Tony, er, Dr Harper has yet to arrive. He's also fully booked today so you'll have to make an appointment.' She went to close the door, but Jake's foot put paid to that.

'We really hope not to take up too much of his time. Shall we come in and wait?'

'There's no point, officer. He will arrive just before his first appointment which, for clarity, is not you.'

Bob stepped forward. He glanced at her name badge.

'Ms Pilsbury. You might be the practice manager and you might think your job is to protect your clutch of doctors from their patients or any other inconveniences, but our warrant cards trump your job title. Let us in and we will see Dr Harper as soon as he arrives.'

'Have you got a warrant?'

'Warrants are for searches, not for conversations,' said Bob, as a ten-year-old bottle-green Vauxhall Zafira drove into the car park, its tyres crunching the gravel just before it hit the CID car. 'Ah, Dr Harper I presume.'

A flustered-looking man, mid-fifties, with startled eyes and a salt-and-pepper mop tied back in a ponytail, appeared from the driver's door. Before he could protest, for the second time in as many minutes, Bob thrust his warrant card out.

'Dr Harper? Would you like us to move the car?'

'Well, yes of course. What's going on?' The GP's eyes flicked to his gatekeeper, who was stock-still yet raging on the threshold.

'We'd like a quick chat if you don't mind, Doctor. My colleague here seems to have had a little trouble setting up a meeting so we thought we'd pop along before the rush.'

'Well, I'm not sure . . .'

'Jake, move the car for the good doctor would you. I'll see you inside. That OK, Doc?' Bob didn't wait for a reply, just strode up to the door, edged past Ms Pilsbury with a smile and stood by the reception desk.

Jake followed once he'd re-parked the Avensis, and gave Bob an almost imperceptible shake of his head and smirk as he approached. Dr Harper was not far behind.

'Your room, Doctor?' Bob spotted the right door and walked in before anyone could object. He sat in the patients' chair, leaving Jake the couch and Dr Harper his own spot. Bob took in the BMI charts, breast examination posters and a primary care pathway flow chart on something or other fixed to the walls.

After some frantic whispering between the GP and the manager, he entered, closed the door and sat down. Bob thought that, whilst it was Jake's enquiry, he had the momentum so he would kick off the meeting.

'Thank you for agreeing to see us. We'd like to talk to you about Arthur Moore.'

Dr Harper gave him a blank look.

'Arthur Moore? Sycamore Care Home? You saw him on Tuesday.'

'Detective Sergeant . . .'

'Inspector,' Bob smiled.

'Detective Inspector, I see many, many patients at the Sycamore and about a dozen other homes. I can't recall them all and, even if I could, you know full well that doctor–patient confidentiality precludes me from discussing them.'

'Not if they're dead.' Bob left a silence.

Dr Harper spluttered. 'No, of course, not once they are deceased. Look, what exactly is it you want to know?'

Bob shuffled forward on his chair. 'Everything, Dr Harper. We want to know everything.'

11

Ajee didn't know if there was a hierarchy to who was allocated which rooms and she was not inclined to find out. If she hadn't worked it out for herself already, Neela's pleading that she just kept herself to herself made her do just that.

However, she took some comfort from the fact that she was working on the first floor today. A promotion of sorts. In her mind anyway.

Away from the smell of the kitchen and not having to continually walk past Mrs Peggy's all-seeing glare through her open office door – these were small mercies for which she thanked Allah.

She was shocked when she learnt that she had the whole landing, eight rooms, to look after on her own. Surely that breached the guidelines. Then again, given the way she was being held and treated, it was clear that Mrs Peggy and whoever she reported to had scant regard for rules and regulations.

In most of the rooms lived old men and women at varying stages of dementia. The more lucid would chat away, telling stories of their families, lost husbands, wives and bygone days.

They'd ask Ajee what brought her to England, but she just rolled out her well-rehearsed story of being Turkish and coming over to study and needing to build up some money to send home and put towards her tuition fees. If any of them did the maths they would have quickly worked out that, even if she was paid minimum wage, university would be a decade off, let alone having enough to support a family back home.

Others, like the one in the room she was just entering, existed rather than lived. She just lolled, dribbling in her chair, stirring only briefly each time a tepid beaker of tea or her pureed meals were served. Other than that, she slept.

'Hello, Mary, how are you?' said Ajee as she walked in, more so she didn't shock the old lady than in expectation of a reply. This was her third visit of the day and the scene had not changed. The first two visits had been to get her up, washed and dressed and then give her breakfast. Now it was lunchtime.

'Shepherd's pie?' she said as she placed the covered plate on the table. 'I straighten you up and help you eat.'

Starving as she felt, this was one meal Ajee would not steal. It was impossible to distinguish between the grey lumps of mince and the gunmetal, scarcely mashed potato. It didn't smell much better either.

As she spooned the lukewarm muck into Mary's barely open mouth, she glanced around the room. Aside from the stories the residents told, the only other thing she liked about this prison were the photos. Some would talk her through them, telling edgy stories of wartime adventures or how 'my son is a doctor'. With the mute cohort, Ajee made them up.

She spotted an immaculately dressed man in a picture by Mary's bed. His sandy hair, slightly reddish face and the fact he was wearing what she took to be a police uniform – medals resplendent – suggested he was very important. Mary must be so proud.

There were others. One of a young football player and another playing the guitar. Grandsons?

For a moment she hoped one day to meet these handsome men, then kicked herself. What was she thinking of? She was a prisoner. She was in a living hell. Sure, visitors who came and went would never spot it. Why would they? To the ill-informed, slavery had been abolished centuries ago and, even then, it happened in other countries.

Then another thought flashed through her mind.

'Your son? A policeman? Does he come here?'

What was she doing? Of course she wasn't going to reply, she couldn't. Ajee wondered if she could even hear her.

She spooned another dollop in. If this policeman came to visit Mary, then maybe he would help her. But no. Policemen beat you, locked you up, raped you. She must hide if this man ever came to the home. He must never find her here. She couldn't go to prison and be abused by all the revolting guards. But most of all, she couldn't be sent home.

Her heart raced. *Breathe. Breathe,* she told herself. She calmed for a moment and scraped the last of the food from the plate.

'One more, Mary.' The spoon came out clean but just as Ajee was reaching for the water beaker, Mary started coughing. Her eyes stretched open in pleading panic. Then the wheezing started. Frantic gasps for breath. She grabbed Ajee's right hand, her strength anomalous to her bony frame.

'Help, help. Someone help me,' said Ajee, her struggle to free herself and save the old lady's life fruitless.

Tom Doughty had paid the boy off within minutes of Parfitt leaving his house. He had no idea what, if anything, he'd heard or even how much English he understood. Fifty pounds extra seemed a pittance for his silence though, despite the sex being average at best.

Since then he'd been pacing his lounge, dressed only in a 'Sandals' white towelling bath robe, trying every number he knew to get hold of his middle man. To contact Leigh directly was an unfathomable risk, but Tom was desperate.

His phone nagged him about the thirty missed calls and dozen or so unread texts he'd deliberately ignored. All from journalists or council press officers desperate for a statement.

Once again, the phone rang and rang but thankfully this time did not trip over to answer phone. Eventually it was picked up.

'Hello?'

'Leigh?'

'Who wants to know?'

'It's Tom. What the fuck's gone on?'

'Are you fucking mad, phoning me? You'll get us both nicked.'

'Calm down. Just tell me what happened? They say there's another body in a van.'

'That Polish twat left his mate behind. Fuck knows what's happened to him, but I just lost it when he told me.'

'So you thought you'd cremate him in a van and leave him there. And you tell me about using phones?'

'Calm down. Even if they identify him, they'll never link him to us.'

'What about the other bloke. The one you left?'

'I never left him, the Pole did.'

'You were in fucking charge. YOU left him. What if he talks?'

'He knows nothing. Trust me.'

'Ginge with you?'

'Yep.'

'Get away, hide. Wait to be contacted.' He paused. 'There will be consequences.'

'Fuck you,' said Leigh before the line went dead.

Tom looked at the phone and swore.

Next, he punched out a more familiar number. This time it was picked up in less than a second.

'Hold on,' said the man on the other end, then Tom heard the echo of him talk to others – 'Sorry, I need to take this' – then footsteps and a door creak open then close.

'What is it? I'm in a Gold Group about last night's murders. Where's Parfitt by the way? You know we need the council represented.' Tom heard another door close and presumed the chief constable had found some privacy.

'Don't lecture me,' hissed Tom. 'You need to start earning our silence.'

'I'm listening.'

'Change the narrative of last night. We lost a beloved colleague and friend. Play down the bloody pikey angle. The real tragedy is Loretta.'

'Are you mad? How do you expect me to brush four traveller murders under the carpet? If you bothered to poke your head up from wherever you and Parfitt are hiding, you'd see that the press, community and government are clamouring for answers.'

'I don't expect you to ignore it, but Loretta was an innocent victim . . .'

'Innocent? Of course she was, but don't you think the two women and children deserve that adjective too?'

'It's not the same.'

'Tom, you can't rewrite this one. We need to work together to catch the killers, reassure the communities and return to normality. That includes you.'

'Stuart, you *will* do this. Quash the traveller story and refocus your efforts to investigate Loretta's death, but don't you dare catch her killer.'

'What do you mean "don't catch her killer"? Isn't that what we're expected to do?'

'Just don't. That's all you need to know. Otherwise your press profile might just sky-rocket. For all the wrong reasons.'

'You wouldn't do that.' Tom detected a quiver in Stuart's voice.

'Do you know how old those girls are?'

'I'm assured they are all over sixteen.'

'Is that so? Sometimes it's hard to tell with these immigrants, but you know that's no defence.'

'Tom, that's our secret.'

'I agree. So do as you're told.'

12

The first twenty-four hours of any investigation were more about survival than progress. As a previous Head of Major Crime, Jo knew that better than anyone. So it was no surprise to her when DCI Faisal Hussain jumped at her offer to front the press. Much as she'd like all this to just go away, she had to do something otherwise she'd fold in on herself. Speaking to media would provide both a legitimate displacement activity and an angle in to the investigation.

As she stood behind Brighton Police Station's reception, she didn't envy Faisal trying to make sense of a quintuple-murder enquiry. Christ, she hadn't even known that was a word until a few hours ago. Two mums, two children, plus Loretta Briggs – all dead following a few moments of barbaric violence. Another, probably one of the killers, also dead; and she was sure the post-mortem would decide he'd been murdered too.

She'd heard good things about Faisal and, so far, he was living up to expectations. He'd identified several potential witnesses, allocated them specialist interviewers and made sure they were well looked after. All the scenes were locked down and the combined intelligence functions of Surrey and Sussex were scouring every known database in their search for who'd committed these atrocities. And who was behind them.

Since her call with Parfitt, the 'who was behind them' question was niggling Jo. He and Doughty were practically Nazis. Their own election victory was so against expectations it was being investigated by the Electoral

Commission. But were they really capable of conceiving and executing multiple murders on their own doorstep?

She checked herself in the mirror, flicked some imaginary fluff from her lapel, nodded to press officer Clarissa Heard and stepped through the security door across the lobby and out onto John Street.

As soon as she appeared, the cacophony of bellowed questions hit her. Her eyes smarted against the strobe of flashes. Clarissa stepped forward.

'Ladies and gentlemen, can I ask for quiet please?' She waited until a hush descended, only broken by the shutter-clicks of cameras with ludicrously telescopic lenses. 'Chief Superintendent Howe will read a brief statement then take questions. Please remember, play nice and don't all shout at once.' A guilty titter rippled around the press corps. Jo made a mental note to remind Clarissa to avoid humour in these situations, at all costs.

And Jo would never 'read' a statement. That was one of her pet hates. Look them in the eye, speak from the heart and show them this is personal, not some pre-formed script.

She silently cleared her throat.

'First of all, I want to express my sincere condolences to the family and friends of the two children and two women who were brutally murdered at the Horsdean Travellers' Site in the early hours of this morning. Also, I want to pass my deepest sympathies to all those who knew Loretta Briggs, who was killed close to the site soon after the attack. These were callous and cowardly killings which have not only destroyed the families of those killed but rocked a whole community.

'This is a hate crime; a racist incident. A murder investigation is being led by DCI Faisal Hussain of the Major Crime Team, and I want to assure you that he and I are committed to tracking down those responsible for – and those behind – the attack. We will ensure that justice is served.

'In the meantime, I want to reassure the gypsy and traveller community, and any other communities who feel marginalised or suffer discrimination, that we abhor any crime which targets people for who they are. My officers and I will not stop until we drive intolerance from this city, at every level. In the meantime, I want to appeal for calm and for those affected by these dreadful events to work with us to make sure these killers and their ideology do not win.'

She then gave a brief update on the investigation's progress, such as it was, and offered herself up for questions.

'Chief Superintendent. Mike Taylor, *Daily Post*. Is this attack an inevitable consequence of the people of this city feeling squeezed out by people who have no roots here?'

'Are you suggesting there can be any excuse for killing five people including two defenceless children?'

'I'm just asking a question others will be wondering.'

'Next,' said Jo, turning ever so slightly to show her disdain for the man.

'Sandra Pelling, South Coast TV. With the growth of the British Patriot Party in Brighton and Hove and the rhetoric coming from the city's leaders, do other minority groups need to watch their backs?'

Jo inwardly smiled. That was better.

'The death of so many people should act as a wake-up call for all of us. I am sure those whose language may have, in the past, been inflammatory will be reflecting on the climate they might have created.'

'Will the council leader be speaking to the press do you know, Mrs Howe?'

'That's a matter for him. I'm sure he and his chief executive will be only too keen to condemn these attacks and help us catch the killers.'

'How sure?'

'Next,' said Jo, leaving the question hanging.

'Is the body in the van at the Dyke connected?' came a voice from the back.

Jo was furious. They had deliberately kept that out of their press release and monitored the social media assiduously to make sure none of the well-meaning police tweeters leaked it.

'Sorry, who asked that?' *Buy time*, she thought.

'Dave Gent, *The Oracle*.'

Jo glanced at Clarissa whose shrug confirmed that she had never heard of him. Her husband, Darren, was an *Oracle* reporter. She made a mental note to ask him about Mr Gent later.

'This investigation is fast-moving and I'm not commenting on operational matters for risk of misleading you. Thank you for your questions. We'll notify you of any developments and send you any future press statements.'

She swivelled round, determined not to catch anyone's eye, hurried back across the empty lobby and zapped her way through to the relative sanctuary of the police station.

She was about to debrief the last few minutes with Clarissa when Bob Heaton appeared in the corridor. The ominous look he gave told her whatever he wanted couldn't wait. Her flashed smile made no difference.

'Ma'am. Have you got a minute?'

'Er, sure. Clarissa, can I meet you back in my office please?'

'Sure,' the press officer muttered and walked off, looking puzzled.

'In here,' said Jo, opening an interview room door and holding it for Bob. As it closed she said, 'What is it?'

'Mary Cooke.'

Jo raised an eyebrow, her heart thumping.

'She died this morning.'

'What happened?'

'I'm going up to the home myself in a bit – but DC Briers, Jake, has given me what he knows so far.'

'Which is?'

'I told you about the old chap who died there the other night, didn't I?'

Jo nodded.

'Well, what we've been told is Mary was having her lunch, choked on something and by the time someone came in to check up on her, she was dead on the floor.'

'That's total bollocks,' said Jo.

Bob looked puzzled.

'There is no way on God's earth she was feeding herself. She can't so much as look at a fork let alone use one. What have they said about the person who found her?'

'Apparently it was an agency carer. She raised the alarm, then Peggy Squire rushed in with a couple of others, told them Mary had a DNACPR in place, by which time she was unconscious anyway, so they let her be.'

'Who the hell signed the form then? Phil would have told me if he had.'

'It's the same as Mr Moore. Filled in by the GP and authorised by him the other day.'

'You're kidding me? So this GP signs up two DNACPRs in one week and both die?'

'That's the mystery. I told Jake to find out who else at the home has them in place and, other than a couple of old chaps whose power of attorney authorised them, they couldn't produce any.'

Jo rubbed her eyes, hoping Bob couldn't see her flush. Why did crises in her life always hunt in packs? Couldn't they form an orderly queue?

'You trust Jake to have looked properly? Asked the right questions?'

'He's one of the best.'

Jo thought for a moment.

'So, if Jake did his job properly, either they hid it from him or . . .'

'Or it was signed up retrospectively. I think that's unlikely.'

'Why?'

'Because Jake and I paid the GP concerned a visit this morning.' His smirk told her he had not been ordering a repeat prescription.

'Go on.'

'Let's just say Dr Harper was being evasive, so I showed Jake some old-fashioned doorstepping techniques.'

'Am I to expect a call from Professional Standards?'

Bob paused. 'Probably not, but we left him very clear that he was in our sights. We are due back later today to go through his records. He had a touch of amnesia whilst we were there so we allowed him some time to refresh his memory.'

'So you've got an excuse to go back to see him, but what about the staff members who were involved? I don't trust Peggy Squire but there's a young girl I've got chatty with, Turkish she said. There's something about her. Maybe we can – or rather you can – get into her.'

'Have you got a name?'

'Ajee. Let's hear what she and the others say. Has Phil been told yet?'

'Not as far as I know. Jake's told them we'll take care of that. I thought it might be best coming from you.'

'You're all heart,' mumbled Jo, wondering how she was going to break the news, let alone explain what happened.

Bob's phone bleeped and Jo watched as he retrieved it from his pocket and slipped on his glasses. He went pale as soon as he focused.

'I need to get back up to the home.'

Although in theory Stuart Acers held operational control over the policing of Sussex, the reality was less clear-cut.

Sure, he could call the shots on day-to-day matters but, since 2012, chief constables' powers had been reined in when directly elected Police and Crime Commissioners replaced Police Authorities. The first tranche of PCCs were a combination of would-be MPs and independent, often ex-police, office holders. Since subsequent re-elections, all but a few of the lone wolves had been swept away and political control had grown stronger.

Other than a short period when former chief superintendent Phil Cooke was dubiously elected before his imprisonment for misconduct in a public office and conspiracy to murder, Sussex PCCs were true-blue Conservatives.

Growing regionalisation had weakened Acers' grip too. Since the savage cuts, so many of the sexier departments were shared with neighbouring forces that true control was blurred. Among them were the South East Major Crime Team. A collaboration of the four forces south of the Thames Estuary and east of the New Forest, it was anyone's guess which chief pulled their strings.

In the old days, he'd be straight onto DCI Faisal Hussain to effectively order him to play down the 'accidental' traveller deaths and focus on catching whoever had mown down Loretta Briggs. He knew the SIO would baulk at the idea, and it would probably keep him awake at night, but Acers would weave his request with sufficient veiled threats to make sure he'd soon fall in line.

Now, with most of the senior investigating officers being from the other forces, he struggled to put faces to names, let alone know where their loyalties lay. So, he had the mother of all problems. He had to keep his secret but was sure Doughty would not hesitate to slip his extracurricular indiscretions to the tabloids if he didn't deliver.

It had all started when he was brought back as an urgent replacement for his disgraced predecessor, Helen Ricks. He'd previously left the force under a cloud when Phil Cooke became PCC, so when he was parachuted back in not only did he have to rebuild a shattered force but also banish Cooke's acolytes, of which there were hundreds. That was still a work in progress.

The pressure had been intense and since his wife had left him, following an indiscretion with an intern during his enforced sabbatical at the College of Policing, he'd sought comfort elsewhere.

He'd taken the brothel owner at face value when she told him the girls were over sixteen. In all honesty, he'd have preferred them younger but, as they all looked so youthful, he was happy for his career's sake to go along with it.

He couldn't exactly ask them; their complete lack of English was an added attraction. Not understanding any foreign cries of 'stop' or 'you're hurting me' would surely provide the perfect defence if the worst happened.

Now, he was less certain. He needed to do something, and quickly.

'Marie,' he bellowed.

The young, blonde direct-entry inspector dashed in from the anteroom that served as her office. Marie Shaw had not so much applied to be the chief's staff officer, as been cajoled. Her master's in criminology from Cambridge and the two years thereafter as an analyst with Her Majesty's Revenue and Customs made her the perfect choice, in the complete absence of any applicants, to be Acers' gofer.

The fact that her silky complexion and elfin body – hewn through her triathlon obsession – made her look at least five years younger than she was, was a bonus in Acers eyes.

'Yes, sir,' she said, notebook and pen at the ready.

Acers felt a stirring.

'I need you to get more detail on this business at the travellers' site last night. Find out exactly what the evidence is. I'm not sure the Gold Group had all the information.'

She looked at him curiously.

'How do we know it's not a prank gone wrong? A gas leak? How open-minded is the SIO? All too often detectives leap at the first, most popular, hypothesis without looking at other options. I need to know that's not happening here.'

'But sir, shouldn't we let DCI Hussain settle the investigation down before we start to question it? I mean, it's very early days.'

Acers' Achilles heel was insubordination. Had a bloke, or that bitch Howe, questioned him like this he'd have exploded. His baser instincts prevented him from shattering the microscopic chance of bedding Marie with an ill-timed tirade.

He counted five breaths.

'Marie, sometimes it's best to guide SIOs to focus on what they might be too busy to see. Mr Hussain will be drowning in information, demands; all sorts of pressure. Often just a gentle nudge coming from someone as clever and well connected as you; well, it lifts their vision. You don't need to say it's come from me, but you are in a unique position to help in a non-threatening way. And whilst you're at it, find out how they are getting on with finding who killed Loretta Briggs. I need to keep the council updated.'

'Aren't they connected? Isn't it the same people?'

'The road to hell is paved with assumptions, my dear.'

As Marie turned to leave, Acers continued. 'Marie, can I borrow that notebook of yours for a moment please? I just want to remind myself of the decisions from yesterday's budget meeting.' He knew she used this book, and only this book, to make meticulous notes of all their meetings and discussions.

By the time he remembered to give it back to her, any assertion she might make that she had made an accurate and contemporaneous record of this particular chat would be ripped apart by any self-respecting barrister.

This meeting simply never happened.

13

Jo put the phone down. 'Fuck. Fuck, fuck, fuck.'

'Lovely to see you too,' said Gary Hedges, as he blustered through their office door in full public order uniform.

'Not now,' she said, fighting to keep the quake from her voice.

'What's happened?'

'Just give me a moment,' she said, surreptitiously wiping a stray tear from her cheek.

Gary was a bullish, often tactless, shit but at times like this he could flick on his sensitive switch.

'Phil Cooke's mum's died and I've just had to phone the prison to tell him.'

Jo didn't need to remind Gary that this was the second out-of-the-blue death message she had given their mutual friend.

'Bugger. How did he take it?'

Jo shrugged. 'Two minutes. That's all those Hitlers gave me. She's all he had left other than Kyle. He needs a shoulder to cry on, not a back to watch.' She kicked her desk drawer.

Gary closed the door and wheeled his chair over to Jo.

'Listen, he'll be OK. He'll get through this.'

Jo spun round. 'You blokes. Have you ever thought that sometimes it's better *not* to tough it out? He needs proper help, but he's got no one. Why the fuck did I put him there?'

Gary held her tighter. 'You can pack that in. You know you did the right thing.'

She looked up. 'Thanks, but it kills me every day.'

'Cuppa?'

'Please.'

Gary stood and poked his head round the door. Two minutes later, Fiona walked in with a mug of steaming water and a treacle-black coffee.

Jo sipped the healthier option, coughed and wiped her eyes.

'OK Rambo, what's going on out there?'

'That's more like it. Well, to give it its technical term, fucking carnage. Faisal has closed Horsdean and, suffice to say, it's not gone down well. Some of the families have left but most of the men are refusing to budge. I've got two PSUs up there to support the negotiators but it's getting interesting, to say the least.'

'You can see their point. If my community was attacked by a gang of racist thugs and the old bill tried to uproot me, I'd have something to say about it.'

'True, but we still need to search for evidence to catch said thugs.'

'Anything else?'

'Friends, Families and Travellers representatives are heading here, demanding a meeting to find out what's going on. They want the Leader of the Council too.'

'Shit. Well, I'll see them, but no way is that redneck Doughty stepping foot in here. Directly or indirectly, he's got blood on his hands and putting FFT and him in the same room would be pressing the nuclear button.'

'When I say "heading here" I mean that around five hundred FFT supporters are at the train station about to march on the police station. And word is the British Patriots are gathering for a counter-demonstration.'

'Same old, same old then. The city apparently elects a bunch of racists on wafer-thin promises and no doubt a fair share of vote-rigging and we get the blame when it all goes tits up. You got enough to deal with it?'

'So far. As ever I'm stripping the rest of the force and putting the shout

out for mutual aid from Surrey, Kent and Hampshire, so I think we'll be OK.'

'Great.'

'What do you mean about Doughty having blood on his hands?' continued Gary.

'It might be nothing, but I reckon whoever is behind this are more than just BPP sympathisers.'

'Are you saying . . .'

'I'm saying nothing at the moment, but we need to be very careful who we speak to from now on. I just hope we can trust Faisal. And protect him.'

Ajee couldn't fathom whether her frantic shivers were down to the cold or abject fear.

Although she'd spent much of the last nine months crammed in boats, trucks and smugglers' cellars, at least that was for a purpose. Now her gut told her that having been bundled into this basement closet, she would probably die here.

The clammy walls and total darkness were every bit as terrifying as the perilous dash across the Mediterranean or the ever-present leer of would-be abductors in Athens. It was the powerlessness that panicked her most. As soon as it was obvious Mrs Cooke was dead, two male orderlies had escorted her out of the room on the pretext of giving her a cup of tea to help her with the shock. Once downstairs they bundled her through a door she'd not noticed before, into the blackness and down a set of narrow spiralling stone steps. Had they not gripped her arms so tightly she'd have tripped, no doubt resulting in at best livid facial injuries, at worst shattered limbs.

Once on terra firma, she could hear the clunk of a lock, the squeal of a door and then felt them push her into the void.

'Help me.' She hammered on the door, but her voice sponged to nothing in the emptiness. She hammered again but, unless there was a guard right outside, her pleas would go unheard.

She sank down, her back against the steel door, and wept. What she wouldn't give for her threadbare bunk upstairs, the grunts of Mrs Peggy and the scraps of pureed food.

Her only handle on time was the frequency she'd yielded to her bladder in the rancid bucket in the corner, which she'd only found by tripping over it. She'd need to ration her wees, as she doubted anyone would bother to empty the pail once the urine slopped over.

Bob Heaton was seething by the time he jabbed at the doorbell. Fifteen minutes to battle through the throngs of protestors laying siege to Brighton Police Station. Then, on autopilot, he found himself trying to nose onto the A27 at the Horsdean intersection. It was only by pulling rank at the PC blocking access to the travellers' site that Bob was grudgingly allowed onto the Brighton bypass.

Peggy Squire inched the door open.

'Oh, you,' she grunted.

'Yes. Like *Groundhog Day*. I want you and my DC in your office right now.'

'I'm not sure that's possible officer, I'm very busy.'

'NOW.'

Peggy flinched. Bob rarely raised his voice, not to women anyway, so felt a conflict of shame and relief when she acquiesced.

He followed her in silence to the poky room off the corridor. She inched round the desk and sat, stony-faced, behind it. Bob hit 'redial' and in a moment Jake Briers joined them.

'Shut the door,' said Bob. Jake obeyed. Neither officer sat down.

'Mrs Squire. I am growing sick and tired of having to hotfoot it up here every time one of my officers has the misfortune to investigate a sudden death. These should be straightforward affairs but for some reason, and I've yet to work out what that is, something stinks here.'

'I beg your pardon. I'll have you know this home is spotless.'

'I'm not talking about the wall of piss and shit fumes that hit me every time I step over your threshold. I'm talking about absent staff, dodgy DNACPRs, an evasive GP and a stonewalling manager.'

Peggy baulked at the last insult. Before she could object, Bob continued. 'Before any of us leave, I want to see the carer who was with Mrs Cooke when she died, the food she was being fed, the DNACPR she had in place, her full medical records and those of Arthur Moore. Oh, and the name of your accountant.' Bob threw that last request in just for good measure. He couldn't pinpoint why he'd want that other than experience telling him that where there were dodgy practices, the books often told the tale.

'I'm afraid the member of staff is no longer here. The whole thing upset her so much she didn't even finish her shift. Left us in the lurch to be honest.'

'Well, her name and address then please.'

'I'll have to get that for you. She's from an agency. Not our usual one. It might take me a while to find what you want.'

Bob looked at Jake, then back at Peggy. 'How can you not know who you have on shift? Aren't there some CQC rules around safe recruiting?'

'The Care Quality Commission unfortunately don't live in the real world, officer. They assume we have a set bank of staff who toddle into work on time, work their socks off then book off. The truth is very different. No one wants to work in the care sector these days, so we end up hunting around on a daily basis just to get enough carers to keep us safe. We can't be choosy and we don't always know much about those that do turn up.'

Bob sensed Jake scribbling every word down in his investigator's notebook.

'Surely you have a register of some sorts.'

'We do but unfortunately this girl didn't sign in, and the night sister who saw her arrive has gone on holiday for a couple of weeks.'

'Well I never.'

'I'm not sure I like your tone. We do our best here to provide some dignity to people in their dying days. It's hardly my fault we try to do so with next to no funding and ever-spiralling costs.'

'Spare me the bleeding heart. We'll come back to the carer. I want those records please.'

'I'm so sorry, Dr Harper has taken them. Apparently he needs them for the Coroner.'

'That's our job,' Jake interjected. 'We investigate for the Coroner.'

'Well, you need to speak to the doctor about that.'

'We will. In the meantime, I take it you have your accountant's details, or are they suspiciously unavailable?'

Bob couldn't work out whether that was a smirk or resignation flashing across her face. In any case she scribbled down a name and a company and pushed it across the desk.

'Thank you. Stay here with DC Briers.'

Bob stepped out, scouring his telephone contact list as he walked as far down the corridor as he could to be sure he was beyond eavesdropping distance.

Having navigated through the inevitable gatekeeper, Bob heard the words he was hoping for. 'Director of Adult Services, Kevin Winder.'

'Mr Winder, it's DI Bob Heaton from Brighton and Hove Police. I need you to close a care home down.' Bob set out why he was making this request; something he'd never tried before. He knew there would be questions to answer, perhaps even one asking whether he had the authority to make this approach. What he was not expecting though was the reaction once he'd said which home he was talking about. The vehemence, condescension and bare-faced attempts to bully him took him aback.

'Mr Winder, do you even care that residents are dying? That there are no records to speak of, dubious Do Not Resuscitates in place, a dodgy GP and vanishing staff?'

'Inspector, you have no idea what you are asking and what it involves. Just get back to doing whatever it is you do and leave the things you don't understand to those who do.'

'My job is to protect life and to catch killers. I'll go wherever and do whatever it takes to do that. If that means closing the home myself and arresting you, that is what I'll do.'

'Are you threatening me, officer?'

'Got it in one.' Bob killed the call, immediately tapping on the one number he could rely on to provide the top cover he knew he'd now need.

14

One thing that had always pissed off Jo Howe when she was a senior investigating officer was bosses swanning into the incident room unannounced.

As she climbed the stairs to the Major Incident Suite in the old accommodation block at Lewes Police Headquarters, she hoped DCI Faisal Hussain would be more understanding.

Pacing the corridors of this 24/7 hub of activity felt like a homecoming. Only eighteen months ago she had been the Head of Major Crime and, despite the crippling hours and the ever-ringing phone, those days were among the most enjoyable of her career. It was the closest officers of her rank got to proper policing and, in her team, the nearest she had to comrades.

Her heart swelled as she acknowledged the sincere greetings from passing detectives. Unpopular ex-bosses would only warrant a grunt. She felt loved here.

As she poked her head into the rooms that flanked the short corridor, she wondered if she should have phoned first. She didn't want to distract Faisal, just to catch up before her phone call to Chief Executive Russ Parfitt later. And to warn him.

She found him in the fourth identical room on the right. He was on an animated phone call, the mobile wedged between his ear and shoulder whilst he hammered two-fingered on his keyboard. Jo cleared her throat and he glanced round, somehow nodding her in without dropping the phone.

'Yeah, listen, I can't find it at the moment but I've definitely read it somewhere. I'll get someone to have a good look and call you back. I've got to go, someone's waiting . . . Yeah it'll be this morning, promise.' He dropped the phone on his desk and scooted his chair away, pushing his hands through his immaculately trimmed black hair.

'Bad time?' said Jo.

'Perfect time, ma'am. Gave me an excuse to sack him off.'

'Please, call me Jo.'

Faisal nodded. His host force, Hampshire, clung onto formalities, perhaps because of its military links, but Jo hated all that nonsense.

'You want an update?'

Jo took a seat at the small conference table between the door and Faisal's desk, impressed at how tidy it was. At this stage of one of her own enquiries you'd struggle to know it was made of wood.

'Just the basics. I know you're in the thick of it, so just the headlines and anything I need to know to keep the chief and the council fed and to reassure the community.'

'Good luck with that.'

'Which one?'

'All three.'

Jo paused, inviting Faisal to continue.

'I had the chief's staff officer on the phone yesterday afternoon. Marie Shaw?'

'She's good, for a direct entrant that is.'

Faisal nodded as if that made sense.

'Obviously she wanted an update for the chief, but she kept banging on about hypotheses and other scenarios. Wanted to know whether I was looking at a gas leak, insurance fraud, some sort of industrial accident.'

'Really?'

Faisal nodded. 'I told her all lines of enquiry are open but she seemed to ignore the whole sequence of events. The two seats of fire, the fleeing vans, the burnt-out vehicles and the body on the Dyke.'

'Some health and safety breach,' muttered Jo.

'Exactly. Then she really drilled into the Loretta Briggs death, as if that was the main event.'

Jo tried to stop her shock from showing. It was too early to tell Faisal about Parfitt's comments when she'd first told him of the fire.

'How are you getting on with witnesses at the site?'

'There's no love lost there. We're slowly getting through to a few of the men, but the women won't talk without the nod from their husbands and they all hate the police.'

'Probably second only to the council.'

Faisal shrugged. 'The FLOs are having a hard time but I've found an intermediary from Friends, Families and Travellers, so we are inching to some sort of dialogue.'

'Well done. They've never exactly enjoyed equity, but they definitely feel at the bottom of the pile since the local elections.'

'Sounds familiar,' said Faisal. Jo nodded, hoping she'd not offended the SIO.

'Any closer to suspects?'

'We've got the vans. And the body in the back, who we are sure is one of the attackers but no idea on ID. Some tyre marks on the track out of the site, paint on Loretta's bike but all that does is tie into the burnt-out chassis. In case you were going to ask, no arrests are imminent.'

'What about motives?'

'Take it from me, we are not exactly short of fascists in this city, and that's excluding the NIMBY brigade who think travellers have equal rights, just not in their back yard.'

Jo stood up, walked over to the door and eased it closed. Faisal's reaction was one of both curiosity and concern.

'I'm going to share something with you that, for all of our sakes, I need you to keep to yourself.'

Faisal nodded.

'If this gets out I'll be branded paranoid and you'll be accused of taking your eye off the ball when neither is true. I'm going to ask my support inspector to draw you up a briefing on right-wing extremism in the city. It shouldn't take him long as it's a work in progress with this lot leading the council, but what he will provide over what you'll get from the analysts is highly confidential hunches from senior people within and connected to the council.'

'With respect ma'am, er Jo, hunches aren't much use to me. I need evidence or tangible intelligence.'

'I know what you need, Faisal. I've done your job, remember. This is stuff no one will put their name to but goes to the heart of everything that is wrong in this city. I'm sharing it with you as, once you've read it, you'll appreciate why you must play your cards wedged to your chest. These murders go way beyond a couple of yobs chucking their weight about. They go to the very top.'

Faisal stared at her, as if desperate to ask a question but at a loss what that should be. Jo's ringtone broke the moment.

'Hi, Bob, all OK?'

'Where are you?'

'HQ, just heading back. Why?'

'Can I come and see you when you're here?'

Jo stepped into the corridor and scanned round for a free office. She darted into the one opposite.

'Sure, what is it?'

'I need to show you something re the care home. You're not going to like it.'

Jo gulped. 'On my way.'

* * *

If Ajee slept at all, it was in fits. The chill of the concrete floor had seeped into her bones and the inky blackness that enveloped her stung her eyes.

Shivering, she clambered to her feet and groped her way around the perimeter of her cell to locate the metal bucket. As no one had bothered to bring her food or water in God knows how long, she was confident the dribble in her bladder would not spill over.

Her hands had brushed the first corner when a flood of light assaulted her eyes. Instinctively she dropped to her knees and masked her head in her hands.

'Get up,' a rasping voice ordered. She braved a glimpse and saw an enormous silhouette in the open doorway. The image remained rooted to the spot but she heard, then saw, two others dart towards her.

'What you doing?' she yelped.

The two figures grabbed an arm each and dragged her to her feet. Once she was upright, her wrists were tethered with what felt like a thick cable tie behind her back and a dank sack shrouded her head. Her instinct told her to kick out, but common sense took over and she feigned compliance.

They shoved her towards what she hoped was the door, not a wall, even though that meant she was probably being moved. At least it meant something was happening and she might, as she had countless times over the last year, find a way to escape.

She pedalled to keep up with the men pushing her along. They were silent but she was all too aware of the throaty voice behind, commanding them to hurry up. She was bundled left, then right, then left again before she heard a door grind open and for the first time felt a breath of air kiss her bare arms. Her sight and smell were still obscured by the rancid blackout hood but she could tell she was outside. She couldn't work out why the distant hum of traffic and the cry of the predatory seagulls lifted her heart; then she realised they were the first outdoor sounds she'd heard since George had sent her off in that taxi.

'Wait here.' She felt the grip on each arm needlessly tighten, then heard an engine, like the lorries through Turkey, cough into life. The fumes found their way up the hood and gagged her. Sensing the car, van, whatever it was, draw up, she stepped back, prompting yet more squeezing. They were hurting her now, but she wouldn't give them the satisfaction of crying out.

Doors clunked open and immediately she was thrust forwards and hustled onto another hard floor, this one metal. A van then. The doors slammed behind her, followed by two more slams from what she took to be the driver and passenger sides, then she was flung against the back as the van pulled forward and away.

It was only as she wriggled so her feet were against what she hoped were the doors, and curled her legs ready to strike out, that she realised she was not alone.

The baton strike to her right thigh had an instant effect. Her impulsive scream and immediate paralysis sucked away any further urge to escape.

The van was thrown round bends, sped up, lurched to a halt, accelerated away and Ajee mirrored its erratic movements as she rolled around the floor.

She guessed she'd roller-coastered around for about twenty minutes before she felt that they had turned onto a track of some sort. Although they seemed to be crawling along, it didn't make the ride any smoother and she bounced and fell with every pothole. Thankfully, after a couple more minutes, the van stopped and she heard the left front door unlatch, footsteps and the clang of a gate opening. The van pulled forward, the gate clanged back and the front door slammed shut.

When the back doors opened, she hoped they would take off the hood. She'd learnt from the days cramped in lorries and boat hulls, there's only so much of your own breath you can bear.

They didn't.

Once again, they grabbed her arms and pulled her along the van floor. She tried to gain some footing but her dead leg dragged like a trawler net.

She felt the drop and the excruciating pain as the two guards hoisted her up so she didn't hit the ground.

Barking, somewhere to her left, startled her.

The men marched her along a gravel path, opened a door, pushed her through then closed it, the bolts and bars made fast before they finally removed her hood, shoving her to sit.

Her eyes stung at the light as she tried to take in her surroundings. As her pupils adjusted, the room looked like a sparse farmhouse kitchen. Behind her was a scratched and stained wooden table. She saw she was on one of two refectory benches. To her right was a chipped butler sink, to her left what looked like a bottom-of-the-range Aga. Only three or four storage units remained, the outline of twice that number marked by the contrasting paintwork on the walls. Her heart sank when she spotted the heavy-duty bolts on the Georgian windows.

This may look quaint, but it was every bit a prison as the care home.

'What have I done wrong? Why you bring me here?'

'We need to keep you out of the way,' said the hoarse man now standing right in front of her, his right-hand men standing sentry at each of the two doors. All were dressed in black jeans and various patterned hoodies and had scarves covering their noses and mouths – but she could see they were Caucasian, and the boss could be the other's dad.

'Why? I no trouble.'

'Let's just say we need to sort some problems out. Let the dust settle.'

'Dust settle? As in cleaners?'

'It's a saying. It's better you are out of the way until the police stop sniffing around.'

'A saying?'

The man nodded. 'We're going to stay with you here for a few days until the bosses work out what to do with you.'

'What is this place?'

'No more questions. Think of it as a holiday. You'll sleep upstairs and we'll feed you, so it's better than the home. Don't even think of trying to run though. Even if you manage to get out, which I doubt, there are dogs running loose in the grounds and they ain't that friendly.'

With that, the two mutes closed in on her. One flourished a knife. She flinched back and he giggled as he spun her round and sliced her makeshift handcuffs free.

'Go with them,' the older man ordered.

Ajee's mind was already racing. She'd do what they said for the time being, play the downtrodden slave they thought she was, but from now on, every waking hour would be spent plotting her escape and the freedom she'd promised herself back in Aleppo.

15

'I thought I told you to fucking hide,' said Tom Doughty as he barged through the door, leaving a startled Leigh stumbling back.

'Come in, why don't you.' By now Doughty was scouring every room of the ground-floor flat, checking that they were alone. Satisfied they were, he waited in the galley kitchen for Leigh to join him.

'Is this the best you could do?' said Doughty.

'Why would they come looking in the council leader's gaffs? And why this one? You told me to use it whenever I needed. Well, I fucking needed.'

Tom lurched towards his 'Mr Fixit', but a cautioning hand stopped him in his tracks.

'In your dreams. Now what do you want? Say it quick then fuck off.'

Tom impulsively took a step back, collided with a bar stool then sat on it as if he'd intended to all along.

'You need to tell me what happened. How a couple of firebombs to scare the pikeys ended up with six dead bodies and no doubt a skip-full of evidence leading right back to me.'

Leigh, capitalising on his even greater height advantage now, smirked. 'This is all about you, isn't it? And if I tell you you're as safe as houses, then you'll abandon me like used bog roll. Well, Mr Councillor, who fucking knows, so I guess you'll just have to wait and see, like we all will.'

'They'll only get to me through you, so best we work out how we stop that happening.'

Leigh paced around, Tom followed him with his eyes.

'You told us to cut the fucking gas pipes. Don't make out it was my idea. If you wanted to scare them, why make sure there's propane pissing around when we threw the petrol bombs?'

Leigh was in Tom's blind spot now. He wouldn't stand up though; that would suggest fear or an act of aggression. He knew from Leigh's background how he'd react to either.

'All right, but couldn't you have been more careful?'

'Show some bollocks you tosser,' hissed Leigh. 'This fucking problem is all, yes all, of your making. Next time you want someone to be "more careful", do it your fucking self.'

'Look, let's calm down,' said Tom, scared this might escalate. 'Just tell me what happened.'

'Aside from the fact that those two Polish twats were a fucking liability, it looks like one of them fell as he was running back to the van. The other spineless shite, instead of going back to find him, just put his foot down and shot off after me and Ginge.'

'Did they get him? The pikeys?'

'Fucked if I know. Anyway, I didn't realise any of this but as we were decamping, we hit that bitch on the bike. Fucking Ivan, or whatever his name is, hit her as she came off my roof. I just made straight for the Dyke to dump the van and regroup. That's when I found out we were a man down. I just fucking lost it with Ivan.'

'Why?'

'You just don't do that. You never leave a man out there. Even the dead ones, you bring them back.'

'What did you do, then?' Tom's mind was racing.

Leigh's marble-blue eyes seeped regret. Then he coughed and shrugged.

'I strangled him. Squeezed the fucking life out of him. Chucked him in the back of the van and torched the fucker.'

'And left him there for the police to find him.'

Leigh's rage returned. 'I would ask what you would fucking do, but we both know you'd be a million miles away. Me and Ginge, we tabbed it across the hills. By daybreak we'd put enough fields between us and the vans, deliberately caking ourselves in cow shit, to literally throw the old bill off our scent.'

'Where's Ginge now?'

'Search me.' Leigh's moods were going up and down like Norwich City. It seemed to have dawned on him how many loose ends he'd left.

'Let me get this right. Of the four of you, we've got one dead, one missing presumed dead and one who, let's face it, was never likely to be longlisted for Child Genius, wandering around the south coast for the taking.'

'That Ivan must be dead. The way those pikeys came out after the first explosion, they were not in the mood to invite him in for a cuppa.'

'Then why haven't the police found his body? They've been at the site all day.'

'Maybe they have, they just haven't told you.'

'Trust me, I would know.' Tom flashed a knowing look. 'Now, you lie low and wait. We'll have another job for you soon. Very soon.'

'And if I've had enough?'

'I think we both know that's not an option.'

Jo and Bob were sitting shoulder to shoulder in front of his computer monitor. She couldn't help but smirk at the curious glances they were attracting from the ever-increasing foot traffic passing Bob's door. It's not that she didn't walk the floors regularly, it was just that seeing a chief superintendent and detective inspector huddled, and probably plotting, was fuel for the most outlandish rumours.

'Explain to me again exactly what I'm looking at,' she said, the columns of figures fusing together.

'Patterns, can't you see the patterns?'

'Like in those Magic Eye pictures? Oh, hold on,' she said, jabbing a finger at the screen. 'Isn't that a herd of migrating wildebeest just there?'

Bob shook his head. 'I'm going as slowly as I can.'

Jo swayed back. 'Sorry, go on.'

Bob dragged the cursor down one column, highlighting its contents, then swapped screens and did the same on another spreadsheet. 'This first set of figures show when the three-monthly fee was paid to the home for seven of their residents, including Mary Cooke.'

'Right.'

'And this column here on the other sheet shows when they died.'

'OK.'

He then highlighted a third column. 'And this is when their DNACPR was signed by Dr Harper.'

Jo tracked all three sets of figures back and forward. She could feel Bob's gaze as the penny started to drop.

'Within a week of the home being paid, the DNACPR was signed and within a week of that they were dead?'

'Top of the class.'

'When did each of them move to the home?'

'It varies but all of them had dementia, none had family close by and none had a GP, or if they did, they transferred to Dr Harper soon after moving in.'

'Even Mary? She was local. Surely she had a GP? Couldn't they have continued her care?'

'Primary care is in a right old state. The city has lost four GP practices in the last two years. Mary's closed down just before she moved in to Sycamore so they just registered her with Harper, like ninety per cent of the other residents.'

'When they get paid then, a call goes in to Harper, he cobbles together a DNACPR, then they die?'

'That's what I reckon,' said Bob.

'Doesn't the family get the money back? You know, the portion between death and the end of the quarter.'

'There's a clause that says fees are non-refundable, so no.'

'Is that even legal?'

Bob shrugged his shoulders. 'It's never been tested and who's going to ask, "What happens to my money if Mum dies soon?" Sounds mercenary, doesn't it?'

Jo stood up and gazed out into the office, wrestling with the 'so what' question.

'How do they die then?'

'Not sure at the moment. Most deaths are certified by Dr Harper, as he made sure he saw them recently and always ensured that was to do with the illness he gave as the MCCD.'

'MCC what?'

'Medical Certificate Cause of Death.'

Jo nodded. 'No post-mortem then?'

'Correct. I need to look at all seven. There must be some common features but I'm as sure as I can be that as soon as the eighteen grand lands in the bank, that's the death warrant for the chosen ones.'

'Have we got ourselves our very own Dr Shipman?'

'Too early to say. If we have then Dr Harper has managed to swerve all the reforms brought in following the public inquiry. He must be incredibly well connected.'

It was meant as a joke but when Bob suggested it was possible, Jo's heart sank. It was true what they said about running Brighton and Hove Police: never mind the crisis you're in, as it'll soon be swamped by another far worse just round the corner.

'Where's the money then? I mean, I presume it's not sitting in their current account for a rainy day?'

'Not at all.' Bob flicked to another spreadsheet. 'This shows all the outgoings. There's the usual day-to-day expenses. Staff, food, bills. Then there are some very odd transfers, here.' He pointed to four debits of between ten and thirty thousand to a payee that looked like a high-security password.

'Can you find out who that is?'

'No. But I know a geek who can.'

Jo raised her eyebrow. 'That brings me on to my next question. How have you got all this information so quickly? I mean, medical records and financial transactions aren't exactly open access. I'm guessing you've not troubled a judge to issue a warrant yet.'

Bob shuffled on his seat. 'You know that old adage "don't ask, don't tell"?'

'Be very careful, Bob,' said Jo, switching to ma'am mode. 'I don't mind bailing you out of some things but please don't put me head to head with Her Honour Judge Laing.'

'I thought you liked her.'

'When I'm on her good side. I've seen what she's left of those who've taken her on.'

'Shall I carry on then?'

'Why not just keep me updated with the what, not the how.'

'Then don't ask.'

'Don't worry, I bloody won't.' Jo winked and pulled the door. 'Oh, and well done. Really well done in fact.'

16

Pressure had been building throughout the day and, by mid-afternoon, it was obvious to Jo and the council leadership alike that unless they held the public meeting before the weekend, Brighton and Hove would be ablaze.

As they led the way to the rostrum in Hove Town Hall's council chamber, Doughty and Parfitt's body language laid bare their disdain for both Jo and the gathered crowd. Privately, Jo was loving this. It was no secret that the two megalomaniacs despised the accountability that came with power and there was no better way of deflecting the fire from the police than sharing a platform with the most hated council leader and chief executive in living memory.

The floor rumbled with the boos that greeted them and, as they took their seats, it fell to Councillor Tom Doughty to call for order. It took a good five minutes for anything approaching silence to fall.

Jo scanned the hall and saw some of the usual faces; professional protestors who'd pitch up supporting – or fighting – every cause. She picked out the contingent from Friends, Families and Travellers, whom she had already met. She'd pacified them out of the rage they were perfectly entitled to harbour by assuring them total honesty and her support in effecting real change in the city. How she would achieve that she had no idea, but a promise was a promise.

To be on the safe side though, she'd posted half a dozen cops in a van round the corner.

'Ladies and gentlemen,' said Doughty. 'Thank you for joining us this evening. Just to be clear, we will make a statement, take two questions and that will be it.'

He'd hardly finished the sentence before the yelling started. This was news to the crowd, and to Jo, and it was clear they were not going to be fobbed off.

'You'll fucking answer as many questions as you're asked,' came an incandescent voice from the left-hand side. 'That's if you want to get out of here with your limbs intact.'

Doughty blanched. He turned towards Jo, his eyes pleading for back-up. The clamour just crescendoed: calls for resignation, shouts of 'racist scum' and threats that, had they been made outside the pubs and clubs of West Street, would have earned the maker a night in Hollingbury Custody.

The council security officers, rather than spreading out round the crowd, huddled at the back clearly intent on being first out of the door should it really kick off.

Much as she was enjoying Doughty's terror and Parfitt's passivity, Jo knew that someone had to take control and wrench this farce back on track.

She rose. 'Thank you. Thank you.' The shouts started to abate. A little louder, she continued. 'I'm sorry if Mr Doughty wasn't clear. Of course we will listen to all your questions and, whilst we can't promise to answer each and every one, we will do our best and get back to you on those we need more information on.'

She could feel Doughty's and Parfitt's eyes burning into her, and that just spurred her on. 'I can answer any questions about the policing of this city and its communities, what we will do going forward to maximise your safety and how we will bring those who do you harm to justice. You will understand that I can't answer any questions on the ongoing investigation except to say that we have the very best team under DCI Hussain, working night and day to bring who committed and was behind these atrocious murders to justice, whoever and wherever they are.' She sensed her instinctive glance to the men on her left did not go unnoticed by them or the floor. 'Mr Doughty and Parfitt will be happy to deal with council policy and equality.'

Having served that ace, she took her seat. Before either Doughty or Parfitt could speak, questions were shouted from the floor.

'I've got one for the councillor,' the loudest voice said. Jo recognised the twenty-something woman by her multiple facial piercings and flowing technicolour skirt as being the spokesperson of the FFT delegation.

This should be fun, she thought.

'Can you tell us why you have disbanded the council's Gypsy and Roma team at the same time that you abandoned the plans to build a second designated transit site, and whether you will review those plans?'

Doughty stood up. 'My dear.' He paused for the shouts of 'shame' to die down, looking at Parfitt as if to understand what he'd said wrong. 'I'm not sure if you keep up with the news, but we're in the middle of a recession. We simply do not have the money for frivolous projects. The council can barely afford to meet the needs of its own people, let alone providing for every lifestyle that blows into the city.'

The young woman let the rest of the crowd howl their disgust. Jo stared at him in disbelief and his shrug betrayed his genuine ignorance.

When she could be heard again, the young woman, with serene cogency, continued. 'Have you any idea how unlawful and racist just about every syllable of that answer was? Is there any wonder why this city, your council, is developing a national reputation for being a force of hate?'

Parfitt stood. 'That, young lady, is outrageous. We are merely exercising common sense. We have to balance the books and support people who come from here. If that means we have to make tough decisions, then we will.'

The crowd erupted once more in outrage. Jo sprung to her feet.

'Please, I know you may not agree with these gentlemen's views, but please can you keep calm and allow others to ask questions?' Her pleading did the trick again. As she was about to sit down, a swarthy-looking man helped an elderly woman – eighty if she was a day – towards the front. He looked at Jo and she picked up that one of them wanted to say something. As they eased their way through the crowd, Jo saw tears in both of their eyes. She raised her hand.

'Can we let this lady ask the next question?'

Silence swept the room.

The couple hobbled to the centre of the platform and looked up at the councillor and chief executive. In a booming voice that belied her frail looks, the old lady spoke.

'Mr Parfitt, you talk about this being the city of common sense and supporting people who come from here. Mr Doughty, you've been quoted as saying that basic council services for travellers are frivolous. You say similar things about the black communities, the gay communities, even the disabled and elderly. The other night two of my daughters and two of my grandchildren were murdered by thugs who are empowered by your hate. My sons-in-law lost their wives and children. Where is the common sense in that? What is it about us that makes you abandon us to the mercy of fascists? You asked this lady here if she keeps up with the news. Do you keep up with history? Are my beautiful daughters and grandchildren the first to fall victim to your Nazi propaganda? How many more will you see die before you are satisfied your work is done? And one more question. Why have none of you, except the chief superintendent, condemned the attacks, only the unfortunate death of your white middle-class colleague? Why?'

The crowd erupted and this time nothing Jo could do pacified them. Instead, raging, she bundled the two men out of a side door knowing they were too bigoted for any of what they'd just heard to make a jot of difference.

17

Despite her age, Ajee was not naive.

The last twenty-four hours locked in the creaking, draughty farmhouse was infinitely preferable to the cycle of work, sleep, work at the care home – but it was obvious that it wouldn't last for ever. She guessed that this was a staging post whilst they thought how best to hide her since Mrs Cooke's death. She'd promised them she'd say nothing if the police interviewed her, but they'd not listened, so here she was.

For now, as well as a rickety, musty bed, she had unlimited access to a tiny bathroom which boasted a cracked and shit-stained avocado toilet, a matching sink with lime-scaled chrome taps and a handheld shower over a scummed bathtub. If she'd expected hot water, she'd have been disappointed. Luckily she was not so presumptuous.

As she stood naked, shivering, under the dribbling water she wondered what was next and whether escape would ever be an option. She rubbed the hair-encrusted soap over her goosebumps and pondered whether now was her best chance. Then a dog bark brought her back to reality. Even if she could avoid the snarling predators, she had no idea where she was, and she'd pushed her luck once already by fleeing across open country from the lorry.

No, she'd use this opportunity to plan. She just hoped they'd give her time to do that.

She turned off the trickle and stepped out, wrapping the sandpaper-rough towel around her freezing body. She was about to pad back to her room, hoping none of the leering guards were on the landing, when a noise outside jolted her.

Statue-still, she strained her ears. The distant crunching of tyres on gravel grew slowly louder and closer. Then the engine idled and the distinctive sound of the same gate as yesterday being hauled open sent an even deeper chill through her than the shower.

She darted into the bedroom, a splinter from the bare floorboards stabbing the ball of her right foot. Ignoring the pain, she edged to the window, just in time to see the gate close behind a blue tatty van that she assumed was the one she'd been dumped in yesterday.

It parked by the front door and two men in muscle-for-hire uniforms – black fleeces, black combats, black tactical boots – stepped out. She lost sight of them and assumed that one of her jailers had let them in.

Ajee scrambled into the blue jeans and sweatshirt they'd swapped her uniform for, fighting to swallow the dread that was coursing through her. There seemed no doubt she was on the move. She'd not eaten since just before dusk and her stomach was remonstrating with her, yet when she heard footsteps creaking up the stairs she felt sick.

The bedroom door was flung open and the guard who'd fed her last night was briefly framed in the opening. He stepped aside and the two from the van, now wearing balaclavas, seemed to fill the room.

'Come with us,' said one, whilst the other, holding a black hood and some strips of plastic, grabbed her. In a moment her wrists were clamped together behind her and the world had gone black once more.

As they hauled her out to the landing, she recognised her guard's voice. 'Careful,' and the men seemed to obey as she was now just coaxed down the stairs.

The van journey was identical to the day before. Ajee felt just as claustrophobic, just as battered and just as terrified. Farting and belching from her left reminded her that, of course, she was not alone. That, and the memory of baton on bone, dissuaded her from any idea of breaking out this time.

She fought back tears as hopelessness swept over her, but no way was she going to show them how terrified she was. Whatever they had in store for her couldn't be worse than seeing her mother raped and burnt alive then her father and brother executed on the banks of the Queiq river.

Suddenly she was flung forward as the van stopped, the flatulent guard booting her away.

Again, the front doors opened then slammed and a few seconds later she was hauled out and bundled through a gate. Another nursing home? The same?

The guards seemed desperate to get her across what seemed to be a yard and in through a door. Finally, after she had been pushed into a room and onto a wooden chair, someone yanked her hood off.

She blinked and allowed her eyes to adjust to take in a small lounge. Two three-seater marigold settees formed an 'L' shape in the opposite corner, each with pastel multi-coloured throws neatly draped across them. In between was a low glass coffee table with bottles of water, a box of tissues and a stack of pornographic magazines, neatly stacked. To her left was a glass cabinet with bottles she presumed were spirits. Next to that hummed a small fridge.

Ajee tried to process what this all meant. The low lighting and red flock wallpaper gave no clue as to where she was.

The two men stepped aside when a woman, mid-forties, white and busty, breezed in. Ajee lowered her eyes but not before she spotted the newcomer's grey roots and telltale fake tan.

'You may leave us now.' Ajee sensed the two thugs obey.

'Look at me, my dear,' the woman said. Ajee knew she was talking to her but pretended she didn't understand.

'You girl, look up, will you?' Ajee raised her gaze and could see that this woman had once been quite beautiful.

'What is your name?'

'Ajee,' she quaked.

'Speak up.'

'Ajee. My name is Ajee.'

The woman had taken a seat on one of the settees and held a clipboard and a small digital camera.

'You can call me Suzanne. You will stay here now and work for me.'

'Like before? Care for old people?'

Suzanne burst out laughing. 'In a manner of speaking.'

Ajee couldn't work out what was so funny.

A flash smarted her eyes and she saw Suzanne examine the back of the camera and frown. 'That won't do. Let's get you cleaned up, into some better clothes, then we'll try again.'

'Why you need photo, Mrs Suzanne?'

'So our customers know what's on offer.'

Ajee frowned. Puzzled.

'Never mind. Let's get you looking presentable and ready to start work . . .' Suzanne glanced at her watch and stood up, 'by lunchtime, say? Follow me.'

Ajee shuffled behind, deeper into the house, or whatever it was. It was only when they arrived on the first floor that the wheezing grunts from behind one of the doors brought a lightning strike of realisation.

18

The arrests themselves couldn't have been less dramatic if Bob had tried. Two officers to each address, gentle knocks on each door, a few mumbled words and the GP and accountant were escorted to the waiting unmarked cars and away to custody.

He'd be amazed if any of the neighbours had spotted what could be the beginning of the end of two illustrious careers and the first step to years in prison.

Now, two hours later, the equally unobtrusive searches complete, Bob and Jo were sitting expectantly in the remote viewing room waiting for the interviews to commence.

'Who's the brief?' asked Jo, pointing her pencil at the monitor towards the shabby-looking man sitting to Dr Harper's left.

'Dunno ma'am. Some legal rep, although I'm surprised the good doc couldn't convince one of the actual solicitors to turn out themselves.'

Jo shrugged and then fell silent whilst DC Jake Briers ran through the interview preamble and caution, for the benefit of the tape. Bob had considered joining the young detective but suspected his foot-in-the-door approach at the surgery two days earlier might not have been the strongest foundation for the rapport Jake was after.

'Dr Harper, you've been arrested on suspicion of conspiracy to murder, forgery and misconduct in a public office. I intend to ask you some questions about that. Your legal rep has been provided with pre-interview disclosure.'

Before the doctor could reply, the lawyer chipped in. 'My client has prepared a statement which he has asked me to read out, after which he will exercise his right to silence and make no comment to any further questions.'

Bob and Jo exchanged resigned looks.

'Told you so. Happens every time,' said Bob.

The rep continued. 'I am Dr Anthony Harper, a medical doctor in general practice at the Goldstone Medical Centre in Hove. As part of my practice, I visit the Sycamore Care Home in Upper Drive, Hove. I have been told that a number of their residents have died with Do Not Resuscitate Orders in place and that the police regard those to be forged or made by me on grounds other than the health, well-being and dignity of the patient. I completely refute this allegation and can say that each DNACPR was put in place in accordance with the guidance from the General Medical Council, British Medical Association and the Department of Health and Social Care. Each was a clinical decision with appropriate consultation and I stand by my practice. I wish to make no further comment at this stage.'

'Oh well that's bloody fine then,' said Jo. 'Let's just call up all the grieving relatives and tell them it's all tickety-boo because the clever doctor says so.'

'Shall we listen to Jake's questions, ma'am?' said Bob.

Jo flounced back in her chair, wearing a scowl that could freeze oil.

Unperturbed by the attempt to close the interview down, Jake plodded on. Despite his junior years, Bob was proud that he'd anticipated this and had devised questions and an approach that would give Harper every opportunity to set out his stall, thus robbing him of the chance to conjure up an explanation in court.

Bob and Jo watched as he diligently went through each death, asking pointed questions about medical conditions, mental capacity, powers of attorney, advocates, the lot. To each question came the robotic, and slightly bored, 'No comment.'

'Arrogant fuck,' spat Jo.

'Love you too, ma'am,' replied Bob. 'You've got to admit, dull as this is, Jake's doing a cracking job. I mean, it was only a few days ago he'd not even heard of a DNACPR. Now he's weaving his way around the law and best practice like a Court of Protection judge.'

'I'll give you that. Any jury will surely see that an innocent man, especially a doctor for Christ's sake, would be desperate to answer those questions.'

'Let's hope so. But the more he blanks, the harder his defence team will have to work.'

Forty-five minutes in and Jake wrapped it all up.

'Can I go home now?' asked the GP.

'No,' replied Jake.

'Why not?'

'No comment,' he replied.

Bob winced at this flash of immaturity.

Next up was Thomas Bradshaw, the accountant.

The fact that he alone was sitting in front of Jake and his co-interviewer told Bob this was likely to be a wholly different affair. Although he'd felt Harper had been foolish not to answer the basics, Bradshaw was crazy to decline a solicitor.

'This should be good,' he said as Jo slopped his coffee in front of him. 'Thanks.'

Jake had barely finished his introduction when the moustachioed prisoner raged.

'You've bloody got me out of bed at some ungodly hour, made me miss my tee-time on some trumped-up charge of money laundering without a shred of evidence.'

'Mr Bradshaw, before you go on, are you sure you don't want a solicitor?'

'Do I buggery. Listen to me, sonny.' He was wagging his finger now. 'I'm a perfectly respectable accountant who plays golf with the chief constable . . .'

'That's blown his respectability argument out of the water,' quipped Jo.

'. . . and I'll have you know that all the major city companies, including care homes, are my clients. Do you honestly think that I need to dirty my hands with laundering money, as you say, when I make a perfectly respectable living the proper way?'

'All we need you to do is explain some of these transactions. Shall we go through them one by one?'

'Is this really necessary? I'm sure a mere detective constable would struggle to grasp the intricacies of corporate accounting. I wouldn't want to bamboozle you.'

'Oh, to wipe that pompous smirk off his face,' said Jo.

'I guess Jake forgot to mention his previous profession,' said Bob.

'What?' said Jo.

Bob told her.

'Oh, brilliant. Pass the sodding popcorn,' said Jo as she settled back for the show to commence.

When DC Jake Briers tapped on her door, Jo almost felt sorry for the lad. The assured disposition that he'd worn in the interview had been overtaken by fidgets and shuffles.

'Come in, come in,' she said, gesturing for him to sit in Gary's chair opposite. Bob was standing, leaning against Jo's desk. 'Relax, Jake. We're all coppers here.' She saw his shoulders loosen a little but his lips remained dry and his eyes refused to connect with hers. 'You did really well in there, didn't he Bob?'

'Taught him all I know.' Bob winked at the DC. 'Seriously Jake, you turned that supercilious accountant inside out. Between you and me, I had to bring the chief super up to speed on some of the finer details you asked, but I think she got the gist.'

The DC flipped his gaze between the two senior officers, unsure what game he was a reluctant spectator at.

'Jake. What you need to know about DI Heaton is that he can be a complete twat sometimes. No, that's not right. He's a complete twat all the time.'

Finally, Jake cracked a smile and Jo sensed he was ready to get down to business.

'Thanks ma'am. It's what I used to do. Forensic accounting that is. I try not to tell people that as they think I'm a bit of a nerd.'

'But with the likes of Bradshaw, it pays to play your cards close to your chest, eh?' said Bob.

'Seems that way,' said Jake.

'OK, so give me the headlines,' said Jo.

'Well, it's early days,' continued Jake, 'but the trail that's starting to emerge is not one I'd expect to see in a legitimate business. Obviously, we are looking at an umbrella company, Maximus Care Ltd, with a number of care homes sitting beneath it. These run more or less independently but under the same business model.'

'Is that legal?' asked Jo. 'From a tax perspective I mean.'

'Yes, absolutely and you'd expect to see some commonality between them in terms of income and outgoings. Fees, staffing costs, catering, general running costs, that sort of thing.'

'I'm sensing there's a but coming.'

Jake flipped open his laptop and called up a spreadsheet, then wheeled his chair over so Jo and Bob could see the screen. Jo flashed Bob a look of panic; clearly Jake didn't understand the concept of 'headlines', but she daren't cut him off mid-stream.

'I've taken the liberty of requesting a model care home financial profile from the City of London Police. For comparison purposes.'

Jo and Bob swapped nods.

Jake switched between spreadsheets and, rather like when Bob had showed her the rudimentary ones, they meant less than nothing to her. 'Can you, you know, cut to the chase, Jake? In laymen's terms. For the DI's sake of course.'

Bob shook his head but remained silent.

'What this shows is that the turnover of Maximus Care Ltd as a group, and of five of their homes, is on average sixty-three per cent higher than comparative businesses. We're lucky as, the way the income is paid, it has to show in the books – which means it has to go somewhere too.'

'So far.'

'The nature and value of expenses is what I'd anticipate given the resident numbers and the nature of their care, and this is borne out by the control model too. So, given that, you'd expect to see pretty impressive profits at the end of the year.'

Jake looked at Jo, as if waiting for a light bulb to flicker. After thirty seconds or so of nothing, he changed tack.

'More money in equals greater turnover. Same money out equals equivalent business expenses. Turnover minus expenses equals profit.'

'Yes, yes. That's what I was going to say,' said Jo.

'Except that's not what we are seeing. There are huge sums of money being paid out. The one who receives the most, in terms of the dodgy transactions, is a company called Expede.'

'And this relates to every home?'

'Five so far, yes. The money comes in and then a dubious invoice comes in and the money is paid out within days. All their other invoices wait the full twenty-eight days before payment but these are settled almost straight away.'

'And what do we know about Expede?'

'That's what I need to dig a little deeper on. It appears to be a subsidiary of a bigger company. No named directors at Company House, just other institutions and trusts and it's been dissolved.'

'And is *that* illegal?' asked Jo, hoping to get back on familiar territory.

'Only if it's a ruse for money laundering, tax evasion or the funds are being used for organised crime, that sort of thing.'

'And before you ask, ma'am,' said Bob, 'Jake's onto it and we'll let you know as soon as we know more. It won't be quick though.'

'Sure,' said Jo, grateful that the DI had predicted her inevitable impatience. 'However, do you know yet whether all the residents in the homes are self-funders or whether any are paid for by the council?'

'Some and some, but the self-funders are paying around £1,200 per week – on a rolling three months in advance basis – whilst the council pay £760. Most homes use the difference to provide equitable care for all, but there's no evidence of that here. In fact, what I'm seeing so far is that the self-funders survive an average of six months and the social care residents live a lifestyle that costs around £500.'

'What's that mean in terms of laundered money then?' asked Bob.

'Don't hold me to this, but Sycamore have lost twelve residents this year. If, for argument's sake, they've died within a month of arriving or a month of their next fee being paid – and that's being generous – that's eight weeks' unused fees each. So eight times £1,200 is £9,600. Multiply that by the twelve residents and that's £115,200 being shipped out for God knows what.'

Jo shook her head in bewilderment. 'And is that what you're seeing so far?'

'There or thereabouts.'

'So, if every home is scamming people at the same level, that's . . .'

'£576,000. And you can bet if this is going into organised crime it's not just Maximus Care who are a front,' said Jake. 'Any self-respecting criminal enterprise will spread the risk not just across multiple legitimate businesses, but across sectors too. My conservative guess is that this racket is reaping upwards of three million a year.'

'What would that fund?' asked Bob.

'It's anyone's guess,' said Jo. 'But a de facto political coup and the muscle to enforce it can't come cheap.'

'You can't be serious,' said Bob.

'I'm sorry, you've lost me,' interjected Jake.

'That's not a bad thing,' said Jo. 'The less you know, the more impartial you'll be. I need you to focus on just this investigation for now, Jake. I want to know where that money is going and who's using it for what. And you report to DI Heaton and me. No one else. If anyone asks what you're doing, make something up – Bob, you can help him with that – but if the money is going where I think it is, it's no exaggeration to say our lives might depend on no one finding out until we're ready. Understand?'

'Perfectly,' said Bob, who then looked at a numbed Jake. 'We both do.'

19

It didn't take much to persuade Jo Howe to gatecrash a Major Crime Team briefing. It wasn't so long ago that these would be her showpieces where, despite all the technology and the plethora of analysts that underpinned any modern-day investigation, pennies dropped and light bulbs flickered.

The last such briefing she'd actually run herself was during the enquiry into Harry Cooke's murder – maybe one she was slightly too close to lead, given her clandestine affair with his father years previously. It was also the moment her and many others' lives changed for ever. She wondered if the psychological scars would ever heal.

Back then she detested senior officers lurking at the back of these scheduled groupthinks – the presence of a boss could easily clam a rookie detective up – but now she was that boss, she'd find a reason to break her own rule.

And with Operation Steward, the name randomly assigned to the murder of four travellers – Mary and Saoirse O'Connor, and Theresa and Patrick Smith – the death by dangerous driving of Loretta Briggs and the murder of the man in the van, she had more reason than most.

She eased the door open to hear Faisal start the briefing with the usual instructions about keeping phones off, listening to everyone and not leaving anything unsaid at the end. 'Don't mind me,' she murmured as she found a spare desk to perch on at the back. Several familiar faces turned and smiled in her direction.

She was pleased when Faisal made no more of her intrusion than a polite 'ma'am'. This was his show and he needed to keep everyone focused on the task in hand.

'Let's kick off with anything from the scene. Witnesses first please. Nigel, any update?' said Faisal.

DS Nigel Hughes was the office manager and saw every piece of paper the investigation generated. Usually, he'd give an overview and then individual DCs or civilian investigators could chip in with more detail or soft information – gut feelings and the like that they'd be reluctant to write down.

'Nothing forensically to note. SOCO have picked up a few shards of glass and a smashed lighter but, with the state of the place, there's nothing to say that they're connected just yet. We're slowly getting there with the residents though. I've allocated actions to speak to those most likely to have something useful to say to the most diplomatic of the team but, as you'll understand, we aren't overly blessed with those.' This was met with shouts of 'rude' and 'cheek'.

'Some will say that's why you're office-based, Nige,' said Faisal which, in turn, was met with laughter.

Jo smiled too. Despite the gravity of what the MCT dealt with every day, good-natured banter was their lifebelt and never undermined their resolve to get the job done.

Nigel continued. 'Those who did see anything only glimpsed the vans making off and the aftermath. Certainly no one saw any faces or could give any form of description. We've got a couple of people who talk about the way the vans were being driven after Loretta was hit, but nothing to take us much further. Obviously, we've got the chassis of the vans so ID'ing those is not an issue.'

'Anyone have anything to add?' said Faisal. After a moment of silence, he moved on.

'Talk to me about the vans. Have we got their life history yet?'

An intelligence officer whom Jo did not recognise cleared her throat. 'First the VW, the one the body was recovered from. The plates, such as we can make out, relate to an identical make and model which is currently parked up on the owner's drive in the posh end of York.'

'A ringer then,' said Faisal.

'Yes, boss. We've managed to read the Vehicle Identification Number from the bulkhead. This shows as being lost/stolen from Newhaven. It was nicked from the railway station car park a week ago and no ANPR hits since.'

'Any hits on the false plates?'

'Not until the night of the attack and then on cameras on the A259 and A27 towards Brighton. My guess is that it was kept in a lock-up or similar close to Newhaven in the meantime.'

'We need to find where that is. Nigel, can you raise actions around that please? We've got very little else so let's follow what we have.'

Nigel nodded and scribbled in his notebook.

The intelligence officer continued. 'The Renault is more interesting.' Jo was struck by how even more alert the already attentive team became. 'That too was on false plates but this one was not stolen. It's shown as no current keeper with the last owner recorded as Expede Solutions Ltd., who transferred the vehicle last September after it had been on a Statutory Off Road Notification since that July.'

Jo gagged on her hot water. 'Sorry, but how are you spelling Expede?'

The DC turned round and double-took when she saw who'd asked the question. 'E-X-P-E-D-E, ma'am.'

'Sorry Faisal, do you mind?' The DCI shrugged. 'What do you know about them?'

'That's where it's getting tricky. The Company House Records just take me down a rabbit hole, but they seem to have been dissolved in January and the directors are all offshore companies so I've not got any further on them just yet. I've requested their accounts.'

'Have they come to light in any other investigations?' asked Jo.

'Not that I can tell.'

'Thanks. Faisal, can we have a chat afterwards? I might have something.'

'Can you say it now? I like everything shared at these briefings.'

'I know you do, but no,' Jo replied, tapping out a message for Bob Heaton to get himself up to HQ, ASAP.

Fifteen minutes after the briefing, Jo, Faisal and Bob were gathered round the circular conference table in what, for the duration of the investigation, served as Faisal's office.

Bob and Faisal looked equally bewildered as they waited for Jo to speak.

'I'm so sorry to spring this on you both, especially you Faisal. I'd have exploded if someone threw a curveball like that in one of my briefings.'

Faisal shrugged. Jo looked at Bob and they both smirked. Bob spoke first.

'Faisal, what you need to know about Mrs Howe is firstly she hates being called Mrs Howe. Secondly, if Mrs Howe says or does something you wish she hadn't, in public you suck it up, but in private, like now, you give her both barrels and talk it out.'

Faisal's brow furrowed and he switched his focus to Jo and then back to Bob.

'He's right,' said Jo. 'I'm becoming bloody impetuous these days and unless I can rely on people to call me out on that, I'm stuffed.'

'These days?'

Jo glared at him. Of all people, he should know what had changed.

Faisal broke the silence. 'Thanks for the ground rules, but honestly it's fine. I was just taken aback a little when you latched onto that company name. I thought it would be good for everyone to hear but I understand some things can't be shared.'

'OK, so long as we are good. Bob, to bring you up to speed, one of the vans used in the firebombing of the travellers' site was once owned by Expede . . .' She looked at Faisal for help.

He turned a page of his notebook. 'Expede Solutions Ltd.'

'That's it. Ring a bell?'

Bob always looked in such pain when he was thinking hard. 'One of the dodgy suppliers to the care homes?'

'Correct,' Jo replied. Then, between them, they took Faisal through Jake Briers' findings and the suspicion that frail nursing home residents were being killed for profit.

'You think there could be a link?' said Faisal. 'I mean, it could just be a coincidence.'

'It could be and maybe I'm being paranoid, but there are things going on in this city that just don't add up and I would love to bottom them out.'

'Things?'

'None of this goes further than this room for now. I have reason to believe that the British Patriot Party use more than politics to drive their fascist agenda. I think they're not averse to crime, up to and including murder.'

'It's a bit of a stretch linking the care home deaths to politics, isn't it? I mean crime, for sure, but I can't see the council being involved in bumping people off,' said Bob.

'Why not? They have to fund their ethnic cleansing campaign somehow.'

'Ethnic cleansing? That's a bit tabloid, isn't it?'

'All I'm asking is for both of you to look into it. Share what you can between you, and just keep your minds open to the possibility there could be more to both your investigations than you're seeing.'

20

Having left the two detectives to absorb her fledgling theory, Jo had every intention of heading back to Brighton Police Station but found herself passing the A23 turn-off and heading for Hove.

Every other time she'd visited Sycamore Care Home, it felt like a chore, but now the desire that she used to feel at the outset of every investigation burnt white hot. She deliberately ignored the inconvenient facts that Mary's death was not hers to investigate, and that she was far too senior to get her hands dirty anyway.

She waited by a van then grabbed the door as another visitor came out. Once inside she realised she'd no cover story. She couldn't afford to have Peggy Squire, the manager, know she was police, but she needed to ask enough questions – preferably of Ajee – to get some clue as to what was going on.

She opted not to sign in this time. No point in laying a trail. First, she crept to the manager's office, and, to her relief, the room was empty. She thought about rummaging through the mountains of paperwork scattered across the desk, but it would be a miracle if she found anything before she was caught.

Instead, she nosed through the corridors, lounge and dining room on the off-chance that Ajee would be scampering around. She'd be bound to know what had happened and, from their last conversation, it seemed she was warming up to talk.

Having navigated the warren of corridors on the ground floor – sorely aware her knowledge of the home only extended to the entrance hall and

Mary's first-floor room – she bumped into a care worker not dissimilar in age and appearance to Ajee, emptying commodes in the sluice room.

'Oh, I'm sorry, I seem to be lost,' she said, prompting the girl to spin round, shock in her eyes.

'You should not be here,' said the girl.

Jo thought she'd struggle to find a credible reason for looking for a dead resident, so took a chance. 'Actually, I'm looking for a friend of mine who works here. You might know her. Ajee?'

If the girl had looked startled before, now she was positively terrified. 'I know no Ajee. Now you should leave.'

Red rag to a bull, Jo stood her ground. 'Ajee. Turkish girl, maybe? You must know her.'

'Turkish?'

'So you do know her then. When is she working next?'

'I not know. Please go. No questions. Please leave.'

Jo knew she was making the girl even more scared but soldiered on anyway. 'What is your name? Please, I only want to help.'

'Ajee not work here any more. That's all I say.' The girl made for the door and Jo stepped to one side.

'Where is she then?'

'I cannot say. Please go.'

Jo watched as the girl ran down the corridor, flashing a look back. Jo stood for a moment and watched her disappear, then turned and walked the opposite way. As she reached the turn in the corridor, she found herself face to face with Peggy Squire with a very familiar young man. Both looked shocked to see her – then, simultaneously, the manager said, 'Mrs Howe, can I help you?' as Jake Briers blurted, 'Morning, ma'am.'

Peggy looked at both Jo and Jake. 'Ma'am? So you're police too? Unless you have a warrant, I think we should all go to my office so you can explain why you're snooping around my care home.'

They dutifully followed, Jo just being able to hiss to Jake, 'Leave this to me,' as Peggy unclipped the two-way radio from her belt. 'Leo, Vlad,

I've found an intruder in the building. Can you meet me in my office in five minutes? And call Mr O'Keefe to let him know the trespasser seems to be a senior police officer. He might want to come down or at least make some calls.'

As they approached the manager's office, Jo's mind galloped. She'd need her sharpest wits to get out of this one, but had not a single clue how.

21

The more Tom Doughty crossed Jo Howe, the angrier he became. As if it wasn't bad enough her bursting into his meetings with that pussy Russ Parfitt and taking delight in some foreigner leading the hunt for Loretta Briggs' killer, now she'd been caught snooping around one of his care homes.

It was only by chance that Tom was with Leigh O'Keefe when the call came through. He could tell by Leigh flicking glances at him that whatever the caller was telling him was not only a big deal, but that it would land on his plate.

It had seemed a suitably remote place to meet his enforcer, especially as Leigh needed to lie low, but the problem with choosing the café at One Garden in Stanmer Park was that, with its mix of yummy mummies and empty-nesters, he'd have to keep his voice down.

When Leigh had finished repeating what Leo had told him, Tom fought every urge not to erupt. It was only a mini-football rolling against his foot that reminded him that here was not the place.

'What the hell has she said?' demanded Tom.

'Some bull . . . rubbish about looking for her DC.'

'But you say she's been visiting a resident for months. How didn't we know that?'

Leigh shrugged. 'No one thought to ask.'

Tom sipped his tea to prevent an outburst. 'How come we don't seem to know that we are looking after the imprisoned PCC's mother nor that the current city police commander is popping in delivering flowers and TLC?'

'You asked me to keep my distance from the day-to-day goings-on . . .'

'Quit the case for the defence. We can deal with who cocked up later, now we have to fix this.'

'You also need to know that Mrs Cooke died the other day.'

Tom was lost for words for a moment. 'What, as in passed away peacefully in her sleep or,' he lowered his voice, 'did we help her along?'

Leigh said nothing.

'Jesus Christ,' said Tom. 'I need time to work out what we do now. One thing's for certain, the cash cow these homes have become is not something I'm giving up without a fight.'

Chief Constable Stuart Acers was ambling back to his office from the Sussex Police HQ canteen, flicking the last remnants of chocolate brownie from his tie, when his phone buzzed. He was about to take it out of his pocket when Paul Davids, the Head of Corporate Development, called from his office. The chief checked his stride and turned into Davids' office.

'Sir, I just wondered if I might run these resource projections past you before the Force Command Team meeting tomorrow,' said Davids in his delightful, received pronunciation.

'Of course,' said the chief, just as the phone buzzed again. And again. And again. Stuart giggled. 'Someone's keen to get hold of me.' He took out his phone and the lock screen lit up. As it did, his face blanched. He turned and made a beeline for his office, calling out 'Another time Paul' as he disappeared down the corridor.

Ignoring his PA, who seemed desperate to hand him a sheaf of papers, and the sergeant perched on a chair awaiting his promotion appointment, Acers darted into his office and slammed the door.

Slumping in his chair, he opened the phone up fully. The pictures were murky, but unmistakably him. Even naked he was easily identifiable. Whoever took them had made sure of that, just as they'd made sure that the girl he was with looked terrified, in pain and very, very young. He could argue being duped into thinking she was eighteen, but no one would buy that.

He cupped his head in his hands, his mind convulsing with what it all meant. He didn't have to wait long. The phone buzzed again, this time a call, and the name on the screen had a menace about it.

'Yes, Tom,' said Stuart.

'You got the pictures?'

'What the hell do you want?'

'I thought you'd be asking a little nicer than that. After all, you're not in the best position to get all prissy.'

Just then someone knocked on Stuart's door.

'NOT NOW,' he shouted.

'You need to calm down, Stuart,' said Tom. 'People might think something's bothering you.'

'Tell me what this is about.'

'How many times have I told you about controlling Jo Howe?'

'What's she done now?'

'She's snooping round where she's no business. You don't need to know more than that, but enough is enough.'

'How can I control her if I don't know what she's done?' said Stuart as he turned his chair, envying the serenity of Malling Down in the distance.

'All you need to know is that she seems to have too much time on her hands and needs a proper job.'

'I'm not with you.'

'Oh, I think you are, but I'll put it in plain English. Unless you move her out of Brighton by the end of the week, those little snaps, and there are more, will be on every news app in the free world.'

An icy chill washed through Stuart.

'Are you still there?' asked Tom.

Stuart remembered to breathe.

'You wouldn't. I mean, you can't. I mean . . .'

'Stuart, of course I won't.' Acers relaxed. 'If you do as I say. If not, you'll see first-hand exactly what I can do. She's gone by Saturday or you are. Clear?'

'Clear,' Stuart mumbled, his mind anything but.

Half a dozen phone calls and two hours later, Acers had it all planned. Jo Howe would not like it, she'd know something was up, and the rest of the force would think he'd lost his marbles but, for all that, he didn't care. The only person who mattered was him and unless he succumbed to this blackmail he'd be out of his job and most likely in a cell this time next week.

When he emerged from his office, his PA was still lurking but it seemed, from the empty chair outside, that the sergeant's promotion would have to wait another day.

'I'll deal with that lot later,' he said, waving away the pile of files. 'Get me Jo Howe in here now.' His PA looked at her watch. 'Yes I know it's six-thirty, just get her in here.'

Forty-five minutes later, which felt like twice that, there was a stern rap on his door.

'Come in,' he called.

Jo Howe, looking as thunderous as he'd ever seen her, barged past him. He'd not seen her in running gear before and he had to remind himself she was married and, with what he was about to do, he'd have no chance.

'Sir, sorry about my appearance but you've dragged me back from home.'

He'd be buggered if she expected an apology.

'I need to let you know before I announce it tomorrow. I'm moving you out of Brighton.'

She looked genuinely shocked, as if the writing hadn't been on the wall. Uninvited, she grabbed the nearest conference table chair and sat down.

Stuart let it pass.

'But why?'

'You know why, but for your sake I'll never make that public knowledge.'

'I see. It's Phil Cooke all over again. A chief superintendent embarrasses you so out they go. Is that how you work?'

'How dare you bring his name into this. Anyway, it so happens there is a genuine opportunity that requires strong leadership.'

'Bullshit.'

One more, and he'd have her.

'Have you heard of the National Law Enforcement Data Service?'

'NLEDS? Of course I have. The overdue replacement for the Police National Computer.'

'Good, well it looks like the wait might be coming to an end. Terry Baker at the Police Digital Service is touting for pilot forces from next year. I've volunteered us and we have to set up a project team, led at a senior level.'

'Sounds fascinating,' she said.

'And that's you.'

'You want to pay me ninety grand per year to run an IT project? Why not get someone in who knows what they're doing and gives a toss for half that?'

'Because you're going to do it. From Monday.'

'You have got to be kidding me. This isn't me. I'll be crap at it. Please, choose someone else and let me get on with what I love.'

'Jo, you're sounding desperate now and it doesn't suit you. Monday morning, and that's final.'

Jo sprung up from the chair, knocking it onto its back. Without picking it up, she grabbed the door handle, turned and locked eyes with the chief. 'Fuck you . . . . SIR,' she said, and burst out of the office.

Acers stood for a moment, disgusted with himself, then tapped out two words on his phone: *All done*. He sent it to Tom, praying he'd keep his side of the bargain.

22

Ajee woke, aching and sore. She ran to the basin and dry-retched. The disgust and shame she felt drove her to a darker abyss than she'd been in since she saw her family brutally murdered. When she started her journey, she hadn't been running to anything in particular; just anywhere that wasn't Aleppo.

Before she'd been put to work last night, one of the other girls had told her to zone out completely. To take herself to a happy place. The problem was, it had been so long since Ajee had been happy, she couldn't think of anywhere. The men – six or seven, she'd lost count – had been all ages, shapes and sizes but one thing they had in common: they had no regard for her as a human being.

The only positive of being here was that she had her own room. Granted, she was expected to live, sleep and, worst of all, work in there but at least there was more privacy than the nursing home. The room was not much wider than the battered queen-size bed and cabinet, with a tiny wardrobe somehow squeezed in. To wash between clients, there was barely a gym locker-sized cupboard which, with the aid of a noisy Saniflo toilet, a sink and an impossibly tight shower cubicle, masqueraded as an en suite.

Suzanne, the brothel manager or whatever she was, had told her that water was rationed, but Ajee had already decided that this was one rule she'd push against.

She sat on the side of the bed gazing out of the window, which looked out to a mildew-stained wall and rusty fire escape. She'd already tried the window latch, but it had been doctored to only open a few centimetres, which was a few more than the door which was locked from the outside.

Ajee wept silently.

Fleeing Aleppo had been a no-brainer; she'd lost her family to those evil soldiers, and her childhood sweetheart, whom Assad's troops had snatched, either had a bullet in his head or had been forced to fight against those he loved.

Since then, she'd been too gullible. Time and again she'd trusted just about everyone she'd come across. The 'aid agency' in Athens, the helpful 'uncle' in Italy and the 'kind' lorry drivers through mainland Europe. Of course, they had all wanted paying for their time, and the risk to themselves, but she'd been suckered in by their feigned altruism. Even Mr George, who seemed to have randomly struck up a conversation and seemed like a harmless grandad, was just another greedy self-obsessed trafficker.

Despite being trapped and at the mercy of her captors and the revolting men who saw her as meat, she knew if she had any hope of breaking out of this cycle of incarceration and abuse, she needed to develop more cunning. Wallowing in self-pity would just bring more pain. She looked around her cramped quarters, which were the sum of her world, and vowed that this would be the last place anyone trapped her.

Bearing all the guilt she usually did when she had to abandon a family weekend for some police emergency, Jo had left home before Darren and the boys had woken, leaving a note claiming she'd been called in. She'd put them through so much recently and, despite home being the only place she felt truly safe, had an unscratchable itch to prove herself as being more than the inept liability she felt in both her professional and personal lives.

She wondered why she'd kept from Darren that she'd been stripped of her command the night before. She felt like one of those Japanese pretenders who, despite losing their job, got up at the usual time, dressed in a suit and tie and caught the same train into the city, so ashamed were they of revealing their unemployed status to their family. She'd have to tell him soon – after all, as a journalist it wouldn't take him long to spot that someone else was ranting in the *Argus* about Brighton's crime and disorder.

He might also notice that her phone wouldn't be ringing quite so often.

Sitting in her white Ford Focus, not twenty metres from the entrance to Sycamore Care Home at 5.45 a.m. on a Saturday was hardly covert. Then again, asking for a full-blown surveillance team for this fishing expedition was a non-starter. All she could hope was that those she was spying on had no reason to suspect anyone might be watching.

Her plan, such as it was, had been to see the shift change over and tail one of the off-going night staff before confronting them to find out where Ajee was. She reckoned, by no more than gut feeling, that staff worked twelve-hour shifts so should be handing over sometime between 6 and 8 a.m. She had no idea how many there would be, or whether any drove to and from work.

As she was slouched in the driver's seat, she remembered why she'd opted for the more overt branches of CID. She had the patience of a gnat and only a slightly higher concentration span. That was bad enough then, but now?

She glanced at her watch, then tapped it to check it was working. Two and half hours here was going to be unbearable.

She glanced over to Hove recreation ground and saw the first of the dog walkers. Her sons Ciaran, five, and Liam, four, had been nagging her about getting a dog since Christmas. Of course, their pleas came with all the promises to walk the mutt and play with it but, their ages aside, Jo knew that would fall to her. Perhaps with this new IT project she might have the time.

God, she was freezing.

Her attention was snatched back by movement outside the home. The brief thrill was soon doused when she saw it was two smooching lads, staggering back from a night on the town. She bet their Saturday morning was about to become far more exciting than hers.

She settled back.

Just then her phone rang. Darren.

'Hi, love,' she answered, trying to effect the sound of someone amid a crisis rather than staring at a gate.

'Where are you? I woke up and you'd gone.'

'I got called in. Didn't you hear the phone?' She hated lying to him but he'd understand. Maybe.

'No. What is it?'

'Just a custody extension. I shouldn't be more than a couple of hours. Are the boys up?'

'No, not yet. How about you bring bacon sandwiches when you come back?'

'Great idea. Gotta go. Love you.'

'Love you too.'

Custody extension? Where had that come from? Not bad though as they were fairly frequent, brisk to deal with and dull enough not to evoke too many questions. She banked that one in case she needed it again.

As time went on, the traffic, joggers and dog walkers increased. She wondered whether she should have secreted herself in the back seat but ditched that idea. No one was paying her any attention anyway, but if they did that would have looked suspicious.

Seven o'clock came and went. Still no movement. Not even going into the home. Maybe it was still too early, but then again she noticed a couple of middle-aged women in what looked like carers' uniforms wander into a care home a few doors down. Still, different homes, different rules?

At 7.30 a.m., her FaceTime rang. Darren again. No doubt the boys wanting to say good morning and ask when she was bringing breakfast back. Her heart broke when she ended the call, but how would she explain the image of her in the car with a park in the background rather than in Brighton custody block debating some villain's immediate future? She salved her conscience with a brief, *Can't talk. Busy XXX* text but as soon as she sent it she was consumed with guilt. She owed it to Darren to let him know she was safe. For stunning reasons, he worried.

The Upper Drive was heaving with traffic now. Jo wondered where all these people were going this early on a Saturday, but she was more concerned that the line of cars, vans and buses were seriously blocking her view. She bobbed around in her car to get an angle, but stopped when she realised she might draw attention to herself.

8 a.m. and a postman came up the road and into the entrance. A minute later, he came back into view and up the next driveway.

Just when she thought she'd call it a morning, a car overtook the line of traffic heading down the hill, then slowed to cut back in, bringing it parallel to Jo. She angled her head away but not so much that she couldn't glimpse the driver as the car turned left into Sycamore.

Peggy Squire. The manager. What a weird manoeuvre to bypass the traffic jam, but perfect for Jo's purposes. As she watched her disappear up the drive, a thought flashed.

She gave it ten minutes, then dialled a number.

'Sycamore Care Home. Manager speaking.'

Jo affected what she knew was a truly dreadful Spanish accent. 'Good morning. Is this Sycamore?'

'Yes, how can I help?'

'Yes, good morning. I been sent, how you say, job advert for your home.'

'For here?' Peggy interrupted.

'*Sí*, from Indeed Recruitment. They say you want night staff.'

'We aren't recruiting, my dear.'

'Yes, I have advert. I need to know, I have baby you see. I need to know your night shift. What are the er, the hours?'

'But we don't need anyone.'

Jo cursed herself but carried on anyway.

'Yes please. When your night shift finish?'

'7 a.m. Our shifts are seven to seven, night and day, but we have no vacancies.'

'Every day?'

'Yes, every day. Who did you say sent you the advert?'

'Oh, that's no good. My husband, he leave for work at six-thirty. I sorry to waste your time.'

Jo put the phone down and looked over at the Sycamore. She guessed there must be forty rooms, minimum. Forty rooms. Forty elderly frail residents, all needing care, yet – she checked her watch – 8.20 a.m. and no one had come in for or gone home from their shift.

Where were all the staff?

With everything that had been going on, Russ Parfitt had been counting down the days to the weekend. Like any chief executive, he'd known what he was getting into when he took the massive salary and the free rein over the city's services. It even helped, but was by no means a prerequisite, that he was ideologically aligned with the current administration. The Electoral Commission investigation into how an extreme right-wing party could have clinched a radical hotbed such as Brighton hung over the council still. If they were astute enough to find any evidence, it wouldn't come back to him as he'd been appointed after the event.

It was one thing being in tune with their agenda, but quite another to be charged with implementing it. Most political parties kicked their manifesto into the long grass once elected, but this lot seemed to think the hoodwinked people of Brighton and Hove had a divine right to expect them to deliver. Even more bizarre as that manifesto was, by any interpretation, warlike.

With the travellers' and Loretta's death, the copper stabbed outside the mosque and a whole host of other headline-grabbing illustrations of how the city was changing, this week had been about the worst in his thirty years in local government.

He knew he'd been a git to Heather and the kids, and was determined to make it up to them. Two days of family time. Walks on the South Downs, some crazy golf at Hove Lagoon maybe, even a trip to the Odeon if there was a movie they'd all like.

Full of anticipation for the next forty-eight hours, he'd wandered downstairs and into the kitchen intent on firing up the coffee machine, when the front-gate buzzer brought him back to the present. Not buzzing once but constantly, and it was frankly pissing him off.

'All right, all right,' he muttered as he went over to the intercom unit. His heart plummeted when he saw Tom Doughty's raging face glaring at him on the video screen. 'Come in,' he sighed as he clicked the switch, opening the gates.

Before his boss parked, Russ reached the front door, opened it and, simultaneously, called upstairs, 'Sorry, Tom's here. Won't be long,' more in hope than expectation.

He stood in the doorway as Tom half-mounted the immaculate lawn, ploughing two twenty-inch furrows in its pristine surface. Russ was gagging to say something but the thunder on Tom's face convinced him to save that.

The council leader got out of the car, slammed the door and marched past Russ.

'Do come in,' Russ whispered as he followed his boss into the office. He closed the door and was about to ask what was up when Doughty exploded.

'We've got a problem. A fucking big problem.'

Parfitt ran through the dozens of issues that could be in his head. Doughty continued.

'Nursing homes. Those fucking nursing homes. Someone, or should I say that Jo Howe specimen, is smelling a rat. Did you know that one of the people we didn't resuscitate was Phil Cooke's mum?'

'How would I know that?'

'Because you're the fucking chief executive and you have both the Coroner and the Director of Adult Services on speed dial. So the question is, how wouldn't you know?'

'And why's that a problem?' said Russ, taking a seat in the hope Tom would follow suit. He didn't.

'Because Jo-bloody-Howe has been visiting her and kind of noticed when she was no longer alive to take callers. And here's the punchline: as well as the accountant and GP being nicked because some DI has got the bit between his teeth, Howe was caught snooping around the home yesterday with some piss-poor excuse of looking for a DC.'

'Maybe she was?'

'You are kidding me? Of course she wasn't. Anyway, I've dealt with her. I sent Acers some pics that persuaded him to take some bloody action. She's in a new job from Monday.'

'So, all good then.'

'You wish. This morning the manager of Sycamore gets a call from someone asking about shift times.'

'How's that connected?'

'I don't know, but the caller said they'd been sent a job advert from an agency and wanted to know if the job was suitable. We've never advertised a job there. We don't need to, do we?'

'Let's take a breath,' said Russ. 'Are you sure you're not overthinking this? I mean, it could be a set of unfortunate coincidences and you've done the right thing in getting Acers to deal with her. Why don't we just see how things pan out?'

'But what if she is onto us? I mean, she's already dropping some not-so-subtle hints about those gypsies. It won't take her long to work out who ordered the march on the mosque. How long do you think it will be before her or one of her goons follows the money back to the care homes? Then what?'

'Tom, sit down. We need to think rationally. Let me get you a coffee and we can talk it through.'

Tom huffed, then took the vacant chair whilst Russ went to the kitchen, returning five minutes later with two Americanos.

'We have to go back to basics,' he said, assuming control over the leader. 'Your, our, *long-term* plan is to return Brighton and Hove to the white, tax-paying, Christian, heterosexual majority. That involves a lot of politics and a little more direct persuasion. The trick is to keep the two apart. Let onlookers, be it the police, press or political opponents, believe that we are the responsible face of patriotism. We will do what the people elected us to do by peaceful means. The more, shall we say, unsavoury elements of the cause are nothing to do with us. On occasions we must even condemn what they do.'

Tom thought for a moment and Russ tried to read how he would react. In essence he was telling the councillor to calm the fuck down and grow up. Would he spot that?

Finally, he spoke. 'It's not that easy.'

'How so? Just keep at arm's length.'

'But so much of what's happening, who's doing it, comes back to me. Sure, we set up shell companies to finance the bigger ambitions, but it only takes one person to turn against us and everything leads to my door. How do I dam the dyke after it bursts?'

'You don't. You do it now before the storm. Work out where, or rather who, your weak links are and get rid of them. And tear up the paper trail.'

'But how can I be sure that will protect me?'

'It's a risk but all you can do is be as thorough as possible. If you deal with the potential traitors, get rid of everyone who might come looking and destroy or re-route the evidence, you'll be watertight. In fact any two of those three would do it.'

'Well, I've already got rid of Jo Howe, so there's a start.'

Russ eyed him. 'You think her moving jobs is "getting rid of her"? That's not going to stop her. She's not the sort of person to be put off the scent that easily.'

'You mean . . . ?'

Russ nodded. 'You need to do it properly. And soon.'

23

The First Major Anthony Blake sensed something was wrong was when the shrill alarm failed to make his teeth grind as he opened the front door. It wasn't the first time the damn thing had packed up though. The intermittent power cuts were the price to pay for living in the middle of nowhere. When he retired from the Royal Engineers, his wife Felicity had insisted on the stereotypical post-army rural life as payback for dragging her round the world's hellholes for twenty-five years.

The second thing was the faint but distinct smell of body odour that hung in the hallway.

He eased the suitcases down, and turned, hoping the Airport Cars cab was still in sight – no luck there. He whispered to Felicity, 'Stay here, get your phone out and don't come in until I call you.'

'What's wrong, dear?' she said, the effects of jet lag slurring her otherwise crisp tones.

'Probably nothing but let me check.'

His military training and instincts kicked in as if the previous ten years' retirement had not happened. He scanned the hallway, which seemed pretty much as they'd left it, but he wasn't taking anything for granted. The first door to his right, the lounge, was ajar. Was that how they'd left it?

He swung the panelled door open, wedging himself against the wall, and peered in. Nothing. Crouching down in case an attacker was gearing up for a head strike or shot, he darted in and to the side. A quick scan confirmed his worst thoughts. Whilst the room was clear, it was trashed. But not in the usual way.

The ochre sofa cushions were lined up on the floor in a bed shape. The slate-coloured knitted throws were bunched up at the end and by the side were a stack of plates, stained with the remnants of several meals, and cups with varying levels of brown liquid. He picked one up to smell it. Its tepid touch warned him that whoever had been living here wasn't far away.

He moved back into the hallway, glancing to the front door. Where the hell had Felicity gone? *Never mind,* he inwardly sighed, *so long as she's out of the way.*

Blake edged his way further along the hallway, weighing up whether to tackle the open or closed doors first. He opted for the open doors as they presented the greatest risk of surprise. With his antennae up, he should be able to react to an opening door, however stealthy the intruder thought they were being.

As he approached the kitchen, a memory flashed from some TV documentary where he'd heard a police officer tell the camera that this was the worst kind of room to talk to volatile suspects in. Without exception, with their array of knives, glasses and often scalding liquids, they were a ready armoury.

Still, he thought, he had no option. He was tired, hungry and just wanted an English cup of tea.

As he tiptoed to the door, he stopped in his tracks. What was that? A muffled cry? He shook the thought away. There it was again and from the kitchen.

He sidled to the door and strained his hearing. Nothing now. Nothing except the ubiquitous birdsong that was usually white noise but was now sonorous.

This time, he decided, he'd abandon stealth and choose shock and awe, praying that whoever was on the other side of the open door was more terrified than him. For no reason but habit, he counted *three, two, one* in his head then burst in.

Blake froze.

It was Felicity's pleading, petrified face that he first registered. Then the wiry, bearded, tramp-like man behind her, his left hand clamping her round the mouth to his chest, his right holding what Anthony recognised as his own over-and-under Beretta 695 twelve-gauge shotgun.

'Let her go and put the gun down,' snapped Anthony, his hands up and open towards the clearly terrified man. 'We can sort this out.' He took a step forward.

'Get back,' said the man, the barrels of the gun waving precariously in the vague direction of Anthony's torso.

Felicity's desperate eyes gave him the same instruction.

'Listen chap, there's no need for this. OK, you've used our place for bed and board. That's OK, we won't tell the police. Let her go and you can be on your way. I've even got some cash to help you find somewhere more suitable.'

The man flicked his eyes from Anthony to the back door, as if considering whether escape was the best option.

'Look, I'll show you,' said Anthony as he reached into his inside jacket pocket.

He never heard the boom. Nor registered the dozen balls of shot crash through his ribcage and obliterate his heart and lungs.

Whichever way you looked at it, Sergeant Andy Dunkers was a shit magnet. Like his father before him, he was incapable of setting foot outside the police station without some catastrophe befalling him. It was not that he was inept, far from it; it was just if trouble was going to find someone, it would find Andy.

Having recently returned to the Dog Unit, via Firearms and Brighton Response, he wore his new stripes with pride. He was back with the animals he adored chasing the bad guys with, and life could not be better.

Driving from Turners Hill towards Haywards Heath, he took in the beauty of Wakehurst Place – Kew Garden's home in the country – and the

South of England Showground, promising to bring his baby son up here on his next day off.

'Hotel Delta 191, are you free for a grade 1 in Horsted Keynes?'

As if by reflex, Andy opened his microphone. 'Yes. ETA about five minutes, what have you got?'

'It's an SFI at Splinter Cottage. One casualty with gunshot wounds to the chest. The injured man's wife is the informant who is in deep trauma but says the offender has made off across the fields behind the cottage. Can you start making? ARVs are en route so don't put yourself in danger.'

'Roger,' he replied. Spontaneous Firearms Incidents had been his bread and butter during his short stint on Firearms. Driving the Armed Response Vehicles at ludicrous speeds across the county hardly put you in the right frame of mind to calmly face a lunatic with a gun though.

'Wake up, Chimp, we've got a job,' he called to his firearms support dog in the back.

Flicking the blues and twos, he overtook two cars and a van and powered his way towards the RV point, a cottage half a mile from the scene.

He knew the area well, having been brought up in nearby Lindfield, so was able to exploit the rat runs a stranger would miss. But negotiating the thirty-degree bends at somewhere approaching fifty miles per hour would take more than local knowledge to survive should a Massey Ferguson tractor be coming the other way.

The radio traffic was frenetic with updates, estimated times of arrival and commanders reeling out the necessary form of words to confirm firearms were authorised.

The controller cut in. 'For the information of all units attending the SFI, we've managed to escort paramedics to the scene and confirm the male is deceased. Further, from his wife, it's believed the offender escaped with the firearm, a double-barrelled shotgun.'

A chorus of 'roger that' and 'received over' followed.

Andy's instinct was not to dwell on the personal tragedy. He would later, but for now he only had headspace to think about catching the killer and keeping himself and everyone else safe.

Just as he slowed for a T-junction, Andy caught a movement from behind the hedgerow to his right. Intuition told him it was more than livestock. Pulling his car across the road to block oncoming traffic, he clambered over to the passenger side of the car and, as quietly as he could, clicked open the door.

'Ssh Chimp, it's OK,' he whispered as the dog growled in anticipation of some action.

Once out of the car, Andy crept round to the back and eased open the rear door, slipping Chimp's lead on as the dog jumped down.

'Good boy,' Andy said, patting Chimp's nape.

He crept back down the road, certain that whoever was on the other side of the hedge, if indeed there was anyone, would have spotted him stop and would be waiting.

Suddenly he heard shuffling coming from the same direction as he'd seen the earlier movement.

'Police with dog. Stay where you are or I'll let the dog go,' he shouted. No response.

'This is your last chance. Stay where you are and show yourself with your hands up, or I'll release the dog.' Half a dozen yards away, he spotted a hole in the hedge, big enough for Chimp, should he need it.

Then came the distinctive sound of someone breaking cover and frantic panting quickly fading into the near distance.

Andy unclipped the lead and said, 'Find him, Chimp.'

The dog bolted like a clay pigeon from a trap, zipping through the hedge gap. Andy ran up the lane to find a suitable access, but his world ended when a gunshot echoed.

'Fuck, no,' he said, sprinting towards a gate. 'Fuck, no, Chimp.' The tears stung as desperation drove him on.

Vaulting the gate in one go, he ran back along the field. He heard himself crying 'No, no' as he scoured the field for movement. Anything that would mean his buddy was OK.

'Chimp. Chimp. Here boy,' his cracked voice bellowed.

As he rounded a bush, he saw a dark mass fifty or so yards away. 'Move, please move,' he pleaded as he exploded into a sprint. As he closed the gap, he thought the movement he saw was an illusion at first but as he got nearer, he realised there was a God after all. His tears of panic became tears of hysterical laughter.

Chimp was prostrate but his tail was wagging like a fly swat, his jaws clamped on the fugitive's right arm. The more the gunman wriggled, the more the dog bit down. Chimp loved tug-o'-war games.

Andy ran over, noting the shotgun was just out of reach.

'Chimp, leave,' he ordered. He fell on the erstwhile gunman, his whole body weight pinning the man to the ground, his head centimetres away from a huge moist cowpat.

Andy unclipped his handcuffs and squeezed them onto his prisoner.

He spouted out the scripted words of arrest for murder and the caution, before saying into his lapel radio, 'Hotel Delta 191, one in custody for murder. Can I have transport and medic for the prisoner? Chimp's had an early lunch.'

'Roger Hotel Delta 191,' said the controller. 'By the way, were you going to tell anyone you were in pursuit?'

'I'm telling you now,' he replied with a smile.

24

Bob Heaton wasn't sure what shocked him more as he sat across from Jo in her new office. The fact that she'd been arbitrarily stripped of her command overnight, or what she was suggesting.

'Let me just check I've got this right. You spent Saturday morning sitting outside the Sycamore and because you didn't see anyone you reckon we should make a completely fallacious arrest to find out what's going on.'

'See, you do get it. Don't doubt yourself, you're really quite clever,' Jo smiled.

Bob looked around the naked office: just Jo's shoulder bag on the floor and laptop on the desk. Not even her family photos up yet.

'Shouldn't you be getting your head round this new "opportunity" the chief has gifted you rather than chipping away at the care home investigation? *My* care home investigation.'

'Yes, I absolutely should. So, are you going to do it?'

Bob had lost count of the number of similar conversations he'd had with Jo, but not the hundred per cent she'd always won.

'Are you going to provide me with top cover when it all goes wrong?'

'Bob, trust me. It won't go wrong. All you need to do is get Jake to arrest a care worker on suspicion of gross negligence manslaughter, get them in an interview room then find out what the hell is going on in there.'

'But just picking on any care worker is a bit of a gamble, isn't it? I mean, what if they're new, or don't know anything? Or worse, what if they are part of it?'

'But what if they are none of those things? We won't know unless we try.'

'We?'

'OK, you. But I'm with you in spirit. You in?'

Bob shook his head in exasperation. He was never a pushover, except in the face of this woman.

'When I retire from this job, you owe me a Range Rover of my choice as a present. Is that a deal?'

'We'll see. Thanks Bob. You know it makes sense.'

Bob had decided, almost the moment he left Jo's office, that he would not inflict this dodgy arrest on young Jake. He had his career ahead of him and Bob had already lost his once, so he'd take the risk himself. He would, however, take Jake with him given that he was doing the legwork on the enquiry.

Having told Jake that the chief constable expected inspectors to make arrests, something Bob made up on the hoof, the DC seemed to accept riding shotgun as they arrived at what should be shift changeover, 7 a.m.

Bob led the way up to the door. He pressed the buzzer expecting to be kept waiting, but almost immediately Peggy Squire opened it.

'Oh, it's you,' she said. 'What do you want?'

'To come in,' said Bob as he barged his way through.

'I beg your pardon. You can't just walk in here unannounced.'

'Yes I can. We are here to speak to the carer who fed Mrs Cooke her lunch the day she died.'

'I've already told you, she doesn't work here any more.'

'You did. Trouble is, I don't believe you. Jake, can you go with Mrs Squire so she can show you the personnel records? I'm just going to talk to the staff.'

Jake made straight for the office whilst Bob headed for the lounge.

'What? Stop. You can't . . . Where are you going?' The manager hopped between the two, as if she was trying to fathom where the greatest risk lay.

As Bob walked into the lounge, he almost bumped into a girl, late teens, African or Caribbean appearance, who looked flustered on seeing him.

'Hello,' he said, in his best 'kind uncle' voice. 'I'm a police officer. Can I ask your name?'

The girl tried to turn but Bob took her arm. 'What's the rush? I just want a word.'

'You're hurting me,' she replied.

'I'm sorry but I need to ask you some questions. You speak English?'

'Enough.'

Bob felt her relax so chanced letting go. 'It's OK.'

'What you want? I very busy.'

'What's your name?'

She hesitated.

'Don't make one up. I'll know. Are you Ajee?' Bob asked, knowing full well that she wasn't. The girl tensed though.

'No, no. Not Ajee.'

Bob feigned a sceptical look. 'Really? You look like her.'

'I know no Ajee. I swear.'

'Then what's your name? Your real name.'

'Neela.'

'Mmm, we'll go with that for now. So, Neela, tell me how Mrs Cooke died.'

'Who is Mrs Cooke?'

Bob was genuinely exasperated. 'Don't play games. Mrs Cooke. Mary Cooke. Room 15. Died the other lunchtime. Don't tell me you don't know about that.'

'I'm sorry. I cannot help. You have to ask Mrs Peggy.'

Just then, Jake came into Bob's view at the open door. He made eye contact and Bob read that it was time to leave.

Bob straightened himself up, taking his hands from his pockets as he did so. 'Neela, I'm arresting you on suspicion of gross negligence manslaughter.

You do not have to say anything. But it may harm your defence if you do not mention when questioned something which you later rely on in court. Anything you do say may be given in evidence.'

'What are you saying? Why you arrest me? I've done nothing wrong,' she replied, her arms flailing.

Jake moved quickly to join his boss and took hold of Neela's arm.

Bob moved closer to her and murmured, 'You'll be OK, I promise,' just as Peggy Squire burst into the room.

'Just what the hell do you think you're doing?'

'I believe this woman was involved in Mary Cooke's death so she's under arrest.'

'You can't do that. We're short-staffed as it is.'

Bob shrugged as they walked past her. 'I'm sorry, that's not my problem. We'll get her back to you as soon as we can.'

25

Jo detested her new role. Life in the Project Office ran at turtle-pace. The IT geeks she was surrounded by treated targets as mere aspirations, despite the new technology they were designing having the potential to make front-line officers' lives simpler and safer. However, their sluggishness gave her the opportunity to stick her nose in elsewhere.

Naively, the chief constable had ignored her since she started, so no one seemed remotely interested in what she was up to.

By the second lunchtime, she was bored. Try as she might, with every Gantt chart she pondered her mind drifted to the murders and how she should be there putting things right. She daren't gaze out at the chalk of Cuilfail Hill which rose above Lewes, as that bore too many similarities to Newhaven cliffs where she saw and did things no one ever should.

She resisted the urge to call Gary Hedges, as he would be up to his neck in his own new position as the acting divisional commander. When she was originally given the job it had been over his head, so she didn't want to interfere now he had his moment.

Instead, she took a stroll to the other side of the HQ campus and, not by chance, found herself wandering into the Major Incident Suite. As she walked through the door, pleased her access card still worked here, a few of the less familiar officers gave her furtive looks; it seemed rumours of why she'd been moved were flowing and some weren't sure whether they should be too friendly. Older hands, however, welcomed her like a long-lost mother, some even hugging her.

She wasn't sure whether she'd be a distraction, given the murder of the retired army officer which another team had recently picked up but, as the offender had been arrested, interviewed, charged and remanded in short order, she guessed it would not be too frenetic.

However, when she popped her head round Faisal's door, he was the picture of agitation; phone wedged between his shoulder and ear whilst simultaneously hammering his keyboard with one hand and rummaging through a file with the other. Knowing what she'd need at times like this – other than a meddling senior officer to disappear – she leant over his shoulder, grabbed his Eastleigh FC mug and, when he spun round, mouthed 'coffee?' He grinned and nodded.

A couple of minutes later, carrying his coffee and her hot water, she returned. Faisal was now off the phone but still flustered.

'You OK?' asked Jo.

'Just when you think you're on an even keel, a squall hits broadside threatening to capsize you.'

'Love the maritime references.'

'It's my Southampton roots,' he smiled.

'Why the Eastleigh FC mug then?'

'I like to keep my expectations low, then you can't be disappointed. The Saints would drive me insane.'

'What's happening? Looks like you're up against it.'

'You could say that – in fact, you might be interested in this.'

She waited whilst he slurped his drink. 'That OK?' she asked. 'White with one.'

'How did you know?' he replied.

'I used to be a detective. Well, that and the list on the fridge door which says how everyone takes their drinks.'

Faisal laughed and shook his head.

'Well?' said Jo.

'Oh right, yes. You heard about Major Blake who disturbed an intruder and was killed with his own gun?'

'Yep. Is that your job too?'

'No. Well it wasn't. We're still working that one out.'

Jo was even more curious now. Murders rarely changed hands mid-flow. 'Go on.'

'Well, the bloke they've charged is Szymon Nowak. Obviously when he was brought in he had his DNA, fingerprints and photograph taken and he's not on the system. Not in the UK anyway.'

Jo really hoped this was going somewhere. Other than the tragedy itself and the sharp eyes of the arresting officer, this was run of the mill. Most people could commit murder in the right circumstances, so a disproportionate number of killers had no previous convictions.

Faisal took another slug of coffee, as if to build the tension. 'But, when his DNA is compared against outstanding profiles on the database, hey presto, we got a hit.'

'And?'

'Do you remember the remains of the lighter we found at the travellers' site on Op Steward?'

'Yes.' *Get on with it*, she silently urged.

'Well, we got a DNA hit off the flint wheel. And it's him. Szymon Nowak.'

Faisal wore the expression of a magician who'd just re-joined a sawn-in-half woman.

Jo looked at him for a moment. This was huge. Why hadn't he told her before? Then she realised: he'd probably told Gary.

'I take it you are trying to eliminate any innocent explanations as to why the lighter was there? Sorry, that sounded patronising.'

'Not at all. Yes, that's what we are doing at the moment and, so far, it looks like it was dropped there on the night. Whatever though, we've got more than enough to interview him. I'm going to have him produced from Lewes Prison.'

'Christ, that's amazing. What about any other links? I mean, who are his associates?'

'We're working on that. Listen, I know you're no longer at Brighton but, given your early interest and of course your knowledge of the city, do you think it might be an idea if I kept you abreast of any developments? Off the record of course.'

Jo finished her drink and stood. 'That would be a fabulous idea.' As she left the office her heart did a little skip.

There was nothing Tom Doughty despised more than cold-callers to his Hanover home. He'd just about excused Russ Parfitt when he turned up unannounced to tell him about Loretta and the four travellers' deaths, even though explaining away his guest might have been tricky to anyone else.

The last person he wanted here was the thug hammering on his door now. Tom flung the door open. 'Get in. What do you want?'

'You'll fucking thank me when I tell you. Well, maybe not, but you need to know.'

Tom checked the street before slamming the door and ushering Leigh into the lounge. 'Sit down.'

'No. You need to see this.'

As Leigh fiddled with his phone Tom's irritation bubbled to the surface but, with gargantuan will, he kept it from exploding.

Finally, his infuriating fixer thrust his mobile out. 'Read this.'

The article on the BBC website was short and to the point. A headline which read *Man Remanded for Army Major Murder*. A standard custody photograph of a scruffy oik who looked like one of the tribe of homeless Tom vowed to eradicate was sitting above some bland paragraphs which told readers that *A thirty-five-year-old man, Szymon Nowak, of no fixed address, appeared at Brighton Magistrates' Court yesterday charged with the murder of retired Royal Engineers Major, Anthony Blake. He spoke only to confirm his name. He did not enter a plea and was remanded in custody to appear at Lewes Crown Court by video link tomorrow.*

Tom read it twice, then looked at Leigh. 'What's that got to do with me?'

'Everything. You know I said that twat left his oppo behind at the site?'

'The bloke you strangled?'

'Yes, him. Well, I thought that the pikeys must have slotted the other geezer and somehow got rid of him. What with the old bill not mentioning him.'

The penny not so much dropped as plummeted. 'Don't say what I think you're going to say.'

'That's him. In that photo.'

Tom sat down before his legs gave way. 'How the hell did he get away? Christ, what are we going to do about it?'

'I'm not being funny but you're usually the ideas man. Fuck knows how he's managed to end up shooting some Rupert from the Sappers, but he needs to know to keep his gob shut.'

'What if it's too late?' said Tom, desperate now.

'Then we're fucked. But with your permission, we've got several friendlies in Lewes nick – with and without keys. We can always make sure of his silence. Want me to sort that?'

Tom looked up, just marginally more optimistic. 'I can put a call in too. Just do what you need to.'

As Jake Briers indicated right at the Dyke Road roundabout, Bob said, 'Take the left.'

'Don't tell me Brighton Custody is closed again,' said the DC.

'I've no idea. We're not going there.'

Jake looked at his boss in the rear-view mirror, about to argue, but Bob insisted. 'Left.'

He turned to Neela, who seemed oblivious to the debate between the two officers. 'Listen, here's what's happening. I'm de-arresting you so, technically, you're free to go.' She looked at him blankly as Jake glared in the mirror, slowing the car down.

'Keep going, Jake.' He turned back to Neela. 'As I say, you're free to go but I'd advise against jumping out of a moving car, so maybe I can explain.

When I arrested you, I believed you were involved in Mrs Cooke's death. Now I don't. I won't trouble you with why I changed my mind, but I think it might be useful for you and me to chat about Sycamore, Mrs Squire and what's actually going on there. Is that OK?'

Jake chipped in. 'Boss, some idea where we are going would be helpful.'

'Hangleton Victim Suite.'

'You sure it's free?'

Bob just smiled. 'What do you think?'

'Anyway, Neela. We're guessing that things aren't all they seem to be at the home. So, I reckon whilst we've got an excuse to have you out of there for a while, you might want to tell us. What do you think?'

Neela made a grab for the door handle, terror written across her face.

'Child locks,' said Bob, thankful they were set. 'Listen, you're not in any trouble, we just need to know what's happening. I'm guessing you know but maybe your papers to be in this country aren't all they should be. Am I right?'

Neela spat on the floor.

'Thought so,' said Bob, looking out of the window and seeing they were only a couple of minutes away from the anonymous police bungalow. 'You can pack that in, and when we get where we are going you are going to walk calmly up to the door. When we get in, we'll get you something to eat and drink then we can have a good chat. The alternative is that I have another change of mind about my grounds to arrest you and we go to custody.'

Neela glared at him. 'The choice is yours,' he added as Jake pulled up at the suite.

26

Over the days Ajee had been put to work she'd established there was a hierarchy which, by default, she was at the bottom of. Fraternisation with the other girls was actively discouraged but, given the way the rooms had been crammed into this many-times converted Regency town house, could not be avoided completely.

Suzanne, the manager, had a kinder heart than Peggy Squire, but she still insisted on rotas to use the kitchen and the small lounge. Even then, one of the trustee girls, those who had earned all the privileges on offer, monitored every word spoken.

During fine weather, Ajee took any opportunity to walk round the gated back yard, rather like how she imagined prisoners would in high-security jails. Again, there was no privacy though.

Her main aim was to escape the daily horror of servicing countless repellent men, but she knew from the hefty bars and bolts that kept them all in, and the ferocity of the men charged with dishing out the punishments if they tried to flee, this had to be a longer-term objective.

All she could do for now was whatever it took to elevate herself to trustee status.

Whilst the trustees still had to endure the clients, Ajee noticed that it was not so often and tended to be with the less disgusting specimens. She'd even heard that a couple of the most senior ones were reserved for the VIPs – police officers, politicians and celebrities, although she'd never seen any of those for herself. They got to go on errands too, albeit with strict return times and horrendous consequences threatened if they breached that trust.

One lunchtime, Ajee deliberately lingered in the galley kitchen when the other girls made their way back to work. Knowing she'd miss the headcount, she predicted that Suzanne would come looking for her. She heard footsteps in the hallway so busied herself washing up a chipped dinner plate.

The door opened. 'There you are. Come on, get back to work,' said Suzanne.

'I'm sorry Miss Suzanne, I need to clean. I worry about sickness. The girls get ill, we all get ill. Then what?'

Suzanne held the door, encouraging Ajee to hurry up. 'Indeed, but you have work to do. We have a queue of clients waiting.'

The thought of what waited made Ajee gag. 'And we make the men ill, they go elsewhere.'

'Come on, my dear. It's clean enough.'

'Maybe I help,' Ajee suggested, wondering how long she could procrastinate for. 'This many girls in one place. You need them well. If they not well, they not work. I was nurse in my home country. I could do health checks. Make sure all girls fit and well.'

Suzanne closed the door, so only Ajee could hear. 'My dear, it might have escaped your notice, but the vast majority of you came from care homes and want to be nurses. A nurse in this country is a lot different than just a carer, you know. You're no more a nurse than I am.'

'I didn't graduate but I did my training. I not a carer, I a nurse and would be working in Aleppo Hospital now if I did not have to escape.'

'Look, I haven't got time for this. Back to your room. I need you to entertain one of our regular VIPs. Two have turned up wanting the same girl, so one will have to have you. Out you go. Quick quick.'

Ajee had been in her room for no more than a couple of minutes when a trustee opened the door, taking a handful of cash from the man who stepped out of the shadows. Important people in her country had stature. If this was the best Britain could offer, it was a wonder how they'd managed to conquer an empire. He looked edgy, scanning the walls and ceiling as if checking for something.

She watched in disgust as the diminutive man removed his blue blazer, throwing it on the chair by the door, revealing a snow-white shirt with funny little loops above each breast pocket and on the shoulders, and a belly that bulged over his black trousers.

As he started to remove them, she lay on the bed, closed her eyes and searched in vain for a happier place.

For years, Jo had monitored suspect interviews through the hardwiring between cell blocks and the SIO office. Now, through secure Wi-Fi, senior investigating officers could observe any video-recorded interview remotely, wherever in the world they took place.

The text from Bob to say the interview was about to start left her just ten minutes to get her head around the technology. Faisal once again came up trumps and emailed her a 'senior officers' aide memoire' probably more usually referred to as an 'idiots' guide', on how to log on and watch. She closed her office door, sat back down and worked her way through the numbered steps.

After a couple of attempts she saw she had to enter her network login. She'd rather have done this anonymously but knew trust never truly extended to any level of the organisation.

She stared impatiently at the window which insisted she had to 'wait for access', which meant Bob had to click a permission box at his end.

In a moment, the screen filled with an image of what looked like a lounge, with a teenager or young woman – Jo couldn't work out which – fidgeting on the edge of a grey three-seater settee filling most of the picture. In front of her was a low table with three glasses of water and a tissue box. In the corner of Jo's screen was a second image from a fisheye lens showing the whole room, which revealed Bob and Jake sitting on low easy chairs opposite the girl.

After some questions from Bob to check the girl had all she needed, he started the interview.

'Neela, we asked you to come here today to help us understand a little of what's been going on at Sycamore Care Home. Do you understand?'

Neela paused, wiped a tear then replied, 'Yes, I understand.'

'And you know you're not in any trouble,' said Jake.

'That is what you told me,' she replied, with just an edge of doubt.

Bob continued. 'First of all, tell me about how you arrived in the UK.'

Between sobs and searching for the right words, Neela described how she'd fled Sudan for the promise of a better life in Egypt, only to find she was one of thousands of illegal migrants, crammed in detention camps waiting for who knew what. Hearing of the squalid conditions, the rapes, beatings and how Neela slept amongst babies' corpses, Jo was thankful her sobs were muffled by her closed door.

Bob gently nudged her along with words of encouragement. Neela spoke unprompted for about half an hour as she talked of her escapes from camps, being herded onto tiny crafts that were twice intercepted by the Egyptian navy, resulting in her re-incarceration. Only on the third attempt was she successful, although being one of only six from the original sixty who'd survived four days drifting on the capsized boat's hull didn't sound much like success to Jo.

Eventually fishermen dumped her in Italy and she spent a year making her way across mainland Europe to Calais where, having sold the last of her belongings and dignity, she raised enough money for about two square metres in the back of a freight lorry bound for the UK.

After what seemed like hours on the road once they'd landed, men with dogs forced everyone off the lorry into a disused barn, where they were made to wait with no food or water. As it got dark, a fleet of minibuses arrived and they were herded in, given a cover story about fruit-picking and ordered to stay silent whilst they were driven off.

About an hour later, and in pitch black, Neela and five others were delivered into the hands of Peggy Squire at the Sycamore Care Home where over the last six months, she'd lived, slept, but mostly worked.

Bob coaxed her to describe the conditions, who was in charge, why she couldn't leave and what happened to the others. With varying degrees of emotion, she answered clearly and, so far as Jo could make out, truthfully. As if by telepathy, just as Jo willed Bob to ask a specific question, he did.

'Where is Ajee?'

'Ajee? She's gone.'

'Gone?'

'Like Farah. They take her away.'

'Where to?'

Neela hesitated. Jake coaxed her. 'Where are Farah and Ajee?'

She looked at each officer in turn, then answered. 'I not know for sure but I think they become *almawmis*.'

Bob and Jake looked at one another.

'Whore. They work as whores,' she clarified.

'Where?'

Neela shrugged, then broke down.

'Neela, thank you. We're going to stop now and give you a break. I promise you though, we will look after you and no one will hurt you again.'

Jo's screen went blank yet she stared at its blackness through her tears, hoping Bob would be true to his word.

27

It had taken Acting Chief Superintendent Gary Hedges less time than he'd anticipated to secure a meeting with the Chief Executive and Leader of the Council. He'd rather wished it hadn't, as he knew he'd be in for a rough ride given their last spat over his refusal to authorise police to remove protestors from the council chamber. However, as he'd messed up his last stab at becoming the divisional commander by misreading the politics, he was determined for a fresh start.

Learning from Jo's experience he arrived at Hove Town Hall five minutes early, checked in at the reception desk and settled down on one of the chairs for the inevitable wait that was Parfitt and Doughty's petty game.

He'd just opened the emails on his phone when the receptionist called over. 'Mr Hedges, you can go up. I'll click you through the gate. Do you know your way?'

'Er, thank you. Yes, yes, I know where to go.'

'Smashing, Debbie will meet you at the top of the stairs and let you through.'

'Thank you,' said Gary as he stuffed his phone back into his bag and made for the security gates.

When he reached the top of the stairs, as promised, Debbie was waiting, her huge smile lighting up his day. He'd always had a soft spot for the long-suffering PA, especially given the dignity she'd shown in the replacement of Penny Raw with Russ Parfitt.

'Gary, how lovely to see you. Those new epaulettes certainly suit you.

Are they there to stay?' she said as she stepped aside the open door.

'Hiya, that's not my decision. Hopefully Jo will be back soon but, in the meantime, I'll try not to lose them.'

'Mr Acers will have me to deal with if that happens,' she sniggered, touching Gary's arm as he passed.

'I'll warn him,' replied Gary.

As they walked into the council directors' inner sanctum, Gary saw Parfitt and Doughty stand up from Russ's conference table and move as one to the door.

'Gary, welcome and congratulations,' said Russ, wearing a smile that was struggling to reach his eyes. He took Parfitt's outstretched hand and then shook Doughty's; the latter seemed even more disingenuous in his welcome than Parfitt. 'Welcome,' the councillor mumbled.

Gary stepped into the office and, obeying Russ's flourished hand, took a seat opposite the two men.

'Gary, can I get you a coffee? "Black, no sugar and as close to treacle as you can", if I remember correctly,' said Debbie.

'Impressive. Yes please.'

Once she'd brought the coffee through, she left and closed the door.

Tom kicked off. 'So glad you could join us. We were all a bit shocked when Jo left so quickly, but I suppose what the chief constable wants, the chief constable gets.'

Gary nodded.

'Shall we start by dealing with the elephant in the room? Those protestors. We didn't see eye to eye on that issue, but what world would it be if we all agreed? You have your job to do, I have mine.'

'Thank you. Maybe I should have explained things a little better.'

'And maybe we should have too,' said Russ. 'Anyway, that's in the past. The Leader and I are really looking forward to working with you. A fresh start. It's good to have a man who really knows the city at the helm.'

'Even if you are a Taff,' said Doughty.

Russ glared at him.

'As I was saying, a strong leader, a perfect role model and one who understands what the people of Brighton and Hove want.'

The flattery was making Gary feel more and more uncomfortable. Previously he'd made a good job of avoiding the city's politics, swerving all that to Jo and, before her, Phil. But if he genuinely wanted promotion – and he was having second thoughts – there would be no escape from these two slimeballs. He hated everything they stood for and, despite what they said, was sure they had some hold over the chief.

Was he strong enough to stand firm without detonating his career in the process?

Jo hadn't been this excited at work since her first day as Head of Major Crime. Given that she'd been shafted so recently she felt almost guilty for feeling so skittish, but today was a big day.

Having popped into her own office and cleared the three emails waiting for her – none coming close to her pay grade – she dashed over to see Faisal for a final catch-up before the show started. As she walked along the corridor to his office, he was coming out of an unmarked doorway that Jo knew to be the intelligence cell.

'Great timing,' he said, looking about as elated as she felt. She followed him into his office and they both sat.

'When's the interview?' Jo asked.

'They are arriving at the prison about now so by the time they book him out, then travelling time to Brighton Custody,' Faisal cached his watch, 'hopefully the solicitor will be waiting, so say fifteen minutes for disclosure, an hour or so for the two of them to come up with an explanation. I reckon we'll be ready to go by eleven.'

'And you don't mind me watching?'

'Sure,' said Faisal. 'Anyway, there's more than the DNA now.'

'Wow. Tell me more.'

'Off the record?'

'Like we agreed,' she said, willing him to spit it out.

'When Szymon Nowak was arrested, he had a phone on him. It was out of charge, but Digital Forensics breathed life back into it. I won't bore you with all the details, but it puts him – or at least the phone – at Horsdean at the time of the attack.'

'That's great.'

'There's more,' Faisal continued. 'We've managed to dig deep into the phone and found that about an hour beforehand, the phone was "shaking hands" with three others. Those three were all switched off around the same time, but Szymon Nowak seems to have forgotten to do the same.'

'Right?'

'Two of those phones aren't of much interest. They seem to have been used just that night, so maybe bought for a single operation. We found the remains of one in the burnt-out van, so probably that's one of them, but even the boffins can't get anything from that.'

'And the third?'

'Well, this is the exciting bit. That's unregistered too, but we've traced some activity after the other two went dead. It receives a call. Not a long one but a call nonetheless.'

'Please Faisal, put me out of my misery.'

'From Tom Doughty.'

'*The* Tom . . .'

'Yep. So, we then do some work on him and guess who he phones straight after?'

'Tell me,' she pleaded.

'The chief constable. Seems he calls him a lot. Could be nothing but equally, it could be significant. Anyway, we then do some work on Doughty's car and other calls and now we think the person who he called, and then met, was an ex-squaddie called Leigh O'Keefe. Nasty piece of work and fully paid-up member of the British Patriot Party. Intel says he's their go-to enforcer.'

'That's incredible. I mean, that changes everything right? It shows a link between the murders and the Leader of the Council. This is dynamite.'

'It's promising, but we've more to do. That was definitely off the record, yes?'

Jo flung up a three-finger salute. 'Guide's honour. Will you put that to Nowak when he's interviewed?'

'Not directly. We'll see what he tells us first.'

'This is going to be fabulous,' said Jo, just as Faisal's phone rang.

She was still grinning when it dawned on her that Faisal was not.

'I see. Right. OK, I'm on my way.'

Jo's stomach turned to lead, and she studied Faisal as he ended the call.

'What? What's happened?'

'It's Szymon Nowak. He's dead.'

'Dead?'

'Attacked in his cell. Looks like he's had his throat cut. I'm going down there now.'

Jo hated pulling rank, so was grateful that Faisal didn't even try to suggest that she stay behind. Sensing that he was a little apprehensive though, she did reassure him that if anyone asked, she'd given a direct order. That seemed to pacify him.

As Faisal pulled off the A277 into the prison complex, both scoured the forecourts for a parking space. As with most dour and imposing Victorian prisons, the place hadn't been designed with the motor car in mind. And, as the inmate population soared following the 'prison works' policies of the 1990s, every square inch of land was swallowed up with new cell blocks and facilities to meet the demand. The upshot was that they had to abandon the car in a pay-and-display behind County Hall and walk back.

Having traipsed through all the various checks and security measures, which, to Jo's amusement, drew comments of her being 'Faisal's assistant' rather than his boss, they arrived on the wing ten minutes later, their escort never more than two paces away.

The catcalls and oinks almost drowned out the banging on what seemed to be every cell door as they walked.

As a rule, police usually ventured no further than the legal visits area so, when Jo saw the archaic parallel landings with netting across the voids and the line of firmly closed heavy metal cell doors, it took her aback. Her immediate thoughts went to Phil and Kyle and the knowledge that at that very moment they would be trapped in a place just like this. Because of her.

As they neared a barrier of police tape, the prison officer predicted their question. 'We've isolated the landing one cell either side of where he died, and all the men are banged up so there's no scene contamination.' It struck Jo that this wouldn't have been the first crime scene this seasoned warder had to manage, and it wouldn't be the last.

Both Faisal and Jo paused beside the police officer guarding the scene, donned their forensic suits, signed the log then ducked under the tape.

As crime scenes went, this was one of the most compact and contained Jo had ever seen and most of it was sprayed in blood.

The body, dressed only in stained boxer shorts that might have once been white, lay face down taking up all but a strip of floor space. She could just make out the gaping wound which seemed to extend around the neck. The blood pooled deeply beneath the cut, but she could also see blood spattered up the opposite wall and ceiling, coating a box of cereal, kettle, small TV set and Bible which was open at Isaiah.

There was only bedding on the top bunk, and just one mug, toothbrush and pair of trainers, so far as Jo could see.

'Hi, Dean,' said Faisal to the crime scene manager crouched in the corner below the tiny, cracked window.

'Oh, hello boss. Do you want a briefing? Oh, hi Jo. I thought . . .'

'What have I told you about thinking, Dean?' cut in Jo.

Dean Gartrell looked like he was about to reply so Jo continued. 'Is there somewhere we can go?'

'We've got the next cell for our kit,' said Dean, leading the way.

'What have we got?' asked Faisal, as the three of them crammed among the boxes and bags of crime scene investigation equipment in the vacant cell.

'Forensically, not a great deal.'

'What are you talking about?' said Faisal. 'It looks like a Hammer Horror film set in there.'

'Sure, but it doesn't tell us much more than we already knew. The blood pattern is consistent with the injury. No sign of the body having been moved and there are more fingerprints in there than on the Shard's lift buttons. And none in blood, nor footprints.'

'Typical,' said Faisal. 'We'll have to wait for pathology and any DNA work then, so let's see how the other enquiries are going.'

Jo followed Faisal out of the cell to the tape, where they removed their coveralls and signed out, then along to the wing office.

As they walked into the goldfish-bowl room at the end of the landing, DS Nigel Hughes looked up, as did a very sheepish senior prison officer opposite him.

'Guv. Ma'am,' said Hughes. 'Excellent timing. Can I introduce Mr Ronan. He's just helping me with some anomalies. Mr Ronan, this is DCI Hussain and Chief Superintendent Howe. Maybe you could explain to them what you've just told me.' The prison officer looked at Hughes as if pleading not to confess his sins to the headmaster. With all three pairs of eyes drilling into him, he spoke.

'Mr Nowak was supposed to be sharing a cell but, for some reason and I can't work out why, his cellmate was moved to A Wing about six o'clock last night.'

'Is that unusual?' Jo asked.

'It's not unheard of, but usually that's to accommodate a more suitable cellmate or if there's been beef between the two, but there doesn't seem to be any of that.'

'Who was the other prisoner?' Faisal asked.

'A Mr Fuller. An old bloke awaiting sentence for causing death by dangerous driving. Spends most of his time either on the phone or crying on his bunk.'

'And no one due to move in?'

'No.'

'Tell them about the CCTV,' said DS Hughes.

'Usually the landings are covered by CCTV, but for a couple of hours early this morning this wing's system was down.'

'As in, not working at all?' checked Jo.

Ronan nodded.

'And what caused that?' asked Faisal.

'That's being checked.'

'If it was working, what would you be showing us now?' asked Jo.

Ronan fidgeted on his chair. 'I guess I'd be showing you someone going into Mr Nowak's cell then coming out covered in blood.'

'We'd see the killer?'

'Yes.'

'Presuming the killer is an inmate, and I'm not ruling out the alternative, someone will have let him in,' said Jo.

Ronan nodded.

'A member of staff?'

Ronan nodded again. 'Probably.'

'And someone will also have known that the CCTV was down. At the time I mean.'

'I guess so.'

'Sod it,' said Faisal. 'I'm getting a whole team down here. I want every prisoner on the wing interviewed and I want details of any member of staff who was in the jail last night in my hands in the next thirty minutes.'

'But . . .' said Ronan.

'No buts,' said Faisal. 'Someone here has allowed – or rather enabled – this to happen and I will find out who.'

Jo remained with Ronan and Hughes whilst Faisal stepped outside to put his machine into motion.

'It's going to be in everyone's interest to cooperate,' she said.

'You really need to talk to the Number One Governor if you're going to disrupt the routines to this degree,' said Ronan.

Jo fixed his gaze. 'We're investigating a murder here. A murder with a significant dollop of collusion, at the very least. If we need to close the whole prison down, that's what we will do.'

Ronan was about to retort when Hughes chipped in. 'I wouldn't take her on, mate. I've seen what's left of those who've tried.' He shook his head. 'Not pretty.'

The prison officer slipped back in his chair. Faisal stepped back in. 'Jo, we're done here for now. Let's leave it to Nigel until the others get down here. Apparently we've got to pop in to see the Number One Governor on the way out.'

'Good luck with that,' mumbled Ronan as Jo turned to leave.

An hour later, after what was probably the most obstructive meeting Jo had ever experienced with someone notionally on her side of the law, she and Faisal stepped out into the sunlight.

'What a complete wanker,' said Faisal before adding, 'excuse my language.'

Jo laughed. 'Is that the best you can do? In fairness, prison governors are forever looking over their shoulder. It doesn't take much for them to be posted overnight to some God-awful place like Dartmoor or the Isle of Sheppey. So having a dead cert of an inside job in his nick is bound to make him jumpy.'

'But if I get even a hint of him obstructing us, I'll nick him myself.'

'Yes,' said Jo. 'I think you made that crystal clear.'

'Fancy a cup of tea?'

'Where have you got in mind?'

'Kingston Snack Bar?'

'What, the burger van on the roundabout? Classy.'

'Read the reviews boss, you'll be impressed.'

'As I only drink hot water, I'm sure it will be fine.'

They walked away from the prison to Faisal's car, chatting through their theories of what had happened to Szymon Nowak and more importantly, why.

As they approached, Faisal pointed his key fob to the car and, other than a brief flash of the hazard lights, nothing happened.

'Didn't you lock it?' Jo asked.

'I swear I did.'

'I'm always doing that. Darren, my husband, goes mad.'

Both laughed then got in and Faisal started the engine and pulled away, the conversation edging precariously towards the merits of women drivers.

They cruised through the green traffic light, onto the A277, driving back past the prison towards Kingston Roundabout. As they passed the national speed limit sign, Faisal floored the accelerator. 'Boy racer,' said Jo. 'The roundabout is only round the bend.'

'Just trying to get that bloody governor out of my system.'

'I know. Another supercilious wanker here to make our lives a misery,' said Jo. 'Try picturing him sitting on the toilet. Works wonders when I imagine Stuart Acers that way.'

Faisal glanced at her. 'I know a great therapist who can help you, you know.'

Jo glanced to see if he was serious as it wouldn't be the first time she'd thought of that. But Faisal was staring straight ahead.

The traffic was clear as they approached the left-hand bend which signalled the roundabout's approach, but Faisal needed to ease off before they met the main A27.

Suddenly Jo could see him stamping the brake pedal, but, if anything, they were speeding up.

'Christ, Faisal. Slow down,' Jo said as the tyres screamed into the turn.

'I can't. The brakes . . .' His look was one of sheer terror.

Jo pulled up on the handbrake, hoping that would at least have some effect.

It didn't.

Faisal wrenched into a lower gear but the gears just shrieked in protest.

Jo screamed as the car careered towards the roundabout, the traffic lights on red.

The last thing she heard was Faisal's yelling 'FUUUCCCKKK' a second before the word SCANIA bore down on them and crashed through the window.

28

The call came into Chief Constable Acers within fifteen minutes of the first officers arriving at the crash. They'd recognised Jo straight away and confirmed Faisal's identity by his warrant card around his neck and the Police National Computer check on his registration number.

Two minutes later, Acers was sprinting along the corridor towards his car. With the A27 closed in both directions, he had no idea how he would get to the Royal Sussex County Hospital but he put his faith in his blue lights, sirens and satnav.

Once he was on the road, he called his Hampshire counterpart who assured Stuart that she would be making her way from Winchester with similar urgency.

His staff officer, Marie Shaw, called next with the grim update from the scene. Paramedics were still working on Faisal, who had taken the brunt of the forty-tonne lorry slamming into him. The air ambulance was arriving with a doctor on board, and they were battling to stabilise the DCI to airlift him to hospital.

Jo was already being blue-lighted to the emergency department. She was drifting in and out of consciousness but miraculously looked like she was going to survive. Marie had called Jo's husband Darren and a police car was on its way to rush him to the hospital. Hampshire were doing the same for Faisal's wife.

Acers instructed Marie to ensure the incident log was restricted and, to stem rumours, a force-wide email to be circulated informing staff of the briefest of details.

As his satnav guided him towards the village of Offham, he ended the call with Marie and mulled over how he should deal with Darren when he saw him at the hospital. He was the head of the organisation, but no doubt Jo would have poisoned her husband against him. He'd have to face that if it came to it. Just then, his phone rang and his heart nose-dived.

'Tom, not a great time,' he said, hoping the sirens would underline his message.

'It's the perfect time,' said Doughty. 'I thought I told you to sideline Jo Howe.'

'Christ, can't we do this later? I'm dealing with an emergency.' Acers fought the urge to reveal what had happened. The councillor would find out soon enough.

'No. Those pictures are just a click away from going viral. Why is Howe still sticking her nose in?'

'I don't know what you mean. I've moved her to an IT project. I did as you asked.'

'Then tell me why she was at Lewes Prison with that Paki.'

Acers winced at the shameless racism. He obeyed the satnav and turned left towards Plumpton, home of the agricultural college and racecourse.

'Why would she be up at Lewes Prison?'

'Don't you know what your own officers are doing? A prisoner was killed there last night and her and Hussain have been up there throwing their weight around. She's getting too close.'

'Look, I really don't know what you're getting at, but I'll find out and get back to you.'

Acers nearly oversteered the second bend and only by snatching the wheel at the last moment did he avoid ploughing into a fenceless cornfield.

'Make sure you do. Oh, and Stuart?'

'Yes?'

'Tell them both to get well soon. They really should check their car over before they drive off.'

Acers stared at the phone, which sneered 'Call Ended'.

29

It always struck Bob that the National Referral Mechanism must have been named by committee. Stripped of its newspeak, it was a system for identifying victims of modern slavery and getting them the right support. An army of civil servants had made it sound like some Third Reich automated screening process.

Once he'd explained that to Neela and assured her she would be safe, she was more confident and was, for the next forty-five days at least, safely housed with all the emotional and practical support and free legal advice she needed.

Now Bob's main concern was to persuade her to tell him everything she knew so he could firstly save Ajee – and many like her – and secondly put those who plied this evil behind bars.

As he sat in the Salvation Army Hostel lounge on the outskirts of Portsmouth, he waited anxiously. The staff here were pleasant enough, but all viewed him with suspicious eyes. After all, white middle-aged men were often the root of the exploitation and abuse those lucky enough to have found sanctuary here had suffered. And, in most of the residents' home countries, the last person you trusted was a police officer.

The clock on the mantelpiece tick-tocked away, mocking him as to how long he was being forced to wait. He resisted the temptation to glance at it or at his watch, as he didn't want to give those who were no doubt watching him the satisfaction of seeing his growing impatience.

The lorries trundling past juddered the ill-fitted double glazing. He wondered how many of those were carrying a desperate human cargo like Ajee and Neela.

The muted voices outside were just a little too quiet for him to hear whether he was being gossiped about – or whether that was just how victims of modern slavery spoke to one another, so scared were they of being overheard.

He was desperate for a wee but couldn't decide whether he was too proud or too apprehensive to ask anyone. He'd sit it out.

The door opened and Neela walked in accompanied by a man in his thirties. Neela nodded to Bob and wordlessly sat in the easy chair opposite whilst the man extended his hand.

'Michael Iwahu,' he said, in a home counties accent that belied his street-casual look. 'I'm Neela's solicitor.'

Bob of all people knew the dangers of stereotyping, but Iwahu's Nike tracksuit bottoms and red, stained and crumpled hoodie would fool anyone into thinking he was the client.

'Oh, pleased to meet you Mr Iwahu,' said Bob, accepting the solicitor's handshake. 'DI Bob Heaton. Sussex Police.'

'Yes, I know.'

Bob turned to Neela, who looked much the smarter of the two. Since he'd last seen her, she bore the signs of having been well fed and benefitting from a bath and hairdresser's scissors.

'Neela, thank you for agreeing to see me again. It seems you're being looked after and,' he nodded to the solicitor, 'have some professional support.'

Neela managed an almost-whispered 'Yes,' whilst she nibbled her nails.

Bob continued. 'Now you're safe, I'd really like to turn my attention to the two things I emailed your solicitor about. Firstly, I want to find out why so many people are dying in the homes and secondly, where Ajee is. Can you help me with those?'

Mr Iwahu chipped in. 'DI Heaton, I know you appreciate the trauma

Neela has been through, not just here in the UK but throughout her escape from Sudan. Much of that has been at the hands of people who she's trusted and more still by people in authority. You'll forgive her for being disinclined to answer any questions.'

Bob felt a trapdoor snap open beneath him. All this way, for what? Bloody solicitors.

Iwahu carried on. 'But, I have had the opportunity to spend a good deal of time with Neela and she has provided me with substantial details pertaining to your enquiries. She has authorised me to read, then hand to you, a prepared statement, on the proviso you guarantee she doesn't face any prosecution relating to her illegal entry to the UK. I can assure you, other than some minor shoplifting to survive, she's not committed any other criminal offences whilst she's been here.'

'Mr Iwahu, I'm sure you have explained that the protections within the Modern Slavery Act almost certainly apply to Neela and, outside of that, I'm frankly not interested if anyone is forced to steal to feed themselves or their family.

'Thank you. In that case, this is what Neela wants to say.'

Unlike the terse prisoners' prepared statements police officers were used to, this one went on for nearly forty-five minutes, was rammed with detail and, if true, was the first direct evidence Bob had that his hunches had been right. And that Ajee was in mortal danger.

He took the statement, scribbled his signature on the receipt Iwahu had proffered, bid farewell to Neela and hurried from the house, desperate to update Jo.

30

There were days when Tom Doughty seriously questioned his own judgement in appointing Russ Parfitt as his chief executive. And today was one of those.

He'd known Russ since their days on the football terraces and was always impressed by how he could whip up a rival firm to meet for a fight at some remote spot, as if arranging to buy a used car. In those days they'd shared values and beliefs and, whilst he was pretty sure they still did, since becoming a family man Parfitt's bottle had gone.

The first text came just minutes after Doughty's call with the chief constable. The next about a minute after that, followed by three missed calls all with increasingly desperate voicemails, all with the same general vibe: *What the hell have you done?*

It was no surprise then that as he pulled into his parking space in Hove Town Hall's underground car park, Parfitt was waiting for him.

Tom eased himself out of his Range Rover, pretending not to see Russ hopping foot to foot by the adjacent bay. He walked away from the car and grinned as Parfitt shouted, 'Why don't you answer your phone? We're in the shit and you need to get us out of it.'

Doughty spun round, taking the opportunity to check they were alone amongst the parade of top-of-the-range cars. 'What the fuck are you on about?'

'You know what I'm talking about. You've gone too far this time. Two senior police officers – both who you detest – fighting for their lives in hospital and the doctoring of an unmarked cop car that has no chance of standing up to the most cursory of inspections. How are we going to get around this?'

Doughty checked again, then grabbed Parfitt by the throat and pushed him between a black Jaguar and a white Tesla SUV to the back wall.

'If you ever fucking talk to me like that again, you piece of shit, you'll be picking wheelchairs out of a catalogue.'

Parfitt's eyes bulged as his face took on the colour of an aubergine. His attempts to loosen Doughty's grip were futile.

'I don't know what you think you know but whatever it is, you keep it to yourself or you'll find out how hard it is to grass from an acid-burnt mouth. Understand?'

Parfitt nodded furiously and Doughty dropped him to the ground. As the chief executive spluttered at his feet, Doughty landed a well-aimed kidney kick and stomped off, turning briefly. 'Make sure you do.'

Instead of heading to his office, Doughty dashed back up the ramp and onto the street. He tapped out a perfunctory *Clear this afternoon's diary* text and, with his head down, walked as quickly as he could the short distance to the flat Leigh had claimed.

Resisting a head-swivel which would surely have drawn attention if his manic pace hadn't, he pressed the ground-floor buzzer.

'Yes,' came the sharp voice through the intercom.

'It's me.'

The door clicked and Doughty slid in. Leigh had already opened the flat door and Tom darted in there too.

He found his enforcer pacing the carpet, face like thunder. 'Why the fuck, every time we do a job, do you make contact? Do you want to get us nicked?'

With anyone else Tom would have responded as he had with Russ, but he knew he'd come off a very poor second if he tried that with Leigh. 'I wouldn't if I didn't have to, but I've already had Russ Parfitt accuse me of being involved. I mean, Jesus, it was an accident. Mechanical fault at best.

That's what people will believe, won't they? I mean, that's what I told you to make it look like. You did that, didn't you?'

Leigh was still walking up and down. 'You know I did. I'm a professional and the lads who did the work are too, but you gave us bugger all time. I mean, who gives anyone an hour to find a car and do the brakes?'

'It was out of my control. It was the best I could do to get the governor to delay them that long. They needed sorting.'

'I get that but was it really such a rush?'

'It was the only chance to get that bitch and Paki at the same time. They're both too smart and, if we could only get one, the other would put the pieces together and we'd be stuffed.'

'What's next then? I mean, you can't go round bumping off coppers and expect the trail never to come back to you.'

Tom stopped his temper getting the better of him and took a breath. 'We need to crack on with the big one. No one can get in the way of that. I don't give a shit what happens after. Get it right and it'll be like the shockwaves from 9/11 all over again.'

'You keep talking about "the big one", like you're on some fucking movie set. If it's that fucking big, I hope you've got a plan as, presuming you want me to be a part of it, it ain't happening with just an hour's notice.'

Tom dared to fix his stare. 'This whole project is the plan. We are that far,' he held his thumb and forefinger an inch apart, 'from having the finances, the people and the fall guy – or girl – in place. If, and it's a big if, I decide you can be anywhere near it, you'll be told. Until then, you better hope you live up to your CV – as by my calculations you have six people's blood on your hands. In fact you're close to double figures.'

Leigh closed the gap between them in the blink of an eye, his nose almost touching Tom's. 'And that elusive one to take me to the perfect ten might be closer than you think.'

Tom thrust him away and dodged as Leigh launched at him.

'Pack it in,' Tom said.

'I could snap your pudgy neck like it's fucking kindling,' snarled Leigh.

Tom believed him. He needed a different tack.

'Look, we're both angry. We don't like each other too much, but we're in too deep.'

Leigh considered this then nodded.

'I'm worried about Parfitt. He's either losing his nerve or he never had it in the first place. Every time I ask him to do something he spends more time finding reasons why he can't than just getting on with it.'

'That sounds more like your area than mine. Just sack the fucker.'

'No chance. He knows too much. No, we need to remind him where his priorities lie. We're running out of time. I've an idea how to get him back onside. And I need your help.'

Having spent fifteen minutes setting out to Leigh exactly what he wanted him to do, Tom left the flat and inched open the communal front door. He checked left and right before hotfooting it back to Hove Town Hall.

In his haste, he didn't spot the grey unmarked police Toyota Corolla parked across the road by the bus stop. But the occupants spotted him and their camera clicked like a grasshopper.

31

When the sleek traffic car jarred to a halt outside the emergency department, Darren Howe was out in a second. Running to the 'walking patients' entrance, he barged into a craggy-faced man in hospital pyjamas, cigarette in one hand, drip-stand in the other.

'Fucking look out,' said the patient, but Darren kept running, not seeing Acting Chief Superintendent Gary Hedges in his path. As Gary put his arm out, Darren was a millisecond away from landing him a right hook before he realised.

'Sorry mate. Where is she?'

'It's OK. She's OK. Just take a moment, then we'll go up to see her.'

They stepped inside the hospital and Gary ushered Darren to a family room which seemed to have been reserved for them.

'Have a seat and get your breath back.'

Darren did as he was told but couldn't help fidgeting his fingers and searching Gary's face for some clue to the truth.

'Just tell me, Gary. What happened? How is she?'

'We don't really know exactly, but it seems that Faisal Hussain pulled out onto a roundabout and the lorry driver didn't have a chance to stop. We're guessing there must have been a mechanical fault as the lights were on red, there were no skid marks and the lorry driver said Faisal looked at him really scared like just before impact.'

'Christ. How's Jo?'

'As well as she could be. Faisal took the impact so she could be a lot worse. She's breathing on her own. Her right arm and ribs are bruised to fuck but the MRI scan hasn't picked up any internal injuries. God knows how.'

'And Faisal?'

Gary glanced away. 'Let's just worry about Jo for now. You ready to see her?'

Darren stood up and headed for the door, terrified of what this would mean for her, if she survived that is. The walk to the surgical ward probably only took five minutes but with the warren of corridors and glacier-slow lifts, it felt like hours.

Finally, they arrived at the ward and Gary breezed past the nurses' station and nodded at a uniform PC standing by the side room's door as he escorted Darren in.

The sight of his beloved Jo, battered, bruised and wired up like a fuse box, made Darren choke. Couldn't someone have at least swabbed the dried blood from her face?

He went to her bedside and was about to hug her, when she croaked, 'Not tonight, darling. I've got a headache.' Despite the levity, both their faces glistened with tears.

'Not again,' replied Darren, relief flooding through him as he rested his hand on hers.

Darren wished they could be alone. After what she'd been through before, he knew she needed to vent and bawl but, with Gary here, she'd bottle it all up and that would only catapult her recovery back months. 'How are you?'

'I've a feeling digging that fish pond might have to wait but, apart from that, I think the word is bloody lucky.'

'That's two words,' said Darren.

'Pedant. Have you heard about Faisal? No one's saying anything to me.'

Darren glanced round at Gary who avoided his gaze. He turned back. 'No, nothing. What happened?'

'I can't remember much after we left the prison.'

'The prison?'

'Tell you later,' she whispered. 'I think we were going for a cup of tea, but after that it's a blank.'

'That's probably the shock. What shall I tell the boys?'

'You'll think of something, but I better not see them until I've put my face on. Don't want to scare them.'

Just then, Darren heard a gasp behind him. He turned and saw Gary staring at his phone. 'Everything OK, Gary?'

'What? Oh, yes. Well not really.'

'Gary, what's happened?' croaked Jo.

'Nothing. Honestly.'

'Don't give me that,' she said. 'What's happened?'

Gary's eyes pooled, then he looked up. 'It's Faisal. He died on the operating table ten minutes ago.'

Bob couldn't work out whether it was the nose-to-tail traffic on the Chichester bypass or Jo ghosting him that frustrated him more.

He had big news and was bursting to tell her, and it wasn't as if she had a proper job any more. What could be more important in the world of stage plans and critical paths than taking a call from him? She knew where he was going, so this was just plain rude – as, he was sure, were the increasingly curt voicemails he had left.

Finally, as the traffic started to ease, he decided she could just bloody wait. She might be a chief superintendent, but he was long past being anyone's doormat. He decided to call someone who'd appreciate – and not have the option of ignoring – his call.

'Hi, Jake. It's DI Heaton. Are you free to speak?'

'Er, well yes ,I suppose so.'

'Well pardon me for interrupting your day. It's great news, confirms all we thought.'

'Er, boss haven't you heard?'

'Heard? What? No, I've been holed up with Neela and her brief. Just on my way back now. What have I missed?'

'Can you pull over? I'll hang on.'

A whirlwind of possibilities ricocheted around Bob's head. 'Yeah, there's a petrol station coming up. Hold on.'

Bob swung right into the oncoming fast lane, returned the horn from the white van bearing down on him with a middle finger, overtook three cars and swerved back across into the petrol station, finding a space by the air and water dispenser.

'I've stopped, so tell me.'

'Are you OK? I mean, I heard horns blaring.'

'Yep, I'm fine, just some overexcited plasterer. What's happened?'

'It's Mrs Howe. She's been in a car crash just outside Lewes.'

'Oh my God. Is she OK?'

'I'm not sure. She's at the RSCH and her husband was blue-lighted there. Everyone's gutted.'

'I bet. I'll head straight there.'

'There's more.'

'More?'

Jake paused and for a moment Bob thought he'd lost the signal.

'You there, Jake?'

'Yes. It's DCI Hussain. You know the Hampshire SIO on Op Steward?'

'Yes, yes. What about him?'

'He died in the crash. Not many of us knew him but we're all gutted.'

Bob went icy cold and struggled to speak at first. 'Are you sure?' *What a stupid question.*

'Yes, there's a force-wide email.'

'Shit, I'll have a read. Who's at the nick, from the command team?'

'A couple of the uniformed chief inspectors, but Mr Hedges is at the hospital.'

'Look, take care and I'll be back soon.'

'Sir, you said you had news.'

'That can wait.'

He put the phone down and sat for a moment to regain his composure.

He didn't know Faisal well, but policing was one of those communities where when one fell, everyone else stumbled. Did he have a wife? Kids? Bob hated himself for not knowing.

There was next to nothing he didn't know about Jo, on the other hand. She was like his high-flying kid sister. Since last year and all they'd been through, not least his time in prison and the horror on the clifftop, an unbreakable bond had formed. She'd even shared her big secret about why she felt obliged to visit Phil's mum.

Christ, if she died too, he might as well give up on this pig of a life.

It had been about an hour since Darren arrived and already Jo was flagging.

The news about Faisal had rocked her and it was all she could do not to sob her heart out. Only the physical agony that would bring prevented her breaking down completely.

The nurse who'd popped in ten minutes ago had checked her blood pressure and temperature, noted the array of numbers flashing and flickering on the monitor, examined her drip and asked if she needed anything. When she replied, 'A new arm, back and head,' the nurse smirked, seemingly reassured.

She deliberately closed her eyes so Darren and Gary would think she was asleep, but she could hear them nattering first about Faisal and how little they knew about him, then drifting into the competing merits of football over rugby and vice versa. They'd only met a couple of times before, but she knew they'd get on; bloke's blokes on the surface but Teletubbies beneath.

Aside from their muttering, the only sounds were her machine and the occasional trolley, phone ringing or a buzzer coming from outside in the main ward. Her hatred of hospitals was waning, for now. She was sure it would return once she was better though. Then a tsunami of guilt coursed through her for being so positive about a future that had been robbed from Faisal. If she'd not insisted on going to the prison with him, he'd still be alive. His children being orphaned and his wife widowed was down to her and she'd never forgive herself for that. She silently sobbed and was about to drop off to sleep, for real this time, when the door crashed open. She jolted and the current of pain that detonated through her made her cry out.

Darren and Gary rushed to her side, checking she was OK, leaving Stuart Acers framed against the closed door. He remained there for a moment, as if he'd come into the wrong room. Jo reassured her de facto carers she was fine, so the men joined her in staring at the chief constable.

'Hello, Jo,' he said. 'How are you?'

'Better than Faisal.'

'Yes, of course. The Hampshire Chief Constable, Libby Paisley, is on her way over with DCI Hussain's wife.'

'Good. I'd like to meet Mrs Hussain when I can.'

'We'll see about that.'

'Is that a problem?'

'Gary, Mr Howe, could you leave us a moment?'

'I'd like them to stay please, Chief,' said Jo. This was not how a welfare visit was supposed to open.

'And I'd like them to leave.'

Gary looked conflicted. They both knew how much Acers hated Jo, and Gary no doubt wanted to support her. On the other hand, this was a disciplined service and if the chief said go, you went.

'It's OK, Gary, go and get a coffee or something.'

'And you please, Mr Howe,' said the chief as Gary slid out.

'I'm not one of your minions, so I'll stay here with my wife.'

'Jo, tell him.'

Jo half shrugged. 'He's his own person, Chief. Sorry.'

Acers conceded that battle and barged past Darren. The chief fumbled in his shoulder bag and pulled out a sheaf of papers. 'First of all, I need to know why you were at Lewes Prison with DCI Hussain.'

Jo looked at Darren, then back at the chief. 'Is this an interview? Do I need my Superintendents' Association rep here?'

'I'm just asking you to account for your movements today. Why were you at a murder scene that had nothing to do with you?'

Darren interrupted. 'This sounds like an interview to me, Jo. Is there anyone I should call?'

Acers glared at him. 'Keep the fuck out of this.'

Jo saw her husband tense. 'Leave it, Darren.' He slunk back.

'As my husband says, whatever you call it, and whatever those are in your hands, I'm not continuing this conversation without the appropriate support.'

'Just answer my question, Chief Superintendent.'

'For Christ's sake, can't you see she's injured and just lost a colleague? Can't this wait?' Darren was boiling up again.

'I don't know what your job is, Mr Howe' – Acers looked him up and down – 'but the police have rules and regulations and if a senior officer asks a question they expect an answer.' He tapped his epaulette. 'And I'm the most senior there is.'

Jo shuffled in her bed, wincing at the pain. 'Let's just get this over with. I'm not answering any questions so if we are done, then please let me rest. If not, get to the point.'

Acers shuffled his papers again, seemingly looking for the right one. He scanned a single sheet which Jo could not make out, then read from it. 'Chief Superintendent Howe, following an allegation that you neglected your duties and disobeyed lawful orders, in accordance with Regulation 11 of the Police (Conduct) Regulations 2020 you are hereby suspended from duty with immediate effect.'

As he reached for a pen, Jo yelled out as Darren launched himself at Acers. She lay helpless and watched in horror as her husband grabbed the chief constable round the neck and crashed him into a trolley, then landed two vicious punches to his head.

'What the hell is going on,' came a shout from the door. Jo looked up helplessly from the career-ending brawl being battled out in front of her.

Bob Heaton grabbed Darren and hurled him off the chief constable, now slumped, battered and shocked on the floor.

'Christ, Darren, what's all this about?'

'Ask that tosser,' Darren replied, jabbing his finger at the chief. Acers just whimpered on the ground.

Jo saw Bob pick up a piece of crumpled paper by the chief's foot. He scanned it then looked at his boss, hatred in his eyes.

'Arrest him, DI Heaton,' croaked the chief. 'He assaulted me. Arrest him.'

'With respect, sir,' Bob looked again at the suspension notice in his hands, 'if you want him arrested, you fucking do it. If you can remember the caution that is.'

32

As she gripped the banister with her relatively good arm, Jo wondered whether she should have listened to Darren and not discharged herself from hospital after just two days. If it had been the other way round, she would have insisted he listened to the doctors. But it wasn't, so she didn't.

Laying there just 'getting rest', as they advised, seemed a complete waste of her life. She dismissed any notion of coincidence and knew Faisal's death was connected to everything else that was keeping her awake.

She tried to avoid the creaky stair but misjudged her footing and as soon as it gave her away, Darren dashed from the lounge.

'What are you doing? If you need something, I'll bring it up.'

'Those four walls are driving me insane. Anyway, don't they say you should keep moving to ease aches and pains?'

'You need to rest.'

'Help me into the lounge,' she said.

She eased herself into the recliner orthopaedic chair they'd managed to find on Gumtree for £50. Jo reckoned they could sell it on for eighty quid once they had no use for it.

'Where are the boys?' she asked suddenly, realising she'd not needed to fend off their octopus hugs as soon as she'd appeared.

'They're with my mum. She promised to bring them back dog-tired and with critical sugar levels.'

Jo laughed. 'Have you heard anything today?'

'What, about lumping Acers? No.'

'All I'm saying is if they offer a caution, just take it. Grit your teeth and apologise, then it will go away.'

'But I'll still have a criminal record, won't I?'

'Yes, but it's better than the alternative. And it'll teach you I don't need a minder.'

'But who the fuck suspends someone in hospital? It reminded me of when that ref red-carded a player as he was being stretchered off the pitch.'

Jo grinned. Always a football analogy. She felt her phone buzz in her dressing-gown pocket. It was a rarity these days, so she took it out to see who was calling.

'Bob,' she mouthed to Darren, who replied with the international hand signal for *Would you like a drink?* Jo nodded and accepted the call.

'Hi, stranger,' she said.

'Why aren't you in hospital? Mr Hedges and I went to see you and they said you'd discharged yourself.'

'Don't you start. The way Darren's harping on about it, I'm tempted to see if they'll have me back.'

'Are you up for visitors?'

'Are you allowed to see me? I'm suspended don't forget.'

'That's what I said to Mr Hedges, but he said . . . Now let me get this right. "Fuck 'em."'

'Stop it. My ribs are killing me already.'

'So can we? Gary and I have got lots to update you on. Even though we shouldn't.'

'Yes sure. It'll be good to see some friendly faces.'

Darren's inquisitive look as he came through the door, mug in each hand, needed no words.

'Hold on, Bob.' She held the phone away from her mouth. 'Bob and Gary are coming round.'

Darren's brow furrowed and he mouthed *really?* Jo shrugged, signifying the fait accompli. She returned to Bob. 'How long?'

'Half an hour?'

'OK. Take us as you find us.' She looked at Darren who just shook his head.

She ended the call. 'Are you sure this is a good idea?' said Darren.

'What could I say?'

'Try no.'

'But he said they've got things to update me on. We might find out what happened and it's not like anyone else is going to tell us.'

'How's that going to help?'

'Brakes don't fail for no reason. Perhaps they are going to tell us why. It might just help me understand more 'cos at the moment I can't help thinking it should be me in the morgue, not Faisal.' Before Darren could embrace her, she hobbled out of the room and upstairs, her head pounding and her eyes streaming.

Thirty-one minutes later the doorbell rang and Darren jumped up to answer it.

'Sorry we're late,' Jo heard Bob say from the hallway.

'No respect,' Darren joked, as he closed the door.

The three men walked into the lounge and Jo went to stand up.

'Please, don't get up on my account,' said Gary.

Jo settled back as they made small talk whilst Darren took the drinks order, returning a few minutes later with a tray stacked with mugs and biscuits.

Jo cut straight to the chase. 'How's Faisal's family? Are they being looked after?'

'Seems Hampshire have a more humane chief than us. Mrs Paisley has been to see them every day and put an inspector at their beck and call. No news on the funeral yet. The Independent Office for Police Conduct are being their usual tardy selves in the investigation, but I've got a mate I used to crew up with in South Wales who works for them now,' said Gary.

'Can you get me Mrs Hussain's number? I really want to talk to her. If she feels the same that is.'

'Leave it with me.'

'What do we know about the crash?' asked Jo.

Gary looked at everyone in turn. 'This goes no further. Got it?'

They all nodded their agreement. Jo was glad the other two trusted Darren, despite him being a journalist.

'These are just initial findings so far, right? The car's data shows that Faisal was keeping to the speed limit on the whole journey, short as it was. As he approached the bend just before the roundabout, that's when he started to brake but they didn't engage. He then tries again and again as the car picks up speed down the slight decline just before the roundabout traffic lights. Still nothing. The lights are on red and had been for about twenty seconds, meaning the lorry that hit you was on a long green, so was picking up speed. That's when it happened.'

'How's the driver? They told me he wasn't injured but was very shaken up.'

'Still is. He's feeling massively guilty but he'll be fine.'

'It was mechanical then?' asked Jo.

'Sort of.'

Jo and Darren looked at each other. Curious.

'Go on,' Jo said, noticing that Bob was showing no surprise, glad that Gary had already taken him into his confidence.

'Well, about fifteen minutes before Faisal started the engine, someone managed to disable the lock and alarm and interfere with the brakes. They've not cut the pipes, as in the old days, but they've done something technical that's meant they were compromised.'

'Hold on. Fifteen minutes? We should have been out of the prison by then. Christ, who knew we were there anyway? Only Faisal's team.'

'And just about every prison officer in the jail,' corrected Bob.

Gary continued. 'And my fella at the IOPC says that whatever they did wasn't random. They knew what they were doing.'

'Whoever did this then was either after Faisal, me or both of us. Knew we were in the prison and when we were leaving. But we were on our way out long before then. Until . . .'

'Until?' said Darren.

'Until we were summoned to see the Number One Governor for what amounted to an hour's rant.'

'What are you saying?' Darren asked.

'I don't know, but what if that was a delaying tactic? I mean, we'd asked some pretty probing questions and, what with Nowak being investigated for the Op Steward murders, maybe someone wanted to throw us off the trail.'

'What, so he calls you in just so someone has time to doctor the car?'

Jo shrugged. 'It's a possibility. They've got CCTV covering the outside so they will have seen where we've come from. These plain cars stick out like a vicar in a lingerie shop. It wouldn't take long to find it round there, do what they need to do, then get the message back that it's safe to let us go.'

'But what if you spotted them tampering?' Darren loved playing detective.

'It's a risk but my mate said they wouldn't have needed long,' said Gary. 'It seems the brakes would only fail once he'd reached a certain speed.'

'They must have involved not only the wing staff, but the governor too.'

All three were staring at Jo. She took stock for a moment. 'No, this is something much more than trying to derail an investigation that any SIO could pick up. This is personal. This is about me.' A swell of nausea overcame her and she rushed as quickly as her aching body would allow to the toilet, making it just in time.

33

Tom Doughty was not taking any of Russ Parfitt's calls since the mêlée in the car park and was only communicating with him by the tersest of emails. In some ways, it was a relief to Russ – but knowing Tom as he did, he knew there would be the almightiest storm after this relative calm.

Still, thought Russ as he walked across Church Road to buy his lunch from Bagelman opposite the town hall, he'd enjoy the silence whilst it lasted.

Having left the shop, he waited patiently for the stream of buses, cars and suicidal cyclists to pass. As he stepped into the road, thinking that the blue Volvo was giving way, it sped up then stopped beside him. An unseen hand flung open the left rear passenger door and a voice from within called out, 'Mr Parfitt, a word please.'

'But . . . I'm . . .'

'Get in.' Russ was about to argue but, as he spotted the huge driver start to unfold himself from the car, he did as he was told, his heart pounding.

The car glided away as Russ's eyes adjusted to the gloom. He picked out a front seat passenger as well as the driver. The man beside him put his arm round his shoulder.

'First of all, don't worry. We're not going to hurt you. We know you're a busy man, so we'll get you back so no one notices you've gone.'

'What the hell do you want then?'

'In good time. As I was saying, we're not going to hurt you. Not yet. In fact, not at all if you do as you're told.'

Russ gulped, tried to reply, but decided silence was the best option in that moment.

The driver made light work of Church Road, turned left into Hove Street then crossed the Kingsway before nestling between the run-down King Alfred swimming centre and the promenade.

'What are we doing here?' asked Russ.

The man in the back half-turned in his seat so he was looking at the chief executive. 'I want to show you something, then we're going to have a little chat.'

He produced an iPad and it lit up, the first frame of a video ready and waiting to be tapped to play.

He instantly recognised Dyke Road Park, not half a mile from where he lived. The video was date-stamped the day before and he quickly picked out his daughters running around the climbing frames, racing by the look of it. The camera switched, changed angles and zoomed in on Heather, sitting on a bench chatting to an athletic-looking black man, younger than her. They were deep in animated conversation then simultaneously burst out laughing.

Anger boiled inside Parfitt. What the fuck was she doing with him? She'd be grovelling for forgiveness when he got home, that was for sure.

'Keep watching,' said the man as the camera swivelled back to the girls. Now they were on adjacent swings, making desperately hard work of getting the things to move. A white man then moved into frame and whispered something to each girl. Initially they looked perturbed but then the six-year-old laughed, the younger girl copying. The man then pushed each in turn making them go higher and higher, their laughter shriller each time.

The camera zoomed in on the man, whose smile vanished and who stared deep into the lens. Then it swung back and Russ was disgusted to see Heather having a whale of a time with her new black friend, of all people. The screen went blank.

The man in the front passenger seat then turned round. Parfitt immediately saw it was the white man who'd been pushing the swings. His expression was every bit as menacing as when he'd locked onto the camera.

The man in the back then spoke. 'So you see, Mr Parfitt, we not only know where you live but we can get to your beautiful little girls, even under the nose of their mum. Although I think she was thinking of getting under something else, don't you?'

Russ tensed.

'Calm down, it's only my little joke. Now, the point of that was to remind you who you work for. To help you regain focus. There are a few things we need you to do over the next couple of weeks to prove your loyalty. I understand there are some big plans afoot and we need to know if you're on board or not.' He handed Parfitt a piece of paper with a single-spaced list of bullet points which filled the page. Parfitt scanned it in horror.

'You want me to do all this? I mean, most of it's illegal, the rest impossible, especially in a fortnight. I can't do this.'

'Oh, that's such a shame. Still, if you don't, I'm sure those little girls would love to spend some more time with my friend here. They did seem to be having fun, didn't they? In fact, I doubt they'd even think of him as the kind of stranger you'll have warned them about, do you? More a loving uncle. Very safe.'

Russ went to grab the man's throat but found his wrist in a vice-like grip.

'Now now. Let's not get excited. It's only a little test. And if you mention any of this to your wife, we'll know. And if that happens, I'm sure she'd just love to be more acquainted with her new friend. I bet she'd love a real man, what do you think Toby?'

The driver turned his head, grinning. Unmistakably the shit who'd had Heather eating out of his hands.

'Just do what's on that sheet of paper and nothing will change. Don't and your life will be ashes. Understand?'

Russ mumbled, 'Yes,' whilst frantically searching for a third way, realising there simply wasn't one.

Jo sat on the edge of the bath and sobbed.

The enormity of her realisation had taken her by surprise. She'd been through so much over the last year, and her life had been at stake before, but this was more calculated. Other threats had been in the moment; this was a deliberate targeting which she knew would not stop just because they'd failed once, not until she was dead.

Worse though, she'd put Faisal in the line of fire and now his young family had to live with the consequences. How could she ever forgive herself?

'Can I come in?' whispered Darren.

'Sure,' she said, wiping her eyes.

'Hey, what's this about?' he said, sitting beside her, his hand on her knee.

'Nothing.'

'It's going to be hard, but you're safe now. Shall I tell them to come back another time?'

'No, I'll be fine. They're risking a lot by being here. Best let them get it all out in one visit. Give me a minute and I'll be down.'

'They've just told me Acers hasn't even reported me punching him.'

'Really? What about the PC outside or the nurses? Surely they'll ask questions?'

'Seems he told them he'd slipped, hence the noise.'

Jo pondered this. 'That's very odd. Acers has lots of traits, but forgiveness isn't one of them. I wonder what he's up to.'

'Maybe he's just embarrassed he suspended you in your hospital bed.'

'That's another thing he doesn't do. No, there's a reason he doesn't want your arse. Come on, let's go down.'

Jo pecked him on the cheek, and they put on their happy faces and went back to Gary and Bob.

'You OK?' asked Bob.

'Sure,' she smiled.

'You want to hear what Neela told me?'

'Yes of course!'

'Well, I say "Neela told me" – she wouldn't actually speak to me.'

'Bugger,' said Jo.

'But her solicitor handed me this.' He proffered the prepared statement but she waved it away.

'Just the headlines for now.'

'OK. Right, first things first, the Sycamore, and probably all the other homes Maximus Care run, are staffed by almost entirely trafficked girls from just about anywhere.'

'You're kidding.'

'No, and whilst it might look all dandy to visitors – like you . . .'

Darren threw her a look.

'I'll explain later.' How the hell was she going to explain that to him? 'Carry on.'

'Some of the girls are brought in en masse. Usually handpicked in Calais, thrown onto lorries, taken to remote RV points, then bussed into the homes late at night. There they are kept prisoner in locked quarters well out of sight, hot-bedding and fed next to nothing. The only time they come out is to work, and that can be up to fourteen hours a day.'

'Why don't they just leave? I mean, the doors aren't locked.'

'Simple. They've got no documentation, no money and there are blokes always around watching them. The most powerful reason though is that the few who have tried were spirited away.'

'To where?'

'Well, that's where our luck was in. I said *some* of the girls came in that way.'

'You did.'

Bob took a sip of his tea.

'Others – still migrants mind – are picked up from the homeless community, schmoozed by some old charmer, offered a job then taken to the home where the same thing happens.'

Jo was getting frustrated with Bob stringing this out. 'I know all the other stuff from your initial interview. Why's this bit lucky?'

'Because, seems they're not very good at tracking their staff. About a month ago, a girl was brought in by this second route and put to work. What they didn't realise was that she'd originally worked in another care home, having been bussed there as Neela was. She tried to escape so was locked in some dark room, taken out to a farmhouse, scrubbed up and then taken out to work in a brothel. Had to service eight to ten blokes a day. All were completely vile and most were perverted or just plain violent. Anyway, somehow she managed to escape this time, lived on the streets but found herself back at square one via the old fella.'

'And told Neela all of this?'

'Yep, so on top of her being scared stiff, Neela gave enough to help me work out roughly where the brothels are.'

'Plural?'

'Seems so.'

'Where?'

'Russell Road, Clarence Square area, I think.'

'Is that what we think has happened to Ajee?'

'That seems likely, as it's not only those who try to get away who disappear. It's anyone connected with one of the DNACPR deaths. They get spirited away too.'

'And Ajee was?'

'Yep. Mrs Cooke of all people.'

'Hold on, I'm definitely missing something here,' said Darren.

Gary touched his shoulder. 'I'm sure your missus will fill you in, but can you let Bob finish? We shouldn't be here and we need to get going before we're missed.'

Darren grunted and sank back in his chair.

'How much did she know about the deaths?' said Jo.

'She's a little shaky on some of the details but, when a resident came in, the first thing that would happen is Peggy Squire—'

'The manager,' Jo clarified for Gary and Darren.

'Yep. Peggy would welcome them, get them settled and then spend some time with the family. Those who either didn't have any or whose family were in a rush to go, well she'd call Dr Harper . . .'

'The one on bail?'

'Yes. He'd come round either that day or the day after. The next thing, the staff were told that if that person suffered any medical episode they were to do nothing but call the manager.'

'Were they told why?'

'No, but they knew that if they didn't do as they were told, they'd be shipped off or handed over to immigration.'

Gary spoke up. 'That's not that unusual. My gran went into a home, effectively to die. She didn't want anyone jumping up and down on her chest if anything happened. She reckoned if it was her time to go, she should just go.'

'Yes boss, and that happens all the time,' said Bob. 'It's fine providing the person has capacity, knows what they are agreeing to and the family have been informed. Doctors can sign these on behalf of patients in certain circumstances – but these cases aren't like that. The residents hadn't given any indication that's what they wanted. No family have been informed let alone consulted, and their medical history doesn't indicate that a DNACPR would be in their best interests.'

'And it's always new residents?' said Jo.

'Not always. According to Neela, they always die within the first month or around the three month mark.'

Gary chipped in again. 'I get this, but assuming they are letting them die to stash away their money, how do they know they will die in that time? I mean, it's a bit random.'

'Neela said they think Peggy Squire messes around with their meds to bring on an episode, or they feed those on a liquid diet lumpy food. Just enough to make them gag, then nature takes its course and no one does anything to stop it.'

'Is that what happened to Mary Cooke? The food?'

'I expect so,' said Bob.

'So Mary was murdered?' said Jo. 'And Neela is prepared to make a statement about this. Yes?'

'That's the bad news. Her brief said we could forget any notion of her being a witness. She's terrified and wants to put all this behind her.'

'So she's happy to see others die. Other girls locked into slavery and then shipped off to prostitution? You need to go back and tell her,' said Jo.

'That's just not possible, ma'am,' said Bob, the formal address indicating that he was about to reverse the pulling of rank. 'Mr Iwahu said it was a one-time visit and we both know there's nothing I can do about that. On the bright side, we now know what's going on for sure. All we have to do is prove it.'

Gary stood up. 'Come on Bob, time to go.' His abruptness took Jo by surprise but, on second thoughts, he had his career to think about and the sooner he could be back on home ground, the better. She pulled herself to her feet, Bob and Darren following suit. The men all shook hands and Bob and Gary gave Jo a gentle hug.

'It'll be OK,' said Gary.

Jo shrugged. 'Not for Faisal it won't. Make sure they find out who did this. And who killed those women and children. Don't forget them.'

As they got to the front door, Bob left first then Gary had a poorly feigned Columbo moment. 'Oh, Jo. Just one more thing. Bob, I'll see you in the car.'

Darren took the hint too and went back to the lounge.

'What is it?'

'I had a bizarre meeting with Parfitt and Doughty the other day.'

'In what way bizarre?'

'They were sickeningly friendly. Tom called me something like "a role

210

model who understands what Brighton and Hove wants". How should I handle them?'

'Like a hedgehog on heat. All they need to eradicate anyone who's not like them is a divisional commander who is either onside or impotent. Don't be either.'

'But I'm not as savvy as you or Phil. I do the transactional stuff and leave the diplomacy to others.'

'Well, now you've got that pip below the crown on your shoulder, you have to step up. You can do this. Just remember, they will never do anything or say anything – particularly to you – if it doesn't suit their purpose. And if you don't play ball? Well, you've seen what happens if you get too close to the truth.'

'You're serious that it was them?'

'I've absolutely no doubt. And I think they've got something on Acers too.'

'No!'

'Think about it. The grief he's given us, me being moved, the suspension. It's all linked. Watch your back, your front and your sides, Gary. And, if you find you're getting an easy ride, you must be missing something.'

'Jesus.'

'On the bright side, apart from your gender, you've got something I haven't.'

'Oh, what's that?'

'Not what, who.'

Gary looked puzzled.

'You've got a mole in their camp.'

'Have I?'

'Come on. Don't tell me you're the only one not to notice how Debbie drools every time you step foot in the town hall.'

This made him blush and, for once, speechless.

'Use her. There's no love lost between her and the BPP. She'll see you as an ally so treat her as one.'

34

The last rapist had left a full fifteen minutes ago, yet despite pumping what seemed like half a bottle of cheap perfume, Ajee could still smell him.

Some of the other girls called the disgusting men they had to service, clients or customers. Some even referred to the frequent flyers as regulars, as if they were steady boyfriends. Ajee, on the other hand, called them what they were. Only the most pig-ignorant would believe that the girls who were hot-housed here consented to even the most benign acts. And those were few and far between.

Subtle giveaways like the ever-warm bed, the bruises that never faded and the dead look in the girls' eyes were enough to bring home the exploitation these monsters paid for. Oh how she'd love to meet their wives and reveal what 'working late' actually meant – although they probably already knew, but felt it was safer not to mention it.

Ajee had been there long enough to know that it wouldn't be long before the next rapist was shown to her room. As ever she'd show no warmth but take in every little detail so, when she was finally free, she could hunt them down and wreak revenge one way or another. She'd never be a victim again.

She stopped spraying. Who was it for anyway? She'd never get the man's stench from her skin so by freshening the room, she was only preparing it for the next one. Well, he could suck it all in. She hoped it made him puke like they did her, then she'd leave that for the next one too.

She was sitting on the bed, conjuring up happier times with her family, when the door burst open.

'Come quickly,' said Suzanne.

Ajee was confused. Was she going somewhere? She grabbed a jumper but Suzanne said, 'No, I need you now,' as she ran back out of the room. Ajee followed more by instinct than obedience and saw the brothel manager dart into a room at the top of the stairs.

When she took in the scene that greeted her, Ajee gagged.

The unconscious girl must have been no more that seventeen, but that was only a guess as the beetroot swelling closed both eyes, her nose was split and Ajee could count at least three teeth missing. Her ripped cream chiffon robe was soaked in blood and the bite marks to her neck, her exposed breast and the grip marks to both arms were further brutal testimony to the ferocity of whatever had happened in here.

'Help her then,' said Suzanne. 'You wanted to be the nurse, so nurse her.'

'She needs hospital, not nurse,' argued Ajee. 'Call ambulance.'

'We both know that's not going to happen,' said Suzanne as she grabbed Ajee by the arm and spun her towards the girl. Ajee realised that the only hope this poor waif had would come from her.

Ajee checked she was breathing and then her pulse. Both weak, but regular. She then murmured words of comfort and reassurance in her ear.

'Speak up. No whispering,' barked Suzanne.

'Sorry,' replied Ajee, as she checked her injuries and vital signs. 'I need bandages. Water. You get me those?'

Suzanne huffed, stepped out then, to Ajee's disgust, locked the door. She took advantage of Suzanne's brief absence to talk to the girl again. 'My name is Ajee. I'm a nurse but I'm like you. They keep me here too. I look after you and do my best to get a doctor. If you can hear me, make them think you very bad. That is only chance.' Ajee wasn't sure but thought she heard a grunt of acknowledgement.

The key turned in the lock and a thunderous-looking Suzanne stormed back in, hurling a grubby first aid kit on the bed.

'Careful,' said Ajee before she could stop herself.

'Don't you dare talk to me like that. How long will you be? You've both got work to do.'

Ajee stopped what she was doing. 'She cannot work. She not work for long time. She needs hospital.'

'I don't think so. You're both here to earn money. If you can't do that, you're no good to us.'

'She could die.'

'We'll all die one day.'

Ajee seethed but kept working on her patient, cleaning wounds, checking for internal injuries – such as she could – and dressing what cuts she was able, offering comforting words all the time.

After about ten minutes, Ajee heard a male voice in the hallway.

'Suzanne. A word.'

'Stay here and keep quiet,' Suzanne instructed, as she left the room. This time she didn't close the door so Ajee strained to listen as best she could.

She could only catch the odd word, but enough to string together some kind of meaning.

The man was saying that whoever had done this had been sorted, whatever that meant. He seemed to be overruling Suzanne on putting the girl back to work straight away. Something about damaged assets and that someone might report the injuries. He did agree that she wouldn't be going to a hospital and there would be no doctor. She heard her own name mentioned but agonisingly couldn't work out what they were saying about her. The last thing she did pick up was the man saying, 'It'll take me about an hour but make sure they're ready.'

As the door moved, Ajee was quick to busy herself dressing more wounds, hoping Suzanne didn't realise she'd been listening.

'You need to get her ready. You're both going somewhere.'

'Where?' Ajee replied, panic rising.

'That's none of your concern but, against my better judgement, it's been decided Farah can't be looked after here and that you are going to nurse her so she can get back to work. Three days, at the most.'

'Three days? She needs more.'

'Three days and if she's not well enough then she will be disposed of and you'll be back here making up for lost time and earnings.'

Ajee went to shout her objections but Suzanne had already gone.

35

It had been a week since Jo had been suspended and whilst she was starting to feel physically stronger, other than Gary and Bob, Sussex Police had been strangely silent.

No contact from the Professional Standards Department, none from her ACC who, as her line manager, had a duty to keep her up to speed and, suspiciously, even the local Superintendents' Association weren't returning her calls. Luckily, when she was a DC, she had worked with Vince Mitchell who was now the Association's national lead for standards. He'd called straight back and, terrier that he was, promised to get to the bottom of what was going on.

Good luck with that, she thought.

She spent far too long than was good for her mulling over how, despite the promises she made to herself last year, work had again consumed her life. She'd barely had enough time for Darren and the boys but the promises she made herself to catch up with her younger sister, Frances, who was fighting her own battles with addiction – rooted in the abuse she'd suffered as a child by a family 'friend' – had long withered away. Perhaps now was the time?

As she was sitting gazing out of the lounge window, she saw a dustcart trundle up the road. All flashing lights, whirrs and clatters as obscenely chirpy blokes laughed and joked whilst they hauled bins back and forward. She spotted her own bin still on the driveway, so fearing the stench that would emanate in a fortnight's time if they didn't take it, she hauled herself up and out of the front door, heaved the wheelie bin with her good arm and left it on the kerb.

'Just in time,' she said to the approaching binman.

'Lucky you,' he said as he went to take it.

Just then a call from the cab stopped him. 'Not that one. That's on the list.'

'Sorry love,' said the binman as he put the still-full bin back where Jo had left it.

'What do you mean?'

'You're on the list.'

'What list?'

'It's a list we get. People whose bins we're not to take.'

Jo stood, incensed. 'Why the hell would I be on your list?'

'Dunno love. Could be a breach of some regulation. Maybe you're behind with your council tax. We just get the list, not the reasons. You need to phone the council.'

'This is outrageous. Can't you just take it and I'll sort it out for next time?'

'Sorry. It's . . .'

'Don't tell me, more than your job's worth.'

He shrugged and sauntered down the road as if all were well in the world.

Jo stormed back indoors and grabbed her laptop. She was about to Google the bins helpline, or whatever the hell it was called, when an email caught her eye.

Urgent Change of School Allocation.

She tabbed over and opened it, re-reading it several times in disbelief.

Dear Mr and Mrs Howe

It is with much regret that, due to over-subscription, it has become necessary to withdraw the school place previously allocated to Liam from next September.

Unfortunately, North Hove Primary School no longer has capacity so Liam will be allocated a place at Lewes Road Primary School. We are sure Liam will be very happy at this excellent school. We regret that this decision can only be appealed on severe hardship grounds. Should you feel you will suffer such consequences please appeal through the relevant portal <u>www.brighton&hovecc.uk/schoolappealsportal</u>.

Yours sincerely
S. T. Whitehead
Schools Admissions Manager

What the fuck? Jo clicked on the link but was curtly informed, *The requested page could not be found.*

She went back to Google and hammered in search terms but felt she was plunging down Alice's rabbit hole.

There was something about the morning Daily Management Meeting that warmed Gary Hedges' heart. Despite the bullshit that was his bread and butter since he'd become the acting divisional commander – performance scrutinies, policy working groups, review and reflection seminars – talking operational policing with those who still did the job they'd joined for was what he did best.

He was such a fixture at Brighton and Hove that the inspectors and chief inspectors forgave him meddling at levels way below his rank. Deciding how many cops would have their duties changed for the FA Cup replay that no one had predicted was probably the job of an inspector – chief inspector at a push – but Gary's pedigree and popularity gave him the right to give a number everyone would work to.

He was in a rush today so as he walked into the conference room at 9.29, he'd not had the chance to read the briefing sheet. He'd wing it. It would be fine.

'Morning, all,' he said as he took in the usual crowd gathered around the oval beech table that dominated the huge room.

They all put their phones down and waited for the briefing to appear on the smart board.

Gary suppressed a gasp when he read the first item.

Update on acid attack (genitals) Clarence Square.

Feigning he knew all about it, he turned to DI Parikh. 'Sapna, where are we with this?' he asked, hoping she'd give some of the basics too.

'Not much further. As we know, the bloke himself isn't giving any details of the attack, but it seems he was targeted. We just don't know why. He's got one caution for a domestic ABH two years ago but other than that he's not known to us. Given the nature of the attack it's probably to send a message. Maybe the partner of someone he's having an affair with. It's anyone's guess, but what we do know is that he was dumped there after the attack. It happened elsewhere.'

'CCTV?'

'There was a malfunction and all that night's data has been wiped. We're still working on any private CCTV and house to house.'

'There's a bloody coincidence. Keep me updated. Next item?'

DI Bob Heaton cleared his throat. 'Just a bit of news on Op Steward. First of all, DCI Hussain's replacement has had to pull off it to run the murder of that teacher in Maidstone that's all over the news. Major Crime are trying to free up another DCI but, in the meantime, I've been asked to step up, so I'm acting SIO for the foreseeable.'

'Bloody hell, we'll all need Equity cards soon,' said Gary.

'The update I can give so far is that we've now established a firm link between Szymon Nowak and the attack, and we're working on some covert lines of enquiry to identify further suspects.' Everyone knew not to probe further. 'However, I just want to thank the neighbourhood teams for the brilliant work with the community. The family liaison officers are feeding back that everyone is feeling well supported from the police, if not from the council. They're particularly pleased the Coroner fast-tracked the independent post-mortems to release the bodies. I'm told the council leadership are not so happy, but there you go.'

Gary scribbled a note to himself.

Bob continued. 'Which brings me on to the funerals tomorrow.

Obviously they want huge traditional traveller ones with all the horses, carriages and pizzazz that they frankly deserve. The problem is the council are refusing the road closures or suspension of parking restrictions. We've assured the families we will work on them but they are digging their heels in.' He looked at Gary. 'Boss, can you have a word? The fact is they'll have the funerals anyway, it's just it would be great if they can do so without a fight.'

'Leave it with me.'

The licensing inspector was next. 'Can I make a bid for a sergeant and six on overtime from eight tonight please?'

'What's that for?' asked Gary.

'I've had a call from the council licensing team. They are planning on issuing closure notices on two pubs and a club in Kemp Town this evening.'

'Bloody hell. Which ones?'

The inspector told them.

'They're the busiest gay venues in the city. What are their grounds?'

'Drug use and dealing, and lewd and indecent behaviour.'

'And do we have the same view?'

The inspector looked sheepish. 'Well, no to be honest. All our checks suggest they are three of the best-run establishments in the city. I've asked for some more detail and my team are rechecking, but it's all come out of the blue.'

'Can we object, or just get them to delay?'

'We can try but as you know, they have the same powers as us and, even if we don't agree, we have to be there to prevent a breach of the peace.'

'Jesus,' said Gary. 'I'll add it to my list for Russ Parfitt.'

A voice piped up from the back. 'You know how bad things come in threes, guv.'

Gary looked up and saw one of the tactical enforcement sergeants wearing a tense smile.

'Go on,' said Gary.

'We're supporting Environmental Health in enforcing an injunction to clear the homeless tents on Victoria Gardens.'

'I'm not being funny but why am I only just hearing this?'

'Sorry guv, but it only came in this morning.' She fidgeted. 'It is on the DMM sheet.'

Gary took that one on the chin.

'When are you doing that?'

'In about forty-five minutes, so can you excuse me?'

She'd stood up and started to walk out when Gary stopped her.

'Hold on. How many of you? There must be twenty tents down there and who knows how many in each.'

'Luckily we've got a team on a training day, so we are starting with two sergeants and twelve PCs. We'll call if we need back-up.'

Gary put his head in his hands. 'Off you go then. Can the rest of you crack on through the rest? I've got some calls to make.'

36

Jo had lost track of how many messages she had left for the refuse department and the schools allocation officer the previous day, not to mention bombarding just about every council officer, and councillor, she could think of to find out what the hell was going on.

None had replied, as she'd anticipated, and she was going to spend the afternoon doing exactly the same again once she had returned from the travellers' funerals.

She hadn't got close to the O'Connor and Smith families but as a mum and a police officer – albeit a suspended one – she felt a burning need to pay her respects. Whatever she was going through at the moment was nothing to their families' pain – nor Faisal's.

She parked on the road outside her house, having returned from dropping Ciaran off at school and Liam at playgroup – dreading what the school run would look like if the council got their way in splitting them up. Checking her watch, she calculated she had enough time for a soak in the bath before dressing in something suitable, meeting Darren by the station, then driving up to see the cortege leave the Horsdean site.

While the water was running, she grabbed her iPad to catch up on the David Attenborough documentary she'd be dying to watch for months. Once the bath bomb had dissolved and the water was at a hazardous temperature and depth, she rested the tablet on the bath tray and lowered herself in.

Almost immediately, the peace was shattered by what sounded like a low loader or a skip delivery. Either way, she guessed they'd be gone soon.

Sure enough, five minutes later, tranquillity returned.

Only for about ten minutes though as, once again, Attenborough was drowned out by a squad of pneumatic drills whose racket and reverberation pulsated through the walls and triggered a mini-tsunami in the bathwater.

'For Christ's sake,' Jo said to nobody, giving up on the pampering idea. She unplugged the bath, wrapped herself in her dressing gown and headed to the bedroom to do her hair and get dressed. The noise was relentless and she just prayed it would be over before the boys came home with their grandma.

Forty-five minutes later there was still no sign of the work finishing and Jo presumed it was a neighbour having their drive relaid. She was gearing up to give whoever they were working for a piece of her mind. A message on the road WhatsApp group wouldn't have gone amiss. She knew she'd let it go though, reminding herself again about the bereaved families she'd be seeing today.

As she was ready earlier than planned, she decided to head off to the station and grab a paper and drink at one of the cafés nearby. She searched for her car keys and phone, set the alarm then stepped out into the fresh air.

As she crossed her narrow driveway, she was horrified at what greeted her.

Across Benett Drive, smack bang outside her house, was a trench, six foot wide by about four feet deep. Men gripping drills for all they were worth, dumper truck drivers ferrying spoil to a waiting lorry whilst the obligatory army of supervisors looked on.

'Where's my car?' Jo said to one man who seemed to be particularly unoccupied.

'What's that, love?' he replied.

'I'm not your . . . Never mind, where's the Qashqai that was just here?'

'Dunno love, I'm not from round here.'

'What's that got to do with anything?'

'I dunno where the council pound is.'

Rage bubbled inside Jo. 'Are you saying it's been towed?'

'Yeah, it was right where we needed to dig. Ignored the notices apparently.'

'What notices? I've only just parked it there. THERE WERE NO NOTICES.'

The man took a step towards her and removed his hard hat. 'Don't get all PMT with me, love. You got a problem with this, contact the council. I just dig roads.'

Jo took a deep breath, accepting that she was taking it out on the wrong Neanderthal.

'What are you digging for though?'

'Sorry, love. We're just digging the trench. No idea who's coming along after.'

Jo spun round, whipped out her phone and ordered an Uber.

Whilst Bob had kept himself up to date with Operation Steward, he needed to get his head round everything if he was to make a decent fist as stand-in SIO. Most of the forensic progress centred around the discarded lighter which had led to Nowak, so a literal dead end. The trawl for witnesses was equally arid, as was the identity of the dead body found in the burnt-out van.

The other scraps they had gleaned though were starting to come together into a sparse patchwork that, with a fair wind, would breathe a new lease of life into the enquiry. It wasn't glory Bob was after, it was justice for the O'Connors and Smiths and a legacy for Faisal.

Given the sensitivities of what he hoped DS Nigel Hughes might reveal, Bob insisted this meeting was just the two of them. Covert policing was called that for a reason and all detectives accepted that there were some things they would never need to know.

Bob and Nigel were both old school so there were no PowerPoint slides or fancy association charts. Just a couple of seasoned detectives sitting across from one another, their notebooks open in front of them with each page folded down the middle – left side for information, right side for actions.

Nigel kicked off with bringing Bob up to speed on how the phone Nowak had was linked, through another, to a call made to Tom Doughty just after the attack. Bob was flabbergasted.

'We've had directed surveillance on this O'Keefe bloke and, just after the governors' crash, Doughty visited him at a flat in Hove. He seemed to be in a bit of a panic but left a lot calmer. Oh, and Doughty phoned the chief just before that.'

'Do you think the chief's involved?'

Nigel paused a moment. 'I'm not even sure Doughty's involved but they are all lines of enquiry.'

'Anything else?'

'The financials. We've had a look at the Expede outfit. The previous owners of the van and the supplier to the care home?'

'Yep, I know who they are.'

'Sorry. They're really interesting. On the face of it they are a typical shell company. Registered off shore, no discernible UK business, cash flow in and out and very little trace either way.'

'Except from the care homes.'

'Correct. And a couple of others. You remember Simon McCartney, the BPP leader?'

Bob nodded.

'Well, when he was up for contempt of court, it was a mystery how he funded his defence. He had a top KC who, so it goes, wouldn't even represent his own mum pro bono. And McCartney didn't have a pot to piss in.'

'And?'

'It's taken some tracking but Expede, through a more circuitous route than a London cabbie could find, picked up the tab. And it was well north of three hundred thousand.'

Bob whistled. 'And where did that come from originally?'

'Still looking into that, but there are also connections with the financing of other countries' neo-Nazi groups and some of the post-referendum targeting of non-white people here.'

'So, they're basically a far-right cash cow.'

'Pretty much. Just a good job they ain't smart enough to hide themselves properly.'

'Don't hate them for that, Nigel. If it wasn't for the stupid ones, we'd be out of a job.'

The Uber had picked up Darren on route then dropped Jo and him at the top of Patcham, just a five-minute walk from Horsdean.

'You OK to walk from here?' said the cabbie.

'Sure,' said Jo. 'I bet all the road closures are mucking up your day.'

'There're no closures so far as we've been told. Still, half the city seems to be coming up here to pay their respects. Have a good day, and say a prayer from me.'

'Thanks,' they both muttered. As they walked away from the departing Skoda, they were both taken aback by the throngs of people: men, women and a surprising number of children, heading the same way as them. Most were dressed in funeral-black but some of the children were in school uniform. The floral displays some of the adults had clearly spent a fortune on were stunning. Reds, whites and blues. Some arranged as caravans, others with the victims' names picked out in the beautiful blooms.

As the groups crossed the A27 bridge, Jo noticed the faded floral tribute to Loretta Briggs in the centre of the roundabout. In contrast to the arrangements being carried for the travellers, Loretta's memorial consisted of tatty supermarket bunches, some with their yellow 'reduced' labels still attached. All except one – a huge display in traditional traveller style saying, 'GOD BLESS.'

The crowds lining the track from the main road to the site were five deep and ironically Jo was glad the carnage outside their house had prompted her to head off earlier, otherwise they'd get nowhere near.

Having policed Irish traveller funerals before, Jo knew these were huge affairs with hundreds of friends and family coming from across the country, even the water, to pay their respects. A few years ago, after a gypsy father of three was killed on a building site, the whole city had been brought to a standstill to allow the funeral procession to St Mary's Catholic Church near Preston Park, followed by the traditional tour of the young man's favourite haunts. The crowd, led by six stunning white horses pulling the carriage, had ambled at a snail's pace and it took them three hours to reach the cemetery. Police from all over the county were drafted in to make this happen. Road closures had brought gridlock, but few complained.

Today, Jo was shocked to see just a PC and PCSO hanging around the junction with the A27, sipping coffee from Styrofoam cups, clearly bought from the burger van that had been a fixture there for decades.

'Don't, Jo,' said Darren as she marched up to them, but she was livid.

The PC recognised her first, pulling himself up to a pitiful attention, coffee cup still in hand. He whispered to the PCSO who looked blank but followed suit.

'Hello, ma'am. I wasn't expecting to see you here.'

'Clearly not. Can't you show a little respect? Put the cups down and stand like you're professionals.'

The PC hesitated, then said, 'With respect, ma'am, aren't you sus—'

'Don't you dare. It doesn't take a police officer to see what a disgrace you two look. Just one to have the balls to tell you. When are the rest coming up?'

'Rest?'

'Yes. These are busy roads. There's probably a few hundred mourners down at the site. When are the others coming up here to help them out safely?'

'There's no one else. It's just us.'

'That's a big ask,' she replied.

The PC shrugged. 'Just a deterrent, that's all we've been told.'

'Against what, exactly?'

The PC was clearly bored with the conversation. 'If you don't mind, ma'am, we've got work to do.'

Jo made a mental note of the PC's number and name. When she

returned to work, as she was sure she would, they'd be having a very one-sided chat.

Jo walked back to where Darren was standing, where the lane met the roundabout by the exit from the A27. This was the funnel into the city for any traffic coming from the west, so cars and trucks thundered up the slip road in their droves and queued, often impatiently, for a gap to pull into.

'What was all that about?' said Darren.

'We just had a little tête-à-tête about standards. Do you realise that from a strength of nearly eight hundred, Gary could only muster those two? It's going to be carnage.'

'Leave it,' said Darren. 'That's his problem, not yours.'

Jo estimated there must be about two hundred in this area alone. She hated to think how many were along the route and outside the church. She prayed Gary had thought this through.

Just then a hush fell on the crowd, followed by the sound of hooves echoing through the still air to her left. The only other sounds were the click of the press cameras and rumble of traffic from the A27 below.

Jo craned her neck to catch a glimpse as the cortege approached. She gasped in awe as four snow-white shire horses, fitted with glossed bridles and majestic, black-plumed headdresses, appeared in slow unison. Similar configurations followed on. Each pulled identical white-framed carriages enclosed in crystal-clear glass and adorned with stunning posies and floral tributes. As they drew close, Jo saw that two contained tiny ivory-coloured coffins and two, larger chestnut ones.

Her thoughts went straight to the hate and brutality that had made this necessary, and to Faisal. Suspended or not, she had to get justice for all the innocents about to be committed to their God.

Onlookers threw flowers in their path and on the roofs. The impeccably dressed entourage that followed spread far into the distance and, as they neared, the wailing amplified and the grief felt physical.

Jo glanced at the two officers, who seemed more tense than before. They had positioned themselves behind the crowd and she could see the

PC muttering into his radio. She only hoped he was calling for back-up.

The front carriage reached the roundabout and the driver seemed puzzled. The traffic was relentless and none were showing the decency to pause for the procession. Jo watched with a professional eye, wondering how this was going to play out. She would have expected the officers to move forward, step into the road and hold the traffic for the few minutes it would take for the hearses to clear the roundabout.

But they remained rooted to their spots.

She felt the mourners become more and more impatient and even spotted some bunching, which was always the precursor to a crush. And with sixteen horses, probably weighing upwards of 800kg each, it was clear which species would come off worse.

'Come on,' came a shout from the rear.

'Fucking move it,' another rang out, which triggered some arguing back. A couple of the horses whinnied and pawed the ground. Jo was ashamed to be a police officer with this impotence playing out in front of her. She looked over at the two officers again, then all of a sudden felt for them. Their body language indicated that they weren't being intransigent out of choice – they were acting on orders.

Gary Hedges had countless strengths. He was level-headed, had an IQ of 130, was renowned as the force's most accomplished public order and firearms commander, and was a gifted cook. However, none of that made a jot of difference as he stood in the operational command suite, notionally in charge of the policing of the travellers' funeral.

He rarely allowed spectators in his domain during the live phase of an operation. At large events he welcomed his counterparts from the other emergency services, as well as the council event planners and the tactical commanders from the contracted private security company, but only if they had a job to do. On those occasions, all needed to be there and all knew the rules.

He was Gold, so his word was final.

Today though, not only did he have a fraction of the officers he needed, but his every decision was being watched over by the chief constable, who had invited the council leader and chief executive along. Gary had started to object but got nowhere.

He tried to ask Parfitt why he'd not returned his calls, but that was met with silence too.

One part of him though was grateful they were here. It was they who had refused road closures. They who had declined contracting private stewards. They who had insisted, 'We don't lock down the city for normal people's funerals, so we won't for this lot.'

No sooner had they received the message that the cortege was moving than they were told it had ground to a halt.

'Charlie Bravo Seven Five,' came the plea over the radio loudspeaker. 'We need to close the roundabout otherwise we are going to have a crush. Permission to stop the traffic.'

To his shame, Gary glanced at the chief and his guests. The stern look from Acers and Doughty forced him to shake his head at the expectant radio operator.

'Charlie Bravo Seven Five, from Gold that's a negative.'

'Charlie Bravo Seven Five, can you confirm that's Gold's decision? It's getting dangerous up here.'

'Keep it open,' mumbled Gary.

'Charlie Bravo Seven Five, that's his decision.'

He felt sick. If only there was CCTV coverage, then surely the three people who had no business here would see for themselves.

All he could do was wait. And hope.

The dignity of this funeral was not so much ebbing away as gushing.

The crowd had gone beyond agitated to raging. This was the first junction of the procession. At this rate it would take them until the middle of next week to reach the church. Jo was tempted to phone Gary to find out what the hell was going on, but what good would that do?

Just then, two men broke off from the front of the procession and stormed over to the officers. The way the crowd parted suggested they were leaders in the travelling community. Most mourners stopped their arguing and watched what was about to play out.

'You two. Instead of just fecking standing there, sort this fecking mess out.'

'I'm sorry sir, I've been told not to.'

'Fecking told? Fecking told?' said the larger of the men, who looked like he could pick up both the PC and the PCSO in one hand. 'If I told you to fecking jump over that bridge, would you fecking do it?'

'Sir, I must ask you to moderate your language,' said the PC.

The smaller of the men, who nevertheless dwarfed the officer, guffawed from the pit of his belly. 'Or fecking what?'

'I'll need to arrest you.'

Now the crowd joined in with a combination of sarcastic laughter and threats.

'I can't stand by and watch this,' said Jo.

'What are you doing? You can't go over there. They'll kill you,' said Darren.

'I'm going to do better than that,' she said as she pushed her way back through the crowd, away from where the action was promising to erupt.

Few took much notice as they responded to her very British 'Excuse me' and 'I'm so sorry' until she reached the kerb. Still no one watched as she gauged the traffic coming up the slip road. This could go one of two ways, she thought.

Judging the gaps and the relative speeds, she spotted her opportunity as a Porsche convertible passed.

Taking a huge breath, she made herself as big as she could, stepped off the pavement and marched to smack in the middle of the road.

She threw her hand up in the air, just like she'd been taught in training school, and faced down the as-yet-unseen driver of the Lidl lorry thundering towards her.

She barely heard Darren's shout of 'NO,' as the blast of the horn and the groan then hiss of brakes deafened her. For a moment she was back in the car with Faisal just before the lorry slammed in to them.

The smoke spewing from the tyres made her gag, and only then did she realise the world around her had stopped and all the mourners' eyes were on her.

As the truck bore down on her, all she could think of was her boys.

Gary was still deploring his own weakness when the radio burst into life.

'Charlie Bravo Seven Five, assistance at Horsdean. Urgent assistance at Horsdean.'

The radio operator clicked into emergency mode, needing no prompting from Gary or anyone else. 'Charlie Bravo Seven Five, we've got units making. What have you got, over?'

'Charlie Bravo Seven Five, the traffic on the roundabout has been stopped. The procession is on the move but it's carnage up here.'

'Charlie Bravo Seven Five, are you in physical danger?'

'Negative, it's just we can't control the cortege.'

'Find out how the traffic was stopped,' said Gary.

The radio operator asked the question and had to ask Charlie Bravo Seven Five to repeat the answer.

'It's Chief Superintendent Howe. She's in the middle of the roundabout stopping the traffic and the cortege is flooding through.'

Gary blinked and his mind raced. What the hell was she doing up there? Then he smirked at the thought of her standing like King Canute, single-handedly creating the mother of all traffic jams to let the travellers grieve.

It was clear that Acers, Doughty and Parfitt were thinking the same, but none saw the funny side.

'What the hell is going on, Gary?' bellowed the chief constable, before turning to the other two and saying, 'I'm so sorry, we will sort this.'

'You better had,' said Doughty. 'You know the consequences if you don't.'

Acers turned back to Gary. 'Get her out of there.'

'How, sir?'

'Christ man, do I have to do your job for you?' He pushed Gary to one side, stepped up to the radio operator and muttered his instructions. She checked she'd heard him right, shrugged then issued the orders, and for the avoidance of doubt, who they were from.

After a few tense minutes of silence, the radio clicked into life again.

'Charlie Bravo Seven Five. One in custody for obstruction of the highway, impersonating a police officer and to prevent a breach of the peace. To confirm, the prisoner's name is Mrs Joanne Howe. Can I have transport to Hollingbury Custody Centre please?'

37

Ajee had managed to negotiate a few more days tending to Farah at the farmhouse. Even the powers that be accepted that they had underestimated how long it would take for those injuries to heal. Initially, Ajee had tried to persuade them on what would be in Farah's best interests. When it became clear they couldn't care less what was good for her, she changed approach and talked of Farah as a damaged asset who would drive down customer satisfaction in their commodity which could, in turn, affect confidence.

It sounded like they were selling furniture rather than human beings, but Ajee needed to appeal to their warped priorities rather than their non-existent humanity.

Over the week they'd been together, the two women had developed a strong bond. Despite the horrific circumstances that had thrown them into the situation, Ajee enjoyed the responsibility of tending Farah's wounds and sharing stories of their escapes from their homelands and what had happened when they'd arrived in the UK. When it became apparent that both had been enslaved at the Sycamore Care Home, they talked long into the night about the conditions there, the evil Peggy Squire, the strange men who'd come in from time to time and the mysterious Dr Harper.

As they were sitting on the bed after their meagre lunch of bread and marmalade, Ajee anointing Farah's cuts, they chatted.

'Why they move you?' asked Ajee.

'They caught me with a phone. I call my auntie. She no pick up but they caught me,' replied Farah.

'How you get a phone?'

'I can get anything. I very good – how you say – pickpocket. I take a visitor's phone. I know how to break into it.'

'Wow. I'd have no idea.'

'Why would you? This my secret. My way out. These people see me as meat for dirty men. They stupid. Could make more if they used my true talents.'

'Could you steal a guard's phone?' asked Ajee.

'Sure. I should try?'

'If you want.'

'OK. We keep it for a whilst then tell him he drop it.'

Ajee giggled.

'Anyway, why you not at Sycamore?'

'I not sure. An old lady choked one day. They not let me give CPR and she died. She was lovely but only had one visitor. I feel sorry for her. Anyway, then they take me here, then to the house.'

'That's sad. It happen often though. What the lady called?'

'Mrs Cooke. Mary.'

Farah gasped. 'Not Mary! I used to look after her. I think her son an important policeman but he in prison now.'

'Prison? Why?'

'I don't know. Lots of rumours I don't know what to believe, so I believe none.'

Ajee nodded.

Farah continued. 'A nice lady came to visit. She care for Mary but didn't talk much.'

'I met her I think.' Ajee described Jo to a tee.

'Yes, I think that the lady. Many people died like that. Many we could have saved but Dr Harper said we shouldn't. I feel so bad, but what could we do?'

Both sat and stared at the floor, lost in their own guilt.

Ajee heard footsteps outside and ran to the door. 'Hello. Farah needs the toilet. It's her period.' They'd already worked out that the men who guarded them rarely entered a conversation if it was about women's issues, so they played this to their advantage. True to form, the key turned in the lock and the brusque guard stood to one side. Farah and Ajee winked at each other.

He stood just inside the door whilst Farah hobbled to the toilet opposite. Ajee ignored the guard and tidied away her medical kit, waiting for her friend to return.

Five minutes later, she heard the toilet flush and the door creak open. Ajee looked up and saw Farah stagger across the hall clutching her stomach. As she passed the guard, she stumbled and grabbed him to prevent her falling.

'I'm so sorry,' she said. 'My period hurt so much.'

He coloured up and wordlessly ushered her into the room, stepping out then locking it closed.

Farah waited a moment, then pulled out a Samsung S10 from her waistband, grinning like a birthday girl.

'You got it,' Ajee giggled in a whisper.

'Easy-peasy,' said Farah.

'Open it, open it,' said Ajee.

Farah held the phone to her chest. 'Be patient, my friend,' she said, then both hugged each other and giggled.

Farah angled the phone to the light and squinted, tilting it as she did so. Then she traced a pattern over the screen. 'Tada!' she said, turning the device round to show Ajee the app icons.

They huddled round it, searching for pictures of the man, shocked to see cutesy family photos of him, presumably his wife and two little girls posing on a stony beach. They read through some of his messages and saw that whoever the woman in the pictures was, she wasn't his only love interest.

'Let's see the news,' said Ajee.

Farah clicked over to the BBC News app.

The image that greeted them stunned them both.

The headline read: *Disgraced Senior Cop Arrested at Gypsy Funeral.* Beneath was a picture of an attractive English woman being held by a male police officer who looked angry and, in the background, a parade of people dressed in black walking behind horse-drawn carriages.

Ajee scanned the article and saw the woman was called Joanne Howe and until recently, she'd been the head of Brighton and Hove Police.

'That the lady who visit Mrs Cooke,' she said.

'Yes, yes it is. She a police lady,' said Farah.

'Maybe we find her, she help us. She's a kind lady.'

38

For all the years Jo had locked up prisoners – drunks, thieves, rapists, killers, the lot – she now realised she'd had no idea what it actually felt like once the cell door slammed. Alone and scared for what must be three hours now.

She was sitting on the moulded bench/bed, the two-inch-thick blue wipe-clean mattress doing no more than taking the edge off its hardness. She breathed heavily, then regretted it. The stench was suffocating. On other days, the pungent cocktail of sweat, feet, urine, Jeyes Fluid and reheated microwave meals was a passing sensation as she made her way from cell to interview room and vice versa.

Now, with that gagging blend heavy in the cell's still air, she wondered whether she would ever rid her hair and skin of its fetor.

Silently she sobbed. How had she ended up here? She'd only tried to do the right thing. et, in a few short weeks, she'd lost her command, effectively killed a colleague,, been suspended and was now almost certain to end up with a criminal record and no job. It had just seemed the right thing to do, so why hadn't that PC done it? People would have been killed if she'd not intervened to let the procession pass. That was week one of initial police training.

Then to arrest her for it? That must have come from Gary. Her friend. Or so she'd thought. The PC wouldn't have had the balls to do it himself. Despite her not technically being an officer, he would have appreciated the enormity of nicking her. There must have been an order. She was just thankful she was able to convince Darren to keep back. He had his own problems, already having punched the chief constable.

The headache that had blitzed as she was booked in by the bumbling custody officer now zeroed in behind her eyes, and the flickering fluorescence against the gardenia-washed walls and ceiling made it all the more agonising. She walked over to the recessed sink and swilled her face with water, making the mistake of glancing into the adjacent stainless-steel toilet bowl and seeing the faecal streaks left by a previous guest.

Obstruction of the highway. Impersonating a police officer. Breach of the peace. How dare they eke out three offences from one simple act. Then she remembered the dozens of times she'd done the same. Spread betting they called it and, now she was on the receiving end, she saw how cynical it was.

Above the oaths being screamed by the woman in the next cell and the incessant door banging by someone further away, she heard the jangle of keys, then the slam of the gate that she imagined was about ten yards down the corridor to her left. Each blast of noise drilled more pain into her throbbing head.

She saw the spyhole darken, then her cell door opened. A flouncy custody assistant stood in the opening.

'Come with me. You're being released,' she said, all matter of fact.

Jo didn't move. 'Released? Why?'

The jailer shrugged. 'No idea, but get your skates on before they change their minds.'

Jo stood and followed the woman out of the door and down the corridor to the charge desks.

She took in the hustle of the room they called the Bridge, as prisoners – some fighting, some resigned, most spaced-out – waited to be booked in whilst others like her were being freed.

She was guided to a waiting sergeant who had the look of someone in the middle of a double shift.

'It's been decided to NFA you,' said the vaguely familiar custody officer.

'You're letting me go? Who decided that? The CPS?'

The sergeant looked to her left. Jo followed her gaze and saw the arresting PC standing a few feet away. He stepped forward.

'No. Command actually,' he muttered. Then he moved closer. 'I just want to say, I'm really sorry about all this.'

The custody officer coughed. 'Cut the chit-chat. Just return Mrs Howe's property and get her out of here.'

The PC did as he was told, then silently showed a bewildered Jo out into the fresh air.

As soon as she was out of sight, she switched on her phone. She tabbed down to Gary's personal number and WhatsApped.

We need to talk. Now.

Tom Doughty had barely held it together once Jo Howe had buggered up their plans of granting no special favours to the travellers. His spotters had told him that once she stopped the traffic, the cortege had spilt onto the roundabout and then clogged up the city for a good three hours.

He'd seethed as he had to listen to the radio messages confirming exactly what he'd been determined not to have happen. Parfitt had been of little help; he'd thought he might be a bit more dynamic since the little ultimatum they'd given him. Instead, he'd just stood and sucked up Acers' platitudes about peaceful gatherings and respecting the bereaved.

He ached for a reason to get out of this sweatbox of a control room with all its squawking radios and acronyms and, once Gary Hedges had excused himself to make a call, he grabbed Acers and Parfitt.

'Find us an office,' said Doughty.

The chief nodded and disappeared, returning two minutes later. 'This way.' He led the way through two sets of double doors and into a room that, from the graphs on the wall, seemed to belong to someone whose job was to keep the building running.

Doughty closed the door and left no gap for either to speak.

'Can you see now why we did what we did outside the prison?' He glared at them both.

Acers interrupted. 'Keep your voice down. These walls are paper thin.'

Quieter, Doughty continued. 'That woman is a fucking maverick. Every bloody turn she's there with her fucking tripwire. What's the matter with you, Stuart? You seem to have lost sight of what's at stake for you.'

'I'm not sure what else I can do. You said move her, I moved her. You said suspend her, I suspended her . . .'

'And got lumped by her husband in the process,' said Parfitt.

'You can shut up,' said Doughty. 'You haven't covered yourself in glory either.' He turned back to the chief. 'It's not good enough, Stuart. I'm serious about those photos, and I'm this far from sending them.'

'What do you expect me to do? I can't sack her . . .'

'Surely you can now. She's going to have a criminal record,' said Parfitt.

'Well, yes. If it gets to court.'

'It bloody better,' said Doughty. 'You need to start getting more creative.'

'Even if I could get rid of her, what's to stop her pulling stunts like today anyway?'

'That's why I said you need to be creative. She's getting too close.'

'And you're getting paranoid,' said Acers. 'Today wasn't about you. From what I heard she just wanted to get things moving.'

'If you believe that, you're more of an idiot than I took you for.'

Acers looked like he was going to explode when Parfitt touched his arm.

'Tom, I'll work with the chief constable to ensure Mrs Howe is no longer a problem. To anyone.'

In fairness to Gary, he'd been about as contrite as Jo had ever known him when he returned her call as she walked down Crowhurst Road from custody. He'd agreed to meet her as soon as possible, but not in Brighton.

She asked the cab driver to drop her off just short of The Green Welly Café in the Anglo-Saxon village of Ditchling, five miles north of Brighton, tucked in the shadow of the South Downs. Despite its quaint feel, it was a monstrous rat run for those wanting to avoid the A23, so its beauty was blemished by nose-to-tail traffic battling through its narrow streets.

Jo passed the stationary cars waiting at the mini-roundabout, crossed Keymer Road, and walked inside.

Gary was already there, as was her drink.

'Christ Jo, what a bloody mess,' he said, skipping the usual banter.

Jo checked for eavesdroppers then launched into him. 'What the hell were you playing at? Jesus Christ, Gary, how crap have you become? Never mind ordering my arrest, what about the fag-packet planning? You're so much better than this.'

Gary slapped the table. 'Hold on there. You have no idea what's been going on and how hard it's been.'

Jo raised an eyebrow and Gary tempered. 'Look, I know you've been through shit, but what I mean is that, since you've gone, Doughty and his lapdog haven't given me a second's peace and, well, I've no idea what they've got on Acers but he can't bend over backwards quick enough for them.'

Jo sipped her water. 'It's always been them and us, Gary. What I'm on about is that you are the best events commander in the force, yet for a massive traveller funeral, you have just a PC and PCSO – who frankly were worse than useless – no road closures and no contingencies. And when I take some action to stop a crush and a riot, I find myself in the cells.'

'Finished?'

'For now.'

'Want to hear what really happened?'

'Go on.' Jo slumped back and slurped her hot water again.

'The council flatly refused any road closures, parking restriction or stewarding . . .'

Jo went to speak but Gary raised his hand.

'They even refused to discuss the funeral at the Safety Advisory Group. They told us it was a matter for us. Reactive policing, they called it.'

'And you just sucked it up.'

'What do you think? I fought tooth and nail, but I could tell that their events staff had been expressly forbidden from making any compromises.'

'From the top?'

Gary nodded.

'What about our staffing? You could have flooded the city.'

'I tried but Acers vetoed it.'

Jo shook her head. 'Then push back. Push back on all of them. If it had gone tits up this morning, it wouldn't have been them in the dock.'

'Yeah, I know.' Gary looked broken but Jo pressed on anyway.

'And don't tell me it was that waste of a PC who decided to arrest his old boss. What was that all about?'

'Now that really was nothing to do with me.'

'How so?'

'I kid you not, the chief literally whispered the order to the radio operator. Luckily she had the presence of mind to get him to repeat it, then typed it on the log. There was no way I could rescind that.'

'I thought you were Gold. You were in charge, not him.'

'Technically, it was a lawful order.'

'What?'

Gary paused. 'In fairness, you were obstructing the highway and impersonating a police officer. Sort of.'

'Well obviously not, as I've been NFAd. I bet you didn't know that.'

'Know it? I instructed it.'

'Does you-know-who know?'

Gary looked at his phone. 'It seems not.'

Jo pushed her chair back from the table and looked underneath. 'Well, perhaps you have grown a pair after all.'

'Seriously Jo, that Doughty is one evil bastard. I've heard he's got some master plan and it's more than just pissing off some travellers. He's ethnically cleansing the city. I just don't know how to manage him. Especially with Acers in his pocket. I really could do with you back.'

'That's not going to happen for a while. Just stall him as much as you can. Speak to Bob too. I'm pretty sure they are making some progress on Op Steward. He was infuriatingly coy when I spoke to him yesterday. He said the strands are coming together linking the care home deaths with the trafficking, with Op Steward and with Doughty.'

'But to what end?'

'That's the missing link. It can't be to just further the city's political leaning. There has to be something bigger. Just keep watching, listening and, for Christ's sake, keep faith.'

'Any chance you could keep your head down whilst I do that then? You are the blue touch paper.'

'I think you're right. I'm going to do some volunteering until I get back to work. Help those less fortunate than me.'

'Why does that sound so ominous?'

'Trust me, Gary. It's time for me to put something back.'

39

Since they had found what they hoped would be a friendly police officer on the outside, Ajee and Farah had plotted day and night as to how they were going to find her. Ajee had returned the phone to the guard – Leo, according to his texts – with a flirty smile after an hour, and he'd seemed to accept that he had dropped it. Having downloaded some software that would obliterate their search history, they were confident the thug would be none the wiser.

If they thought they could risk it, they would have hung onto it for longer, but an hour was enough for their purposes. They'd Googled the life out of 'Jo Howe', 'Chief Superintendent Howe', 'Joanne Howe' and dozens of other permutations.

This was one feisty woman who surely deserved an award for bravery after what she'd done the previous year. They struggled to find out where she lived but they thought they had enough to track her down.

They settled on a plan, the only remaining detail being who would execute it. Both thought the other should as, if it was successful, it would bring that person freedom. For the one remaining – well, they dared not speculate.

In the end, despite the fact she had still not recovered from her injuries, Ajee persuaded Farah she should be the one. They'd used the phone to scope the local area and discover where they might find help or, at least, somewhere to hide. They plumped for Brightside Haven, *The UK's foremost support and refuge service for survivors of human trafficking and modern slavery*, if their website was to be believed.

They'd scoured Leo's messages and worked out who his shift partner was: Vlad. It was pure fortune that they'd been so chatty about their night shifts and how they shared sleep times.

Tonight seemed as good a time as any. It was now or a lifetime of rape and exploitation for the pair of them. Ajee prayed for forgiveness for what she was about to do and tried to fight the repulsion it would bring. Long after dark, they hugged and wished each other *Allah Yehmeek*. Ajee removed her bra and made sure her T-shirt hugged her contours.

'Guard, I need the bathroom,' called Ajee, praying the guard who came was Leo who they'd learnt so much about, and that Vlad didn't wake up. Farah pretended to sleep as the door swung open, keys still in the lock.

'Quickly,' said Leo, whom Ajee was sure must have been sleeping too.

'So sorry,' she said as she squeezed past him, deliberately brushing his arm with her breasts, but closing her eyes in self-disgust. 'I hope I didn't wake you,' she said.

She stepped into the bathroom opposite, leaving the door ajar. She left it a few seconds then squealed out, 'Get it out!' before darting back out into the corridor.

She grabbed Leo by his hand and pulled him towards the bathroom. 'A spider.' She didn't have to fake shaking with fear.

'For God's sake,' said Leo as he surrendered to her pulling him. When he was in and clear of the door, Ajee threw herself back, pointing. 'In the sink.'

Leo moved forward to check. 'There's nothing there.'

When he turned round, Ajee had already taken off her T-shirt and was blocking his exit. She hoped he'd presume her shivering was due to the cold. 'Silly me. How can I repay you?' she said, forcing a smile.

He looked her up and down and she could see him flush. 'Shshsh,' she whispered and stepped forward to take his right hand, then cupped it over her naked left breast. 'Nice and quiet.'

She girded herself for the one thing she would never do with the rapists sent to her room. Holding his palm against her, with her free hand she reached up and pulled his head towards hers, opened her mouth and, forcing down the bile, kissed him.

After about thirty seconds, Ajee heard the faintest chink of metal on metal coming from the hallway. Terrified that he would hear too, she broke from the kiss, turned his head and whispered all the things she would let him do to her.

She knew Farah was agile, even with her wounds, so *inshallah* wouldn't need long to escape. Ajee could only keep up the disgusting pretence so long and calculated that she need only spin this out for a couple more minutes before she could invoke her exit plan.

Happy that all was now quiet, she kissed Leo for what she hoped would be the last time, feeling the growing bulge through his trousers. She slowly turned him round so his back was against the sink and hers towards the toilet. As she did so, she glanced at the metal toilet brush stand and gauged the movement she'd need to do what was necessary.

The circling made it easy, that and the fact Leo had just one thing on his mind. Once she was in the right position, she swung out her left leg and clattered the stainless-steel accessory onto the stone tiled floor, making an ear-splitting clang.

Ajee broke off, feigned panic in her eyes. 'I'm so sorry. Forgive me please.'

Leo looked startled for a second then started to pull Ajee back towards him. Her heart pitched; she couldn't go through with this.

Then, Allah answered her prayers. 'You OK up there?' came a sleepy but resonant call.

'Yes, all fine,' replied the guard, as he pushed Ajee back and made for the door.

'I so sorry,' mouthed Ajee, as she put her shirt back on and edged past him, back to the room. She glanced down and the keys were still there. She prayed Farah was not. Leo slammed and locked the bedroom door.

Relief surged through Ajee as she saw she was alone. She darted to the window, checked it was shut and hoped no one would notice it was no longer locked.

Alone, she collapsed on the floor and wept. For Farah and her freedom, and in terror of what they would do to her.

As police funerals went, Faisal's was just about the worst Bob could ever have imagined. The Islamic rites themselves were dignified, beautiful in fact. But it was the utter grief and devastation of Faisal's wife, children, parents and siblings that did it for him. He hadn't known the DCI that well but, after hearing all the incredible testimonies of what an honourable and good man he was, Bob wished he had.

Jo had been there too and he'd intended to catch up with her, but he spotted her dodging Stuart Acers and her body language yelled that they shouldn't be seen together.

On his way back from Southampton, his phone rang. Nigel Hughes. He tapped 'accept' on the steering wheel.

'Hi, Nigel, I'm driving.'

'Yes, sorry boss. I won't keep you long. Just to say, could you pop in and see me when you get back? You are coming back, aren't you?'

'No, I thought I'd nip on the Isle of Wight ferry and grab a few days away! Of course I am. What's it about?'

'I'll tell you the details when you get here but, as a teaser, there's some very interesting movement on Expede's accounts. Jake Briers is joining us too. Also, there's been three more deaths in care homes overnight. Certified by?'

'Dr Harper?'

'Congratulations, you've beaten the Chaser.'

'How the hell is he getting away with it? Post Shipman, this shouldn't be happening. I'll be there the second I can.' Bob pressed 'end call', and tossed around hypotheses of what, if anything, this could mean.

* * *

Two hours later, Bob, Nigel and Jake were gathered round the conference table in the SIO office.

'Jake, you go first,' said Bob.

'Over the last twenty-four hours, we've had three deaths. All exactly the same profile as before. New residents, DNACPR signed by Harper, then what would otherwise be seen as natural deaths.'

'I thought Harper's bail conditions forbade him from attending any care home?' said Nigel.

Jake and Bob looked at one another. 'They did, but he appealed that on the grounds that it would cause undue suffering to the residents,' said Bob.

'What, the residents he's systematically killing?' said Nigel.

Bob shook his head in despair. 'Tell me about the residents,' he said.

'They all arrived at the three homes over the last week.'

'Causes of death?'

'One choking and two heart failures. Deaths all certified by Dr Harper. They're being reviewed by an independent doctor as per the Shipman rules.'

'Truly independent this time?'

'Yep, out of area,' said Jake.

'Are we arranging forensic post-mortems?' Bob asked Jake.

'Yes boss. Should be tomorrow.'

'Fine,' said Bob. 'Keep me updated.' He looked at Nigel. 'And the accounts?'

'Well, they've been pretty dormant for the last few weeks. But, over the last forty-eight hours, we're seeing huge influxes of cash, some we are pretty certain relate to the deaths Jake's investigating, but some from elsewhere in the country too. I'm onto the relevant forces to see if there are any similar trends. But, we are also seeing significant withdrawals. It's taking a bit of effort to follow it all, but we think we've found a link to groups who've supplied nitromethane and potassium chlorate in the past.'

Jake looked puzzled.

'Both of those are chemicals on the government's list of regulated substances. You need an explosives precursors and poisons licence to even possess them, let alone buy them,' said Nigel.

Jake's brow furrowed.

'They're used for making bombs.'

As soon as Leo and Vlad found out that Farah had escaped, Ajee had prayed for death.

First of all, Leo finished what she'd started and Vlad joined in when he'd finished. Both would suffer gravely for allowing Farah to run off, so they seemed to have decided to take what they could before whatever punishment awaited them.

Next, she was left cuffed – wrist and ankles – naked and freezing in a bare room next to the one she and Farah had slept in. She lay on the bare floorboards, her ear to the wood, straining to pick up any words or movement from downstairs.

By the time they came, she was gagging with thirst and, despite the fear in her belly, ravenous. But she'd known better than to call out. The same when she had been desperate for the toilet, and the faeces in which she was now sitting obliterated any remaining dignity.

Suzanne and the man whom she'd discovered was called Leigh simultaneously gagged when they opened the door.

'Get her cleaned up,' Leigh shouted down the hallway.

Straight away, Leo hobbled in. His face was bloodied, bruised and swollen, almost as much as Farah's had been, and his left fingers were roughly bandaged together. Using his good hand, he grabbed Ajee by the arm and dragged her along the floor to the bathroom. Suzanne and Leigh said nothing, just watched in disgust.

Leo flung her in the bath, then turned the cold shower on her. 'Scrub it off. All of it,' he said as he deliberately sprayed it in her face every time she went to speak. When he deemed her clean enough, he turned the water off and threw a threadbare hand towel in her direction. 'Dry yourself, you whore,' he grunted.

'Hurry up in there,' came Leigh's voice, stopping the guard in his tracks.

'This isn't fucking over,' Leo hissed as he dragged her out of the bath and back to the room.

'Cover her up,' Suzanne insisted, and Leo went next door, returning with a coarse blue blanket which he dropped in front of her. She looked at it, then up at Leigh, moving her cuffed hands towards him so he'd get the message.

'Cut the ties,' he ordered. 'She ain't going anywhere.' Leo did as he was told and Ajee grabbed the rotten blanket and wrapped it round her, a fig leaf against the cold and shame.

Leigh started. 'The next time you open your mouth will be to tell us where the fuck that other bitch has gone.'

Ajee stared him down. 'Farah.'

'What?'

'Farah. She has a name. Call her by her name.'

This wrong-footed Leigh for a moment – then, to Ajee's surprise, he relented. 'Where's Farah?'

Small victories.

'I don't know. I come back from the bathroom and she gone.' Leo reddened and turned away.

Suzanne looked between him and Ajee. 'What's going on?'

Ajee shrugged.

'Never mind that, we've lost an asset and we need her back. Not to mention the breach in security in having one of our scum running around talking to God knows who. Don't tell me you didn't plan this together. Where is she?'

'I don't know,' Ajee insisted, and it was true. At that particular moment, she had no idea where her new friend was, but she knew roughly where she was heading.

The interrogation continued for around two hours. Throughout,

Suzanne stood motionless, and only nodded or shook her head in approval or otherwise at whatever violation the men decided on.

Despite the ferocity of the beatings, Ajee drew strength from this small sign that they wanted to keep her alive. The only thing that troubled her about that was why.

40

Jo was serious about volunteering.

Despite the criminal charges being dropped, there was still the small matter of the misconduct allegations. And there seemed no way that Acers would rescind her suspension whilst the sun rose in the east.

The fact was that she was scared. Scared of what was being conspired around her. Scared that someone, probably Doughty or Parfitt – or both – was waging a war against her family. Scared that she would lose her job.

The hours snowballed into days. She just sat at home stewing over the past horrors, how she was still failing so many families and, most worrying of all, what the future might hold. Could she carry on? She was wary of calling Gary or Bob, two of the only people she could trust, because of the risk of igniting their careers on the embers of hers. Darren and the boys were great when they were home, but they'd soon tire of her moping around.

She definitely needed something to occupy her brain before it withered. There were plenty of care homes in walking distance – she still hadn't collected the car and wouldn't until the council admitted fault – but she couldn't be sure which were run by Maximus. Walk into the wrong one and she'd be rumbled straight away.

Her thoughts turned to Ajee, and that lovely girl before her. What was her name? Something beginning with F. Or was it S? Then what Neela had told Bob. And she thought her life was bad.

When she'd been on secondment to Liberia, helping build an ethical and accountable police force, she took pride in actually doing something about the atrocities the world witnessed on their televisions rather than sitting idly by.

On that thought, she abandoned the washing up and Googled 'Trafficking charities near me'. Aside from the half a dozen that weren't anywhere near her, even by the most optimistic cabbie's definition, she was drawn to Brightside Haven. *The UK's foremost support and refuge service for survivors of human trafficking and modern slavery.*

Clicking the link, then *About us*, she found that they had only started up in 2016, and their mission chimed perfectly with what she felt was crucial: *To provide long-term, safe, restorative environments for human trafficking and slavery survivors.*

That was it in a nutshell, and the fact they were based in Dyke Road, Brighton nailed it.

She clicked on the *Volunteer* link and completed the online form, which was scant to the extreme.

Rather than putting the laptop aside, she spent the next hour researching human trafficking and was surprised how little she, a professional police officer, knew. A total of 40.3 million people worldwide were in modern slavery, and 24.9 million in forced labour. On top of that, 4.8 million people were victims of forced sexual exploitation.

She dropped back in her chair, the enormity of the problem winding her. Then her phone rang.

'Jo Howe.'

'Ah, Mrs Howe, this is Carrie Allen from Brightside Haven. You've applied to volunteer with us?'

'Wow. That was quick. Yes, I did.'

'This is a global emergency,' replied Carrie. 'There really is no time to waste.'

Jo smirked. 'Yes, I'm sorry, it's just . . . Well, I'm so glad you called me back and I'm happy to help any way I can.'

'It's not as simple as that. These people we rescue and support are the most vulnerable you'll come across. We don't take just anyone, you know.'

'Very wise,' Jo replied.

'Before I ask you to interview, would you be good enough to tell me a bit about yourself?'

Jo thought about lying for a moment, but she really wanted to do this. And, in any case, she was so well known in the city, especially since the arrest, she doubted she'd be lucky to stay anonymous twice. She cantered through her CV and interests.

Once she'd finished, Carrie Allen said nothing. 'Hello, are you there?' checked Jo.

'Yes, yes. I'm sorry, it's just not every day we have senior police officers offering to volunteer.'

'Do I get an interview then?'

Ms Allen cleared her throat. 'Well, yes I think so. Please understand though that we like to carry those out at our applicants' homes. I'll be straight with you; we've had some people try to infiltrate us in the past. We find that visiting people at home gives us a . . . well, let's just say we get a clearer picture of the sort of person we are taking on. You understand?'

'More than most, I think Ms Allen.'

'Oh, please call me Carrie.'

'Thank you. I suspect also, *Carrie*, you're rather reluctant for people to see your offices until you're sure.'

'Quite. Quite.' Jo could almost see the grin in her voice. 'I think we are going to get on very well, Mrs Howe.'

'Oh, please call me Jo.'

Carrie chuckled. 'OK. *Jo*. When are you available? I could come round this afternoon if it suits you.'

'That would be perfect. If you could make it before two-thirty though. I have the school run and then this house becomes a war zone. Oh God, I'm so sorry, that was most inappropriate.'

Carrie belly-laughed this time. 'Jo, I'm very much looking forward to working with you.'

'Subject to interview and vetting, surely.'

'Absolutely. Subject to those. See you at two o'clock.'

'Looking forward to it,' said Jo. 'I'll put the kettle on.'

41

The barman at the Plough, in Pyecombe, looked nonplussed when Tom handed over a £10 note for the two pints. Nowadays almost everyone paid contactless.

'Something wrong with that?' he said.

'Er, no, not at all, sir. I'll get your change.'

The lad returned with a handful of coins which Doughty promptly slotted into the Royal British Legion charity box, inwardly scowling at the Refugee Crisis one.

'Fucking students,' he mumbled as he returned to the corner table where Leigh was sitting tapping at his phone.

'You might as well be dressed as a wandering minstrel playing the lute,' said Leigh.

'What?'

'You can't go anywhere without making a show of yourself. The less we do to be remembered, the better. That's how it works.'

Tom grunted. 'Can you fucking—'

'There you go again, keep your voice down.' Leigh sipped his beer.

Tom lowered his volume but not his ire. 'Can you believe Acers had that bloody Jo Howe in the palm of his hands and then released her?'

'Strictly speaking that wasn't his decision, but I get the point. Why are you so worried about her?'

Tom leant in closer. 'Because she's the only one we can't manipulate. Acers is a piece of piss. As soon as we dangled those kids in front of him, he's on the hook. We snapped him again the other day. Gary

Hedges is old school. Put him in a fist fight and he'll come out on top. But he's weak. Malleable. He's too thick to work out when he's being had.'

'And Howe?'

'She's probably the cleverest, wiliest cop I've met. Outwardly she's all sweetness and light. Even plays the dumb woman when it suits her. But that's an act. We misjudge her at our peril. Look at her now. She's suspended, been arrested and outwardly fucked, but she's still there. Digging away, causing us problems.'

'How do you know? She stopped some traffic, that's all.'

'Trust me,' said Doughty.

Both men paused as a family of four pushed past to the restaurant area, the one with the huge 'Birthday Girl' and '9 Today' badges skipping ahead, the mum, dad and grumpy teenage boy glued to his phone bringing up the rear.

'If she's that much of a problem, we need to deal with her,' said Leigh.

'You were supposed to do that last time,' said Tom.

'We've had this discussion. With more timing, we would have come up with something better.'

'If we can, we should have another go, but only,' he paused for effect, 'only if we can do it in a way that doesn't bring more scrutiny. We've already got them crawling around the care homes and getting close to your fiasco with the gyppos.'

Leigh looked down.

'And it won't take them long to link the crash to their prison visit. I can't have what's coming buggered up by revenge.'

'That's good to hear. Keep your eye on the prize. I've lost too many good men chasing officers' petty reprisals.'

Just then the door opened and a man of indeterminate age, average height, average build, average everything, walked in. Tom didn't give him a second glance until he shook Leigh's hand.

'Leigh.'

'Jimmy, great to see you. This is Tom. He's the governor.' Jimmy nodded in Doughty's direction.

'Get you a pint?' said Tom. If this was the ex-SAS ordnance and logistics expert and the best the British Army could muster, it was a wonder the country won any wars.

'Pint of Harvey's.'

His accent was as nondescript as the rest of him, yet Leigh had mentioned the best bloke was a Scouser. Jimmy better not be second choice.

Tom went to the bar, paid by card and came back. As he arrived at the table, the two military men stopped talking. He put the beer down in front of Jimmy and was about to talk when Leigh interjected.

'This is the bloke I was telling you about,' he said.

'You sure?' said Tom. He turned briefly to Jimmy. 'No offence mate, but he said you were,' he lowered his voice, 'ex-special forces.' He looked him up and down.

Jimmy went to stand up, but Leigh stopped him. 'Is this bloke some fucking joke?' he said to Leigh, then turned to Tom. 'You either want me or you don't. Your choice.'

'Jimmy, it's OK. He's got a lot on his plate.' Leigh scowled at Tom. 'You not believing he could stand up in a stiff breeze is exactly the point. No one notices people like Jimmy. No one would be able to describe him let alone suspect him after the op.'

Leigh was right; he'd heard before that the best soldiers hid in plain sight. But Tom was still not sure.

'You said he was a Scouser. He's as Brighton as you.'

Jimmy raised his eyes to the ceiling and said nothing.

'If he's in Brighton, he sounds Brighton. If he's in Newcastle, he's a Geordie. Belfast, he's from there. If it's Afghan, he's pure Taliban.'

Tom stared at Jimmy, totally bewildered. 'Let's talk business.'

42

As day broke, Farah cowered in the abandoned shepherd's hut, battling the wisdom of returning to Brighton. Anywhere else would have provided her with the cloak of anonymity and, *inshallah*, no one would be looking for her. They'd be looking for her here though.

But she'd made a promise and she'd never go back on that. Anyway, each time she wavered she imagined what Ajee was going through, and she owed it to that woman to save her. Her photographic memory had saved her many times during her exodus to England and now she would rely on it to spot faces in crowds before they spotted her. Her life depended on it.

As she emerged into the crisp morning air, she blinked at the bright sunlight. How could a country have such beautiful skies, yet its people be so cold, she wondered. Her eyes focused and she took in the Brighton and Hove skyline. The TV mast on the hill to her left. The azure sea with white crests ahead. The sails of the wind farm far on the horizon and the bizarre pole with a saucer sliding up and down, incongruous to its surroundings yet dominating.

She wondered if this was how a warlord felt as he readied his troops for the final push. She could certainly do with an army by her side now.

She was thankful to whoever had ignored the *Do Not Leave Donations Here* sign outside the hospice charity shop she passed in a place called Hassocks yesterday. Some of the bags' contents were frankly an insult, but the black puffer jacket and Adidas trainers were a perfect fit and just what she needed for warmth and speed.

Finally, she could ditch her moccasins.

Wrapping the coat around herself, she surveyed the landscape between her and the city and worked out her best approach. She'd managed to flee across deserts and battle zones before, so navigating a few South Downs footpaths whilst dodging unnecessary crowds should be a doddle.

She knew all about not drawing attention to herself, so worried that her wild hair might stand out after two days on the run, she'd carefully pulled out the cord from the shoes she discarded and used that to tame it into a tight ponytail.

Meandering along the bridleways, past what looked like a marble-domed Sikh memorial, Farah avoided overly curious cattle and sheep, eventually reaching a brow. Beneath her was a caravan site. She counted the burnt-out skeletons of four mobile homes, the ground around them scorched like a ransacked village. Elsewhere children played and open-back trucks came and went. Unsure of the reception a strange girl from a foreign land would receive, she skirted the area and, using her natural sense of direction, weaved her way into the city centre, hopefully unnoticed.

Now the hard work began. She had three missions and had no idea whether she'd achieve any of them. One, find Brightside Haven and get help. Two, find Chief Superintendent Joanne Howe and get her to put a stop to the horror she, Ajee and all the others were living. Three, don't get caught.

She was used to living on her wits so those, and Allah, would guide her. But one thing was for sure: she'd rather die than go back to the mercy of those men. And she'd kill to make sure she wouldn't.

Jo was sure that Carrie Allen would forgive the mess. To her mind there was nothing that pointed more to a suppressed upbringing than children whose home was immaculately sterile. But that didn't stop her whirling round cramming toys, games and clothes into every cubbyhole to feign order.

At 2 p.m. on the dot, the doorbell rang. One last check in the mirror, then Jo ambled to let Carrie in.

'Lovely to see you,' she said, a little too loudly. 'Do come in.'

'Thank you for inviting me at such short notice. I was so excited when we spoke and, like I said, volunteers of your calibre don't crop up every day.'

Jo brushed that off with the nervous giggle that infuriated Darren. *Take the bloody compliment*, he'd say.

Once drinks had been offered, made and served, the two women sat opposite each other in the lounge.

Carrie was not as Jo had imagined on the phone. Her plummy inflection suggested a mid-fifties, twinset-and-pearls blue-rinser. She should have known better. This was Brighton. She was a good few years younger and her flourish of blonde hair, satin skin and high cheekbones, together with her pastel lemon summer dress patterned with pink roses gave her the look of a Hollywood film star. Not your typical charity worker, thought Jo then scolded herself for stereotyping.

As her guest sipped her tulsi tea, Jo watched nervously. She couldn't remember when she'd been gifted the box of herbal infusions, nor whether they had a use-by date – she dared not check – but was just grateful she'd not decluttered the kitchen over the last two years or so. To her relief, Carrie didn't wince.

'I appreciate your availability may be temporary. For your sake I hope it is. Not for ours though.'

Jo sniggered at that.

'But, if I tell you a little about the charity, maybe we could discuss where you might fit in.'

'Yes, of course.'

'As you have no doubt seen on our website, we were founded in late 2016 and, whilst we are based here in Brighton, our reach is much wider. Our aim is to provide a safe refuge for women, and men, who find themselves trafficked into the UK and/or trapped into forced labour. The prejudice and discrimination these poor people suffer is frankly disgraceful – a blot on our privileged culture. What they have been through to get here is unimaginable. Our aim is to help them heal, settle and hopefully build a new life.'

'That sounds incredibly ambitious. You must have support from so many quarters. I mean, healthcare, counselling, legal services to name but three. Where do you house the people you help?'

'Let's just say, our volunteers bring a variety of skills and help in different ways. I can't divulge exactly where we have lodgings but there are some very generous people in the city with more houseroom than they need.' Carrie pointedly cast her eyes around the room.

'Oh, I don't think I could take anyone in here, if that's what you were . . .'

'No, no, I wasn't thinking that for one minute,' she answered – although her expression said she absolutely was.

'I'm afraid I'm not a doctor, nurse, psychiatrist. Nothing like that. But I suppose I do know a little about criminal law, particularly how we, I mean the police, operate. And I can do the basics too. Talk to people, make them feel they matter and, feel free to correct me, make a passable cup of tea.'

Carrie's smile gave nothing away.

'Certainly your knowledge and background are areas we are lacking at the moment. So many of our clients come from countries where the last people they can trust are the police. I've lost count of the number of stories I've heard of beatings, corruption, people just disappearing and summary executions. Despite what the tabloids would have us believe, we really do have the most compassionate police service in the world.'

Jo did not mention the most recent chief constables.

'I've seen that first-hand over the years,' said Jo. 'People come here and their ingrained mistrust of us not only makes our life all the more difficult, it puts them in danger too. Just everyday things like trying to convince a woman whose husband beats and rapes her to come with us to a safe haven, or convincing a runaway child that we won't return them to their impending forced marriage, is nigh on impossible.'

'Precisely. Listen, I know you are short of time so let's cut to the chase. You'll not be surprised that I have used the time since we spoke on the telephone to carry out some due diligence and, having met you, I can tell you're genuine. I've spoken to the trustees and we are all agreed we'd love you to join us. We were thinking you could go out with our street teams, you know, literally finding people to take in as well as being available during the debriefing stage to provide specialist advice and reassurance.'

Jo thought for a moment. She realised she didn't have a picture of exactly what she wanted to do and this felt like a huge commitment. But Carrie made a compelling case and there was no doubt the service Brightside Haven provided was sorely needed. And, for now, the one thing she had was time. She might even find Ajee.

'I accept,' she said, with a beaming smile. She stood up, her code for any meeting being drawn to a close. Carrie took the hint.

'That's amazing. Thank you so much. We'll be in touch with the arrangements but please, remember, this is voluntary so don't feel pressure to take on any more than you're able. Any help you can offer will be incredible.'

'Thank you. I'll remember that,' said Jo as she shook Carrie's hand. 'I'm really looking forward to working with you.'

Jo checked her watch as she watched her new friend stride down the drive. Time to dash across the park to pick the boys up.

43

Doughty had insisted on meeting Parfitt at the chief executive's house. He knew he was taking liberties but, if anyone was becoming suspicious, it was known that the pair often worked there so hopefully that wouldn't add to their misgivings. And with Heather and the children out, he knew they wouldn't be overheard.

His trust in his right-hand man was gushing away and he knew that, before long, he would have to irrevocably break their bond.

'Right,' he said, glaring at Parfitt. 'I need you to free up some more funds.'

'It's not that easy, you know.'

Doughty glared at him.

'I mean it can be done, of course it can.'

'Good.'

'But we have to be careful. I'm sure no one is onto us but if they are, the unusual patterns of money coming in and withdrawals is what they'll pick up on. Expede's spending has been all but dormant for months. The money from the care homes has been steady and unremarkable, but over the last few weeks we've hoisted a massive red flag.'

Every syllable that Russ uttered wound Tom up even tighter. He was forever finding reasons not to do things, rather than making them happen. He'd honestly thought that the scare they'd given him about his wife and kids would have brought him back on side, but it seemed to have had the opposite effect.

'Now listen. Your job in all this is to make sure the finances and the infrastructure are in place. That's all. When this thing goes off, you'll be nowhere near, so just do as you're asked. I don't want to hear what *might* go wrong or who *might* find out. Just make sure none of this comes back to us.' He held Russ's gaze.

'You keep saying "this" and "it" but you refuse to tell me what *it* is. I mean, don't I have a right to know?'

'No, you don't. It will be safer all round that way.'

Tom could tell this wounded Russ. And he was glad.

'You don't trust me? Is that what all this prevarication is about?' said Russ.

'Honestly? No I don't. I think all this is getting too heavy for you. The pikeys. The copper at the mosque. That twat in the prison. The Paki cop. Am I right?'

Russ waited for a beat too long. 'Not at all. It's all means to an end, right?'

'It is but, if you can't stomach that, you'll become a liability if you find out what the main event is. All you need to know is that it will swing public opinion right on our side. I promise you.'

Sweat broke out on Russ's top lip, further evidence of him being a weak link. Ever since he'd met Jimmy, the special forces guy, Tom had realised the mentality needed to pull this off. Clear, unswerving loyalty to the mission, driven by a heart of ice. Russ had neither of those, and why should he? Sure, he espoused the same values as Tom, but he was a desk jockey. A bureaucrat. The toughest battles he'd fought had been over points of order in the council chamber. He'd need to be dealt with soon but for now he served a purpose. Once that was out of the way, he'd have to go.

'Don't worry, Russ. No one but me and a couple others know the whole plan. It's huge and too many people knowing what they don't need to risks everything – but we'll all benefit. Others don't know what you're doing and that's to protect you all. Just do what you've been asked to and wait to be told what you need to know. Soon it will all be over, and we can all get on with an incredible new life.'

Tom forgave himself that last fib.

* * *

266

Putting the phone down, Acers sat alone in his office pondering how to extricate himself from Doughty and his threats, yet knowing he never could. He'd been told to wait for another call, so that's all he could do.

Each time he thought he'd found an escape hatch, it was padlocked. All in all, he thought he was a good chief constable, and a pretty decent human being too. Sure, he liked younger girls, but not kids. Never kids. And who was to say what a child was, anyway? He'd read somewhere that across the world the age of consent varied between eleven and twenty-one. And he'd never go with an eleven-year-old.

Not knowingly, anyway.

He knew he'd been foolish to visit a place that he'd not checked out. It was recommended, for sure, but maybe he shouldn't trust those online forums so readily. He'd never prove the girl he was photographed with was over sixteen, and he doubted anyone could prove she wasn't. But who needed proof these days? Bloody social media just needed 280 poisonous characters and that was you convicted in the court of public outrage. And there was no appeal.

He gazed out at the white chalk face of Malling Down and the River Ouse that snaked through the County Town of East Sussex. Some days he managed to stay positive; others, like today, he weighed up whether it would be less painless to throw himself off that cliff or into the murky water.

He keyed at his laptop, not for the first time researching whether there was any way he could reverse Gary Hedges' decision to release Jo Howe without charge. Sure, it was petty to order her arrest in the first place and she'd probably be acquitted – if it ever got that far – but at least having criminal charges hanging over her, trivial as they were, would appease Doughty for a while, keep her suspended and strengthen his position.

His phone jolted him. Looking at the screen, he breathed a sigh of relief. Bill Sansom, the prison governor.

'Bill, how's it going?'

'Morning, Stuart. Not so bad, you?'

'Had better days, had worse,' Acers lied. 'Listen, if it's about the murder enquiry, I'm a bit behind the curve of that just now. Can I call you back when I've found out the state of play?'

'It's not about that, Stu.'

He hated being called that. He swung his chair round subconsciously to face the prison. 'Oh!'

'Mate, we are releasing a prisoner on a home detention curfew tomorrow.'

'And you're telling me that, why exactly? I mean, that's like me saying we're dealing with a road crash.'

'Just listen.' Acers' brow furrowed at the change in tone. 'He's coming out for a specific purpose and there's something you need to do when he does.'

'Me?'

'Yes, you.'

'OK,' said Acers, stringing out the K. 'Who is he?'

'None of your business, but you do need to know what he's going to do. He's a hacker. Doing three years for infiltrating the Home Office intranet and changing immigration data in advance of the Brexit vote.'

'And?'

'And when he's out, he's got a specific task and you need to inject some intelligence into your own systems to move things along.'

'I can't just submit intel without a source and provenance. We have to show where it's come from and that it's reliable.'

'You'll find a way. Anyway, surely if it's about children at risk, thresholds must be lower.'

Acers felt like a woodpecker was hacking its way out of his chest. Was this about him?

'I need more.'

Sansom explained exactly what the hacker would do – on pain of recall to prison if he messed it up – and what Acers must do within a day of the release.

He gulped. 'And if I refuse?'

Sansom laughed. 'Stu, you won't. I've seen the photos and if they get out, I can't exactly promise you the warmest of welcomes in my little hotel here.'

'What photos?'

'Don't take the piss. You know what photos, just as you know how they got to that DCI's car. Just do as you're told and everything will be fine. Don't let us down.'

'Us?'

'Us. Despite you being an obnoxious nonce, I quite like you. I'd hate to see you in general population on B Wing. They're really not very nice up there.'

The phone went dead, along with any trace of hope Acers had of getting out of this.

44

Jo didn't know why she was surprised to have been invited for her first shift so soon, nor that it was during the day, but she was.

The speed with which Carrie had responded to her application, then interviewed her, should have been a sign that Brightside Haven didn't mess about. She was surprised that, despite her credentials, the vetting wasn't more thorough. Was she being paranoid? Then again, this was a voluntary set-up and perhaps they just didn't do bureaucracy – certainly not with the obsession of the police, anyway.

As Jo walked to the Clock Tower to meet Nadia, her mentor for the shift, she suddenly realised she had no idea who to look for. She had all sorts of stereotypes of what a Ukrainian refugee might look like, but this was Brighton, and she of all people knew you couldn't assume anyone's background or lifestyle from their appearance.

She was stood outside Leon Café, looking up at the imposing Victorian monument, when she heard a voice behind her. 'Jo?'

She turned round and saw a six-foot, rake-thin woman who, if Jo was pushed, she'd have put in her late twenties, but could just have easily been ten years older. Her black-and-pink New Balance running top and leggings and scrunched-back hair finished off her ultra-marathon look.

'Hello, you must be Nadia.'

'I am. It is lovely to meet you. It's so good to have more mature volunteers.' Nadia glanced Jo up and down. 'Some of the younger girls, they need a mother figure.' Jo didn't know whether to be offended or laugh out loud at her frankness. She chose a polite smile.

'And you. It's fabulous that you are able to show people that there is a way out.'

Nadia nodded. 'For some.'

Conscious of the lack of induction, as they walked down to the seafront, Jo probed Nadia as much as she could without appearing rude. She quickly learnt that daylight hours were the best time to find those who were in the UK illegally and trying to make ends meet.

'We might find a few begging with the homeless people, but most aren't,' said Nadia. 'Today, I take you round the places we find them, so you know.' She looked down at Jo's sandals.

'They no good,' she remarked.

'What's wrong with them?'

'You can't run in those. You need trainers. Like me.' She pointed at her own Nike Airs. 'Sometimes, the slave masters or their muscle, they chase us. We have to get away.'

That would be out of character. Throughout her whole working life it had been ingrained in her to run towards, rather than away from trouble, despite the toll that had brought on her. She figured she'd have to fight that instinct, otherwise she'd put Nadia in danger.

'Wait there, I'll get some.' Ten minutes later, Jo emerged from Sports Direct with a pair of cheap but perfectly functional trainers on her feet and her discarded sandals tucked in her bag. Nadia nodded her approval then took Jo on a tour of the city she thought she knew so well. Seeing it through an ex-slave's eyes was profound.

They weaved their way around the backs of the hotels and restaurants that edged the coast road. Nadia seemed to sense when it was safe to approach the stinking yards which served as delivery bays, and they often saw groups of emaciated, filthy men and women bunched together sharing cigarettes or just muttering in foreign languages. More often than not a man stood menacingly between them and the exit.

What shocked Jo more than seeing these pathetic souls' pitiful existence was that they were not just behind the fried chicken or kebab shops, but the £500-plus per night hotels and the restaurants where you needed a reference to book.

How many times had she and Darren been inadvertently fed or served by one of these impoverished people? She felt sickened.

'What do we do about them?' Jo asked, desperate for her warrant card back.

'Nothing for now. We take note, we gather information then, when we can, we try to rescue one or two. But it's very dangerous. We have to plan.'

'But look at them. How can we leave them like this?'

'Jo, you must understand. If we run in, that will be no good to anyone.'

'But . . .'

'No. Come, we must move before we are seen.'

From there, Nadia took Jo along West Street, Brighton's nightlife-central. She pointed out bar workers, security staff and charity canvassers; all, she said, were in some form of slavery. Next, they walked up Queen's Road towards the railway station and meandered round the streets that led off it.

'I've never noticed so many nail bars,' Jo said to her shame.

'Many have slaves. They live in the back, work for their food and rent. Sometimes twelve hours a day. One day we will rescue them. One day.'

As they crossed the junction outside the station, a horn sounded and Nadia pulled the bewildered Jo back on the pavement, narrowly saving her from the front wheels of a GB Nextday Deliveries van. 'Careful,' she said. 'We don't want them to kill you before you save them.'

'What do you mean?'

'You shop online?'

'Doesn't everyone?'

'How do you think they deliver so cheap?'

Jo stared at the disappearing van. 'You're kidding me.'

Nadia shook her head. 'Even them.'

'My dear,' came a refined voice behind them.

Both women looked round and, straight away, Nadia embraced the immaculately dressed man, who could easily have been her father. He looked like one of those retired city-folk who never quite managed to divest themselves of the starch and shine of their former lives.

'George, how lovely to see you. Jo, this is George. He's one of our volunteers. George, meet Jo. She's new so I'm just showing her the sights.'

'How lovely to meet you. It's so heartening to know some people still care enough to give up their time.'

'Nice to meet you too,' said Jo, trying not to be shocked that he too didn't fit her stereotype.

'George, he's very generous man. He helps the homeless people who have nowhere to go. He find safe places for them.'

'Really,' said Jo, remembering Neela's interview.

George laughed. 'One does what one can. I'm sure you understand, Jo.'

'I'm certainly beginning to,' she replied, watching the glint briefly vanish from George's eyes.

'Good, good,' he muttered. 'Anyway, I must dash. Take care, both of you.'

As he marched off, Nadia looked puzzled. 'How strange, I usually can't get rid of him.'

'Maybe I was cramping your style,' offered Jo.

When Doughty walked in, Leigh and Jimmy were sitting at the table. He almost checked his shoe for dog shit, such was the look they gave him.

He was glad they were no longer using any flat linked to him. Jimmy had ready access to a network of safe houses around the country and it just so happened one of those was in Burgess Hill, a stone's throw from Brighton.

It was the most basic of apartments. One bedroom, a lounge with a kitchenette in the corner opposite the transom window and a toilet/bathroom. No shower. The decor would have been sneered at even in the 1970s and the boiler trickled out hot water as and when it fancied.

Leigh commuted there each day, varying his mode of transport between train, bus and car – never by a direct route.

'Do you have to keep coming up here?' said Leigh. 'I told you, we'd let you know when there was an update. And guess what, there's no fucking update.'

'I need to know how it's all going. Have you found a carrier yet?'

'One thing at a time,' said Leigh.

Doughty ran his fingers through his hair. He was all too aware that he'd encroached into their world, but finding the right mule in time was pretty critical to make the whole operation a success and misdirect the gullible public.

'Look, just stop what you're doing.'

They both looked at each other, shared a shake of the head and turned to face Doughty. He was the paymaster, after all.

'We've got just under two weeks. There's no slippage on that. If this doesn't happen on Saturday week, it doesn't happen at all. Not for another year anyway, and none of us know where we'll be then. I know you think I'm panicking but having the gear in place is not enough.'

'We have done this sort of thing before, you know,' said Jimmy.

Doughty hated to think what this vanilla soldier could do – had done – so he let his insolence go.

'I know that but, see it from my point of view. My whole career – my whole life – has led up to this. The pendulum has swung so far to the wokes, it's almost rotating. Natural superiority is being usurped to protect the feelings of the underclass. We pussyfoot around whilst others stamp all over our rights and traditions. If any of us ever stood against a black, disabled, jihadi or lesbian in an election or interview, we'd have no chance. Not because they are the better candidate – how could they be – but so no one gets offended. It's got so that normal people are too frightened to speak out. We can't help being white, hard-working, able-bodied, heterosexual men but we spend our lives apologising for who we are. We need to show the public what these people are really like; make them believe that jihad is alive and kicking.'

'Sermon over?' said Leigh.

'Look, what we are doing will make the doubters sit up and listen. It'll bring the majority together against an enemy in our midst. We cannot fail.'

'Clearly not,' mumbled Leigh. 'Look, let me play devil's advocate for a moment. We will be ready so don't worry about that. We are hardwired to deliver missions as per the brief and on time. And with the money you've promised us, we'd be mad not to. But, what if it all backfires?'

'How do you mean?'

'What if we do what you want, it's breaking news all over the world – and it will be – and it has the opposite effect? Targeting one group of marginalised people with another, well why will that make people come running to your side?'

'But they hate each other anyway, and people will see us as the only party who can stop the killing.'

'But you're hardly the party of moderation. How are you going to sell your new peace-loving credentials to an already petrified country?'

'Just leave the politics to me and find me a courier.'

'We've already thought of that,' revealed Jimmy.

'What? Who? Why didn't you say?' said Doughty.

'That's your problem. You're so busy planning nirvana you can't see what's under your nose. Or who.'

Doughty's mind raced. What were they talking about?'

'We've got just the person already and the last I saw she's going fucking nowhere.'

45

The insistent knock could only mean one thing. The cadence that said *We're not going away* struck terror into anyone who heard it and today it was Russ Parfitt's turn.

'Who the hell is that?' asked Heather as she sat bolt upright, instinctively covering herself with the duvet.

The bedside clock read 5.30 a.m. and Russ threw his legs out of bed, fixed on getting to the door before they woke the girls up. 'How the hell should I know?' he replied, although he instinctively did. Grabbing his dressing gown, he ran out onto the landing and took the stairs two at a time, calling, 'I'm coming, I'm coming.' He picked up the door keys from the letter table in the hall.

As he opened the front door, the scene that met him was straight off a TV drama. Front and centre was a detective he knew as Bob someone. He'd been all over the news last year when he was charged, then released, for killing a drug dealer. Next to him was a young detective, and in an arc behind them were four uniformed officers, encased in body armour and with enough equipment hanging off their belts to see them through SAS selection.

'Can I help you?' said Russ, reflecting that they were about to help themselves whatever he said.

'Mr Parfitt, I'm DI Heaton from Brighton and Hove Police and this is my colleague, DC Briers. We have a warrant to search this house. May we come in?'

'Can I say no?' he mumbled as he stood to one side.

'Not really,' said DC Briers, which seemed to annoy the DI.

'Who else is here?' asked Bob Heaton.

'Apart from the Massed Bands of the Household Cavalry, just me, the wife and my two little girls. What the hell's this about?'

'Mr Parfitt, this is serious. We are investigating an allegation that you have been downloading and distributing child abuse images. I need to tell you now that I'm arresting you for those offences,' Bob cautioned him.

'What the hell are you talking about?'

'All will be explained but, in the meantime, I have this warrant and we are going to search the premises and seize anything that might be evidence of an offence. Go with DC Briers, get your wife and daughters up and bring them downstairs.'

'I will not.'

'Your choice.' Heaton turned to the two burliest uniform officers. 'Could you go and get Mrs Parfitt and the children down here please?'

'No, no,' said Parfitt. 'You'll scare the life out of them.' He turned to Briers. 'This way.'

A few minutes later, Heather and the bleary-eyed girls walked down the stairs hand in hand.

'Daddy, what's happening?' said the eldest as she twiddled her toy rabbit in her free hand. 'What are these policemen doing here?'

Heather glared at Russ. 'Don't worry, darling. They just need to talk to Daddy. Mummy will look after you.' She grabbed the girls' hands and pulled them into the lounge. Briers followed and Bob waited until they were out of earshot.

'We've had some intelligence that you've been downloading child abuse images . . .' said Heaton.

'Kiddy porn, you mean.'

'We prefer "child abuse images". Kiddy porn rather makes light of babies being raped on camera, don't you think? Anyway, we are going to search the house and take away anything that is capable of holding data. So that's computer equipment, phones, tablets, memory devices. That sort of thing. Also, anything that might be evidence of the allegation, so financial records and the like.'

'You're bloody not,' bellowed Parfitt.

'We are, and for your children's sake, you might want to keep your voice down.'

'Don't you . . .'

Bob put his finger to his lips and, finally, Parfitt got the message.

'That's better. Your wife and children will be allowed to go to a friend or relative, but we'd be grateful if you stay and observe the search.'

'And if I don't want to?'

'You *are* under arrest so if you'd prefer not to stay – and the search will all be videoed – then we'll take you to custody and you can wait in a cell until we are ready to interview you.'

As the uniformed officers brought in handfuls of property bags, torches and tools, Briers led Heather and the girls from the lounge. It broke Russ's heart to see his daughters red-eyed and deliberately avoiding his gaze.

'They're just going to get dressed and then to Mrs Parfitt's sister's,' said the young officer.

Heaton turned to a woman sergeant. 'Diane, do you mind going with them?'

'That's hardly necessary,' said Heather.

'I'm afraid it is,' said Bob. 'You're not suspected of anything, but we can't have you taking anything that might be evidence with you. It's just procedure, I'm afraid.'

'For Christ's sake, Inspector, isn't there another way you could do this?' Parfitt demanded.

'Not really,' he replied. 'We'll be as quick as we can and cause as little disruption as possible, but these are serious matters and, well, you're a prominent person so we can't be seen to afford you special favours.'

Once Heather and the girls had left in tears, the search started in earnest. Russ followed the searchers round, with DC Briers by his side throughout. After the first room – his office – he'd given up complaining about how much they were taking and the mess they left. He'd not expected them to dismantle light switches and phone sockets and empty bins but, then again, he'd never been in this situation before.

It took four hours, once they'd gone through the outhouses, his car, and every inch of the house. The evidence bags piled up in the hallway to such an extent that he thought they'd call in a removals van to take them away.

'When will I get all this back? There's my life and my work on those devices.'

'When we've finished with them. As regards your work, given your position and the nature of the offences, we will have to inform the council, so I would imagine they'll suspend you.'

'You are joking,' said Parfitt. 'You'll find nothing on any of these, but you're quite happy to destroy my career, not to mention my marriage.'

Bob shrugged. 'We're done. We'll get this lot loaded up then we'll take you to custody. I'm assuming you'll behave yourself so we won't need to handcuff you?'

'Don't be ridiculous.'

It took a further half an hour for the bags to be removed and for Russ to satisfy himself that the house was secure.

'Ready,' he said before setting the alarm.

As he pulled on the door to check it was locked, a voice called out.

'Mr Parfitt, what are you under arrest for?'

He turned and found himself staring into the lens of a long-range camera, wedged between the railings.

'What the hell . . .' he sneered at Heaton, but could immediately tell that the bank of reporters were as much a shock to him as anyone.

'Russ, why are they taking your laptops?' said another voice as the cameras clicked.

'Get in the car,' said Heaton as he bundled Russ through the back door.

Briers started the engine and followed the marked vans out of the drive, the reporters flocking around the plain car.

'Get your head down if you want,' said Heaton.

'Not on your life. I've nothing to hide,' he replied.

'Let's hope for your sake that you're right,' said Bob as they accelerated towards the custody centre.

Unlike last time Farah had been on the streets of Brighton, now she was actively trying to find a police officer. Not just anyone: Jo Howe.

She'd spent the last four years finding food, transport, shelter, even traffickers, but each time she had a network of people in her position to draw on. This time, she had just her wits and the vaguest of local knowledge.

She sheltered from the rain under the park café's awning. It dawned on her that she had no idea whether this Howe woman would help or whether she'd be like all the rest and hand her over to the Border Force. Had she misjudged a few kind words at the care home? Then what would happen to Ajee?

She banished the negativity. This was their only hope though, and she were running out of time.

Just then, a convoy of trucks trundled into the park. Most were stacked with metal fencing, but others carried scaffolding and what looked like packed-up marquees. She couldn't stay here. Whatever this was about, the place would be crawling with workmen soon.

She went into the toilets, winced at the freezing water that spurted from the tap marked 'hot', but scrubbed her face and hands with it anyway. She sighed as she took in her dishevelled hair in the polished metal which served as a vandal-proof mirror. Tying it back up, she accepted that she was as presentable as she'd ever be, so set off.

In a city this size, she knew she'd have next to no chance of just bumping into Jo, so she decided she'd do what most people do. Turn to Mr Google.

The only trouble was she didn't have a phone, but that was easily solved.

She found a barely smoked cigarette surprisingly quickly. She wasn't a smoker, but this would be a tool of her trade. She picked it up, wiped off the grime then turned on her act.

Her mark was a young man who was busying himself unloading one of the smaller lorries, whilst multitasking on a phone call. She'd spotted him stamp out a cigarette a few seconds earlier. Waiting until he'd finished the call, she watched where he put the phone then flounced up to him, a huge smile lighting up her face.

'Eh, my darling? Do you have a light? I've lost mine and I'm gagging.'

The man looked round to check she was talking to him, then grinned back. 'Gagging are you?'

'Cheeky.' She waved the cigarette in his eyeline.

''Course I have, love,' he said, reaching into his left-hand pocket, the opposite one from where the phone was, and pulling out a grubby-looking orange Bic lighter.

Farah moved in close as he held it up to light it. She steadied the cigarette between her lips with her left hand, lightly touching the lad on his right hip. 'Oh I'm sorry, it won't light,' she said, moving in closer and swiftly dipping her hand in his pocket and out as she deliberately stumbled. 'Oh sorry. There you go, all lit. Thank you. Have a lovely day.' She winked as she slipped the phone in her puffer jacket.

'Be lucky, love,' he called after her.

'I have already been,' she mumbled to herself as she skipped across the park and away.

They'd left Ajee alone for the last day or so, but still there was no sign of her being taken back to the other house. She should have been relieved but, in some way, both things unnerved her. Her experience, from George chancing upon her when she was begging in Hove to now, was that nothing they did was without purpose, and it was never in kindness either.

Sleep was hard to come by, especially as she had no idea whether Farah had made it away safely. If she thought what had happened to her since the escape was bad, she hated to think of the punishment that would be meted out to Farah if she was caught.

Gazing out of the window to the field beyond, Ajee searched for the family of deer who often grazed and gambolled by the far hedge. To her, they were a metaphor for love and freedom. Two things she'd been promised when she came to England but had yet to find. In some ways the evil here was worse than in her homeland. At least you could argue those fighting in Syria believed in something, however misguided that was. Here, she was imprisoned, abused and commodified for money and money alone.

Just as she saw a movement in the distance, her door was flung open. Ajee spun round and self-consciously wrapped her robe tighter, seeing the man they called Leigh with another man she'd not seen before in the doorway.

Her fear must have flashed through her eyes as Leigh stepped forward, the other man remaining framed in the door. 'It's OK. No one's going to hurt you.'

'Why I believe you?'

'Good point, but from now on if my friend and I hear that anyone has laid a finger on you, they will answer to us.'

'Am I going back to that place?'

'No, you're not.'

'Are you going to free me?'

Leigh sat on the bed and tapped the space next to him. 'Come over here. Don't be frightened.' Ajee walked over and sat, leaving a modest space between them. 'Listen, something has come up and we have been looking for just the right person to help us. We think that's you.'

'What is it?' said Ajee, her anxiety sky-rocketing.

'We'll give you all the details later, but the most important thing is for you to relax, get plenty of rest and build yourself up. It's nothing to worry about but you'll need your strength.'

'Can't you tell me more?'

'Not yet. In good time.'

The men left and Ajee heard the door lock. Abandoning deer-spotting, she threw herself on her bed and, for no reason she could figure, sobbed.

46

Bob had always thought that once he was promoted to inspector, his days of interviewing prisoners would be behind him, yet here he was again. It wasn't a requirement for DIs to interview chief executives when they were in custody for paedophile crime – no one had thought to write that protocol down – but it just made sense.

He allowed DC Jake Briers to operate the recording equipment but insisted that he would take the lead. If Jake was put out by that, he didn't show it.

Like the cocksure accountant who, unbeknown to him, would soon be back in here facing eye-watering money-laundering charges with a whacking account freezing order to go with them, Parfitt declined a solicitor. So, he sat facing the two detectives in the soundproof room, probably oblivious to the depth of trouble he was in.

Once they'd dealt with the preamble, Bob was out of the blocks.

'Mr Parfitt, you've been arrested on suspicion of downloading and distributing child abuse images. Is there anything you want to say to us about that?'

'I have no idea what this is about. You're wasting everyone's time and once you examine what you've taken from me, you'll see I'm completely innocent.'

'Can you just confirm that you have sole use of the items on this exhibit list?'

Parfitt scanned down the handwritten sheet and pointed out what was his, what was his wife's and what they shared.

'That means, anything we find on those items you've said you have sole use of, is down to you?'

'Yes, but you won't.'

'Let's look at what we can deal with at the moment.' Bob produced a page from a spreadsheet, identified it and turned it round to show Parfitt. 'Can you confirm that this number here is your credit card number?'

'It looks familiar,' said Parfitt.

'Well, it matches the one you had in your wallet when you were arrested and our enquiries show it's registered to you at your address.'

'Well, it must be then.'

'Good. And do you recognise these transactions?' He ran his finger down each row and read out their contents for the recording.

'Not offhand.'

'These payees then?'

Bob pointed to seven different account names repeated many times over thirty-five entries. All were suffixed with .com or .org.

'No. Should I?'

'Well, given that each of these sites are specifically pay-per-download child abuse sites, where people buy images, videos and access to live shows – I'll leave you to guess what they're about – and you seem to be a loyal customer, I'd imagine you have a bit of a clue.'

'Inspector, I know nothing about this, the sites or any of my cards being used to buy filth. I've got two young girls, you know.'

'I wondered when you'd bring them up. You know we will have to look at their safety, don't you?'

Parfitt stood up and banged his hands on the table. 'What the hell are you insinuating?' Neither officer moved.

'Sit down,' said Bob, so the tape would clearly show who the aggressor was. Parfitt obeyed.

'I'm not insinuating anything, but given the information we received, what we've found so far and your denials, we have a duty to safeguard your children so, before you go, we'll be asking you to sign what we call a voluntary agreement not to live or have unsupervised access to your girls. Just until, or if, we can clear you.'

Parfitt was about to explode again but this time Bob's raised palm dissuaded him.

'Who the hell provide you with this,' he air-quoted, 'information?'

'I can tell you it was Crimestoppers, so was provided anonymously.'

'You've arrested me on anonymous information? And you're going to deny my children their father too?'

'No. We arrested you because we found you've been buying child abuse images. We'll check your computer and the times the purchases were made. If there is sufficient evidence, you'll be charged and you might go to prison. If not, you won't.'

Parfitt's eyes filled up and he shook his head. 'This can't be happening. I haven't done any of this. I'm being fitted up.'

'Now hang on a minute,' said Jake.

'Not by you. I think you're being had over.'

'Why would anyone fit you up? And how?'

'I've no idea how but I've got a pretty good idea who, and why.'

Bob and Jake exchanged a glance. This wasn't in the interview plan but was too good not to probe.

'I think you better explain,' said Bob.

Parfitt looked between the two, seemingly weighing up his options.

'If I tell you this, my life is over.'

'Seems to me you need to come up with something pretty good to keep you out of jail.'

'You need to protect my wife and kids. Not just me.'

'Aren't you being a bit overdramatic?' said Bob.

'No. They've been threatened already.'

'By who?'

'By some blokes working for Tom Doughty.'

Bob leant in, truly puzzled. 'Doughty? You and him are as tight as a sailor's hitch. Why would he threaten you?'

'You've no idea, have you? Not a clue what that man is capable of and what he's planning.'

Bob checked that the equipment was still recording.

'Tell us.'

For the next thirty minutes, Bob and Jake sat and listened as Parfitt talked them through Tom Doughty, the tyrant. He started with how they'd fixed the election, his off-the-scale extremism and the reign of terror he presided over. Parfitt accepted he shared some of Tom's views and that they had known each other since their football hooliganism days. Then he laid out the councillor's role in the travellers' murders, the deaths that followed from that, the mosque riot, the campaign against Jo Howe – whom Doughty saw as the biggest threat to his ambitions – the care homes, the trafficked women and the prostitution.

When he finished, Bob chipped in. 'I don't understand someone so vehemently fascist bringing in migrants. I mean, isn't that what you fight against?'

'It's not about ideals. Well, it started out as that. It's about power and money. He doesn't see these immigrants as anything other than a means to make money. Just as he has no compunction against killing the old boys and girls in the care homes. It's all about what they are worth to him and whether they can finance his megalomania. They are commodities, plain and simple.'

'But I still don't know why he's threatened your kids or you think he's fitted you up here.'

'He's put a shot across my bows a few times recently. Questioned my commitment to the cause. The cause? I'm just trying to run a council according to whatever party is in power. I can't commit to any cause; I just implement his crazy edicts in as legal and as palatable a way as possible. He sees that as weakness and said if I don't prove my allegiance then he'll harm Heather and the girls. Even played me a video to show how close he could get.'

'What's he getting you to do?'

'Just some minor stuff for now. I've been told to bugger up Jo Howe's life as much as I can for starters. She'll tell you what we've done, but that's nothing. Just irritations in the scheme of things. It's my loyalty test. He's got some massive plan brewing and, whilst he won't tell me what it is, I'm having to free up six-figure sums to pay various people to make it happen.'

'Tell me more about this "massive plan".'

'I wish I could help you, I really do, but he's deliberately keeping me out of the loop – but it's supposed to bring hearts and minds across to his cause.'

'You need to find out,' said Bob. It wasn't a question.

'How can I? I can't exactly go back to work and, if he is behind this, he's certainly not going to throw his arms open and welcome me back into the fold now.'

'Try.'

'You could always ask Stuart Acers.'

'What?'

'I've said too much, forget it.'

Bob wagged his finger, oblivious to the two cameras picking up his every move. 'You don't get to say that. What about Acers?'

'He's got him just where he wants him. And the prison governor. And the hospital chief exec. Everyone in any position of power is either one of Doughty's cronies or he's got something on them that makes them dance to his tune.'

'And which camp does Acers fall into?'

'Put it this way, I don't know his politics, but I've seen proof of how he gets his jollies.'

Bob turned to Jake. 'This goes no further,' he said, then turned back to Parfitt. 'I need to stop the interview. You'll have to go back in your cell whilst I take some advice. I'd say it's the safest place for you.'

Once Parfitt was locked back up, Bob sent Jake to the office, whilst he racked his brains as to whom he could call. In the end it was a no-brainer, suspended or otherwise.

Jo picked up on the second ring. She listened patiently and without interruption as Bob explained all that Parfitt had said, how that fitted in with what they already knew and why he kind of believed him. When he finished, Jo paused for so long that Bob wondered if he'd lost the signal. 'Jo, are you still there?'

'Yes, yes. I'm just thinking. OK, the first rule is whatever carnage is happening, our job is to stop it getting any worse. Our . . . your first priority is to find out what this plan is and stop it happening. I'm guessing it's more than killing a few travellers or a DCI, so it's going to be huge. Find out and stop it. And Bob?'

'Yes?'

'We have to do this under the radar and the chief constable cannot find out until it's time. Here's the plan.'

47

For no reason other than spite, Jo wanted to make this meeting as inconvenient as humanly possible. She would have gone out of the county if she didn't have another Brightside shift that afternoon, so the Lido Café next to Worthing Pier would have to do. But they'd sit outside.

She deliberately arrived a quarter of an hour early so she could get her hot water and not feel obliged to buy the specimen she was meeting anything. Luckily it was a beautiful day and the salty sea air and squawk of the diving seagulls enlivened her otherwise grumpy mood. But she was looking forward to this.

Bang on time, Russ Parfitt shuffled into view, glanced around and saw Jo. She didn't stand. His England football shirt, crumpled khaki cargo shorts, and blue flip-flops he'd obviously decorated in at some time, looked positively vagrant.

'Is it safe here?' he asked, as he scoured the toddlers playing on the mini-amusements which packed where the old outdoor pool used to be.

'Apart from you being so close to kids, I think we might be OK.'

He took the seat opposite and looked at her drink. 'Get one if you want,' she said.

'No, you're OK. Why did you want to meet? I mean, we're both suspended, but other than that, what have we got to talk about?'

Jo glared at him, holding his stare for a fraction longer than necessary. He was a shadow of the misogynistic bully she was used to locking horns with, and she'd play that for all she could.

'Let's start with saving your liberty, your reputation and, if Mrs P is stupid enough, your family.'

Instead of the usual volley back, his eyes pleaded. 'You can do that?'

'If I choose.'

'But you're not at work at the moment. How can you help?'

'It's because I'm not at work that I'm probably the only one who can. But it doesn't come for free.'

'I don't understand.'

'How could you when you're as thick as pig shit and nothing but Doughty's lapdog? And talking of shit, do you have any idea how deep you are in?'

Parfitt's eyes filled and he started to fidget with a plastic stirrer that had been left on the table. Jo left the silence for him to fill. Eventually, he did.

'I'll do whatever it takes. I promise you I've never even looked at those kinds of sites, let alone paid to go on them or downloaded pictures. You have to believe me.'

'I don't have to. For what it's worth, and he'll kill me for saying this, Bob Heaton's bought your stitch-up excuse. I'd rather see the evidence but as I trust Bob's instincts, you might be of use.'

'For God's sake, Jo, you're talking in riddles.'

'Let me explain. What you are going to do is way outside the rules. That's why, against my better judgement, I'm the one who will tell you what to do and the only one you'll talk to. See, technically, I'm not a police officer at the moment and the rules I'd be breaking only apply to sworn officers.' That wasn't strictly true, but Parfitt didn't need to know the Police Conduct Regulations fine print.

'I've told Bob Heaton all I know. I just need my life – my family – back.'

Jo shook her head at the order of his priorities. 'You don't deserve them. I know what you've told Bob, but you're going to have to work for your freedom.'

'Have I got a choice?'

'There are always choices, but they all come with consequences. You can do what I say and, providing you're telling the truth about the images, you might emerge with the scraps of your sorry life. Or you can choose not to, and you'll go to prison – where they really don't like your sort – lose your family, house, job of course and whatever reputation you think you have. Frankly, your life as you know it will be vapour. See, choices.' She smiled and was delighted he didn't.

'What do I have to do?' he said in resignation.

'Tell me more about this "master plan".'

'I don't know. I told Bob, Doughty doesn't trust me. All I know is that he's got some military guy in to help Leigh.'

'Leigh?'

'He's Tom's muscle. Fucking psycho and just about the only one who can tell him what he thinks. He's ex-army and a proper Nazi but they've brought in this ex-special forces bloke. That tells me it's not just another scrap outside the mosque.'

Jo thought about that. Ever since Bob had told her about this so-called plan, she'd assumed whatever it was would be in Brighton. This now confirmed it, and Parfitt was right. You didn't bring in ex-SAS unless you had something cataclysmic in mind.

'And they don't trust you?'

'Don't trust me? Of course they don't, otherwise they wouldn't have set me up with this kiddy porn – sorry, child abuse images – stuff.'

'How do you know it's them? You're not exactly short of enemies.'

'Not with the abilities and connections to do this. You know they're after you too?'

Despite suspecting this, hearing it out loud took Jo aback. She couldn't show it though. She needed to keep Parfitt on the ropes.

'Really?' She hoped her feigned disinterest came through.

'You must have noticed. The school placements? Your car? The bins?'

'That was them? Hardly the hallmark of an army preparing for war, is it?'

'Me actually, and before you go off on one, it was a test. I was told to make your life miserable to see if I was loyal to Doughty. They threatened my kids if I didn't fall in line.'

'Well, you're going to have to win back some trust, and pretty quickly.'

Parfitt's face blanched. 'What, go back to them? Are you mad? They're not the kind of people who give second chances.'

'Your choice.' Jo prayed he'd take the bait as, despite her outward nonchalance, without the compromised chief constable on board, there was no plan B. She went to stand.

'Just a minute. I can try. I can't guarantee anything, but how will you make these images charges disappear if I do?'

'There's no effort prizes for this. You either find out what's going to happen, when, where and who, and you pass that information to me in time for the police to stop it, or you fail. All or nothing.'

'And if I can't?'

'Well, if what you're saying is true, we'll probably find all sorts of hideous things on your hard drive and the financial records to back up the intelligence. I mean, if you're being stitched up by people as clever as you think they are, they're not going to leave it at you being nicked and there being no evidence.'

Parfitt started to shake. 'You think so?'

'A hundred per cent.'

'What can you do about it then? How do you prove it wasn't me?'

She waited for a couple with a toddler in a pushchair to walk past.

'Well, I can't but those clever digital forensic guys can. You'd be amazed.'

Parfitt sneered.

'I know what you're thinking,' she said. 'I don't have to do this because those geeks will find trace of the images being planted anyway.'

'Exactly.'

'That all depends though.'

'On what?'

'On whether anyone asks them to look. Or tells them not to.'

'What? The police would stop them finding the very evidence that could prove I'm innocent? Just because I don't manage to do what you say?'

'As if. The police would never do such a thing.'

Parfitt's shoulders relaxed and Jo leant in.

'But I would. Have we got a deal?'

She could tell Russ was frantically weighing up the options, searching for a third way. His face became tauter and tauter before inevitability hit.

'You've got me over a barrel, you bitch.'

Jo stood and said, 'Now that's just rude,' before walking away, beaming.

48

Farah never struggled cracking phone passcodes and, frankly, didn't know what all the fuss was about. It was just a knack of working out the unlock pattern.

What she couldn't control was the battery power, so she preferred to strike early in the day when most people's phones were at, or close to, full power. That gave her ample time to do whatever she'd stolen it for. She rarely took them for cash alone, although for a decent one, that was often a welcome bonus.

Having worked out that the brothel was somewhere between Brighton city centre and its seafront, she headed over to Hove to keep out of the way.

Checking the O2 signal was strong enough, she settled down on the shingle and set about searching 'Jo Howe' again – and every variation she could think of – for updates.

Her Twitter account showed her as @ChsuptJoHowe and seemed solely for professional purposes. Tweets and retweets about missing people, wanted criminals, protests and football matches, and a few commenting on issues of the day. There had been no activity for a couple of weeks.

Instagram drew a blank, as Farah expected from a woman of her age. Few over-thirties mastered the photo-sharing service unless they had kids or professionals doing the heavy lifting.

Facebook though was a different story. It's ubiquity among the forty-plus age group meant two things. Firstly, no self-respecting kid went anywhere near it. Secondly, that age group had no clue of how Meta's algorithms worked, nor that 'privacy' meant nothing of the sort.

Jo's account was locked down so only friends could see her posts. Big tick for that. Not so for letting her friends tag her in their posts and photos though. And boy did they tag.

Farah shook her head in shame at how naive this supposedly super-bright senior police officer was, but it suited her purposes to a tee.

Soon she was able to work out her husband's name and those of her two boys – weren't they cute – and their favourite Greek restaurant in Hove. And that was just the start. Within half an hour, by cross-referencing posts with various other sites and throwing in a few reverse Google Image searches, Farah had worked out where she lived to within a few streets, that she was an erstwhile runner, the car she probably drove and even where she shopped. Crucially, and this was criminal, she knew where her boys went to school.

With the aid of Street View she quickly realised that were she to hang around Jo's neighbourhood she'd be noticed in no time. She needed to be wilier and try to spot her coming in or out, then follow her to somewhere she'd feel safe to bump into her.

She hated herself for it, but it would have to be the school. Ideally, she'd wait until the morning then pick her off without the children but, thinking back to what Ajee must be going through, she didn't have that luxury.

She checked the time, then Googled the school and pre-school and found their pick-up times on the website. Looking at the map, she worked out the quickest route to North Hove School, presuming Jo would collect Liam from the pre-school first, then headed there. It would be tight, but if she could spot her as she walked home, she could work out a pick-up plan.

Trying hard not to pant and ignoring the aches from her injuries, Farah just about made it. She recognised Jo straight away with, if she remembered rightly from the Facebook pictures, Darren. He had Liam on his shoulders and Jo held Ciaran's hand, with his Avengers backpack in the other.

Farah kept well back, using Liam's artificial height to show where the

Howes were headed. *Please don't put him down.*

Thankfully, by cutting across the park, it took no time at all before the happy family turned off Benett Drive into a driveway. Farah made a mental note of the number. As Darren helped Liam down and Jo fumbled with her keys in the lock, Farah hurried past, desperately looking for somewhere she could watch the house from.

It was hopeless. Talk about suburban tranquillity. She'd stand out like a lighthouse here. She walked to the end of the road, checked the map and trotted round the block, ambling when she came back into view. As she did so, Jo jogged out of the house and down the hill.

This wasn't in the plan.

There was nothing for it – Farah would have to follow as best she could and catch up with her when she could engineer a chance bump. She couldn't afford for this woman, probably her only saviour, to think she'd been stalking her.

Jo checked her watch as she speed-walked down the hill towards Church Road. Nadia wasn't around so Carrie had suggested she pair up with George for the afternoon. He usually worked the Hove end of the patch which, given how late she was running, suited her fine. It was also a perfect opportunity to find out more about him. Having met him the other day, she recalled something Neela had said that made Jo distinctly edgy about the old man.

Twenty minutes later she was standing by Palmeira Square, looking around to catch a glimpse of George approaching, when a voice made her jump.

'My dear Jo, are you looking for me?' She spun round and saw the old man who'd seemed a little wrong-footed the other day, beaming behind her.

'Oh, George, you made me jump. Sorry if I'm late, it's just I . . .'

He raised a hand. 'Say nothing of it. We all have lives to lead. Anyway, let's get started. I'd rather like to take a look at some car washes if that's OK. There are several round here and there's one young man who seems to bounce between them. I want to see whether we can work out a strategy to help him. Sometimes the men get forgotten.'

'You're the boss,' said Jo, still curious how piecemeal their approach seemed to be. She decided that if she stuck at this, she'd develop a more efficient model to rescue slaves en masse and lock up those responsible at the same time.

'Let's just cross the road to Tesco. I always like to have some sandwiches in my bag in case the chance arises to coax them away. It's bloody dangerous though, so I usually end up eating them myself. At least you can help me out with that.'

Jo feigned a chuckle. 'I'll wait outside.'

When he went in, Jo took out her phone and idly flicked through.

'Mrs Howe?'

She turned to see a vaguely familiar skinny girl standing behind her.

'Er, yes. Do we know each other?'

'We have met before,' the girl said. Jo couldn't place her or the accent.

'Remind me.'

'You came to the home where I worked. You visit Mrs Cooke. I look after her.'

Jo's heart leapt.

'Ajee? No, you're not Ajee, you're the other one.' This could go one of many ways.

'Farah, but I know Ajee. Ajee help me but she's in great danger. You police lady, you must help.'

Jo went to touch her arm but the girl recoiled. 'I'm sorry. Where is Ajee?' Jo looked around.

'They keep her in big house. I ran away but they will harm her.'

'Calm down. Let's just wait for my friend to come out of the shop and we can go somewhere to talk.'

Farah hopped from foot to foot, looking all around her. 'OK, but quickly,' she said.

'It's fine. I'm so glad you found me.'

Just then a booming voice came. 'Unexpected item in the bloody baggage area! Those damn self-service tills will be the death of me.'

Jo looked round. 'George, before we go off, can we help this girl? It's just that—'

The scream behind her came from nowhere. She turned and saw Farah sprinting away, dodging the buses and taxis as she ran into the road.

'Seems she had other plans,' laughed George.

Jo ran after her, shouting her apologies to the man she'd left standing. The man whom she was sure had made Farah flee.

Her injuries screamed out as she sprinted back along Palmeira Square, desperate to keep Farah in her sights. She sensed a limp in Farah's gait too, but the girl's youth gave her the edge.

'Out of the way,' she yelled at the ambling pedestrians who seemed determined to block both her path and view.

Stretching up to glimpse where she'd gone, Jo caught sight of Farah peeling off right into Salisbury Road. A double pushchair blocked Jo's path so she skipped into the road, not seeing the blue-and-white Streamline Taxi bearing down towards her. The blare of the horn shocked Jo back onto the pavement and she fobbed the gesticulating driver off with a shrug and a silent 'Sorry.'

How long could she carry on? If her back and legs had any say in it, she'd let Farah go, but that wasn't going to happen.

As she turned the corner, a bunch of students were spilling out from the English Language Centre. Ploughing through them, she snatched her mobile phone from her pocket.

'Call Gary Hedges,' she panted at Siri and thankfully it understood. Keeping up an unsustainable pace, she didn't wait for his preamble but yelled, 'Gary, get CCTV to search round Salisbury Road. Get eyes on the ground here. I'm chasing a girl in danger.' She rattled off a description which Gary repeated back.

'I'm on it but aren't you supposed to be injured?' he asked.

'I bloody am. I think she's done a right into Lansdowne Road.'

'Roger that,' he acknowledged, and Jo stepped up a gear, getting to the junction just as Farah took the left into Palmeira Avenue, along the side of Hove Crown Court. A white prison cell van was just turning into the rear yard, delaying Farah enough for Jo's protesting legs to get her within shouting distance.

'Farah, stop. I want to help.'

The girl turned briefly then darted into the oncoming traffic and headed for Eaton Road. A removal truck wouldn't shift, and Jo was able to catch up. She grabbed her by the arm and, to her relief, Farah did not resist.

Between breaths Jo, hanging onto Farah, more to stop herself falling than in restraint said, 'Just give me a minute.' She guided her to a wall.

Eventually her breath returned and the fire in her lungs abated.

'Why did you run? I thought you wanted me to help you.'

'That man. Your friend.'

'What? No. I've only just met him. What about him?'

'He very bad. He takes girls.'

'What, for sex?'

'No, he make girls feel special then sends them to the homes. Then . . .' She shrugged. 'You police lady, right?'

Jo decided it was best not to explain. 'Yes.'

'Why you friends with Mr George then? You like the police in my home country.'

'No, no. Honestly I want to help you. And Ajee.'

Just then a marked police car drew up at the junction. Jo spotted the double take from the driver, then the window gliding down. 'Everything OK, ma'am?' said PC Wendy Relf.

Farah laughed. 'Ma'am? Like a queen.' She mock curtsied.

'Stop it,' smiled Jo. 'Yes, I'm fine thanks. Did you get a call?'

'Hold on,' said Wendy. She pulled the car out of the junction and parked next to them. Jo saw she was on her own. Safer crewing, they called it. One of the most ridiculous misnomers in the police lexicon. Wendy stepped out and walked over. She eyed Farah suspiciously, positioning herself so she couldn't run off again.

'Honestly, it's fine. We were just chatting and then something spooked her. Just a misunderstanding.'

Jo could tell Wendy wasn't buying it but was reluctant to open a can of worms. 'So, what now?' she asked.

Jo thought about that. Farah needed to be off the streets and safe. She just hoped that George was the only bad apple at Brightside, otherwise her only option could make things a whole lot worse. 'Could I ask a big favour of you?' She explained and Wendy smiled.

Farah got in the back of the car and Jo in the front.

'Last time I saw you was at the hospital after Dan Bilkham was stabbed. How is he?' said Jo.

Wendy looked across, her eyes wondering how Jo didn't know.

'He's OK. He'll be off for a few more months but other than being minus a kidney and his spleen, they reckon he'll make a full recovery.'

'Wow, he's lucky,' said Jo.

'He reckons it's the most effective weight-loss plan he's been on,' said Wendy, a twinkle in her eye.

Ten minutes later, they were pulling up outside Jo's house. Not quite long enough for Jo to work out how she'd explain this to Darren.

49

Bob loved being a DI, but it did bind him to the office a bit too much for his liking. Back in the day, he'd liked nothing more than being out either kicking doors in and arresting the bad guys, or playing a cross between chess and hide and seek on surveillance.

It was rare for an SIO to have their Airwave radio chirping away on their desk. In fact, it was rare for an SIO to know how to turn the damn thing on. But, as Bob was double-hatting as intelligence manager, he needed to keep tabs on the operation to discover what Tom Doughty and Leigh O'Keefe were up to, and who this mysterious super-soldier was.

In town they were not hard to follow, as the volume and speed of traffic meant that the surveillance team could blend invisibly into the chaos. However, from time to time, they ventured beyond the city limits and that presented problems. Like today for example.

Not for the first time, O'Keefe had changed cars. There was no common denominator as to where he sourced them from, he just seemed to have an endless supply. Today, it was a grey Nissan Juke – a model whose ubiquity made them as invisible as the surveillance team. Shadows chasing shadows.

From what Bob could make out from the radio transmissions, the car was on the way out of Brighton. O'Keefe – or whoever was driving; they daren't get that close – was taking a suspiciously circuitous route, including heading out to Shoreham then using the cloverleaf roundabout to come back the same way.

By deploying the whole gambit of dry-cleaning – counter-surveillance – techniques, they were making it clear they were up to something. What they didn't account for was the fact that however many red lights they went through, junctions they indicated at yet drove straight on and dead ends they went down, the team had seen them all before and were prepared, so didn't show out.

What they did struggle with were long, narrow, winding country lanes with few if any tributary roads coming off them. Like Blackstone Lane near Henfield, into which the Juke had just made an un-signalled turn.

Bob knew the area well but had probably only driven that particular road once or twice, so could offer little in terms of local knowledge. He'd just have to sit there listening with the map up on his screen, hoping either there was a purpose in the Juke being there – in which case they might be able to fill in the gaps in Parfitt's account – or it was another tactic to see if anyone was following them, and they'd come out the other end.

The team leader, Donna, with whom Bob had a special bond, was as calm as ever.

'Sierra Victor Seven Three, all units top and bottom to deploy foot officers ASAP. Victor Seven Six, vehicle take static point at north end, Victor Seven Eight at the south. Victor Seven Five, Seven Four and I will drive the lane on my command.'

'Victor Seven Eight, have we got NPAS we could deploy?'

'Negative,' sighed Donna.

Bob winced. To request the National Police Air Service to support the operation would risk the chief constable finding out, which he was trying to avoid at all costs. He'd batted off Donna's pleas over the last few days with excuses about them being unavailable, but they really could do with an eye in the sky now.

A few minutes later a volley of confirmations that everyone was in position came over the radio, and Bob knew he could only wait while the painstaking foot-sweep of the tracks and fields played out.

Leigh eased the Juke to a halt by the front door. He and Jimmy had argued on the way up as to whether it was wise to come here again. Jimmy would never visit a venue more than once on an operation, especially with such a critical asset as this one housed. Leigh thought he'd appeased him by dry-cleaning.

Neither had seen any tail, but both knew that didn't mean they weren't there. Nevertheless, they had a job to do and, unlike in the special forces, they didn't have other trained operatives to call on.

Leigh grabbed the bag from the back seat. 'You coming?' he asked Jimmy.

'No need,' he replied. 'I'll stay put in case we get any uninvited callers.'

'Suit yourself,' said Leigh as he walked up to the door.

The guards weren't expecting him – another security tactic – so Leo dropped his playing cards when the front door opened.

'Sorry to have disturbed you,' said Leigh. 'I hope someone's watching her.'

'Yes boss,' said Vlad.

Leigh didn't reply but made straight for the stairs, hoping to catch out the guard outside Ajee's room. He was surprised that he was in position by her locked door, looking reasonably alert. *No doubt the WhatsApp group was functioning well*, he thought.

'Open it,' he said. The guard unlocked the door, closing it again once Leigh was in.

Ajee was curled up on the bed, faced away from the door, hugging herself.

'You warm enough?'

'I'm fine,' she mumbled.

'I can't hear you. Sit up please?'

Slowly, she stretched out and turned to face him, her eyes raw, her expression blank.

Leigh held up the Next bag. 'I bought you a present.' Ajee looked at the bag, then at Leigh, then away. 'Don't be ungrateful. I got you some clothes, smellies and some stuff to do your hair with.'

'I don't take clothes from strange men. Not after last time.'

Leigh shrugged but wasn't going to ask her what she meant. 'Well, I'm afraid you haven't got a choice. This little job we've got for you means you have to look and smell presentable.' He sniffed the air to make the point.

If a bloke had looked at Leigh with the contempt Ajee did, he'd have punched his lights out. But he was a gentleman.

'Just get yourself cleaned up and be ready to go when we say.' He left the room and told the guard to lock up.

As he walked back along the corridor, his phone rang. Shit, hadn't he turned it off? *Christ Tom, not now.*

'Yes?'

'Where are you?'

'At the farmhouse. Why?'

'Are we set?'

'I think so. She's a bit grumpy but she'll do as she's told.'

'How's Jimmy?'

'Fine. Thinks the world's watching him but that's not a bad paranoia, in the scheme of things.'

'Quite. Have we got all the kit?'

'There's a couple more bits coming this afternoon then that's the lot, just needs putting together. Have you sorted out the other manpower?'

'Yes, Bill Sansom has identified some suitable prisoners due out this week. We're picking them up with a "too good to be true" job offer, accommodation thrown in.'

'I hope they're trustworthy.'

'They won't know anything until Saturday morning, so it should be fine.'

Leigh was by the front door now. He finished the call as he stepped out into the bright sunlight, which blinded him just long enough for him not to glimpse the camera lens in the hedge opposite, nor the officer behind it who'd been clicking away at the house, the Juke and its occupant.

50

Darren had been surprisingly sanguine when the police car deposited Jo and Farah outside his house.

He got the hint when they rushed in with little more than 'I'll explain' before they dashed into the dining room. Other than getting them drinks and a plate of biscuits, he made himself and the boys scarce.

Once Jo had convinced Farah that she really didn't know anything about George, just that she'd been put with him for her second Brightside shift, the girl relaxed.

'Ajee and I were going to Brightside for help. Thank Allah we didn't.'

'How did you find me?' asked Jo.

Farah smiled and tapped the side of her nose. 'I'm glad I did. Ajee and I, we saw you on the BBC. You stopped the traffic.'

Jo sighed; she was never going to live that one down. 'You'd better tell me everything about you, Ajee and why you think she's in danger.'

Farah took Jo through, step by step, how she'd arrived in the UK and her journey up to when they had occasionally met at the care home. She even gave some funny anecdotes about Mary Cooke which Jo banked to tell Phil when the time was right. Jo's heart bled when Farah described the rapes and beatings, especially the one that had thrown her and Ajee together.

'They took us to farmhouse for me to recover. Ajee a nurse. They sent her to heal me. We made it look like I still hurt so they not send us back.'

'Where was the farmhouse?'

Farah shrugged. 'Not far but in countryside. No people. No cars. Although some days I hear a busy road and police sirens sometimes. Birds. Deer. Cows. Peaceful. Not like before.'

'Where was that?'

'Very noisy. Lots of people, day and night. Police cars too. All the time. And birds.'

'Seagulls?'

'I don't know. Squawk, squawk.'

'Yep, seagulls. Why do you think Ajee is in such danger?'

'They will punish her for helping me escape. They will hurt her then kill her.'

Jo's mind raced. So much information, but how much was relevant and how much did Bob already know? Who was she kidding that she could keep Farah safe?

'We must find Ajee but also the farmhouse and brothel. Will you help me do that? I'll understand if you don't want to.'

Farah looked at her like she'd gone mad. 'I'll do anything. I don't know these girls, except Ajee, but they are still my sisters. I'm the lucky one. They are being raped and beaten every day in your city. I must stop that happening.'

'You're so brave. But you must be tired. How about I run you a bath then make the spare bed up so you can have a proper sleep?'

Tears filled Farah's eyes. 'Thank you, Mrs Howe.'

'Please call me Jo.'

'Or ma'am?' She stood and curtsied, then convulsed with laughter.

Jo hugged her.

Once Farah was tucked up in bed and she'd explained what was going on to Darren, she texted Bob.

Free to speak? J x

A minute later her phone rang.

'What have you been up to?' said Bob. 'Gary told me you were chasing a runner earlier. In your state?'

Jo explained the afternoon's events and how she'd somehow ended up lodging a refugee.

'Have you ever thought of taking up gardening? It might keep you out of trouble.'

'No time,' she replied. 'Look, there are some victims of serious abuse here. But I've got a lead that could put a stop to it. There are two houses we must find.'

'We?'

'Fair enough, you. The one which operates as a brothel, by the sound of it, is somewhere in the city centre. I'm certain it's in Brighton and I'm thinking somewhere close to the seafront, but also near the shops or pubs from what she could hear.'

'We did have that bloke who had acid poured over his knackers in Clarence Square. Could that be connected? Unfortunately, he still won't say anything about it. Won't even give his name.'

'Well, she did say she heard that her attacker had been sorted, and it fits with her description.'

'Sure,' said Bob. 'But it's a warren of Georgian townhouses round there, as you know. Could be anywhere, even if we're right.'

'It's a start. Better than the other place. All she can say is a farmhouse that may or may not be near a busy road, but otherwise in the middle of nowhere with deer, birds and cows.'

Bob went silent.

'You there?'

'And she's saying this is where Ajee is being held?'

'Was. She might not be there now. But how the hell do we find that?'

'We don't have to, Jo. I know exactly where it is, and we were there not three hours ago.'

This time there was air support. Given the almost indecent lack of light, it would have been fatal attempting such an audacious raid with only drones in the sky.

The intelligence had come together quickly and once the outcome of that day's surveillance and Farah's description of the farmhouse were combined, there were ample grounds to believe that Ajee was being held in the isolated building and could, at any time, come to harm.

That meant Gary Hedges had to act straight away. Ideally, he'd wait until the morning, but she could be dead by then, so the worst-case scenario of a night-time armed assault and rescue was his only option. Just before the 1 a.m. briefing, Bob had spelt out what they knew so far including the layout, from aerial and the surveillance photos, Google Street View and the Land Registry. They had to make a lot of assumptions, but the handpicked specialist firearms officers would know that, and the risks.

Close target reconnaissance teams were already deployed and a ring of armed officers contained the house. None were reporting any discernible movement.

Bob was sitting in the briefing room to the side of the sullen yet laser-attentive specialist firearms officers – SFOs. He could never help reflecting on how this lot resembled special forces gearing up for the last push behind enemy lines, rather than the bobbies that they were.

Gary explained the operation's objectives before handing over to the Tactical Firearms Commander – TFC – Chief Inspector Marion West. A veteran at these jobs, she set out her understanding of the threat and risk and outlined the plan and tactics. In this case the challenge was both methodically clearing the house of threats and trying to find the victim quickly.

Next up was the woman on the ground, the Operational Firearms Commander – OFC. Bob stifled a giggle when she described each officer's position and role as 'dance steps'. He pictured some grotesque mash up of the TV shows *Strictly Come Dancing* and *SAS: Who Dares Wins*.

Whilst not strictly allowed, Bob persuaded the TFC to let him accompany her in the command car.

The twenty grey-clad officers checked their weapons one last time, then boarded their unmarked 4 x 4s and headed off to slip into Blackstone then swiftly leave, victims rescued and slavers in handcuffs, before any of its villagers had rubbed the sleep from their eyes.

Bob took his place in the back of the black Toyota Proace Verso, next to Marion. She was cordial enough in other settings, but Bob found her terrifying when she slipped into TFC mode. 'You stay in the car at all costs. No chit-chat when we get to the target premises and certainly you say nothing on the radio. Understood?'

Bob surpassed a grin. 'Yes, ma'am.'

'And don't fucking call me ma'am.'

'Ma'am.'

She glared at him then turned her attention to her laptop. 'Tosser,' she muttered.

As they turned off the A23 towards Henfield, Bob strained to hear the hushed radio messages. Clipped updates which talked of white, black, green and red sides followed by two-digit numbers which he remembered were window or door identifiers.

'TFC to NPAS 15. Move to the target area,' she said, broaching no discussion.

'NPAS 15 roger. ETA three minutes.'

Bob knew from the briefing that the helicopter had been holding off at the Newhaven coastline, where its presence at this time of night would not spark a second's curiosity.

Bob heard the faint thump thump thump of the rotor blades approaching but could see nothing.

As they sat, blocking the entrance to The Old Vicarage, a stone's throw from the southern end of Blackstone Lane, Bob wished he could see the doors go in and Ajee carried out, like in the movies.

'Don't you hate having all the responsibility but not being there to make a difference?' he asked Marion.

'What did I say?' she replied.

Bob shrugged down in his seat. Clearly Marion wasn't up for a debate on the paradox of command just now.

One last check with the OFC that everyone was in position – on ladders, on the roof, at each window and doorway, and covering from a distance – then Marion gave the command.

'Strike, strike, strike.'

Suddenly the pitch black was bleached with the 1.9 million lumens Nightsun helicopter floodlight, the silence blasted with the explosions of stun grenades and the yell of 'armed police', audible even at their remote holding point.

There was nothing for Bob to do now but fight the urge to rush to the scene and wait for updates.

Shouts of 'clear', 'clear', 'clear' repeated ominously as he pictured the raid team racing through the house in teams of three, checking each room and cubbyhole as they went. *Please, just one positive. Find Ajee for God's sake.*

Thirty seconds, and Bob turned to Marion.

'What's happening?'

Her glare said it all and he slunk back into his shell. The wait was interminable but at least he'd not heard any shots, and Marion seemed calm. Except with him.

The next seven minutes seemed like seventy, and then came the message Bob was dreading.

'OFC, to TFC.'

'TFC, go ahead.'

'Premises clear. Repeat, it's empty. I'll keep a presence here until local units can secure.'

'TFC roger. All units other than those maintaining integrity, stand down and return to HQ for debrief.' She turned to Bob. 'So much for a dead cert.'

Bob wasn't having this conversation. His head was spinning with where she could be, if not here.

* * *

Five miles away another frantic conversation was being held over the telephone.

'It's done,' said Acers, pacing up and down his conservatory, his grey silk dressing gown stretched over his paunch, flicking off his radio with his spare hand.

'Jesus, Stuart, have you any idea how close that was?' said Doughty, sounding more relieved than his trademark raging.

'I know. I'd have told you sooner but I only found out by chance. You'll make sure this doesn't come back to me, won't you?'

'I've got bigger things to worry about before I think about saving your arse. We're going to have to hide her somewhere else until Saturday. You better make sure we don't have a repeat of tonight. That house was hard enough to find, now Christ knows what your lot will find traces of in there. It's you who should be making sure it doesn't come back to me.'

'I'll do what I can.'

It had been a few weeks since Jo's phone had woken her up in the middle of the night. Even so, she still hadn't shaken the Pavlovian jitters that something awful had happened, nor her trigger greeting. 'Chief Superintendent Howe,' she muttered without checking the caller ID.

'I wouldn't let the chief hear you say that,' said Gary Hedges.

'I'll be back,' she said in her worst Terminator voice. 'Give me a sec.'

She swung her legs out of bed and pulled on one of Darren's T-shirts that had landed near the laundry bin. She almost walked into the spare room before remembering Farah was in there. 'One minute,' she said as she crept down the wooden stairs, miscalculating which was the creaky one again.

Once in the kitchen, she dropped the whisper. 'Hi, sorry about that. How did it go?'

'Negative I'm afraid.'

'What, as in no Ajee or no arrests?'

'Both. The place was completely empty. They've cleared out. I've got uniform up there guarding it and we'll get SOCO in first thing, but we're back to square one.'

'But they were there this morning.' She checked her watch. 'Yesterday morning.'

'And they're not now. Sorry.'

'Shit. Is Bob still at work?'

'Yep, he's going frantic.'

'I'm not surprised. It's not just Ajee, it's all the other girls and whatever this plan is.'

'I'll leave you to it. I've got a busy day ahead but call me again if you need me. Oh, and that girl you were chasing. I hope she's not become your house guest.'

'Speak soon,' she said and hung up.

Absent-mindedly she filled the kettle and set it to boil, scouring her mind for ideas. She could only think of one. She checked her watch: 2.30. Sod it, he didn't deserve to sleep.

For a moment, Jo thought the phone would ring out or at least trip to answerphone. Then, 'Russ Parfitt.'

'It's Jo Howe. Are you pissed?'

'No. I was asleep. For Christ's sake, what time is it?'

'Never mind that. Why haven't you got anything back for me yet?'

'Can't this wait until the morning?'

'It is the morning and things are getting urgent. Have you forgotten there's stuff on your computer you wouldn't want attributed to you? Get me a result by midday or Digital Forensics might stop looking for malware.'

'You wouldn't.'

Jo pressed the red icon and stared out of the kitchen window into the blackness. *Where are you, Ajee, and what are those fuckers up to?*

When the guards had burst into her room five hours ago, Ajee had been convinced this was the end.

It was only when they shouted at her to pick up the bag Leigh had

313

given her earlier that she felt more hopeful. Maybe they were being true to their word that she wouldn't be harmed.

'Quick, quick,' they'd said. 'We must go.'

Maybe someone was coming to rescue her. Maybe Farah had got through.

Ajee thought for a moment. How could she delay them? Feign illness? No, look what had happened when she'd done that before.

'One moment,' she pleaded. 'It's cold. Let me put a hoodie on.' She fished about in the bag for the black one she'd seen earlier and made a fist of trying to put it over her head, using the time to think.

One of the guards burst forward, grabbed the top and yanked it down from the bunching around her neck. Ajee felt something give and pulled back but the men dragged her out.

She'd not been in this new room long before she realised she no longer had the necklace her mother had given her to keep her safe. That last connection with the woman she loved and her homeland before the war was gone. She sobbed into her pillow.

After an hour, a guard she'd not seen before came in and ordered her to take a shower. This one had hot water and, if she stood on the edge of the bath, she could just make out the sea through the tiny opening in the transom window. She dried herself, then it struck her: she hadn't felt so clean since George's flat and wondered why, all of a sudden, they were so obsessed with how she looked.

She prayed Allah would look after her.

51

Russ Parfitt couldn't get back to sleep after Jo Howe called him. What the hell was she flapping about? It was before dawn; whatever it was could surely wait until daylight. But he was hardly in a position to argue. Suspended or not, she only had to make one call and he'd be handed round Lewes Prison like pass the bloody parcel.

Ever since Howe had presented him with the fait accompli, he'd been pondering how he was going to break back into Doughty's fold. How do you ingratiate yourself with someone who's practically beaten you up in a car park, said they don't trust you, then stitched you up so it looked like you were the lowest of the low?

And by noon?

He slurped his third cup of coffee, willing a plan to magic itself in his brain.

Fortunately, one of Doughty's habits he rarely broke was spending Thursday and Friday nights in his Hanover house. Those were his nights for picking up young boys. So, not only would he almost certainly be there now, but he'd also be in the most compromising of positions – rather like after the gypsies were killed.

Deciding against a cab or his own car – he was learning a lot about how the police could track people – at 5.00 a.m. Russ set off on foot from his rented bedsit in Kemp Town, taking the alleyways and cut-throughs. He'd expected the streets to be deserted but clearly the early Pride weekend arrivals had other ideas. Men and women drooling over each other, snogging and holding hands. They represented everything he hated about this city and what he and Doughty had vowed to expunge, though the hypocrite politician had since immersed himself in far worse.

He jostled his way through, cursing as he went, arriving at Tom's fifteen minutes later.

He'd decided that a dramatic arrival would have far more leverage than some apologetic ring of the bell. Hammering on the door with both fists, he yelled, 'Tom, let me in. Let me in.'

The door flew open and Russ was shocked to see Leigh scowling at him as he dragged him in by the scruff of his jacket. The door slammed behind him, and Leigh flung him into the lounge.

'For fuck's sake, man, what the hell are you up to?' said Leigh.

Russ took in the scene. Tom was glaring from his armchair. Either side of him were an older, dapper man and a fierce-looking smaller man about Leigh's age.

'I need to see you. To explain.'

'Explain what? And make it quick, we're busy.'

'Not explain so much but reassure you. I want in. It's what we talked about all those years ago. Don't drop me now.'

'Too late. You're weak and a liability. And now we know you're a nonce, you're damaged goods, so fuck off.'

The small scary bloke stepped towards him and the older man looked away. Russ took a pace back but remained focused on Tom.

'You know that's a mistake. I'd never look at that stuff. If that was a warning from you, I'll take it. But please let me back in.'

Leigh tutted. 'Pathetic.'

Tom stood up and walked to the window.

'I'll think about it. We've had a bit of bad luck, so I need to sort that out. Let's get through the weekend first then maybe we can have another chat, but I'm not promising anything.'

'What the fuck . . .' said Leigh.

Tom spun round. 'I've had enough of you. Never forget you're staff, not a decision maker. I can replace you like that.' He clicked his fingers.

'Fucking try it,' Leigh said.

'Don't tempt me. Look, I don't need this fucking grief. I've got enough on my plate and we only just got the girl out in time. Tomorrow can't fail, so make sure she's ready and that twat Acers warns us a bit sooner than yesterday. Got it?'

Leigh looked dumbstruck. So did the others. The smaller man stepped up to Russ, took him by the arm and marched him to the front door. 'You heard none of that. And if I get so much as a breath you've repeated it to anyone, I'll rape your wife and kids whilst you watch, then cut your fucking heart out. Understand?'

Russ nodded just before he was launched out of the door.

Back in the lounge, Leigh was ripping into Tom.

'Why the hell did you say that in front of him? Are you fucking losing it?'

'He's nothing,' said Tom. 'He's a desperate, finished man. All he's worried about is staying out of prison and getting his kids back. Anyway, he won't know what we're talking about.'

'You better be right.'

'Believe it.' He turned to the older man. 'George, you sure this girl talking to Jo Howe was one of the care home girls?'

'Indeed, and Mrs Howe seemed very keen to continue whatever their conversation was about.'

'And what did she look like?' asked Leigh.

George described her the best he could.

'That definitely sounds like the girl who ran off from Blackstone.'

'And just about every illegal,' scoffed Tom. 'More to the point, how do we get Jo Howe to keep her nose out once and for all?'

'Don't dismiss her that easily. If it is her and Howe's caught up with her, that could be how they found the farmhouse.'

'That's in the past. My worry is she'll do something to bugger up tomorrow.'

'I don't know why we can't just finish her,' said Jimmy.

'In good time,' said Leigh.

317

52

The fact that the call had come before 7.30 a.m. told Jo that Parfitt was taking her threat seriously. And so he should. She'd amassed enough respect around the force for most people to do her a favour, and there would be nothing more delightful than seeing a picture of a handcuffed Parfitt being led to a prison van to serve five years of hell.

He promised he had something, so she agreed to meet, even though he dodged the question of whether he'd found out what she'd asked him to. She gave Darren and the boys a kiss goodbye. 'Have a lovely day,' she said, as she picked up her keys.

'Daddy said we can go on the swings later,' said Ciaran.

Jo ached. Why couldn't she leave it and spend the day with those she loved? She owed them all so much. Darren most of all taught her what was important, or tried to. He'd made her look petulant when she'd refused to recover their car from the pound. 'I just thought I'd be the bigger person,' he'd said as he returned £150 poorer.

The traffic to the meet was surprisingly light for a Friday morning.

Jo pulled up next to Parfitt's car on the deserted top level of the Marina multi-storey car park and wound down the passenger window. He did likewise on the driver's side. The warm sea breeze whipped through the car, picking up a crisp packet and landing it on the dashboard.

'Shall we walk?' he asked.

'No, we can talk like this,' said Jo, aware of the tongues that would wag if the two of them were seen together.

'Suit yourself.'

'It better be good.'

'You promise you'll be true to your word.'

'If you deliver, yes. You'll just have to trust me on that.'

'Did something happen yesterday? Were you looking for someone in a house outside the city?'

Jo's interest piqued. 'Go on.'

'And could it have been something that the chief constable knew about?'

'Maybe. Why?'

'And did it go wrong?'

'Stop with the riddles and bloody tell me.'

'I don't know the details, but I managed to see Doughty for a few minutes and he said something like Acers needed to warn them a bit sooner next time.'

Jo turned to face the choppy English Channel, battling to keep the anger and shock off her face. She'd known Acers was tight with Doughty, but leaking operational information? Surely not.

'That's nonsense, why would he do that?'

'One minute,' said Parfitt. He fiddled with something out of sight. 'Here.' He passed a phone across the gap. Jo unclipped her seat belt and leant over to take it.

As she flipped through the photos, she had to turn the handset occasionally to be sure what they showed. Her stomach lurched. 'How long have you had these?' She hung onto the phone.

'Acers will do anything to stop these getting out. I wouldn't mind betting he had something to do with me getting arrested. It's certainly why you're suspended.'

'What? He's doing all this to stop these getting out?'

'Wouldn't you?'

Jo didn't dignify that with a response. 'What about their plan? That's what I told you to find out.'

'All they said was that tomorrow couldn't fail and something like a girl being involved. They got her out just in time.'

Ajee. It had to be Ajee.

Jo jumped out of the car, ran round and wrenched open Parfitt's passenger door. She leant in and grabbed him by the throat. 'What girl? What about the fucking girl?'

Parfitt thrashed in her grip, grabbing at her hands, trying to pull them off. She squeezed harder, then an image that was never far from the surface flashed in her mind, bringing her to her senses. He of all people wasn't worth it.

As she released him, he gagged, coughed and spluttered. 'You mad fucking bitch,' he said.

'Where is she? Tell me.'

'I don't know. I'll try to find out, I promise.'

'Too right you will, now piss off.'

'But my phone.'

'It's evidence,' said Jo as she dashed back round to her open driver's door. She got in, started the engine and screeched a J-turn before speeding off, one destination in mind.

Fifteen minutes later, she was pulling into Sussex Police Headquarters. Before her suspension, her warrant card would have given her access through the gate, but now she'd have to bluff her way in.

'Morning, ma'am,' said the familiar security guard.

Great, he recognises me.

'Oh, hi.' She feigned an embarrassed giggle. 'I've only gone and left my warrant card at home. Be a love and let me through, and I'll get a temporary replacement.'

The guard faltered.

'I'm so sorry, but I've got a meeting with the chief and we all know what he's like if he's kept waiting.' Another chuckle. Now she just had to hope the force didn't issue the private security firm with lists of suspended officers.

He grinned. 'So I've heard. Just this once.'

Jo punched the air below the window as the guard returned to the hut and raised the barrier.

Having squeezed her car into a bay and dodged behind a cleaner through the door to the chief constable's suite, she was up the stairs in seconds.

She stood outside the closed door, filled her lungs and burst in.

'What the hell do you think you're doing?' bawled Acers, as he rose from his conference table. His staff officer looked flustered and remained seated.

'You and I need to talk.'

'You've no right being here. You're suspended from duty, remember?'

'And we all know why, don't we?'

Acers flinched for a microsecond, then was about to round on her again when Jo cut in. 'Marie. Go and get yourself a coffee.'

'How dare you. Stay where you are, Marie. Mrs Howe is just leaving.'

Jo reached in her bag and took out Parfitt's phone. Opening up the photos app, she showed the screen to Acers, just close enough that if he recognised himself in the photos, he'd react.

'Er, on second thoughts Marie, yes we can finish this meeting later.'

Marie hesitated, looking between the two senior officers. Jo flashed her a hint of a reassuring smile and flicked her head. The young inspector gathered her things and almost ran out of the door.

'What the fuck's been going on, Stuart?' She thrust Parfitt's phone in front of him, flicking through the photos.

For the first time, Acers crumbled and his eyes filled. 'I've been so stupid.'

'I'd say raping underage girls is a few levels above stupid, wouldn't you?'

'They assured me she was eighteen.'

'Look at her, for God's sake. Does she look eighteen? LOOK AT HER.'

Acers blubbed.

'You can pack that in too. Even if she was eighteen – which I doubt – what're the chances she's consenting? I mean, does she look like she's having a good time?'

'I know, I know. I'm sorry. They were going to leak them all. I had no choice.'

'So that makes attempting to pervert the course of justice, abuse of authority, providing false intelligence and leaking operational information which could put officers at risk all OK, does it?'

He did not reply.

Jo continued to flick through, examining them properly for the first time. They were all grainy, graphic and sickening. She noticed the girls were different and the date stamps suggested they had been taken over a period of time, some in the last few weeks. She paused on one and was about to swipe on when something caught her eye. She pinched the image open to zoom in. She couldn't see the face but could just make out a double-crescent pendant on a chain. It was hard to tell by the light but it looked silver. *Where had she seen that before?*

'Who's this?' she demanded.

'Don't make me look,' he pleaded.

'Look.'

Acers forced himself to examine the screen.

'I don't know. She's just another one.'

'You disgust me. You're no better than Helen Ricks.'

The mention of Acers' predecessor made him look up with a start. 'I'm nothing like her.'

'In some ways you're worse. What else do you know? What's Doughty up to? I mean, Doughty is behind this, isn't he?'

'I don't know. They're planning something but I've no idea what.'

'My sources say it's something to do with a girl. Maybe tomorrow.'

'Honestly, I have no idea. I'd tell you if I did.'

'Bloody think. Whatever it is, it's tomorrow and it's big. You might actually be able to save a life or two.'

Acers looked a wreck as he sobbed.

Jo stood up and walked over to Acers' desk, partly to stop herself shaking sense into him, partly to think.

She glanced down at a sheaf of papers clipped together in the centre.

'Operation Denham'
Brighton Pride
Saturday 3rd August
operational plan

She checked the date on her phone.

Of course. Since her suspension she'd forgotten. Pride. The event they'd tried to get the courts to ban. The biggest LGBTQ+ event of the year. The one day which exploded every value the British Patriot Party held dear.

'Stuart. Pull yourself together.' She dashed over to him and pulled his shoulders up.

'What the . . .'

'How much do you know about Pride? How involved have the council been in the planning?'

He wiped his eyes. 'I don't know. Gary Hedges is Gold as you well know, but I'd guess it's the same as most years. We'd have been working with them for months.'

'Jesus Christ,' said Jo. This couldn't be much worse. Nearly half a million people parading through the city in various degrees of sobriety and garish dress, then gathering in Preston Park to literally party until dawn. How the hell would they even identify a threat, let alone neutralise it?

'Pull yourself together, Chief. You've got just over twenty-four hours to rescue thousands of people and maybe, just maybe, the shreds of your career.' Jo knew that last bit was impossible. 'But you have to work with me, and the first part is to reinstate me. Now.'

Acers looked up in confusion. 'I can't do that. They'll kill me.'

Jo locked eyes with him. 'You have absolutely no choice. Now you'll do as I say.'

Once he'd taken her warrant card from his top drawer and handed it to her, Jo spent the next hour setting out exactly what the plan was for the following day and what he must do to make it work. He seemed to rally a bit. She knew that would only be temporary, but allowing him the illusion for now was crucial.

'And if you make or receive one phone call without telling me first, to anyone, then I will personally leak the photos, just before I kick your door down and drag you off to custody. Understand?'

His pathetic nod was the best she'd get.

'I'm off to brief Gary.' She pointed a finger at him. 'I mean it.'

His crestfallen face said he'd got the message.

As she was leaving, her phone beeped with a WhatsApp. Bob.

Search at Blackstone finished. Nothing much. Several DNA submissions but they'll take time. Just this necklace found in one of the rooms. The wheel of death whirred interminably over the downloading image. Jo held her phone in the air – as if that would make any difference. A full minute later, the image crisped into sharp focus.

A silver double-crescent pendant.

Jo's heart raced. Now she knew that she'd seen it before, but where? Where?

She took out Parfitt's phone again and compared the necklace on the girl Acers was abusing with the image on her own phone. There was no mistake, they were one and the same.

Then it hit her like an avalanche. She was thrown back to her first meeting with the nervous Asian girl at the Sycamore Care Home, avoiding eye contact and twiddling a necklace.

That necklace. Double crescent. The same necklace.

The girl under Acers was Ajee.

Jo battled every instinct to burst back into the chief's office and kick him into next week.

She had to find Ajee and stop whatever was planned for tomorrow.

But she had no idea how to do either.

53

Jo had kept Farah up all night, scouring the streets around Clarence Square searching for the brothel. They had followed men whom Jo insisted were 'definitely punters', only to find they were merely using the network of Regency mews as cut-throughs to the next pub or back to their cars. Farah had argued that the men who'd abused her and the other captives came in all shapes and sizes, and selecting them on looks alone was futile.

Inspecting each building was just as much a waste of time, and Jo eventually accepted that Farah had only seen where they were kept from the inside.

In a last throw of the dice, Jo even resorted to showing passers-by the picture of the crescent pendant in the hope someone recognised it and led them to Ajee.

They didn't.

It was five-thirty before Jo gave up and reluctantly dropped Farah back at her house. Instead of practising what she preached and getting a few hours' shut-eye, Jo threw on the uniform she'd not been allowed to wear for too many weeks and headed for Brighton Police Station, taking one last chance to tour the streets just on the off-chance.

Ajee's fitful sleep came to an abrupt end when a woman she'd not seen before walked into the room without knocking.

'Morning, love. Time to get you ready,' she said, with far too much chirp for the time of day.

Ajee scowled and turned her back, hoping that her guest would get the message.

'Now, now. We've got a lot to do, so rise and shine. Got to make you look presentable for your big day.'

Like the teenager she had never really had been, Ajee flounced off the bed.

'That's more like it. Right, in the shower, then I'll do your hair and make-up. After that you can try on your new togs.'

'I do my own hair and no make-up,' said Ajee.

'Today you're wearing it, love. Trust me, you're in for a treat. You won't recognise yourself once I've worked my magic.'

Having stretching out her shower for a full fifteen minutes, Ajee returned to the bedroom and succumbed to her makeover. After three quarters of an hour of backcombing and enough blasts of spray to decimate the ozone layer, followed by the not so careful application of a vivid rainbow of basecoats, eyeshadow and blusher, the woman produced a mirror.

Despite her reticence, the unrecognisable image of a wild-haired, technicolour raver staring back at her made Ajee giggle. She wondered what her dad would have said if he'd seen her like this.

'Where am I going? I cannot go like this.'

'Of course you can. You look beautiful. Anyway, you'll soon see, you won't be the only one.' She threw her the bag. 'Pop these on.'

Ajee upended the bag on the bed and a bizarre array of what looked like vibrant pink, green and blue rags, and a tangle of straps and fishnet, fell out.

'Do these have instructions?' she asked, only half joking.

The woman shrugged. 'If you can't work it out, someone my age would have no hope.'

Much to Jo's relief, her warrant card triggered a green light and the police station side door clicked open. She was surprised at the 'first day

326

at school' buzz that surged through her.

She'd phoned Gary the previous afternoon to update him. They'd discussed cancelling the Pride parade and party but, given they had absolutely no idea of the nature of the threat, they agreed that would cause more danger than it would solve.

At least with the event playing out as planned, the police could retain a modicum of control.

As a concession, Gary put out a call for extra spotters, both plain-clothed and uniform, and another six specialist firearms officers. He wasn't convinced they were necessary, but Jo wouldn't shut up until he had.

The looks Jo got from others as she walked up the six flights of stairs to the incident room were a picture to behold. Most who knew of recent events had thought she was finished.

'Hi, Gary,' she said, a little louder than she intended, as she walked into the command suite.

He swivelled round from the terminal where he was squinting at his command log.

'Jo. So glad you could make it,' he said, as if hoping to convince the others that her return to work today had always been the plan.

Contrary to what she'd anticipated, Gary had seemed delighted she was reinstated but livid when she explained the circumstances. 'I'll kick his fucking head in' was his exact response.

There was never any question of Jo taking over command of either the division or Pride at this late stage. Her sole aim was to hover and pick up anything that might suggest what this 'big plan' was, the threat it presented – if any – and of course to find Ajee. She had no idea whether her disappearance and Doughty's plot were connected, but coincidences scared her, and she was petrified.

Gary carried on stabbing the keyboard while Jo took in the plethora of agencies represented in the suite. The quiet, efficient way each beavered away at their individual roles, feeding into one overall commander – Gary – was a hallmark of excellent planning.

Later, the not so great and good would swan in and drop in their two pennies' worth of how things should be. She'd told Stuart Acers he must make an appearance and to ensure Tom Doughty did likewise. The flesh and debauchery on display would turn his stomach, but she craved seeing his face when he saw she was back at work.

More importantly it would give her a greater opportunity to predict what, if anything, he had planned.

54

Ajee had wondered what all the rush was about when she'd been plastered with all this make-up and dressed as a freak show. No one had spoken to her since the funny little lady had left and, other than being thrown a cheese roll and a bottle of water, she'd been left totally alone. They'd gone to a lot of effort, so she decided she'd just sit it out and see. She'd grown used to that.

Her stomach had started to rumble again when the door finally opened. To her horror, it was Leigh and the scary man from the farmhouse. Both looked as icy as before, but there was a hint of excitement in Leigh's eyes.

Neither spoke as they dominated the room, closing the door behind them. The scary man produced a rucksack from a large paper bag. He delicately placed it on the bed then stared at her in a way that fired terror through her every nerve.

The parade itself had passed without incident. The usual bottlenecks as it passed through the Clock Tower junction and the Steine had been managed with the usual panache and good humour. Jo, as ever, was amazed at the audacity of some of the floats. Each represented the struggle of the LGBTQ+ communities for recognition, equality and justice. The city had come a long way since the first Sussex Gay Liberation Front Pride March in 1973 but still had further to go, as the older generation of gay men like Bob would attest to.

For Gary and his counterparts from other agencies, this was an annual party and, whilst none would ever admit to dusting off previous plans and freshening them up, there was a bit of that. Their experience taught them that as soon as the floats reached Preston Park, the nature of the event changed from being essentially traffic and crowd management to one of policing the supply and consumption of drugs and alcohol, and the consequences of overindulgence by thousands of revellers.

So that there could be a hands-on response, for the last few years the planners had established a separate forward control point in the Preston Park Chalet Café, smack in the centre of the park. As agreed with Gary, this is where Jo had now gone, as would the chief constable and Doughty if Gary could persuade them that was their best vantage point. He even had drivers ready to whisk them there.

Jo marvelled at the technology which gave crystal-clear feeds from a whole battery of pop-up CCTV cameras and drones to both this and the main command suite back at the police station. She was starting to feel weary after her night on the streets, but she still scoured the screens for any sign of the unusual and, of course, Ajee.

Jo had promised Gary she'd remain on the radio command channel so each could update the other if the need arose. So far it hadn't. There had been the usual reports of drug dealers dishing out various substances in and around the dance tents, and about half a dozen ambulance calls to those for whom the revelry had become too much.

All seemed to be going to plan. Jo started to worry that she'd misjudged the threat or, worse still, it was happening elsewhere. The familiar feeling that she'd failed again and, by that, even more people would die consumed her. Surely it was time to accept she wasn't up to this.

Suddenly she was hit with a gust of air as the door opened. She turned round and, both to her delight and consternation, in walked Acers and Doughty. Two for the price of one.

The radio operators and forward tactical commanders seemed oblivious to the hike in air pressure as Doughty spotted Jo by the monitors.

'What the hell is she doing here?' he hissed at Acers in a very poor attempt to prevent the others in the room hearing.

'She's back at work,' said Acers, just as Jo had told him to.

'What the hell . . .'

'Mr Doughty, welcome to the operation. I'm so glad you could make it,' said Jo, stepping forward to shake his hand. She didn't pause for breath before introducing everyone by name and role. She knew Doughty wasn't taking a word in, but the ruse shut him up enough for her to take control.

Every few minutes he checked his watch, and he kept flipping his gaze to the screens. Something told Jo it wasn't just her presence that was making him edgy. Finally, after fifteen minutes and yet another time-check, he turned to Acers.

'Stuart, I need to get going. Can you get me a lift back please?'

Jo chipped in, 'Leave that with me. I'll get the car back.'

Doughty looked confused. 'Back? Aren't they still here?'

'I doubt it,' said Jo, smiling at them both. 'We can't have police cars sitting around. Shouldn't be long.' She radioed the command channel with the request that she knew Gary would only pretend to grant.

Jo had returned to examining the screens when she spotted an unguarded emergency access gate ajar. On any other day she'd put that down to partygoers opening it to allow their ticket-less mates to sneak in free of charge. Today though, with everything that had gone on, it might be significant.

Leigh and the scary man had fiddled about with something in the backpack before ordering Ajee to put it on. She sensed something was very wrong so struggled and squirmed, but they overpowered her and in a second, it was tight on her back with a thin body strap fixed around her rainbow T-shirt. Despite not knowing what was in the bag, her every instinct told her she needed to get rid of it.

She was dragged to the van and kicked out. The scary man produced a pistol and jammed it to her forehead. 'Fucking do as you're told or I'll blow your brains out here.' She had no choice but to comply.

If she'd not suffered the reek of dozens of unwashed men in boats and trucks across Europe, she'd have found the journey to the park unbearable, but the suffocating stench of the four men waiting in there as she was bundled in was nothing by comparison.

The scary man took a seat in the back too. After about ten minutes of winding round the back streets, they pulled up. 'Right, you lot. Go through that gap in the fence and just walk into the park.' The men got out of the van and stretched their legs. Before she could follow, he turned to Ajee. 'These guys will look after you, so do as you're told and nothing will happen.' He pulled a small cylinder from the bag's pocket and thrust it into her hand. 'Whatever you do, keep your thumb on this switch unless the police come near.'

Ajee stared at it in horror. 'What is it? And what's in the bag?' she asked, knowing the answer but praying there was some more innocent explanation.

'It's only drugs. Someone will come and take them from you.'

'Why the switch then?'

'It'll destroy the drugs but if that happens, you'll spend the rest of your life paying us back.'

'You're lying. This is a bomb.'

Just then she felt the gun rammed into her ribs. 'Keep your fucking voice down and do as you're told. It's drugs, that's all you need to know. It's what they've been told.' He nodded to the four men huddled in a group.

'But we will all die.'

'Not if you do as you're told.' He pressed the gun in harder to emphasise his point.

With tears streaming down her face, Ajee knew she had no option but to squeeze into the park.

'Zoom in on that,' said Jo. The CCTV operator obeyed immediately and the four pasty, ill-dressed yet well-built men and the brightly dressed Asian girl with wild hair came into focus. All five looked lost and their facial expressions were the polar opposite to the laughing, ruddy and mainly inebriated ones in the crowds around them.

Suddenly, there was something very familiar in the terrified girl's face.

Jo thanked God for her ability to recognise faces, despite any disguise. She mentally stripped back the hair, replaced the party wear with something dowdier and, there she was. Ajee. This didn't make sense. Just then Ajee turned side-on to the camera.

What was that on her back?

Jo melted to the corner of the room and fired off a WhatsApp to Gary telling him to get the feed up on his monitor, and asking the question *What's she carrying?*

After a couple of minutes Gary replied, *Do nothing. I'm putting explo and drugs dogs in.*

Jo typed back. *No, that'll spook them. If it's a bomb it could detonate at the slightest twitch.*

Leave it with me. We do actually plan for this scenario, Gary insisted. Keep out of this.

Get the covert SFOs ready and do NOT lose her. I've got a plan. Jo replied.

55

Jo pocketed her phone, ignoring the incessant buzzing of calls and messages. She didn't need to check that they were from Gary, and she wasn't going to waste time hearing his pleas – or orders – to do nothing stupid.

It all made sense. No wonder Tom Doughty was so twitchy. She approached him on his blind side as he shuffled, flicking his gaze from the screens to his watch. Whatever was going on, he was definitely part of it. Probably behind it.

'Fancy a walk?' she muttered as casually as she could manage, and just loud enough for those close by to hear.

'I beg your pardon?'

Jo swept her hand towards the screens. 'A walk. Fancy seeing things a little closer up? It might be a good time to clear the air too. You know. Chat things through.'

Doughty swivelled his head, as if searching for an emergency exit. 'I, er, I'd love to of course but I think we're about to go soon. Just waiting for the police car to collect us.'

'They'll be ages yet. Come on, let's take a stroll.' Jo had deliberately increased her volume so everyone in the room could hear, but not so much as to make her request sound like a big thing. It wasn't, after all. VIPs often took walkabouts in the park. Jo banked on Doughty knowing this and realising that any refusal would look highly suspicious. He looked at Acers standing next to him, who just shrugged.

'Well, OK. Half an hour. Max.'

'Great, let me just get my stab vest and hat and we'll be off.' Jo walked to the desk, battling against her shaking hands as she tried to insert her radio earpiece. Once it was firmly in, she put her hat on and moved next to one of the radio operators and whispered, 'Keep me updated where that group go, channel 65. Put me on ambient monitoring.'

'Yes ma'am,' the operator said.

'Are we fit then, Tom? Just stick close to me and I'll show you the sights.' She smiled at him whilst zipping up her high-vis jacket.

He'd turned the colour of a bedsheet.

Jo opened the control room door and was hit by a wall of ear-splitting beats of competing music battling with the shouting and singing from the thousands of revellers rammed into the park. The sweet waft of weed made her gag and, at any other time, she'd search out the smoker and take the offending hash off them. Today, the challenge would be finding someone not having a puff.

'Where shall we go?' she asked Tom, rhetorically, knowing her every word would be fed to the controller through her open mike. It would also be recorded, which would be gold dust.

'Making for the Diva dance tent,' she heard through her earpiece.

'Shall we head over here?' she said, pointing towards the middle of the park where an enormous pink marquee took centre stage. She started walking.

'Jo, listen, can't we do this another time? I really should be getting back.' Tom's voice was shaky and he scampered behind like a tardy child.

Jo laughed. 'What, next year? This is a great opportunity for you to see what events policing looks like in practice. And for us to chat without being overheard.'

'Not overhead? Look at all these quee— people.'

'They're not listening to us. Come on, let your hair down.'

'I can hear you, Jo,' came Gary's voice through the earpiece. 'And I'm telling you to get out of there now.'

Shit.

'Let me explain how we police this sort of day,' said Jo to Tom, trying hard to keep a neutral but cheerful expression.

'We have a command structure,' interrupted Gary. 'And I'm in charge, so get the hell out of there.'

Jo kept shoulder-tight to Tom and rambled through how the planning and decisions happened and the role of the council and others in that. Her soliloquy was punctuated with 'excuse us' and 'sorry' every few steps as they weaved through the thickening crowds. She laughed out loud when Tom cringed as a six-foot-three, sixteen-stone, bikini-clad hulk with a full beard wrapped his arms around him. 'Your Amazon package is here. Would you like it round the back?'

Tom pushed him. 'Get off.'

'You don't know what you're missing,' the man called as he skipped off, his friends collapsing with laughter.

'Disgusting,' Tom hissed.

Jo fought off a snigger.

'They're static by the water point,' said the controller. 'Two of the males are huddled and the other two are boxing in the female.'

Jesus, thought Jo as she slowed her pace and worked out a route that would get them closer.

Ajee's legs could hardly carry her. The weight on her back grew heavier and heavier at the realisation that every step could be her last. She tried to tell the four men guarding her that they were in danger, but they were so pig-stupid, they cut her off and just chatted about the payday they were in for.

She saw one of them had an earpiece and he seemed to be responding to orders as they meandered around, then suddenly changed directions or stopped. She was more convinced than ever that this was a bomb but had no idea how it would detonate. Surely, in such a crowd they couldn't rely on a mobile phone signal?

She jammed her thumb harder on the switch.

'Wait here,' said the man who must be receiving instructions. 'You two, watch her and don't fucking wander off.' The two nearest Ajee closed in on her whilst the leader pulled the other man away and whispered frantically.

'What, what?' cried Ajee, causing a couple standing close to turn and look at her, concerned.

'She's OK,' one of the men said, gesturing that she'd had too much to drink. He rammed his head next to her ear. 'Shut the fuck up.'

Ajee trembled with fear and for a second felt her thumb twitch. Still sobbing, she squeezed the switch tighter and prayed to Allah.

'We should do this more often,' Jo said to Tom, her voice wobbling now. 'No wonder we've had our differences. Everything is so formal.' Tom didn't seem to be listening but was scanning around.

'Jo, get him out of there,' hissed Gary. 'She's squeezing something in her hand. I'm certain it's a device. I'm moving covert SFOs in and I need him away. And you of course.'

'It's all about priorities,' she said, intending Tom to take it as a comment on their relationship, when really it was a dig to Gary at her being an afterthought.

Tom's jumpiness was becoming dangerous, so she moved in even tighter, hoping he'd assume it was the press of the crowd that brought this intimacy rather than her determination that he'd not get away.

As they closed in on the water point, unease washed through Jo. This was madness. If Ajee was carrying a bomb, it could detonate in a second. Gary was right. She should get out of there and let him do his job. Of all the people who had even the slightest chance of stopping hundreds of deaths, it was Gary who had the best odds, not her. She needed to retreat and do it now.

Then she thought of Ajee. That poor girl who'd fled everything she'd known and loved for hope. She'd risked her life, time and again, to get to something close to safety. She'd been promised the world, then brutally let down, every step of the journey. Could Jo really let it all end here? She knew Gary had just one option. A critical shot. A bullet straight into her pretty, bright, caring head, stunning the central nervous system so, even in her final milliseconds, she couldn't detonate the device.

An SFO would clamp her hand around the dead man's switch – the button her thumb would now be on which, if released, would explode the bomb – whilst another would execute her with one, two, even three devastating headshots from point-blank range. Her brains, bone and blood would cake everything in a twenty-metre radius.

Jo knew that was the likely outcome, and she mouthed a silent 'sorry' to Darren, Ciaran and Liam. But she had to take the one per cent chance of saving Ajee and, with her, all these innocents bustling against her right now.

She tried to steady her voice as she urged Tom on. Not only did she need to keep close to stop him getting away, but to capture any incriminating comments through her open microphone. She felt like an undercover officer. Outwardly she had to portray a calm 'this is what I do every day' demeanour. Inside, her mind was racing to figure how to get him to incriminate himself in a way the courts would accept. His words and actions might be recorded, but sometimes it was what people did not do as much as what they did.

She had to commit his every move, gesture and silence to memory and hoped she'd be alive to repeat it all in evidence.

She smiled. 'You can see the challenge. All these people. All have waited a year for this, their biggest party, yet there might be a handful amongst them who have other motives.' She casually glanced at him and his face muscles contorted. 'You know, drug dealers, pickpockets, drink spikers. Worse.' Now she glared.

'Yes, yes of course,' he replied, his voice barely audible.

'Can we just get through please?' said Jo, her fluorescence and hat asserting authority. The crowd parted to let them pass then swallowed them up again. Jo was conscious, as her heart jackhammered, that the fixed grin she wore as a mask might give her away. Who smiles like that unless they've had one too many facelifts?

She sensed Doughty inch away from her right shoulder. 'This way, Tom. It's easy to get lost in these crowds.'

'I'm really uncomfortable with all these people around, can we go?'

Jo gave him a shove forward. 'No.' He stared back at her and in that instant, she knew he knew.

'Jo, we're moving in. It's too dangerous. I'm evacuating, so get the hell out of there or at least bloody help us,' said Gary in her earpiece. She saw in the middle distance the crowd being ushered away by yellow-vested officers and security staff, herding them in the opposite direction.

'Something's happening,' said Doughty. 'We should go.'

She gripped his arm and turned him so their noses were almost touching. 'Why? What's the hurry? I thought you wanted to see how we police these things.'

He struggled and shook to loosen her grip, but she'd expected that so squeezed tighter. 'We're going in nice and close to see what the fuss is about. That's what we do, run towards danger.' She homed in on his eyes for a reaction. 'If there is danger, that is. Is there, Tom?'

His mouth gabbled but no words came out, though he shook beneath her grip. She pulled him against the flow of the crowd. As the space cleared in front, she made out the distinctive grouping she'd seen on CCTV and there in the middle was Ajee. Her face expressionless, her eyes dead and her knuckles white around the black tube.

'Jo, what the fuck are you doing?' said Gary.

'Keep moving,' she said, ostensibly to Tom but so Gary could hear.

'No, Jo. We're moving in. We have to neutralise the threat. You know the rules.'

Again, this time for both Tom and Gary, she said, as she pushed Tom further towards the target, 'You can't kill that girl. You have to stop this. If you don't, we're going up with them.'

'You don't understand,' sobbed Tom. 'She's got a bomb. We have to get out of here. We really will die.'

Jo pulled him even closer as they fought the tide of the crowd. 'Yes, we will. And it will be down to you. But you can stop this, can't you? Can't you?'

The crowd was thinning as they pushed through.

'It's gone too far. Please, don't do this.'

'Back off Jo, I can't hold off any longer. Once I get a sterile zone, I'm giving the command.' This just spurred Jo on even further. She had to get to Ajee before the armed officers reached her. Though the sight of her full uniform might just be the excuse whoever had the remote detonator needed to hit the kill switch.

As the ground around her cleared, the incongruous wails of singing and laughter, music and fairground noise floating from elsewhere in the park distracted her. In seconds she and all those around would not just be dead but their disrupted body parts would be catapulted as far as the eye could see. The oblivious partygoers, still revelling now, would be screaming and fleeing in panic, covered in limbs, blood and flesh.

Doughty was using every ounce of his flaccid strength in his attempts to wrestle free and Jo was struggling to keep him under control. 'Keep going, you piece of shit.'

All she needed was to get him close enough to launch him into the arms of another officer. Despite what she'd love to do, she'd never get away with deliberately slaughtering him.

'I'm sorry, I'm so sorry,' he sobbed, turning his head to plead with her as they powered forward.

'Who's behind it?'

'All of us. I'm so sorry.'

'Gary, did you get all that?' she said, making Tom frantically look round for the acting chief superintendent.

'Yes, now clear the area for fuck's sake.'

Just then, she saw something in Doughty's hand, his eyes locked on it. A mobile phone.

'You fucking dare,' she said, as she grabbed his wrist, brought it to her mouth and sank her teeth into his fingers.

'Aarrgh,' he screamed and the phone dropped at their feet. The next seconds would show if he'd managed to send the kill-code, but Jo would know nothing about it if he had.

She gripped him. Nothing.

Her foot on the phone, she propelled him towards a stunned police officer. 'Cuff him and don't let him touch a thing,' she ordered the fresh-faced PC, then she powered through the remnants of the crowd who were now almost past her.

Ajee and the guards appeared frozen at the sudden dispersal and, in some huge stroke of luck, they were all facing away from Jo. She knew what she had to do.

She filled her lungs with what might be her last breath, fixed her sights on Ajee and sprung forward.

At the same time a massive figure, in jeans and a blouson, burst out of nowhere, slipping on a blue baseball cap with a chequered band around it, POLICE emblazoned across the front. Then she saw around half a dozen more fill her vision, revealing their semi-automatic weapons from beneath their jackets. The first was heading straight for Ajee, his pistol at the ready. Jo knew this would be a low-velocity weapon, just enough to kill Ajee without hitting countless more when the round exited.

Jo had maybe three feet on the SFO and she threw herself forward.

As she hit Ajee, she grabbed her left hand and smothered her thumb over the switch it was holding, yelling 'police,' as she fell on top of the girl. As they hit the ground, Jo yelled in Ajee's ear, 'Stay absolutely still. It's me, Jo.'

The explosion Jo wondered if she would hear came in an instant, yet she couldn't understand why her ears stung so viciously. Did you feel pain in death?

Then three more bangs, but she felt nothing and, as she opened her eyes, she saw that Ajee was still in one piece and – thank God – sobbing.

Jo risked looking up and saw three muzzles trained on her and Ajee. She caught sight of the four guards' bodies scattered around, but otherwise there was not a soul within a hundred metres. She knew that the second she moved away, the dead man's switch would do its devastating work. Also, all the time the bomb was live, as soon as they could, one of the SFOs would finish the job they'd been sent to do.

That was NOT going to happen.

'Get back,' she said.

'Stay where you are,' came the furious reply.

'OK, but just get back in case this thing goes off.'

She could see out of the corner of her eye the nearest gunman waver, then heard the order through her earpiece.

'All units back off. Rifle officers have this covered.' Then, 'Jo, stay absolutely still. Don't move a fucking muscle.'

'You've changed your tune,' she replied. 'What happened to me getting the hell out of here?'

Gary clearly wasn't in the mood. 'Just stay put. Bomb Disposal are on their way.'

Jo held Ajee tighter as they lay among the discarded food cartons, plastic glasses and roaches. 'It's OK. We're going to be fine. Just don't move.'

Ajee shook with fear in Jo's grip. 'I'm so sorry.'

'You've nothing to be sorry for. We're going to get through this, then I've got someone who wants to see you.'

Ajee didn't answer, just sobbed.

Jo knew she had to give Ajee a reason to live.

'Farah wants to kick your butt for causing all this fuss.'

'She's OK?' Ajee moved a fraction.

'Yes yes, she's the one who saved you. Now just stay still. It won't be long.'

'You are a good lady, Mrs Jo. What will happen to me?'

'When they've made us safe you will be arrested, but don't worry,' Jo added quickly. 'It's just procedure and I'll make sure you're OK.'

'You promise?'

'I absolutely do.'

* * *

342

It took an hour for Bomb Disposal to arrive at the park and another to disarm the device. Jo had told Ajee to keep her eyes closed as the Kevlar-clad soldier approached and delicately made the bomb safe. Throughout, Jo thought every second would be her last, yet whispered reassuring words to Ajee.

True to what Jo said, as soon as the corporal retreated, three armed officers closed in on Ajee.

'Stay on your front and look at me,' one said from behind his weapon. 'Keep your hands on your head and keep looking at me. You're going to be handcuffed. Do not make any sudden movements. Only do as I say.'

Jo saw another officer approach from the other direction, take one hand off Ajee's head, clip one side of the handcuff to her wrist and then repeat the exercise with her other hand.

'Right, stand up,' said the same officer who'd give the orders. Ajee did as she was told. As they led her away, Jo stood up and took in the scene around her. Armed officers still trained their weapons around but, other than that, the park was deserted. It would be a long time before SOCOs allowed the public back in.

As she started to walk to the control room, Bob was walking towards her between a line of cones – the common approach path. His white forensic suit covered everything but his eyes, but she'd know that gait anywhere. As he approached, she was desperate to hug him, but he kept a safe distance. Ever the detective.

'I've got a message from the Gold commander, ma'am,' he said.

'I can imagine,' she replied.

'He said, now let me get this right, "Tell that mad fucking bitch that if she comes within a mile of me for the next forty-eight hours, I'll finish what should have happened to her." I think that was it.'

Jo nodded. 'Mmm, he's calming down then. I suppose you want me to take my clothes off now,' she said.

'I don't normally ask a woman to do that, but yes please.'

Epilogue

One year later

The City of London Police had cordoned off Old Bailey – the road that lends its name to the Central Criminal Court – at both ends. It was not unusual for a small section of barriers to be erected outside the court's exit, but closing off the whole street was saved for only the denouement of the biggest trials, and they didn't get much bigger than this.

Tom Doughty, Russ Parfitt, Leigh O'Keefe and Dominic Youngman – AKA Jimmy – had stood trial on a bewildering raft of charges including multiple murders, modern slavery, terrorism offences and election fraud. Their cut-throat defence method of blaming each other, and Russ's PA Debbie as the star prosecution witness, had only exacerbated their guilt as well as that of those below them. After a four-month trial, the jury had spent a respectable day and a half to find them all guilty on each charge they faced.

Stuart Acers had faced the same indictment, but after legal argument he pleaded guilty to child abuse offences, corruption and misconduct in a public office.

Dr Harper and Thomas Bradshaw, the accountant, were convicted for their part in the premature deaths in the care homes and of money laundering. Peggy Squire and George Millar faced certain imprisonment too.

Once the judge heard the dozen or so victim impact statements from the bereaved relatives and one each from Ajee and Farah, he went through the motions of listening to the defence counsels' lame pleas of mitigation, before sentencing each of the main players to whole-life sentences, and the lesser ones to terms that would see them in their eighties before they breathed fresh air again. His blistering condemnations summed up the mood of the nation and the anger of those who'd seen all of this unfold.

Jo took Ajee by the arm. 'You ready? Remember what we said, don't answer anything you don't want to.'

'Of course. Just one thing.' Ajee reached inside the neck of her blouse and pulled out her double-crescent pendant, kissed it and left it out for all to see. 'I'm ready.'

They stepped through the doors and even Jo was taken aback by the scene that greeted them. Satellite trucks masked the historic and contemporary buildings in the background, and the road and pavement in front was crammed with journalists and camera crews craning for the best view.

'Ladies and gentlemen, I have a statement to make. Then the government's new Anti-Trafficking and Slavery Commissioner, Ajee Khaled, will say some words. What we have seen today is the British justice system at its best and our democracy at its worst. There is an old adage that goes "The only thing necessary for the triumph of evil is for good men to do nothing". Brighton and Hove bred pure evil in plain sight. These men, who rightly have been condemned to spend the rest of their lives in prison, took advantage of world events to propagate their hate, to subject young girls to rape and slavery, and they killed with abandon. While too many "good men did nothing", this brave young woman beside me, and her friend, fought this evil head-on. These are the very people bigots say have no place in our country. Well, let me tell you this. I would take a thousand Ajees and Farahs over one of these wicked men the jury have convicted today. Thank you. Ajee?'

Ajee stepped forward and looked around, taking in the crowd.

'I came to this country with hope in my heart. I love Syria and always will, but bad men took all I love from me, and I fled to save my life. England is a beautiful country. I was unlucky to fall in with these bad people. I am lucky as, with the help of Mrs Howe, I am now alive and free. So many more aren't. To be asked by the government to help eradicate—' She paused and looked at Jo to check she had the right word. Jo nodded. 'To be asked by the government to help eradicate trafficking and slavery is an honour, and *inshallah* we make a difference. But slavery is not abolished. Trafficked people like Farah and me live and work among you and hate keeps us there.'

She paused then turned to Jo, each of them ignoring the shouted questions as they slid back through the court doors into the calm and serenity of England's foremost crown court. 'Well done, that was great.'

As the door closed behind them, Bob Heaton signalled Jo over. His face was not what she expected of someone who'd had such a clean sweep.

'What is it, Bob?' she asked.

She saw tears in his eyes as he held his phone out for her.

BBC News Alert – Disgraced Police and Crime Commissioner Philip Cooke found dead in prison cell. More follows . . .

Acknowledgements

Tackling human trafficking, modern slavery, euthanasia and neo-Nazi terrorism in a novel was never going to be easy, but, like the themes in my debut, *Bad for Good*, I just had to.

Thankfully, I was blessed with more support than I could have wished for. Many of those who generously leant their knowledge and expertise cannot be named but those who can include my nephew and his wife, Noah and Suzi Bartlett, who gave up life in the UK to work for an amazing charity, Helping Hands, providing much needed sanctuary, support and life's basics to refugees arriving in Athens. Their real stories of the risks and danger those fleeing warzones go through to reach safer havens will never leave me.

Then there are my good friends and former police officers, Andy Cummins and Rich Lancashire who over many years have enlightened me that slavery is still very much alive in all our communities if only we care to look. Step outside and see where the slaves are; they're everywhere. If you're still not sure of the giveaway signs, the incredible charity Unseen lists them here: https://www.unseenuk.org/about-modern-slavery/spot-the-signs/ Please read this and, if you're concerned, about someone, report it. You may well save a life

As ever, you'd not have these pages in your hands were it not for my inspirational agent, David Headley who is quite frankly the busiest man in the world, yet still finds time to coax, and coerce books out of novices like me then find the perfect home for them. David, and the whole team at DHH Literary Agency and Goldsboro Books cheering me on does wonders to appease my imposter syndrome too.

My incredible publishers, Allison and Busby, come next. Their initial belief in my books was followed by indefatigable energy when *Bad for Good* was published. I will be forever grateful for the publicity and promotional effort they put into my debut, making it a bestseller. I know their similar thrust for *Force of Hate* will be equally impressive. Thanks to you all, I'm so lucky you signed me.

Anouche Newman, Dani Brown and Jas Sheridan continue to be incredible at making sure my website and social media is professional and focused and move heaven and earth to help me understand algorithms and Instagram. Maybe one day the penny will drop!

No novel of mine will ever go near David or Susie until it's been thoroughly polished by my essential pre-readers. First, my youngest son Deaglan who puts paid to the myth that family members are too gentle in their feedback. Then, my mentor and good friend Peter James who has a more refined but equally impactive way of suggesting deep editing where he sees the need. Samantha Brownley of the UK Crime Book Club has a laser eye for detail adding her own ingenious creative suggestions along the way. Julia Crouch helped me with structure, character and some grammar that I really should have known before. Crime writer, scientist, ballistics expert and thoroughly nice chap Brian Price applied his forensic eye and not only helped on some of the weaponry and ordnance but also typos that spell-check missed.

I'm often asked how I approach writing such a strong yet realistic woman as Jo. Thanks for that goes to former Assistant Chief Constable Di Roskilly, who knows more about Jo's world than I ever could. This time, I wanted to ensure that Jo did not emerge unscathed from the traumas of *Bad for Good*. Step forward fellow crime writer and eminent clinical psychologist Dr Chris Merritt who helped me shape how she would react and the impact that would have on her and those around her. Chris, if you thought this book was hard, you've got your work cut out next time!

Thanks to everyone who read, fed back on and told your friends about *Bad for Good*. I couldn't believe the response to it and the clamour for book two. Well, here you are.

Last but absolutely most, is my family. My wonderful wife Julie and triplets Conall, Niamh and Deaglan (and Murphy the Dog) deserve medals for putting up with my musings, hours at my desk, self-doubt, and vacant moments when I (honestly) am plotting the next scene. You are my rocks and I am prouder than I ever thought possible of you all. Thanks to for helping put the print on the page and my name on the cover. I never imagined I'd become a writer, not in a million years, but you made it happen and you've all made an old(ish) man very happy.

GRAHAM BARTLETT rose to become chief superintendent and the divisional commander of Brighton and Hove police. His first non-fiction book, *Death Comes Knocking*, was a *Sunday Times* bestseller, co-written with Peter James. Bartlett is a police procedural and crime advisor helping scores of authors and TV writers inject authenticity into their work.

policeadvisor.co.uk